# HOME OF THE BRAVE

Joyce Tracksler

back channel press
portsmouth new hampshire
www.backchannelpress.com

HOME OF THE BRAVE
© 2009 J. Tracksler
ISBN 13: 978-1-934582-21-3
ISBN 10: 1-934582-21-2

This is a work of fiction, although many incidents, names and places, while real, are used fictitiously. Most historical references have been meticulously re-searched, however, a bit of history has been fudged here and there. For purposes of the story-line, some dates have been moved slightly, but not much. The names of many of the characters have been borrowed from friends, and these, while real, have also been used fictitiously, you lucky ducks, you. Any errors, and there certainly might be some, are the fault of the author, and hers alone.

BACK CHANNEL PRESS
170 Mechanic Street
Portsmouth, NH 03801
www.backchannelpress.com
Printed in the United States of America

Original cover design by
bryce creative, kittery point, maine
Book design and layout by Nancy Grossman
Photographs of Meg Biase Lanterna and Skip Lanterna,
property of the author

Library of Congress PCN 2009908201

# DEDICATION

This book is dedicated to Jack

And the *real* Patten family and their generous support of
Fair Tide, Kittery, Maine

... and the *real* Brenda Be and her support of
Hospitality Homes, Boston, Massachusetts

... and the *real* Tricia Tobey and her support of
Fair Tide, Kittery, Maine

... and the staff of the Oncology Unit, York Hospital,
York, Maine

... and the memory of
the *real* Aunt Mary Rose and Uncle Nick

... and all of the men and women who worked at
The Portsmouth Naval Shipyard during World War 2,
and to those who work there now

... and to all of the men and women
who defended our beautiful country in World War 2,
including my Aunt Chub (WAVES), and my uncles
Pat, Norman, Cappy and Phil (Army and Marines),
those who fought for our country in other wars
and to those who defend us now – I thank you all...


*And the star-spangled banner,*
*In triumph shall wave,*
*O'er the land of the free,*
*And the home of the brave.*

# PROLOGUE

**February 4, 1943 – Portsmouth, NH – The Railroad Station –**

The two men hid behind the bulwark of the old wooden wagon and waited...waited until the train had chuffed into the station, disgorged its load of soldiers, sailors, marines and workers, all headed for the Portsmouth Naval Shipyard, and chuffed away, trailing a long streak of oily black smoke.

Also waiting for the train and its passengers, but certainly not hiding, were a group of prostitutes...women who were willing, for a small payment, to entertain any of the soldiers, sailors, Marines and workers in a way that would be mutually pleasing to the seller and the buyer.

After certain negotiations, most of the women left the station, hooked onto the arm of a man.

One woman, who hadn't managed to negotiate to her satisfaction, was left behind, cursing herself for being too difficult to please. "I should'a taken the two dollars and not insisted on two-fifty," she muttered into the night. "Now, I gotta' walk back and try to find a John on the street."

She turned, angrily stalking back along the front of the old wooden wagon. A large and powerful arm grabbed her by the throat and pulled her into the darkness. She tried to scream, to wiggle away, but, alas, the large and powerful arm was much too large and powerful.

No doubt, she should have taken the two bucks.

# CHAPTER ONE

February 7, 1943

THE US GOVERNMENT ANNOUNCED TODAY
THAT SHOE RATIONING WILL START IN TWO DAYS...

The redheaded sailor swung himself down from the train. He adjusted the heavy Navy-issue backpack and settled it more comfortably on his shoulders. All around him, soldiers and sailors were also climbing off the train, relieved that the journey was over and wondering what the coastal towns of Portsmouth, New Hampshire and Kittery, Maine, home to the Portsmouth Naval Shipyard, might hold in store.

The redheaded sailor... a veteran of six month's service, watched the brand-new enlisted men. It was easy to tell right away which ones were fresh meat...they were the ones who looked around in awe. Check out that newbie...his mouth full of teeth, open and gaping. Others, boys who had been around for a while, milled in small groups, sliding a Lucky Strike out of a pocket and lighting it, nonchalant.

Around the corner, squeezing through the opening left by two huge baggage wagons, six women appeared as if by magic. The redheaded sailor was the first to notice them. The women were an assorted lot. Two old, two very young, and two in the middle. The two young ones were scrawny, both with long brown hair bunched into pony-tails. They were crack-ing gum, joking with one another, nudging each other and scrutinizing the crop of doughboys. The middle-aged ones had flat, empty eyes. They looked for the really raw, young ones. The ones with the five-dollar bill tucked into a pocket by a loving mother.  The one with the red sweater immediately latched herself onto a skinny Oakie boy, fresh from a hard-scrabble farm.  She'd give him an evening he'd remember when he was overseas, awash in the mud of an Okinawa beach.

Another, standing with her hands on her hips, tipped her head and looked around, checking out the fleet, so to speak. Making up her mind, she approached a short, stout boy with a fuzzy wisp of a moustache.

Four more women stepped around the corner and came toward the crowd of men.

The redheaded sailor ignored the gaggle of women. He was looking for a familiar face... "Hey! Big Bess!" he waved and hollered at one of the older prostitutes. "Over here! It's me! Red! Remember?" He shoved his way through the group toward the tallest and largest of the girls. She was a mountain of a woman, weighing more than two hundred pounds. She was large, rather than fat. Her flesh was well-distributed with firm, heavy arms, a jutting bosom, and thighs like tree-trunks. Red beamed. He loved them big.

"Hey, Red! You cheap son-of-a-gun!" Big Bess certainly remembered *him.* He'd been great in the sack, laughed a lot, and threw his money around like leaves in the autumn. I've been waitin' for you! Let's you and me get going." She linked his arm in hers, nearly pulling him off his feet. With a bellowing laugh, she yanked him away from the crowd.

He bent and kissed her neck and then nibbled at her earlobe. "Christ, Bess, you yummy woman! You look good enough to eat!"

~~~~~~~~~~~~~~~~~

On December 7, 1941, the Japanese air force bombed Pearl Harbor. Congress responded by declaring war on Ja-pan. On December 11, 1941, Germany and Italy declared war on the United States.

The attack on Pearl Harbor galvanized the American people. The American war machine sprang into around-the-clock action and touched the lives of everyone, whether they lived in cities, farms or small towns. Men between the ages of 18 and 45 – from factory workers to students – joined the armed forces and went off to fight. Folks on the home front, older men, women and children, went to work to support the soldiers in the field.

To keep our boys supplied with what they needed, the United States government instituted a new term called "rationing." No longer could Americans just walk into a store and buy as much sugar, roast beef, butter, or coffee as they wanted, nor could they blithely fill up their cars with gasoline whenever they wished. All these things and more were rationed, which meant that Americans were only allowed to buy a small amount of certain items (even if they could afford to buy more) and only at certain times, to boot. Rationing was introduced because certain things, vital to the war effort, were in short supply. The bulk of these many necessities went first to our men and women fighting for our freedom. The rest was meagerly parceled out in what most Americans thought was a crazy way.

In January, 1942, tires were rationed. Cars were put onto the ration list in February of 1942, and gasoline in May of 1942. Rubber footwear was rationed in October, 1942, and shoes in February of 1943. Food came next. Sugar in May of 1942; coffee in November of 1942; processed foods, fats, canned fish, cheese, canned milk and…the most terrible deprivation of all…meat…were all rationed in March of 1943. Americans tightened their belts, adjusted their attitudes and tried to live normal lives without the things they were once used to. It was annoying to have to do without canned corn, but devastating to have to skimp on coffee, butter and red meat.

Many Americans, to alleviate their hunger and desire for fresh foods and sweets, began Victory Gardens and learned new ways of cooking and food preparation. American housewives prepared a concoction called "Butterless Butter" to put on a baked potato and a dessert called "Butterless Milkless

Cake" (often called Yum-Yum Cake, so that the children would eat it) appeared at the end of family meals.

America was at war.

## SOME STATISTICS FOR
## THE YEARS 1942, 1943 and 1944

|  | 1942 | 1943 | 1944 |
|---|---|---|---|
| New House | $3,775 | $3,600 | $3,475 |
| Average Income | $1,885/yr | $2,041/yr | $2,378/yr |
| New Car | $920 | $900 | $975 |
| Average Rent | $35/mo | $40/mo | $50/mo |
| Movie Ticket | 30 cents | 35 cents | 40 cents |
| Gallon of Gas | 15 cents | 15 cents | 15 cents |
| First Class Stamp | 3 cents | 3 cents | 3 cents |
| Tuition-Harvard | $420/yr | $420/yr | $420/yr |
| Loaf of Bread | 9 cents | 10 cents | 10 cents |
| Dozen Eggs | 21 cents | 21 cents | 21 cents |
| Gallon of Milk | 60 cents | 60 cents | 60 cents |
| 1# Coffee | 45 cents | 46 cents | 46 cents |
| 1# Bacon | 45 cents | 45 cents | 45 cents |
| 10# Sugar | 59 cents | 75 cents | 75 cents |
| 1# Hamburger | 30 cents | 30 cents | 32 cents |

Life Expectancy on average for all three years: 62.9 years

# CHAPTER TWO

**MARCH 8, 1943**
**American forces are attacked by Japanese troops on Hill 700 in Bougainville in a battle that will last 5 days...**

**Throughout the United States, meat is rationed.**

"You seen Big Bess?" The redheaded young sailor, dressed in his whites, again stepped off the train in Portsmouth, New Hampshire.

"Big Bess? She was here a few weeks ago." The tall Spanish-looking woman, her hair piled high on her head, snapped at a slice of gum. Sensing opportunity, she sidled up to the Navy man and fingered the insignia on his blouse, purring. "But she ain't here now. I do a better job than she did. Whaddaya say?"

The young fellow smiled and shook out two Lucky Strikes. He offered one to her. She came even closer, cupped his hand in hers and lit the cigarette. "Cost you two dollars." She drew the smoke into her lungs, pouting her lips so that the sailor would know that she knew how.

"Are you sure Bess isn't around?" He liked Bess. Liked her a lot. They'd had a fantastic week-end that last time. She was fun...cheap and accommodating. A memorable screw just the way he adored them...a woman of full flesh; monumental breasts, heavy calves and a rounded, voluptuous derriere.  A tasty morsel.

"She ain't here." The tall woman finished the cigarette. "Ain't seen her for a few days." She giggled and shrugged. "The night must'a swallowed her up." She gazed around with a practiced eye, noting that the servicemen were quickly pairing up with the rest of the women. She needed a partner for the night and the cash that such a transaction would bring. "Well, what is it, handsome? Yes or no?"

The sailor shrugged, he'd prefer Bess, but…if she wasn't around…one chicken was as good as the next. He dug into his pocket, fished out two dollar bills and followed the Spanish pompadour down the road and into the cheap tenement house.

Afterwards, hungry, Red and the pompadour, who went by the name of Chickie, went to Tedesco's for cheap but tasty bowls of stew, heavy on the potatoes and light on the beef, washed down by a few beers. "Damn good stew," Chickie mumbled, licking up the last of the gravy with a crust of bread.

"Ya can't get stew anywhere back in Niagara Falls," Red speared up the last carrot. "Can't much get any kind'a meat. The butchers are taking this meat rationing thing a little too serious." He burped. "You guys are lucky."

# CHAPTER THREE

May 24, 1943
**Holocaust: Josef Mengele becomes the chief medical officer at Auschwitz Prison.**

In the early morning hours, after a busy night of entertaining the troops, several of the local women gathered at Wolfie's, the local all-night coffee shop.

"Suzie's late," Gladys, one of the older prostitutes, remarked. "She's usually finished by midnight." She sipped at the tepid cup of coffee, wondering how the hell anyone could get coffee to taste this bad.

"Maybe she got a late night special," Maureen, the one with the amazing blonde hair, ventured. "I'd stay later if someone paid me enough."

Gladys, who was slightly overweight, had bad feet and hated to stand on corners for any length of time, rubbed her left ankle. "I'm too old to last much beyond midnight."

"Ya know," Maureen thought back. "I ain't seen Suzie in a couple a' days."

"Me, neither," Helen, the youngest of them, chimed in. "Maybe she's been sick, or on the rag this week."

"I was doing a double with her last week...maybe it was Saturday night." Gladys tried to remember one busy night from the next. "Three guys...they wanted some curvy girls with big bazoomas. Me and Suzie fit the bill."

"Ha! I'll *bet* you filled their bills!" Maureen screeched with laughter at her own joke. Maureen was still as slender as she'd been at sixteen.

Gladys gave her a look of annoyance. "Hey, don't knock a little bit of healthy meat on the bones. Lotta guys love all that."

"Yeah, yeah." Maureen wasn't about to get into a fight. "If you see Suzie, tell her she still owes me five bucks from last week." She yawned, her wide, lipsticked mouth showing strong white teeth. "I gotta pay my rent, ya know."

Helen shook a Chesterfield out of her handbag and then offered cigarettes all around. As the smoke drifted over the table, Helen's face scrunched up.

"She's about the fifth girl that seems to have gone away..." She inhaled deeply, her forehead furrowed. "I mean, where's Big Bess nowadays? And what's her name? The young one who was so fat?" She turned to Maureen. "The one who dressed like a schoolgirl? Ya know, with those little girl dresses?" She's not at the corner where she always is."

The ladies shrugged. "Maybe they found someone who wanted them to go to wherever they were going. Traded this kinda crappy life for the crappy life of a follower." Gladys pushed her chair back. "Maybe they found someone who really...well, maybe...somebody wanted them to stay with them." The other girls looked skeptical. "As for me, I'm hungry. Who wants ta go for a hamburger or some chili at Tedesco's?"

"I'm in." Helen stood up. "Maybe we'll run inta Suzie there. She was always crazy about Tedesco's chili."

~~~~~~~~~~~~~~~~~

The south side of Portsmouth, where most of the bars and areas of debauchery and prostitution were located, had grown considerably in the years since the War started. Empty buildings were re-opened as cheap dance-halls, where a sailor could get a beer and a dancing partner for one dance for less than a quarter. Dingy saloons opened, where blousey, but still attractive hostesses were delighted to share a bottle of ersatz "champagne" with a lonely soldier. There were cheap hotels, renting out sordid rooms by the hour, lonely fly-specked coffee shops and restaurants, a few small grocery stores, gambling houses that ranged from those with dime limits to those whose clientele catered to the men who were either really wealthy, or those who were temporarily flush from fleecing their fellow soldiers. For the ones with cash, there were several upscale restaurants fronting State Street: The Chinese Palace, Salvatore's Steak Restaurant, The Palm Court, The Green Monkey and The Jazz Spot. For those who were not quite so flush, several less-expensive eateries did a good business: Harry's Chili Joint, Chang's, and Tedesco's. Tedesco's, one of the older establishments, distinguished itself further by not only being a restaurant that sold cheap food, but also had a butcher shop in the building that sat next door.

Even with rationing, these places, expensive and inexpensive, seemed to find lobsters, steaks, chicken egg fu yong, pork chops and sweet desserts from somewhere. Most of the customers believed that the owners dealt regularly with "Mr. Black," the euphemism used to explain those who flouted the law and dealt with black market goods. Hey! Rationing was good...after all...our fighting men did need the meat and sugar and rubber more than the average American, didn't they? But, hey...once in a while...what could it hurt if I had a steak or two, too? Right? Right. Most just turned a blind eye and Mr. Black flourished, especially in the cities and towns and training camps where men who were to be shipped overseas might be dead in the war next week. Right?

~~~~~~~~~~~~~~~~

Tricia bent from the waist, touched her sneakered toes, and then did a series of windmills with her arms. The book, *A Lady's' Running Companion*, by Genevra Davis, stressed the value of a good warm-up. Several passers-by glanced at her, wondering what the heck she was up to. It was rare to see anyone dressed the way she was, never mind a young woman. Bare legs ending in athletic socks and sneakers, short pants, and a grey short sleeved tee-shirt. She jogged, bending her knees high, in place. She bent one last time, supple as a willow, and picked up a thin Thermos bottle from the sidewalk in front of her house. She stuck it deep into the pocket of her shorts.

Tricia grinned to herself. If they thought her running was not lady-like, what would they think of her new job? She took two more deep breaths, screwed her long, dark hair into a knot at the back of her neck, secured it with a rubber band and began to run with the slow trot that Mrs. Genevra Davis suggested.

She turned the corner, away from the Kittery Foreside, a neighborhood of old houses, small shops and businesses, and picked up her pace as she headed toward Kittery Point and Seapoint Beach. She remembered Genevra's advice. "Keep your head up and your arms bent. Swing your arms in time to your running feet. Sing to yourself and run to the music in your head. A rousing march or a vigorous hymn is suggested." As her feet pounded the road, ever faster, Tricia allowed the music to accompany her, singing to herself: "I got spurs that jingle, jangle, jingle…as I go ridin' merrily along…" Three cars passed her as she crossed the bridge over Spruce Creek. Two, driven by men, tooted their horns and waved. She waved back, never pausing, her pace ever faster, her feet drumming on the pavement, sweat spilling into her hair. As she rounded the uphill stretch that lead to the beach, she dropped her pace. Mrs. Davis stressed that a successful runner would run for five miles and then slow down, "to save ourselves for the run home…"

The sun rose higher as she stepped onto the beach. Seapoint Beach and its neighbor, Crescent Beach, were small sandy inlets carved out of the granite boulders that edged the Atlantic Ocean in Southern Maine. The dark, oily Maine sand was churning with dogs. Little hairy dogs, yapping and darting at one another. Big, smooth-coated retrievers, joyously leaping into the cold waves, chasing ratty old tennis balls thrown by their owners. Dog lovers and beach strollers stood in clumps, talking with one another, scratching the rumps of their pedigreed poodles and scruffy mutts, reveling in the freedom of the morning sunshine. Normally, Tricia might have been here with them, running along the sands with her mother's dog, Flash. But not this morning. No, poor Flash had been left at the house, wheeking in disappointment. Mrs. Davis did not recommend running with an animal attached.

She waved to a few familiar faces and patted a few furry heads as she left the beach area to renew her run on the scrubby paths that wound through the humpbacked tidal marshes. She was alone again, her feet pumping to an even faster sound in her head. *"He was the boogie-woogie bugle boy of Company B..."* She needed a faster paced song to match her steps.

Even with the preoccupation with her run, Trisha reveled in the beauty of the marsh, the rustle of the yellow-gold reeds and the dark and mysterious winding tidal waters that flushed in and out of the inlet. This was a special place.

She raised her head and noted Eustace Barnes' ancient shack perched on stilts at the edge of the marsh. Old Eustace was a Kittery Point legend. An odd old geezer. A fisherman, lobsterman, handy-man-of-all-trades. Many thought he was as crazy as a loon ... certifiable, and some mothers warned their daughters not to go near him. "There are stories about him...be careful...I heard that some girl was seen with him and was never seen again..."

Eustace lived in a dilapidated shack patched together from old packing cases, discarded pallets, windows found at the dump, bailing wire and string. It was a wonder to all who passed that the place had been standing for years, despite floods, hurricanes and nor'easters.

Since the war started, Eustace had padded his sporadic income by going around to houses, patriotically collecting old tin cans, rags and tags of clothing, and any other venerable pieces of junk that had suddenly – since the war started – become saleable as salvage.

Trisha looked around. The beaten earth in front of the shack was empty. Eustace and his wagon, pulled by his faithful mule, Jezebel, didn't seem to be home.

Trisha paused for a moment, a sharp pain bisecting her at the waist.  Mrs. Davis had warned her that there would come a time when her body rebelled from the punishment of a long run. "Down in the depths" was her term. "A lady will feel exhausted. Listen to your body. Stop for a few moments and walk around in circles. Shake your legs and stretch your foot muscles. The fatigue will slip away. Just like the morning dew." Trisha obediently shook and stretched. She only had a mile to go and then she'd stop properly and drink her water before heading back home.

Mrs. Davis was a wise woman. The tiredness was quickly gone and Trisha's body felt flushed with effervescence, as if she had soda pop in her veins. She shook her shoulders like one of the dogs on the beach and began to jog again, heading for the end of the marsh. There, at the ocean's edge, she'd sit on the ancient stone wall that stood between the marsh area's second stilted shack – presently unoccupied – a shambles, but picturesque nonetheless…often captured by local artists, sometimes beautifully and sometimes not…and the pounding waves. She'd rest there, drink her water, and run home.

Up and go. She began to sing again, unable to keep the Andrews Sisters and their bugle boy out of her head. And then, crinkling her nose, she smelled the rank smell of smoke permeating the air. She stopped slightly, jogging in place. *Smoke? What the heck?* She looked at the sky and the horizon, trying to see over the waving tops of the sedge grasses. She couldn't see any smoke or fire. *What's that smell, then?*

As she got closer, she saw.

*The old shack. My goodness!* Instead of a dilapidated pile of wood, the shack was now a blackened hulk spoiling the beauty of nature. She stopped. The smell was heavy here. It enveloped her, sooty and acrid and somehow sweetish, roiling at her stomach, sickly and clinging. "What the heck?" She walked closer, noting the total devastation. *Must have been some kids out here.* When she was younger, the local kids always gathered on the beach, here or there. No different now. *Maybe they tried to light a bonfire and it got out of hand…* She came closer and nearly tripped over a charcoaled board, nails sticking out. Then she stepped over lumps of debris, kicking at pieces of twisted rubble. Then…

What *was* it? She bent over. A skeleton? A skeleton of some animal? A dog, perhaps? "Ugh!" The word was forced from her mouth and she felt bile in her throat. The poor animal! Tricia shuddered. She picked up a stick and poked, catching the glittery links of the dog's collar and the chain that had been attached. *Poor thing! And what was a dog doing out here?* A small chromium oval on the collar was scratched with crude letters: "Pal". Tricia's eyes filled with tears.

The smell was sharper and sweeter now. Tricia raised her head, walked closer to the shack and touched a warped wall. Whatever had happened, it had happened at least a day or so ago. The wood and debris were cold to her touch. She cocked her head and listened... The warped walls still made mouse-like noises, a crackle and a snapping sound. She shuddered again, hopeful that no small, furry creature might jump out at her. *Thank God no one lives here*, she thought. Her sneak-ered foot clinked against something. Looking down, she saw a cheap metal badge lying on the ground. She bent down and picked it up, turning it over in her hand. It was a toy...a child's toy...a cheap, tin badge with the letters "S H E R I FF" lettered across its five pointed star. *Sheriff, huh?* The metal was cold against her skin. Tricia wondered if it had been dropped by the kids who might have set the fire.

And then she went closer. The stomach-churning sweetish smell was more pungent. She felt frightened and turned around, expecting she knew not what. She was all alone with the roasted skeleton of a dog and afraid.

Should she run back? Tell the police? Do something? But what? She tried to look into the shack, touching the emptiness of a window sill, black and stiff. And what was *that?* There, huddled in a heap on the floor...and over there by what used to be a window... A mattress with...*oh, no! Nooooooo!* And over there! What was *that?*

She stumbled back to the path, running awkwardly with no sense of the rhythm that Mrs. Davis had so carefully taught. Frantic, her feet tripped on a hummock and she fell, sprawling into the grass, fighting hysteria and twisting her ankle. "*Ow! Damnation!*"

The fall stilled her panic. Flat on the ground, she felt her right ankle. It hurt but she wiggled it around. It seemed well enough to stand on. She hauled herself up, clutching at the scraggly reeds. With care, she stepped on her foot, almost forgetting what she had just seen. Her pretty face winced. Dratted ankle hurt! She nursed it, limping a bit, favoring her stronger side. And then she remembered the burned bundles and gasped.

Ankle or no ankle, she had to get the police! She stepped up her pace, turning away from the main path and heading through the underbrush, skirting the beaches. It would cut at least a mile and a half off her journey. Wincing at the pain, she leaped over the hummocks and grass, noting the stumps of the deserted old trolley car line that stuck out of the tidal waters like the rotted teeth of some gigantic monster that lived under the surface. She gasped and turned her head back, almost expecting some boogieman to be running faster than she was, following her and ready to devour her.

Her fright spurred her to nearly superhuman effort. As she ran faster and faster, her brain galloped in time. *"Mine eyes have seen the glory of the coming of the Lord...His truth is marching on!"* The words tumbled out of her mouth, nearly babbling, nearly unbidden. *"Glory! Glory, Hallejul-yah! Glory, Glory, Hallejul-yah!"*

At the beginning of the paved road, she looked up to see old Eustace and his wagon coming towards her. *Eustace! Thank God!* "Eustace! Hey!" She stopped, panting, and waved her arms.

"Whoa, Jezebel! Whoa!" The old man pulled on the reins. The elderly mule turned her grizzly head back, asking just what in the heck was he doing? OK. OK. She'd stop. All he had to do was say so. Snorting with mule-ish disgust, Jezebel kept up her measured pace until her soft muzzle bumped into Tricia's chest. Sighing a grassy sigh, the patient animal pushed her nose against Tricia and stopped dead.

"Ain't you Charlie Tobey's youngest gel?"

"Yes. I'm Tricia." Tricia patted Jezebel's face, eliciting a barnyard gust of mule- breath. *"Eustace! The old house at the end of the road! It's burned up!"*

"Ya don't say?" Eustace's rheumy eyes opened wide. "There's people there. Them's kiddies in there."

"I thought it was empty," Tricia wailed. "But...but...I saw a dead dog and I think...oh, God...maybe a dead person or some dead people!"

"Git up heah, honeybunch and we'll go get help." Eustace was old, but when necessary, he could move with alacrity. "Come on up. Quick, missy."

Tricia quickly climbed up and Eustace backed and filled as he turned the wagon and Jezebel around. Jezebel, who had been anticipating a well-deserved meal, wasn't overjoyed about this. As Eustace swore softly at the mule, Tricia turned, "Did you see the fire? The smoke? The wood is cold, so it must have been yesterday or the day before."

Eustace waved to the load of scrap iron that jangled in the back of the wagon. "I wuzzin't here fer the past three days. Went down Rye way to pick an old barn clean. What in tarnation happened?" Jezebel had come to the realization that her master, for once, meant business and resignedly began to trot back toward town.

Tricia shrugged and touched Eustace's arm for reassurance. "I don't know. I was frightened, Eustace."

"Hmpf." Eustace spat over the side of the wagon. "'Bout a month ago, this fambly from up Aroostock way came and moved in. They wuz keepin' mostly to themselves. Name o' Weasley or Wezey. Man, woman and three little kiddies. He had a boat out in the marshes and went fishin'." He wiped his chin and slapped the reins gently, trying to urge the tired old animal into a faster pace.

"Do you think they were all in the house?"

"Now, child. How the heck would Ole Eustace know that kind a' thing? Juss what did ja see?"

"The dog was in the yard, burned to a crisp. I could tell because of the dog collar." She bent her leg, forgetting about her ankle, and clasped her arms around it, hugging herself as she thought of what she'd seen.

"Yea?"

"I went up to the house. The wood...the house and the walls and everything were cold, but I could smell the smoke and...and...I smelled....it smelled funny. I managed to look inside and then I could see a...a shape...maybe more than one shape...a heap of...I think it was a body. Or maybe more than one body. I didn't go in, but I think there were more..." She shivered in the late morning sunshine.

"Mmmm." Eustace rubbed his whiskers. "Sounds bad, missy. Sounds mighty bad." He looked over at her and shook his head. "You're shivering. You silly girl. Whut you dressed like that for?"

"I'm a runner."

"Say?"

"I run, Eustace. I go out and run for about six miles. Every day."

"Whatchu do that kind o' thing for?" He scratched his head. Although a hard-working man, Eustace only expended energy when he had to, to earn money, to keep warm or to find some wine or food.

"I want to be a marathon runner." Trisha bit her lip. "I want to compete."

"Sounds daffy to me." He shook his grizzly head, muttering to himself about the younger generation and their fool ideas.

They approached the police station and he clucked to Jezebel. "We're here, Jez." The wagon rolled to a neat stop right under the sign that said **Kittery Police Station.** Eustace climbed down and put his hoary hand out to help Tricia to the ground. "Wait a minnit..." He went to the back of the wagon and tossed a cast iron dress form aside, pulling a nose bag out. "Who'd'a think that some blamed ole dress form would be worth ennythin' to the Army?" He muttered about how things were getting mighty funny around here.

He checked the contents of the feed bag, and then strapped the bag onto Jezebel's face. "Here, honey-girl. You wait for us. Old Eustace will be right back." He patted the whiskery muzzle.

Tricia and Eustace opened the door to the police station.

"Hey! Chief! Come on out here! I got a little girl who wants ta tell you a story..."

~~~~~~~~~~~~~~~~~

**June 1, 1943**
**British Airways plane shot down.**
British Overseas Airways Flight 777, on a scheduled passenger flight, was shot down over the Bay of Biscay by German Junkers Ju88's...all 17 people aboard perished, including actor Leslie Howard. There is speculation that the downing was an attempt to kill British Prime Minister Winston Churchill as the Germans may have had erroneous information that he was on board...

The sister towns of Portsmouth, New Hampshire and Kittery, Maine sit opposite one another on the sides of the Piscataqua River. The inlet runs from the Atlantic Ocean into Portsmouth Harbor, skirting an island, smack-dab in the middle of the water between the two states. This island is the site of the Portsmouth Naval Shipyard, affectionately referred to as "the Yard."

Portsmouth and Kittery were originally fishing villages with rich stands of fine timber which could be harvested for masts and boats. The shipbuilding industry followed naturally, as boats could be built here more economically than in any other location. With proximity to the sea and vital locations as guardians of the east coast of the United States, the shipbuilding industry flourished, and so did Portsmouth and Kittery.

Portsmouth became the center of business and commerce, growing into a city, while Kittery remained, except for the Yard, a sleepy fishing village with summer tourist attractions.

The *Falkland* was the first ship constructed in the region for the Royal English Army at Portsmouth in 1649. In May, 1776, the *Raleigh* was built for the American Navy.

In 1789, the Navy became a separate and distinct branch of the service. In 1864, there were 2,500 men on the payroll of the Yard, and more room was needed.

Thus, the little island in the middle, known as Seavey's Island, was purchased by the US Navy on June 12, 1800, and became the first US Naval Shipyard. The first ship built there under the Navy's approval was the sixteen-gun sloop *Ranger*. The *Ranger*, commanded by John Paul Jones, was the first man-o-war to fly the new American flag and the first ship to receive an official salute from a foreign nation.

In 1898, a prison camp was established on Seavey's Island. Prisoners taken in the Spanish-American War were confined there until the terms of settlement were completed. In 1908, the prison was officially commissioned as the United States Naval Prison at Portsmouth. The design of the prison was a nine-day's-wonder to all who watched it rise. Perhaps the architect had delusions of grandeur, or perhaps, as was the belief of many, he drank heavily, for the edifice rose, like a

demented caricature of a Bavarian castle, complete with tur-
rets and pediments, to loom, more than six majestic stories
high, over the surrounding trees and Navy buildings. Even to
this day, the prison is called "the castle." Passers-by, seeing
its excess, wonder why the heck a building more suited to a
Hollywood movie, was constructed in bucolic Kittery.

In 1914, the Navy decided to build its first submarine at the
Shipyard. Completed in 1917, she was the forerunner of a long
line of submarines and the facility was officially designated a
submarine yard by the Secretary of the Navy in 1923.

Before Pearl Harbor, Kittery and Portsmouth were still
sleepy little towns, concerning themselves with boat-building,
fishing, the tourist industry, and business-as-usual at the
Shipyard.

After December 7, 1941, the two towns changed radically
as thousands of workers streamed into the area, seeking jobs
at the Shipyard. At the height of the War, there were more than
twenty thousand men and women, working three shifts around
the clock, employed there.

These thousands of military personnel swelled the
Shipyard's barracks to bursting. All these men, young, virile
and randy, coming to two generally rural and sleepy areas,
changed everything. Thousands and thousands of workers
also spilled into Kittery and Portsmouth, as the Portsmouth
Naval Shipyard began to churn out submarines to protect the
seas and to fight our enemies.

The servicemen and servicewomen and the Shipyard
workers came in by train, by car, by ship. Some of them were
barracked at the Yard, some stayed with relatives. The over-
flow had to sleep elsewhere. Most of them tried to find a room,
an apartment, a bed....somewhere to lay one's head. Widows
and housewives with a spare bedroom quickly furnished it with
the left-over bed from the attic, added a dresser from the
garage and stitched up blackout curtains. The rooms rented
out in a twinkling, and hey...who needed to know that the little
housewife...the widow...the guy who had that extra room on
the third floor....who needed to know that a few bucks
changed hands?  Not the tax man. No sir.  And everyone was
doing it, weren't they? Right? Right.

The barrage of men descended like locusts on Kittery and Portsmouth. Where would they all sleep? Eat? Drink? Have fun? Meet a few women?

~~~~~~~~~~~~~~~~

**USO Opens at Connie Bean Center, Portsmouth!**

**Syphilis rate soars in Seacoast Region!**

The Connie Bean Center, named for a popular local hostess and civic leader, was quickly re-opened as a USO Center. The three-story brick building, centrally located in downtown Portsmouth, was originally opened in 1913 by the Army and Navy Association, in answer to the city's need to supply military men with an alternative recreation site to the waterfront brothels and downtown taverns that dotted the narrow streets. The airy, welcoming rooms were furnished with pool tables, a reading lounge, a chapel, food facilities, lockers and temporary sleeping quarters for servicemen. When the US joined into World War I, the Connie Bean Center was there to comfort and cater to the sailors and soldiers who passed through the Portsmouth Naval Shipyard and the local training camps at Pease Air Force Base. When the War ended, the center was closed, only to reopen in 1937 at the onset of World War II.

The Center, run by the USO, added a wing with a gymnasium and an auditorium. The most popular programs were the twice-weekly dances and the USO shows. The dances were run by a committee of local matrons. The women, selected for their unblemished characters and civic responsibilities, acted like "mothers" to the young and lonely servicemen. They sewed on buttons, helped write letters home, listened to alleviate the loneliness of young men thousands of miles from home and family, and, most important, oversaw the young ladies who acted as hostesses at the dances.

These young girls, the pride of local families, were handpicked for their prettiness, their winning personalities and abilities to dance with and listen to the young soldiers and sailors. There were strict rules governing their behavior, however. These were the "nice" girls of impeccable families. And, by golly, the women heading up the USO Committee would see to it that they *remained* nice girls.

Of course, there were the *other* girls. The ones who lived in cheaply constructed multi-storied houses on the south side of town. And the ones who lived in better circumstances and entertained men with more jingle in their pockets. The ones who worked at the Swedish Massage Center and the few other upscale bordellos. And the ones who lived here and there and rented a room for a two-hour time frame. Over and over and over again. Just keeping the troops happy.

On the highest end of this scale were the prettiest and most cultured ones... These were the ones who entertained men at the very private and expensive Hess Club for Gentlemen.

Every one of the hundreds and hundreds of men who came to Kittery and Portsmouth, and, in less numbers, some few women, who worked at the Yard or waited at the bases to be assigned to fight overseas, could choose where they wanted to spend their time. At the USO...at the Hess Club... on the street...in the bars and taverns....there were so *many* choices. And after all, in a week or so, they'd ship out for France, or Tunisia, or the Philippines...and who knew if they'd be blown up or machine-gunned down by the end of the month. So, why not have a little fun?

# CHAPTER FOUR

SPORTS NEWS: Red Sox player-manager Joe Cronin sent himself up to pinch hit in both games of a double-header. He hit a 3-run home run in each of the games!

# KITTERY GAZETTE
OUR NEWS IS YOUR NEWS • Saturday, May 29, 1943

# ARSON!!!!

**KITTERY POINT FAMILY OF 5 BURNED TO DEATH**
**By GREG STARR, News Editor**
**Kittery Point, Maine. Woman finds bodies in Seapoint Beach marsh shack. Three little children, mother and father murdered! "We are seeking the public's help." Police are baffled.**

On the morning of May 24, 1943, while running on the beach, a Kittery Point resident, Miss Patricia Tobey, smelled smoke and found the charred hulk of a decrepit fishing shack burned to the ground on the salt marshes beyond Seapoint Beach.

"The ashes were cold," she told this reporter. "I saw the body of the

The family's dog in the yard. I looked into the shack and saw the bodies scattered in the house. It was awful!"

The bodies, five of them plus Pal, the family dog, were tentatively identified by neighbor, Eustace Barnes. Barnes, who lives in a stilted house a half-mile from the arson site, told Kittery Police Chief Horace Parks that the family had moved into the shack a few weeks ago.

"They came here from Aroostook way," Barnes said. "Told me that they were starving up there and heard there were jobs down here. He was a fisherman. Poor folks. Who would do this?"

Who would do this indeed? Police Chief Parks and his Deputy, Gideon Balfour, upon arriving at the eerie scene, immediately suspected foul play. Upon examination, they affirmed that there were five bodies inside the shack, four in the front room and one, a female infant, in a back room.

In addition, the family dog was found in the yard, a burned-out pile of bones. A chromium dog-tag with the name "Pal" was found in the ashes.

Chief Parks and Deputy Balfour, both trained in arson techniques at the State Police Academy, were able to confirm that gasoline or kerosene had been splashed on the premises, then, presumably lighted. "The shack, poorly constructed of old wood and tinder-dry in these summer hot days, most likely burst immediately into flames. From the position of the bodies, the occupants were overcome by smoke and fire and never had a chance of surviving." Chief Parks affirmed.

"We have tentatively identified the adult bodies as those of Hiram Wesley and his wife, Florence. The bodies of the children are Absalom Wesley, age 4; Ezekiel Wesley, age 3; and Ruth Wesley, age 6 months." The Bangor police have been contacted for any further information on next-of-kin.

Chief Parks asks all readers to contact him if anyone has any knowledge of this terrible crime. Call KITTERY 4---

Pictures on Page 3. More to follow...

~~~~~~~~~~~~~~~~

The arsonist, reading *The Kittery Gazette* and a similar article in *The Portsmouth News and Bugle*, was delighted. The only disappointing thing was that the article hadn't mentioned the sheriff's badge. Maybe they hadn't noticed it? The arsonist chuckled softly. They'd notice it next time.

~~~~~~~~~~~~~~~~

**May 29, 1943**

**Norman Rockwell's illustration of _"Rosie the Riveter"_ first appears on the cover of the _Saturday Evening Post_...**

"Poor son-of-a-bitches," Horace muttered, watching Doc Brogdon performing the grisly autopsies.

"Not much here to examine," Brogdon grimaced, his gloved hands picking charcoaled shards out of the shapeless bundles. "They're burnt to nothingness. No organs, no skin, no nothing, except these charred bones, and even those are beyond my ability to tell you much." He backed away from the stainless steel table and motioned to his assistant, Audrey Lesta. "Bag these up for whatever reason we might need them later on." His face was a study in sad disgust. "Only thing you can do is bury them and hope they'll enrich the soil." The two men shook their heads.

"No clues, no one saw anything. Just five people dead..."

"And the dog," piped up Audrey, gathering a plastic sheet of brittle shards.

"And the dog." Doc Brogdon agreed with her.

~~~~~~~~~~~~~~~~~

Tricia's first day at work was unusual for several reasons. For one, never before had a woman been hired at the Yard to design the interior of a submarine. This, in itself, was enough to bring every man who could manage into the design area to gawk at her. And if a pretty girl doing what had formerly only been a man's work wasn't enough, it was widely known that this particular girl had found five bodies a day or so ago. Five bodies burned to a crisp. The gawkers watched Tricia carefully. Did her young and unlined face show any stress from stumbling over dead people? Could a pretty little girl cope with all of this?

Charlie Tobey could have answered their questions.

The Tobey family had moved to Kittery Point, Maine when Charlie Tobey took a job as an engineer with the phone company. His wife, Patricia, stayed at home, as most women did in those times, raising a family of four daughters. The

Tobeys were progressive parents; they brought up their girls to think independently and educated them as well as they would have educated sons. The three older sisters were married, but had careers, unusual in the early 1940's. Debbie and Lynn were accountants; Diane was an office manager. Baby Tricia was the most fiercely independent of all. She studied in an unusual sphere and became a designer, specializing in the utilization of spaces.

Even when Tricia was a youngster, everyone wanted her help in putting things neatly into spaces. Most of the women in her family were delighted to let her re-arrange their closets. She'd dump out the entire contents, shoes, belts, sweaters, dresses, and throw everything onto the bed. Ruthless..."Have you worn this rag in the last two years?"...she'd throw the offending garment into a pile on the floor...."This can go to the Thrift Shop. Someone else will appreciate it."...And when she was done, why your dresses all hung facing the same way! Your shoes were stacked in boxes, and each box labeled clearly. Your blouses and sweaters were hung by color, short-sleeved yellow blouses first, then long-sleeved yellow blouses. Short-sleeved white blouses next, followed by long-sleeved white blouses. The hats sat in round boxes, each labeled, on one side of the shelf, and purses, filed on end, on the other side. "And I plan to inspect this closet in three weeks," little Trisha admonished. "And I expect it to be as neat as it is now!" And her way *was* better. Tricia could pack (and neatly) more things into any space better than anyone else. It was an unusual gift. "Great," her sister Debbie acknowledged. "But so what?"

"I'll be a closet designer," little Tricia avowed. "Famous movie starts will hire me to fix their closets."

"Ha!"

"You'll see."

She interfered when Auntie Maude fixed up her kitchen. "Like this, Auntie!" She drew a plan, putting the ice-box out on the porch, the sink under the window near the stove, and the refrigerator close by. "See? They're in a triangular pattern. It will save you steps and make working here easier, Auntie Maude." And it was.

She was constantly playing a game that she called "Shipwreck in the Pantry". She'd barricade herself in her mother's pantry, taking down all the items and re-arranging them in a more systematic way, with less space taken up, thereby allowing her mother to store even more groceries in a smaller space. No clothes closet was safe in the Tobey household...Tricia, no matter how many times she was yelled at...would re-arrange shoes, dresses, coats...and all of the items *did* fit back into the closet in a better, neater, more efficient way.

Her sisters might moan: 'I don't care if it is better. Keep her away from my stuff!' They hated to admit, in their vastly more mature years, that Tricia's re-arranging was certainly better...much better...

And it was, indeed. In the years to come, more and more neighbors and friends asked Tricia to help them better plan spaces. How should the living room be arranged so that everyone can sit in front of the radio and still enjoy the fire-place? If I put in a bathtub, does it go nearer the sink, or nearer the toilet?

How can my Judy put all her wedding presents in her tiny china cabinet?

All fine and dandy, in its own way, but what good was it in the long run? Tricia felt rather satisfied about herself, but how could she earn a living using this kind of talent? She tried the two architectural firms in Portsmouth, but they had no interest in hiring a girl who could clean up closets and arrange kitchens.

But, still...this was what she wanted to do. How would she fit this talent into practicality? What would she do with such a gift? Well...

One day, Tricia went to visit her father at work, Charlie paraded her around, proud of his littlest and most charming child. She was feted by Charlie's boss who served her a cup of warm, milky tea in his office. "So, Trisha, how do you like our place?" Mr. Bessinger beamed, his face gleaming with great avuncular pleasure. *Cute little kid, she was. By golly, all of Charlie's girls were adorable. Too bad Maudie and I didn't have any daughters.*

"It's very nice, Mr. Bessinger, but I think I can re-arrange your mailroom so that the work flows in a more orderly fashion." Tricia's feet dangled from the chair and she clasped her hands together eagerly. Mr. Bessinger's mouth flapped open for a millisecond. Incorrectly interpreting his astonishment for approval, Tricia forged on: "And the storeroom needs some help. Let me come in on Saturday morning and I'll show you how I can arrange your work flow in a better way."

With a gasp, Mr. Bessinger began to laugh. "My goodness gracious! You think you can run my mailroom and my storeroom?"

"No, sir. Not run them, just re-arrange them." Tricia grinned at him, showing him the gap-toothed smile of a child. "Please, Mr. Bessinger, please!"

"I'm just whiz-banged, honey. I never heard of a ....well, why not, by jingo? Why not?"

In five hours, Tricia showed him her plans for a vastly streamlined mailroom. "And you don't really have to spend any money...just re-arrange things a little, hang this chart up and here...see? You always know at any moment where the order is...if it was delivered...what might be holding it up...see?"

And he *did* see. Shaking his head with wonder, Bessinger had the foresight to take this little girl more than half-seriously. Tricia was invited to wander around the entire building...the offices, the switchboard rooms, the soldering and assembly lines...even the cafeteria and rest rooms. "It's going to take me about two weeks, Mr. Bessinger. I have a lot of homework and I have to help mother with chores, but I'll have graphs and reports for you very soon."

And she did. Mr. Bessinger was a wise man. He quickly saw that her spatial grasp and understanding of flow was far, far advanced for a child of her age. Matter of fact, Bessinger thought that Tricia's talents far surpassed most professional adults. "She ought to be encouraged, Tobey," he advised Charlie. "Find her a great engineering school and let her go. She's just amazing!"

And thus, twelve years later, Tricia copped the prize of being hired to re-design the living quarters of the newest submarine to be built at the Portsmouth Naval Shipyard.

The Shipyard was churning out submarines and the technology to build them was improving daily. America needed these stealth underwater vessels and by golly, the Portsmouth Naval Shipyard was complying handily. In the past, it took many months to build and launch such a huge, complex war machine as a submarine. But, with American "can-do" and ingenuity, the Yard managed to improve the completion time to less than 3 months, and, as a matter of pride, launched four submarines in a single day!

And Tricia went to work there. The first day went swimmingly. She spent most of the day with Commander Clay, who led the *SS Burrfish* Project. The Chief Engineer of the sub, a young Lieutenant named Scott Wanner, was absent that day. Wanner was in New York City, attending a chess match. "It's nice that the Navy lets an employee off to play chess," Tricia remarked with some tact and candor.

"It's a special case," Commander Clay chuckled. "Not everyone can swan off to play games, but Scott is a well-recognized chess player...known world-wide...advanced league, or some such. Don't play the game myself...I'm a poker player at heart." His booming voice expressed his humor. "Lose every time, that's me! Chump Clay, I think, is how the swabbies refer to me when my back is turned." He smiled down at Tricia. "But this young man...I understand he has a steel trap mind and can play chess with the best of them." His frosty blue eyes met hers. *By Jove,* he thought, *she has green eyes! Real green eyes. Just like the ocean's flash at twilight. Remarkable!* He pulled his thoughts back to chess. "He's teaching a chess class one night a week to any of the employees who want to learn. I understand there are fifty or more beginners. And he's also trying to have a session once a month for the prisoners here in the Castle. Maybe teach *them* a little bit about chess. Can *you* play chess? Might be interesting..."

"I play a little. My dad taught all of his daughters how to play." She began to laugh, "And I deal a mean hand of poker, too. I've cleaned out my Dad and most of his buddies. Watch out, Commander Clay!"

Clay introduced her to the men in the engineering office, then sat back to watch what transpired. Will they accept her as an equal? Would she be able to handle all of the crap that a group of Navy men might hand out? Could she cope with the swear words? The wolf whistles from the fellows who thought and acted that way? The sexual innuendoes? Would the men only see a pretty face...and dam*nation*, she *was* pretty...With that long, black, shiny hair and those eyes...or could they also see the razor-sharp brain behind the face? Could she dish back all of the bilge that was going to be coming her way? He lit a cigar, listening to the back and forth chit-chat. He nodded...she seemed just fine. He hoped so, for all of their sakes. A lot was on the line here, putting a young woman into this hornets' nest.

~~~~~~~~~~~~~~~~~

**JUNE 12, 1943**
**WWI Liberty Ships back on duty! These doughty relics have been refitted as hospital troop ships bringing home our wounded men and women.**

Alex braced his legs apart, trying not to shift his weight or fall over as the sturdy old ship, the *Buchanan*, fondly called the *Bucket* by all who were on it, foundered in the trough of the wave.On his right side, Carol Abbi-Patricks leaned up against him hard, bolstering his stance with her hip hard against him. On his left, Michelle Rondeau also pushed her curvy body against him, standing square and leaning into the operating table with her arm holding him as still as she could. The doughty little ship leaped into the air, and Alex held the scalpel away from the incision.

"Christ! I almost cut his throat!" Across the table, he met the calm eyes of Eunice O'Connor. The mask hid her mouth, but the crinkles at the edge of her eyes told him that she was smiling with encouragement. He could always count on Eunice...even with her face half-hidden.

"Seems a little bit calmer now." Carol sponged the blood away from Airman Sammy Jordinski's trachea. "Now is a good time. The waves seem less violent. This poor guy needs some help before he dies on the table in front of us." She gave Alex a mild shove. "It's up to you, Doc."

He nodded and took a deep breath. His scalpel descended, gleaming and glittering under the dangling light bulb that lit the crowded quarters they were using as an operating room. Delicate...delicate...the blood welled up in a fountain, but Michelle was there, heavy padded swabs in hand, soaking up the gush of blood and deftly inserting a suction tube.

In complete harmony, like an orchestra that played the most complex musical piece in total unison, the operating team, with Captain George Alexander Patton conducting, competently saved the life of Airman Jordinski.

After the surgery, Corpsmen Alan Bowen, his own arm bandaged from wrist to elbow, and Corpsman Neil Harmon, a gash on his neck showing where an enemy bayonet had struck, together carried the anesthetized body of Airman Jordinski back into the relative peace and stability of sick bay.

~~~~~~~~~~~~~~~~~

Michelle plopped herself down. *"Mon Dieu!* That was a close one." She picked up a sugar cookie from the platter on the table. "He is some genius, our Doctor Patten."

"And gorgeous, too." Carol's shoulders wiggled in admiration. "I'd bite him on his little neck, if he gave me any encouragement."

"You have too many men that you bite!" Michelle's rich laugh rang out. "I am trying to convince him that French women are the best."

"And French women, like you, also have too many men that they are trying to satisfy!" Carol started to count on her fingers. "You're writing to Anthony in the Marines, Shorty in the Navy, um, *Gary* in the Navy, *Eddie* in the Navy....who else?"

"She's got seven or eight on her little French string," Eunice laughed. "And who are you, Carol, to criticize Michelle? How many guys do you write to every week?"

Michelle and Carol drew themselves up. In unison, they chorused: "It's our patriotic duty to keep as many men as happy as we can!"

~~~~~~~~~~~~~~~~~

By virtue of Trisha's brilliance in spatial concepts and innovative ideas, she'd wowed them all. And the worry of Scott Wanner was for naught. He supported her one hundred per cent and made sure that everyone knew that he did. Scott's areas of responsibility were the exterior of the sub and the placement of the weapons that she was to carry. Tricia was responsible for the interior and the crew areas. The Yard, after its first shock, treated Tricia as if she had been a man, just another human being doing a job. After all, the Yard had adjusted to women who welded, women who painted, female sweepers…and every woman who worked at the Yard worked as well, if not better, than the man whom they had replaced. Despite the early grumblings and dire warnings from the older men, it was roundly acknowledged that, by golly, these women could do anything!

And Scott proved to be an admirer of hers from the start, loudly proclaiming her ability right up to the Yard Commander, Admiral Withers. It was a good thing that they got along so well, as they were thrown into close proximity, not only in the tiny hot, stuffy yellow-green painted room that served as their office, but also in the suffocating squeeze of submarine interiors. Tricia spent the best part of her first several days crawling through the Control Room, trying out the sagging hammocks that were to be the beds of the submariners, attempting to cook in the ill-fitted galley and pretending to eat, read and relax while shoved against the three torpedoes that jutted into the minuscule day-room.

It certainly was a positive step for man-kind…or woman-kind… Scott mused, when ladies started wearing slacks. As women left their kitchens to weld, to build, to paint and to hammer, house dresses or skirts and tops simply were not practical for bending and stooping. And so, slacks became acceptable. Now, to be fair, some women really shouldn't be wearing trousers that delineated their buttocks and hips. For some women, these areas should be covered up and disguised as much as possible. But for others…women like Tricia…well!

Behind her, watching the way her khaki-colored slacks fitted her shapely derrière, Scott found himself drawn more and more to this young woman. His thoughts were almost, well, lustful. He found himself thinking of her late at night, when he woke up, thirsty for a drink of cold water and wishing that there was someone...a meaningful someone...waiting for him to climb back into bed. He wondered if she thought of him in the cold, lonely hours of the morning.

Tricia, unaware of the way her wiggles caused discomfort in Scott's midsection, pulled herself out of the narrow opening of the submarine's day-room.

"I don't know how any human beings, much less these husky men, can live in these conditions. Live! *Ha!* They're going to be underwater for weeks or months at a time, trying to acclimate themselves, and they can barely move! None of them can fit into their hammocks...look! Even me...and I'm only five-foot-four...I can't cram my legs and feet into these bunks!" Tricia was livid with disgust. "I have to design a sub where 6 officers and 54 enlisted men can exist in some comfort. I mean, they don't have to be living in luxury, but they do have to be able to thrive." There was anger and frustration in her voice. "We have to rip all of this out and redesign it so that the men can be rested and ready to fight."

"We don't have the time," Scott told her. "These subs have to roll out of here haba-haba."

"Haba-haba? What does that mean?"

"Chop-chop, wickie-wickie...you know, right away." He smiled at her. Damn, but she was cute. "You're going to have to learn a bit of swabbie talk, Tricia. If you want to be like a gob, and not have the mockers," he laughed at her astonished face, "you've got to learn how we speak down here in the pig boats."

"Never!" she averred stoutly. "I'll stick to plain old English."

"Then you'll never know what the gobs are saying about you. They might think you're a scupper or a canary."

"What do those mean?"

"Ah, *now* you want to know, do you?" He reached over and patted her hand, fighting off the desire to grab her and run his hands through her shiny, dark hair. "How about I give you some lessons."

His grin made her stomach do funny things. She wondered if he knew that she thought of him at night. Wondered how his lips would feel. Wondered...ah, nevermind...She harrumphed and made her voice sound businesslike. "Well, even if the subs have to be produced wickie-wockie, or whatever you said, the men need a decent area to live in. I think I can take a day or two and come up with a better sleeping area, common day-room, galley and command station."

"It's too late to do anything about the *Sea Cat*. She's almost finished. But maybe we can re-do the interior of the *Sea Devil*. The plans have been drawn and approved, but nothing has been produced yet."

"How much time do I have?"

"Maybe two or three days," Scott shook his head. "You'd have to re-draw everything, be sure it all is going to fit properly and safely, get it approved and sweet talk the machinists into re-tooling all of the components." His face was skeptical. "This will take a lot of work! The effort will have to be Herculean!"

"Well, wickie-woo-to you!" Her jaw was stubborn. "I plan to get it done, one way or another. No one should be uncomfortable or jammed into a bed that's too short, or have to eat upside down. Even in a submarine."

Scott checked his watch as the Yard whistle blew. "Time to go home. How about you join me for a quick supper and we can both try to redesign the interiors. My work is going on schedule, but I can give you a couple of hours every night until we get this done."

She stood up and grinned, then stuck her hand out to shake his. "You're on, you swabbie, you." He roared with laughter. "If you, a flatlander from Ohio can work overtime, just think what you can do with me, a true-blue Maniac. Let's do it! These guys deserve the best we can offer them!"

And, to the delight of the submariners and officers who were to live on the *Sea Devil,* and the pride of Commander Withers, they did. Even the hardened machinists, fitters and welders were in awe of the new interior. "Christ! It's the first pig boat that can accommodate a six-foot-two swabbie like me!" one of the crewmen crowed. "Everyone will want to be on one of these new subs! Hip-hip-hooray and a donut for Tricia!"

~~~~~~~~~~~~~~~~

On the night that the *Sea Devil* was launched, Scott gave Tricia a present; a wiggly one-year-old Black Lab puppy. "Her name is Hannah," he beamed, "and she's a rescue dog."

"Oh, the darling!" Tricia was nearly knocked over by an eager pink tongue and a lashing, whirling tail. "What's a rescue dog?"

"She was rescued from her former owners. They didn't treat her well."

*"What?"* Tricia knelt, gathering Hannah's silky body in her arms. "How could anyone not treat a dog well, especially a sweetie pie like this?"

"You'd be surprised. One of the men in the Yard rescued her and he has two dogs of his own. He wanted to know if I knew anyone who would take good care of her for the rest of her life." His eyes crinkled. "I said, 'Yeah, I know someone'." His eyes yearned into hers.

Hannah was spilled onto the floor as Tricia flung herself into Scott's arms.

# CHAPTER FIVE

**June 6, 1943**
**The USO at The Connie Bean Center begins a series of USO**
**Camp Shows on Thursday and Saturday nights. Local perform-**
**ers, show-business people from the USO ranks and even Holly-**
**wood and Broadway stars will entertain our troops.**

The entertainers came from everywhere. By train, by automobile, using precious ration points for the gasoline, by foot,
hoping to hitch-hike a ride from some sympathetic driver...
they filed into the Connie Bean Center, their props and music
in hand, ready to perform. Ventriloquists, quick sketch artists,
comedians, opera singers, dance bands, barbershop quartets,
choirs, snake charmers and magicians...they all crowded into
the Portsmouth-Kittery area to do their bit for the boys.

America saw the outpouring of talent that eagerly volun-
teered to entertain the troops. Famous stars, movie queens,
people well-known: Bob Hope, The Andrews Sisters, Jean
Bartell (Miss America 1943), Rudy Vallee, The Ink Spots,
Glenn Miller, Dinah Shore, The Mills Brothers, Bing Crosby,
Mickey Rooney, Jimmy Stewart, Olivia DeHaviland, Joe E.
Brown (who was to lose his son in the war), Al Jolson, Martha
Raye and hundreds of other famous stars entertained soldiers
all over the world. By the end of the war, more than one and a
half *million* performers had contributed their time and talents
to the USO.

One of the most fervent stars entertaining the troops was Marlene Dietrich. Her sister was being held as a prisoner at the Belsen concentration camp. Miss Dietrich took particular pleasure and great personal risk in performing for the troops and thumbing her nose at Hitler. The *Fuehrer,* in anger, had Miss Dietrich's name placed on his infamous death list. Miss Dietrich just laughed and threw back her head, showing the lovely line of her neck and face. "I spit at Hitler!" she averred. "Let's get on with the show!"

The celebrity entertainers gleaned most of the national publicity, but the lesser-known entertainers, local people with talent, those who hoped against hope to be discovered, men and women who just wanted to do their bit, were the backbone of the USO shows and the Camp shows. They became known as "Soldiers in Greasepaint", and many of them faithfully performed six or eight times a day to brighten the lives of our fighting men and women. Sometimes the USO show was performed before an audience of several thousand GIs. Sometimes a group of Greasepaint GIs entertained only six or eight men who were sequestered near a foxhole close to the actual fighting. Wherever they were needed and wanted, these gallant men and women gave of their voices and talents to the war effort. Many even made the ultimate sacrifice, losing their lives on airplanes and under enemy fire.

~~~~~~~~~~~~~~~~~

A committee was drawn up. "If we're going to have a USO here, we're going to do it right," Kittery Town Councilman Joshua Dingley proclaimed. "We'll have the best damn USO in the Yew-Nited Sates!"

"And we'll work together with you," Portsmouth Mayor Ron Leard chimed in. "We'll bring together the folks in Portsmouth and Kittery and give those servicemen only the finest!"

"And women," Grace Sabatino interrupted him.

"And women?" Ron echoed, perplexed

"Women," Grace averred. "There are many women who are in the armed service."

"And who work at the Yard," one of Kittery's oldest residents, Mary Dalzell, sitting in the front row of the chamber, added. "Lots of women are working now. Riveters, welders, painters, in the offices..." She turned to face the audience..."It wasn't this way when I was a pup, but things have changed. Women are to be included equally." She patted her neatly coiffed white hair and nodded firmly to the applause, coming mostly from the women in the audience, and sat down. Councilman Dingley opened his mouth to demur, then noticed that more than three-quarters of the audience *were* women. He was a prudent man, up for re-election in the fall. And not stupid.

"You are absolutely right," he beamed at the audience, paying a special obeisance to Mary Dalzell. She nodded regally to him. He made a mental note to get a photo of Mary and himself printed in the Bugle. It would be worth a lot of votes.

As for the committee, he prudently chose those who would do most of the work for him: Julie Patten, who never shirked from hard work and knew everyone in town; Julie would head up the entertainment. Jacqueline Small, who managed the cafeterias in the York Public Schools. Jacquie would be in charge of the food kitchens to help feed the wives and children of the servicemen who came to temporarily live in the Seacoast area. Grace Sabatino, co-owner of Kittery Gardens and Nurseries, with her experience in gardens and plants, would be a natural to head up victory gardens both in Portsmouth and in Kittery.

In turn, Julie suggested the unusually unorthodox Brenda Be. Most of the committee had heard of or seen Brenda one way or another. Perhaps strolling down State Street, wearing a man's tuxedo and a top hat...perhaps riding a bicycle, wearing an old-fashioned bloomer costume, her hair tied up in a colorful kerchief, perhaps attending a movie or a play, dressed in a Valkyrie outfit, wielding a spear, as if she was going to appear in a rendition of *Aida*...

Julie coughed and tried to sell Brenda's positive attributes. "Brenda, well, she's unique. She's...ahem...the bee's knees on music and the arts. She'll be in charge of culture and classes to learn, oh...maybe getting up a jazz band...that sort of thing. Teaching the men how to play an instrument, showing them how to appreciate music..." Julie looked around, hoping for support.

"She's really, um, peculiar," Mary Dalzell murmured, finger-ing the long rope of pearls that adorned her neck. "She wears... well... sometimes, she wears men's clothing." Mary's face was a study. She wanted to support a woman to handle the job, but did she want to support *this* particular...and peculiar...woman?

"And she smokes cigars. I swear!" A lady in the second row, who wore a green kerchief over her hair and a sour expression on her face, objected. "She's really odd."

"But she's whip-smart," Julie countered. "And who cares what she wears?" She asked the green kerchief, "Can *you* set up a performing art group?" The lady quickly demurred.

"If Julie thinks she can do the job, well, even if she is peculiar...it is the job that we must focus on," Mary threw caution to the winds. Kerchief grudgingly nodded her accep-tance. Julie, pleased that she had overcome this silly little skirmish, nodded pleasantly to the Kerchief. The Queen nodding to the commoner.

"We also have to consider the Negros who are coming more and more to the area," Ron Leard interjected. "Are we going to allow Negroes at the USO?"

"The USO rules say that anyone...anyone in the armed services, is welcome to come to the club." Councilman Dingley referred to a sheaf of papers on the podium. "Other, larger cities have sometimes gotten around this problem by building two separate clubs; one for whites and one for the colored."

"It's really not needed and impractical. And anyway, we can't afford two buildings, Josh," Ron shook his head. "This is 1943. We are all Americans, all working for the same goal. We'll just have to assume that everyone will get along."

"They get along in the Army and the Navy." Julie's words were tart. "They can manage to get along at the Connie Bean Center. How silly!"

"But how about the dancing?" Grace Sabatino asked. "How will we handle that?"

"I have been doing a lot of research," Mayor Leard said. "We need to find a woman...maybe more than one...a colored woman who can sit on the board with us and advise us...well, handle the situation of Negros."

Mary Dalzell raised her hand. "How about Sabina Carter?"

"Who's Sabina Carter?"

"She's head of the National Urban League. She's a local woman, respectably married to a dentist. Doctor Lester Carter has a practice in North Hampton. No one has a harsh word or a problem with the Carters. And Sabina, well...she's...responsible, capable and has horse-sense. She'll help us formulate a sensible and workable solution so that everyone can use the club and not be intimidated or shunned. After all," Mary faced the audience, "these men, whatever their color or wherever they're from...they are fighting the war for us." There was a burst of applause. Mary was very well respected among the women in the Seacoast area. Secure in her position, Mary added; "In everything we do here with and for the USO, we have to ask ourselves, 'Are we fighting Hitler or are we fighting ourselves and America?'" The applause swelled.

Several ladies answered her rhetorical question by calling out, "Hitler!" Mary sat back down, satisfied that she had done a good thing.

"Whew! You certainly wowed them!" Julie whispered. "Where'd you get that clever slogan?"

"Right out of the USO manual!" Mary pointed to page seven. Julie laughed and patted Mary's arm.

Thus, the USO Committee was formed.

## COMMITTEE OF THE
# SEACOAST REGION USO
### PORTSMOUTH, NH and KITTERY, MAINE

Chairmen
Mayor Ronald Leard, Portsmouth
Town Council Chairman Joshua Dingley, Kittery
Secretary – Mary Dalzell


Committee Chairwoman – Julia Fern Patten

Victory Gardens – Grace Sabatino
Food Pantry – Jacqueline Small
USO Shows/Performances – Julia Fern Patten/Deborah Orloff
Urban League Affiliate – Sabina Carter
Hostesses – Candace McClosky
Security and Maintenance – Harold Fessenden

USO Chaplains:
Rabbi Joel Fish and Father Nicholas Calabro

# THE USO AT
## THE CONNIE BEAN CENTER
*presents*

# YOUR SHOW OF SHOWS!
### Saturday Night, June 12, 1943 • Doors Open at 7 PM

## *Starring...*

**Janis Neiman**, singing **"Stormy Weather"**

**The Flying Heibels** on their daring trapeze, featuring
**Christa Heibel, Kathy Fontes, Keith Schlief, Elizabeth Blosser**
& strongman **Charlie the Miner**

Mister Magic, **Kurt Englehardt** & his lovely assistant, **Christina**

The twinkling toes of **Dick & Ursula Bondi**
in a glamorous **Tango**

**The Sounds of the Accordion Named Bob**
with **Frankie Accurso**

**Tap Dance down Broadway**
with the **Knickerbocker Brothers, Sam & Eddie**

**Caricature Sketches** by **Artist Patrick Bee**

Sharpshooter **Captain Dave Holt** & his blazing guns

**Jane Whidden**, singing **"I'll Be Seeing You"**

Strongman **Dick Vermerian** will astound you with
feats of strength

**Laurie & Ted Mooney** dance a **Jitterbug**

**Barbara Fine**, singing **"GI Jive"**

**Timmy & Molly Corcoran** & their **Irish Band**
dance the **Irish Jig**

"The Bells of Saint Mary," a Monolog, by **Mary Ellen Cross**

**Karen Cosgrove** & her **Amazing Poodles**

**Bruce Carlson**, singing **"You'll Never Know"**

**Julie Patten** tap dances to **"The Lullaby of Broadway"**

**Kittery Jug Band Four**
starring **Bryce Adams, Moo MacKinnon, Ruby Stevens,
& Murphy Bush**
& featuring **Jana Ciboroski** on the **washboard**

**"Ma" Fuller,** singing **"Pistol Packin' Mamma"**

**Chris Gallagher** with her **Australian Digeree Doo**

Those Kittery Clowns, **Larry & Marty Graham**

**Paul and June Haven** dance to the **Polka**

**Debbie Higgins** & her performing horse **"Kathleen"**

**The Tumbling Acrobats** of the **Lewis Family:
Christian, Jody, Isabella, Francesca & Little Skip**

# All These...and More!
*And, the sublime sounds of*
Rosie Nunn & her all-girl orchestra!

**Ticket Price: $1.50
Servicemen and women in uniform admitted FREE!**

*Come early! Seats are limited!
Don't miss this show!*

Jan Neiman was the opening act. The opening act of the first USO show ever produced at the Connie Bean Center. A show put together with great speed, using the best of local talent. No wonder she was nervous!

Nervous? Good golly, she was scared stiff! She gulped as she heard the opening notes of her song. She thought of her mother and father out there and slithered out on the stage, imagining how Lena Horne would have performed and praying that she might do one-tenth as well. She wore a silk gown, the color of a just-picked peach, and the color set off her smooth, dark skin. Her hair was up in a glamorous chignon and she'd placed a dark pink Camilla behind her left ear. She looked glamorous, poised and professional.

The audience screamed their welcome. Thinking of how Lena would have done it, she sashayed to the gilt stool in the center of the stage and waited a moment, until the roar subsided. She crossed her long legs, letting the audience glimpse her shapely knee and a few inches above.

The orchestra again played the first bars and Jan wet her lips, prayed and began to sing: "Don't know why…there's no sun up in the sky….stormy weather…"

The audience pounded their hands in applause. Jan bowed, catching sight of a large group of Negro servicemen who were sitting on the right side of the auditorium. The men, as one, stood up, clapping and cheering and calling out "More! More!" Grinning, Jan spread her hands out, as the stagehands behind her brought the complex apparatus on stage for the next act.

"Thank you all and thank you for wanting more. We have such a huge show for you tonight that I have to move on." The audience, in a fine mood, booed and tried to convince her to stay on stage for another song.

"You'll all just have to come back in a few weeks when I'll be singing again." A smile split her face. "I promise I'll rehearse a nice new song for you."

"But Jan", a booming voice came from the other side of the footlights, "I'll be fighting in a few weeks! I need you *now!*"

The audience roared.

Jan, confused and touched, turned to the wings. What should she do?

Connie Bean herself had been standing at the left of the stage. She came out.

Some of the audience, recognizing her, began to applaud and stamp their feet. She shushed them cheerfully. "Isn't Jan marvelous?"

The audience cried out their agreement. "She'll be back, I promise. Wait until the end when we do our finale." Jan smiled at her and six servicemen thought they'd died and gone to Heaven. Connie threw out her hands, appealing to the audience. "But right now, we *have* to move on. Otherwise, we'll be here until tomorrow!" Connie signaled Rosie Nunn and the all-girl band swung themselves into a rousing march. Jan, sensing the moment, threw kisses to the soldiers and, hand-in-hand with Connie, exited the stage.

"And now," Connie called out just as she disappeared, "The wonderful Flying Heibels!"

At that same moment, a whirl of colorful acrobats bounced on, turning cartwheels and leaping into the air to catch the swinging bars of the trapeze that had been let down. A blonde woman, curvy and athletic, dressed in pink spangles and feathers, descended into the middle of the melee on a decorated trapeze, waving to the audience. The answering whistles and stomps were interrupted by a drum-roll and she launched herself into space, turning in mid-air as she flew to the second trapeze. Jan's performance was nearly forgotten in a collective gasp of amazement. The audience settled down to watch and be entertained. The show was on.

~~~~~~~~~~~~~~~~

**June 16, 1943**
**WAR NEWS - MORE THAN A MILLION NEGROS ENLIST!**

The war certainly changed the lives of most Americans, but for two groups – all women and men of color – the change was most profound.

Until the start of the War and the urgent need for workers to replace the young men who had gone off to fight, most women were housewives, staying home to care for families. Only 20 percent of women were in the workforce. By 1944, that number had increased to nearly 40 percent. With many young men in the fighting forces, and even with the Servicemen's Dependent Allowance Act, passed in 1942, the allowances were simply insufficient for the women left behind to raise and feed their families. And thus, women were forced to go to work building bombers and submarines and becoming necessary parts of the war economy. Housewives got a taste of their first paychecks, and discovered that they *liked* it! However satisfying it had been to raise a family, coming home with cash in their pockets was a liberating and exciting thing.

Women of color, who had been employed as field hands in the south and maids or cooks both in the north and the south, left these jobs (generally with undisguised glee) to work in factories, driving trucks and buses and tractors, learning to run offices, becoming nurses or teachers, for once having access to jobs for which they never would have been considered prior to the war. Many joined the war effort directly, enlisting in those branches of the armed forces that accepted them as pilots, drivers, nurses and cryptographers. They, too, liked this heady feeling of being useful and needed, not to mention the salaries that accompanied these new responsibilities.

Many men – both Negro and white – who joined the war effort had never been away from home before they embarked into the maelstrom called basic training. Many, especially those from the south and Appalachian regions, never owned a pair of shoes before. Many were extremely poor and even suffered malnutrition from lack of food or ignorance about basic health. For them, the rigors and companionship of camp came as a surprise – sometimes a good surprise, and sometimes a dreadful surprise.

In the two years starting from the time that Pearl Harbor was attacked, the Negro moved into industrial jobs and into the armed forces faster than in the seventy-five years which preceded the war. Previously shunned from many positions in factories, the urgency of needing workers to man the war machine propelled Negroes into those jobs that they could not have previously hoped for. The top brass in the Army, Navy, Air Force and Marines remembered the bravery and excellence of the colored forces that fought in the Civil War and encouraged Negroes to enlist. And they did with great eagerness and patriotism, serving as combat troops, SEABEAS, corpsmen and, as they fought the enemy, were given the opportunity to become trained and educated into fields where they hadn't been able to previously penetrate.

From the standpoint of women and Negros, their entry into the war was generally a very good thing. From the standpoint of the war effort, the entry of women and Negros into the war effort was *definitely* a very good thing.

And for Jan, watching in the wings as Sam and Eddie Knickerbocker, neighbors from the Puddleduck area of Portsmouth, tap-danced their way into the USO audience's hearts, this USO show was proving to be the best thing since... well...*since!* She couldn't wait until the next show. She'd give them a rendition of *"Takin' a Chance on Love"* that would pull them *all* out of their seats.

~~~~~~~~~~~~~~~~~

**Headline, Washington, DC: Enough VD cases in Washington, DC, to fill Griffith stadium twice-over!**

It was the same in the Portsmouth-Kittery area. Men who should be in fighting good-health were catching VD...there was a serious epidemic of syphilis and gonorrhea cutting into the good health of the men, and even a few women, who were being trained to fight overseas.

Penicillin and the other drugs that could cure venereal diseases were in critically short supply. There wasn't enough medicine produced yet to both cure the men who were still stateside and still supply the injured and maimed who were overseas. Naturally, the bulk of the drugs were sent overseas to save the lives of our fighting men.

The men still in training camps or stationed at the Yard were warned and then warned again, but it was an almost impossible job to convince healthy young men, who might just die in a few weeks or months as they were transferred to combat areas, that they should stay chaste. Most of the young men refused to believe that a case of the clap would ever actually kill them. They were going into battle, for goodness sake! Which would get them first? The Japs, the Krauts, or the clap?

The War Department tried, producing films and printing lurid brochures with graphic photographs describing how certain body parts might just fall off if you were really careless, and the men were all forced to attend the screenings, watch the gory and graphic pictures and read the propaganda. But even the gruesome warnings failed to convince many who were being shipped to the jungles of the Philippines, the arid regions of North Africa or the bombed-out cities of Italy or France that their last days stateside should be pure and virtuous.

The people of the USO did their best, trying to keep the young men in a wholesome environment. The young men themselves, torn between the "good" women and the "prosties", shrugged their uniform-clad shoulders and spent their off-duty hours visiting a bit of both.

Young and impressionable, many of them away from family and home for the first time, these teen-aged soldiers yearned to be mothered, to assuage their loneliness with a home-cooked meal, an evening of wholesome entertainment and a jitterbug or two with a pretty girl who reminded him of his own sweetheart back in Tuscaloosa.

And yet, the glamour and glitter of the dark saloons, peopled with prostitutes, camp girls, and even the local talent, called a siren song. How could they resist the bright lights, gambling halls and soft bosoms that beckoned with sin?

~~~~~~~~~~~~~~~~~

"I really want to help with the war effort." The tall blonde woman, dressed in the latest of styles, perhaps a little too well-dressed, insisted.

*What the hell am I supposed to say to her?* Brenda Be, generally able to cope with *any*thing, nearly cowered. *For*

*Christ's sake! She's the biggest madam in Portsmouth! She owns a whorehouse! Do we really want the head of a house of ill repute helping with the USO?*

"Uh, um, Miss Hess...Is it Miss Hess or Mrs. Hess?" Brenda stalled for time, her brain churning furiously as she thought of how to handle this. *What the heck do I say to a madam?*

The apparition smiled, showing a beautiful set of teeth. *She really was rather pretty*, Brenda noticed. Lovely hair, huge blue eyes, glowing complexion..."Just call me Kathie, spelled with an 'ie' at the end," the apparition said, her voice low and pleasant. Then she grinned. "Look, I know what you're thinking. I'm not a dope, you know."

Brenda had the grace to blush. She shook her head. "I'm at a loss. I don't quite know what to say...um, ah, ...Kathie. I, um..."

"I'm the madam at the whorehouse, is that what you were trying not to say?" Her laugh bellowed out. "You know who I am and why should I deny it?" Uninvited, she hooked one slim ankle around the chair in front of Brenda's desk and sat down. As Brenda struggled, Kathie lit up a cigarette. "Nonetheless, me and my ladies are American patriots. We do our bit for the war effort all the time. You entertain the troops one way, we entertain the troops another way."

Brenda nodded. It was a fair statement. "I guess I never quite thought of it all that way, um, Kathie." *I never dreamed of thinking of it that way!*

"So we all talked and said that we wanted to help out. The girls told me that no one would want us. I know," Kathie's mouth was wry, "that you think we're vermin, but, hey! We fill a need here in this town."

Despite herself, Brenda began to giggle. After a moment, Kathie Hess joined in, bellowing her laughter out. *Maybe this strange broad will give us girls a fair shake!*

"Hell's bells," Brenda said, after she regained her composure, "There must be some way you can help out and have it accepted by the powers-that-be. But I'll be damned if I can think of it right away." She leaned over the desk and stuck out her hand. "I thank you and your....um...employees for trying

to help." Kathie leaned over the desk and put her soft mani-
cured hand into Brenda's. "Let's go out for a cup of coffee,
raise every eyebrow in the building and in the coffee-shop, and
talk about how we can manage this."

~~~~~~~~~~~~~~~~~

The two women walked down State Street, one, a tall,
statuesque blonde, dressed in a costume that shrieked money
and extruded sex, the other outfitted in a man's tuxedo, topped
with a man's bowler hat and sporting an ebony cane.  Men
stopped in their tracks to watch them go by, some watching in
confusion, some doffing their hats and some muttering dire
threats about fancy women.

"Who looks more outlandish, you or me?" Kathie laughed
as a young sailor passed them and did a double-take, not
believing his eyes.

"I'd say we are two very distinctive ladies."

"Where do you want to eat?" Kathie asked as they passed
Wolfie's Café.

"Not here," Brenda made a moue of disgust. "I hear they
serve cat meat here!"

They walked further..."And not here..." as they passed
Tedesco's Meat Market and then Tedesco's Restaurant next
door. "This place makes me shiver." Kathie shrugged. She
wasn't too fussy.

The lurid red dragon of Chang's Restaurant loomed. "How
about this? Chinese food OK?" Kathie asked. Brenda nodded.
They seated themselves on the hard bench of Chang's and
opened the menu. "Egg drop soup and pork lo-mein for me."
Kathie ordered.

The waiter turned to Brenda, who opened her mouth to
order. A series or chirping sounds were emitted. Kathie reared
back in amazement and the waiter's eyes gleamed. *Does she
speak Chinese?* The waiter grinned and nodded his head. He
chirruped back to Brenda, who laughed and spread her hands
out. The waiter joined in her laughter, bowed again and left
them.

"Did you...was that Chi*nese*?"

"Yup." Brenda nodded. "Or I should say Mandarin." She put her hands together in supplication, "'*Zhe no gai?*'" Brenda chortled. "Yes, I speak fluent Mandarin."

"You *do?*"

"I do. I spent some time in the Far East, 'way before all this war and misery."

"Amazing!" Kathie was stupefied. "I thought you were a high hat! But now! I don't think I ever met anyone like you!"

"And I don't think I've ever met anyone like *you!*" Brenda back-handed the compliment. "When you came in my office and offered to help the war effort, I was flabbergasted. I mean...well...you're a *madam!* What could we do with you and your girls without harming ourselves? We try so hard to keep up a respectable front...I mean, how could we even associate with you?"

"And how can you?" Kathie tipped her head sideways. She wasn't going to make it easy.

"I think I have an idea..." Brenda's words were drawn out slowly. The waiter shuffled to their table. Carefully, he placed down two tiny cups, brimful of some hot liquid. He bowed again and then placed a platter with a pile of large green beans in the middle of the table. Brenda spoke with him in his language. He answered back, his voice sing-song, bowed once more and backed away.

"And?" Kathie eyed the cups and poked her finger at the beans.

"This is Chinese wine. You drink it hot and it really warms you up." Brenda winked and sipped from her cup. Kathie watched her, then picked up her own cup and brought it to her lips.

"Yahhgh!" She coughed and sputtered. "Tastes like gasoline!" She gasped.

Brenda laughed harder. "Keep sipping. You'll grow to like it. The beans are lucky beans." She picked up the salt shaker and doused the plate. "Try them. They're sort of salty and chewy. They're supposed to bring good luck."

Kathie tried one. "Mmmm. Not bad." She chewed and swallowed.

Brenda ate another bean. "Soooo. What I think we could do with you and still keep to our own side of propriety is let you have a gambling evening to support the men at war."

"How so?" Kathie asked.

"We'll pick a needy thing. Maybe the men at York Hospital who are recuperating. Maybe some of them need transportation home. Maybe they want their wives to come here so that they can see one another. Maybe they need a car...um...or some new clothing to start their lives again...whatever. Your gambling evening, with all the profits going to the wounded soldiers at York, might earn a thousand dollars...."

"Or more..."

"Or more. More would be excellent."

"Would the Hess Club get any publicity?" Kathie tried to look nonchalant, but Brenda could sense how important this was to her.

"Why not? You would be a part of the war effort, but sort of separate from the USO. If people wanted to attend, they would. If they found this money offensive, well, then they could stay away. I think we can overcome a lot of opposition by saying, 'Hey! The wounded soldiers need these things...the people at the Hess Club want to help. How can you turn them away? They are Americans wanting to help Americans.' What do you think?" She wiggled excitedly on the bench as two silver dishes of food were ceremoniously placed on the table. The waiter placed two sets of chopsticks on the table. Again, he gibbered in his native tongue to Brenda, nodded his head and backed away.

Too excited to eat, Kathie mulled over Brenda's proposition. "I think you've struck gold, my friend. You think your part over and I'll think our part over and we'll meet here in a day or two and define our plans."

Brenda picked up her chopsticks, uncovered her dish and began to eat, uncoiling long strands of a brown, noodle-like food.

Kathie picked up her chopsticks and stabbed at the food on her plate. She giggled. "Screw these things!" She tossed the chopsticks aside and picked up her fork.

For a few moments, the women ate in companionable silence. Then; "Why do you wear those outlandish clothes?" Kathie just had to ask. "These men's pants and hats?"

"I like them. The pants make me feel free. The hats...oh, I just adore hats. I have dozens and dozens of hats...all kinds."

"Tell me more about yourself," Kathie urged. "You're nearly as notorious as I am around Portsmouth."

"Well....it's hard to be as notorious as a lady of ill-repute!" Brenda laughed. Kathie shrugged and leaned forward on the table, listening....

"OK. I'll give you the quick edition of Brenda Be and her life story."

"Yeah, and why is your last name like that? It's weird."

"Listen and I'll tell you..." Brenda's dark eyes sparkled. She lifted her hat off and dark, curly hair spilled down onto her shoulders. Her grin was devilish and Kathie thought that the shape of Brenda's lips, curving and provocative, would drive the customers at the Hess Club crazy. She wondered...if she offered Brenda a job...would she consider it?

"I was born in the mid-west. My parents were part of a circus. Wild, gypsy people. Sort of romantic, if you didn't get too close to them. Romantic, but mean and venal. They'd stab you or exploit you and rob you in any way they could. I wasn't a wanted child. They didn't want a little brat who would have to be cared for and would spoil their toxic games. I grew up being beaten and starved and neglected. They forced me to steal and cheat...and when I was a little older...they tried to force me to...well...to do what you and your girls do..." She raised her dark eyes to Kathie. "I make no judgments about you, Kathie. You are free to live your life as you please, as far as my standards are concerned. But I was a child."

Kathie's hand crept to her mouth. But she said nothing and Brenda continued, tracing a pattern on the tabletop with a chopstick. "I was still very young. They let me get away with disobeying them...you know...not lying with the men that they wanted me to...but, I could tell that they were always arguing and bickering over my disobedience, slapping me, pinching me black and blue. I knew the clock was ticking...their patience could only stretch so far. They wanted the big money I could earn...you know how some men really like to do things with little girls. Once my father nearly....well..." She shrugged. "I knew I would have to get away or they would kill me or I would have to kill them...or kill myself." She sighed. "I know it sounds rather melodramatic...like some movie...but it was real...and terrible....and it was intolerable to me. I stole as much money as I could from them and ran away."

"Really!" Kathie breathed.

"I was always a little bit mature for my age. I got on a train and rode East, going until a glimpse of the ocean told me to stop. I dropped my real last name. Who knows what my real name was anyway...I thought that I would begin to be myself...*Be*-gin to *be*...and, well, it just became Brenda Be." Kathie's face showed that she was impressed. *She certainly must have been one hell of a spunky kid!*

Brenda continued, "I found a place to stay in New York City...found some other people who were *simpatico* to me...I found a little restaurant in Greenwich Village where they played the blues and got a job waiting on tables to keep myself in food and wine." She smiled at some inward memory. "And then I discovered Art...with a capital A. Art changed my life and the way I thought about things. I reveled in painting, in going to museums, learning about artists and their lives...why they used paint as they did...why light mattered so much...I found I had a talent...I could paint, draw, sculpt...all those things flowed from my fingertips onto canvasses and clay." She looked down at her immaculately groomed fingernails, each nail painted a slightly different shade of red... "I made a good living selling my work, and many of my pieces hang in New York and Boston galleries."

"My!"

"Yes. But Art, although very important, wasn't just what I wanted to do for a living." Brenda ate more, paying very little attention to the food. "I wanted to create beauty for *others*.... and how could I do that?"

"How?"

"Within their homes and surroundings. I discovered my talent for making them feel special...fabrics, tabletops, steel furniture, the textures and touch of stone and silk...the colors in a bedroom that made a woman glow in her husband's arms… the feel of the wind as it danced with a filmy splash of curtain…the sweep of a staircase that beckons upward…the ambiance of a kitchen table groaning with fresh fruit and sparking glass…all these things and more…I can create the atmosphere…the background… for my clients to live as they want…" She laughed. "And sometimes, they didn't even know they wanted to live that way until I created a new kind of life for them!"

"*Jimminy!*" Kathie was open-mouthed in tribute. "You make me feel it all…I *see* it!"

"Yes." Brenda was solemn. "I can do that for a client…or a friend…make a life that suits them"

"Are you married? Do you have a lover?" Kathie leaned forward again, safe in the knowledge that there was nothing that she couldn't ask.

"I had a love…" Brenda was wistful. "To quote Edgar Allen Poe: 'I had a love that was more than a love…' He was beautiful and we were as happy as it was possible to be. He looked like a satyr…a faun…a god. He was everything to me, but he had to leave me. I can't talk too much about that time…." She paused, and the pupils of her eyes grew enormous. "He left me with the greatest treasure, however. A son." She smiled down at her empty plate. "I named him Alden. Alden Be. It means loyal friend, and he was the most beautiful child, even if I say so myself," a faint blush stained her cheeks. "But he was! He really was! Rosy and long-limbed, with curly hair and a dimpled smile that would break your heart. He was brilliant and charming, cheerful and funny, yet perceptive and solemn…all these things and more was my son. And he still is." She looked up and the sun shone out of her eyes. "He lives in another city now; he's no longer a child, but a young man. He's making his own way and living his own life. We see one another often and enjoy every moment. But he is free, and I need to be free, and our lives suit us both." She sat back.

"And now, my dear, it is your turn to tell me how you became a madam."

Kathie shook her head in admiration. "Nothing quite so romantic, I assure you. I had a very conventional upbringing…

a good and loving mother and father. We moved a lot because of my father's job, so I made friends quickly and was prepared to lose them as quickly. I was...well, maybe *adjustable* is a good word.

"When I was a young woman, my parents were killed in an accident and I was left with a small legacy. We had just moved to Hackensack, New Jersey and I knew no one, really. And Hackensack...well...Hackensack, I can say with certainty, is the most boring place in the world." She made a face of disgust. "And then, I became infatuated with a man....it's always a man, isn't it?" Her enormous blue eyes looked inward... "I got caught."

"Caught? You mean...?"

"Exactly. Caught like a fish on a line." Kathie grimaced and shrugged. "I wanted to keep the baby, and so I moved north to a place outside of Boston, where no one knew me at all, and tried to pretend I was a widow. I wanted to be respectable." She pushed her plate away. "He was rich. He gave me more money than I could count. But it was a payment so that the baby and I would disappear...go away from his well-ordered life." She sighed. "It was a good business arrangement for me. I admired him, but never really loved him. Maybe it was all a part of punishment for behaving as I did." She shrugged and sipped again at the tiny cup. The Chinese wine tasted mellower this time, warming her tongue and shooting, like liquid flames, down into her breast.

"I lived in an apartment house owned by an older woman. I never gave much thought to her or how she lived until I had the baby...a daughter...and she, the neighbor...her name was Ramona...came up to my apartment with a toy...a pink elephant... that she'd made as a gift. Ramona adored the baby and we became good friends. One night, after a few glasses of wine, she told me that she owned a whorehouse in the South End of Boston. I was shocked and upset." Kathie's mouth was rueful and Brenda chuckled.

"I thought that we'd stop being friends then. A madam wasn't really someone that I wanted to be associated with. I shunned her and ignored her for a few weeks, but then found that I missed her companionship. We became friends again. I figured we could be friends and I didn't have to approve of her life. She could be what she was and I could be what I was."

Brenda nodded, understanding.

"Then, I began to run out of money. Ramona tried to help. She hired a nursemaid for my daughter so I could look for work, but...I just couldn't find a job. Ramona suggested that if I really wanted to earn a lot of money and be home during the day for my little girl...well, she offered me a job."

"As a prostitute?" Brenda's huge eyes were like saucers.

"Yup," Kathie laughed, a guffaw from her belly. "I liked it!"

"You *did?*" Brenda's voice squeaked her disbelief. *Liked it? It was one thing to succumb to an amorous adventure with the man of your dreams, but....to lay with strangers? For money? And she liked it!*

Kathie's laughed tinkled out. "I did. Ramona's place only catered to rich men...powerful men...handsome men...and they were kind and treated me well. I...we...Ramona and I shared an apartment and we had a housekeeper who took care of my daughter when I was working. It might not be for everyone, but for me...well...it was a good life for me."

Brenda tipped her head sideways, thinking...*It might have been fun. Glamorous, certainly...rich and powerful men... jewels...furs...I might have adored it!* "I can see it...I really can." She giggled. "I think I could have taken that path..." She examined Kathie's face closely. Was there a payment to be exacted for reveling in sin? It didn't seem so. Kathie was lovely. Her skin was peaches and cream, her bright blue eyes were clear and sparkling, her teeth straight and pearly and she glowed with good health.

"It was a path strewn with roses." Kathie chuckled. And then her face grew sad. "And then we suffered heartache. Nothing is ever given to you that you don't have to pay for, one way or the other. My dear Ramona contracted tuberculosis. She was always frail. I nursed her devotedly and she died in my arms. She died, leaving me her business and all of her money. She told me that I was really the only friend she had."

"Wow." Brenda shook her head. "And then what?"

"I met a man...an older man...very, very rich and very, very influential. You'd recognize his name if I told you. He and I fell

in love. He was married and it was out of the question that
we'd ever be legitimate anyway." She began to gather her
belongings. "I have to get back to work, but quickly, let me
summarize the rest. Over the years, I had three more daughters... he was their father. I moved my business to Portsmouth. It was an up-and-coming-city with great potential for a
spiffy, exclusive gambling house. One that had extra-special,
um, arrangements for pleasure. It is expensive to come to the
Hess Club. Expensive, but...certainly worth every dollar. My
girls are exceptional. All well-educated, all charming, cultured
and amusing...all beautiful. The men that patronize my gambling house are rich and influential. I'll never have any problems with the law or morality here. I keep a quiet profile."

"What about your daughters? Where are they?"

"I purchased a small, very exclusive boarding school about
six blocks away. All the children, including my four, are board-
ers, all come from very wealthy homes. I have an impeccably
respectable staff, and..." she winked. "And if one of my girls
slips up and wants to keep the child, well...we have a great
arrangement!"

"I didn't think I could be surprised at anything, but this takes
the cake! I have to know more! Can I come and visit you? I'd
adore seeing a whorehouse and when will I ever have this
opportunity again?" Brenda stood up and tossed several bills
onto the table, waving off Kathie's offer to pay. "No, no. My
treat. You pay next time, and there *will* be a next time!" She
turned to the waiter and they embraced, speaking to one
another in Mandarin.

# CHAPTER SIX

**JULY 5, 1943**
**The Allied invasion fleet sails to Sicily.**

The second fire consumed a dairy barn and a small farm-house on Route 1 heading toward York. Eighteen cows and a hired hand, an elderly man named Calef Hammerstone, died most certainly in writhing agony.

Police Chief Horace Parks discovered the shiny tin sheriff's badge lying in the driveway that led to the barn. It was only then that he placed any importance on the similar badge that Tricia Tobey had picked up.

~~~~~~~~~~~~~~~~~

The third fire was discovered on the morning of July sixth. Mrs. Madelyn Monaco, whose husband, Richard, was fighting somewhere in Europe, she wasn't quite sure where…was on her way to work as a newly hired riveter at the Yard. As she drove her six-year-old Chevrolet onto Route 1 early in the morning, she saw a small house just ahead explode with flames. With great presence of mind, Mrs. Monaco leaped out of her car and ran to help. The flames were already devouring the old wooden structure. She could hear screams inside, but there was no way that she could go into the house. She backed up her car, fearing that the flames might also eat up her only transportation, and then drove into the next driveway. She banged on the door, arousing a still-sleeping housewife who immediately called the police. The two women went back to the burning house, hoping against hope that they might be able to rescue someone.

"There are three old ladies in that house!" The neighbor chewed at her lip in frantic panic. "I think they're already goners!"

The house was cherry red and, as they watched in horror, the roof blew itself off. Flames and dark smoke billowed up, soiling the air with particles of wood and shingle.

The Kittery police and the volunteer fire department arrived at the next moment. There really wasn't anything that they could do. Police Chief Parks swore...ripe, earthy words, but was helpless to save the three women who perished.

He did immediately search for the sheriff's badge, and didn't know whether he was pleased to locate yet another one lying on top of the stone well-cover in the front yard. "It's a clue, at least," he told his men. "I mean, we know it was the same son-of-a-bitch who lit the other fires." He was careful to pick it up with his handkerchief in case the arsonist left fingerprints.

His deputy, Aaron Crossfield, muttered, "And where does that get us?"

Parks spat. "Nowhere." He scratched at the back of his neck. "Just means we know it was the same person."

Crossfield watched as cars and the curious stopped. "Here comes the newspaper guys. We gonna tell them this time about the badge?"

"Not yet. We'll keep it under wraps for now." Parks turned to meet Doc Brogdon. "That way, we'll know."

"This has got to stop, Horace." Doc Brogdon, too, swore softly. "We gotta catch this bastard."

"Hmmm." Parks watched Greg Starr, the young reporter and all-around-errand-boy from the Kittery Gazette. Starr had his camera ready and was snapping photos of the still-burning house. Parks ambled over to him. "Hey, Mr. Starr."

"Chief," Starr saluted, worrying that Parks would order him to cease and desist. "Hell of a thing, isn't it?"

"Worse than hell, my boy. I hear that there are at least three bodies inside that mess."

"I have information that the house was owned by Lucille McCutcheon and that she rented to two men from the yard...both of whom are working today and therefore, fine...well, sort of fine, as they don't have any clothes left or a place to live..."

"We'll see that they find a place to stay and get them what they need."

"I'll do a sidebar with this story. I know some kind people will step up and help them get settled. It's the least that the Gazette can do." Greg offered.

"Good boy. Know anything about the ladies who perished here?" The Chief's face sagged with sorrow. "We know Mrs. McCutcheon also rented to two other widows," the Chief freely passed on this information to the reporter.

"Really?" Greg Starr was delighted that Chief Parks wasn't telling him to buzz off. "Do you have their names?"

"Yeah," the Chief took a package of cigarettes out of his pocket and offered one to Starr. The two lit up and watched as the volunteer firemen tried to quell the flames. "I'll tell you, but you'll have to keep this quiet for now. I think I can trust you. This information must be classified." He blew a puff of smoke out. "My wife told me who they were...she knew them... before I left the house."

"Telephone, telegraph and tell-a-woman, huh." Greg waited for more.

"You know it. The poor, damn ladies were a Mrs. Lillian Overton and Mrs. Shirley Zahr. Both born here in Kitt'ry, both married local men who died several years ago. Nice ladies. Belong to the same church as my Fanny."

Greg scribbled in his notebook, blinking hard so as not to laugh at the Chief's words. "Anything else you can tell me, Chief?"

"I want you to do me a teeny favor, Greg." The Chief rocked back and forth on the heels and toes of his shiny black shoes.

"Whatever I can, sir."

"Can you go around and unobtrusively as possible, take pictures of the people who are here? I want to check out who is gawking and who is here."

"Sure. Right away."

The young man sauntered off, still photographing the burning house, taking shots of the firemen and managing to catch, in the background, every face that watched with fascination and horror. Some of the onlookers, he recognized. There was Jimmy Earnest, a man who worked for one of the local churches. He recalled hearing that Earnest was always at the scene of a fire or an automobile accident. He was well-known as a man who never missed a tragedy. And there was Captain Simeon, the restaurant owner. And Eustace Barnes and his mule.

And Nellie...what was her last name? She was always jawing away at the Post Office...ah! Nellie Hogan. He stopped for a moment and wrote down the names in his notebook. He'd heard that arsonists sometimes came back to the fire...is that what the Chief wanted these pictures for? And didn't killers come to the funerals of their victims? He'd ask the Chief and see if he wanted pictures of the mourners when these ladies were waked and buried. If the Chief cooperated with the newspaper, why...he'd do anything at all that he could do to help to catch the bastard who did this.

He flipped to a new page. Behind him, he could hear a very thin woman talking with a very fat man. "We've seen enough here, Augustus."

"I'm rather hungry, my dear. What are we having for lunch?"

"Oh, Augustus. You're going to enjoy my lunch. I've got pork chops and mashed potatoes for you with buttered lima beans." Her pretty, narrow face smiled at him. With wifely devotion

"You sure do know how to keep a man happy, Gladys." His face was wreathed with a smile that stretched from ear to ear...a rather long distance, as it had to travel over one chipmunked cheek to the other. "And did you make any dessert?"

"Of course, you silly goose! I made you a lovely dessert. One of our favorites! An apple custard pie with vanilla sauce and a scoop of vanilla ice cream on the side." The two of them, each thinking their own thoughts on the upcoming prodigious meal, wandered off.

*Sure wish someone was making me that kind of lunch*, Greg was wistful. *Sounds just great!* His elbow was jostled. "Hey, reporter man." A beery breath blew in his face. "Ain't this awful?"

"Oh, Floyd." He recognized the vein-streaked nose of one of Kittery's most infamous drunks. Floyd, despite his penchant for drink, was employed as a cleaner at the local school.

"Yeah." Greg nodded with solemn sadness.

"When're they gonna catch this bastid?" Floyd shook his head and nearly fell over with the effort.

"Soon, I hope. This cannot go on." Greg looked around. He saw Fred, the man from the Esso Station get into his truck and drive off. Greg didn't know Fred's last name. And there was Charlie Casey who was the janitor at the Shapleigh School riding up front with Fred. Charlie was moon-faced, with slanty eyes that were sunk into his suety face. Charlie Chan, they called him. Even the kids called him that. Greg flipped open his notebook and wrote down a few more names.

"Whatcha doon?" Floyd leaned his considerable weight on Greg as he peered at the notebook. Greg noted that not only did Floyd stink from last night's beer, but he also smelled rancid and sweaty. He wondered if Floyd was married. And what might Mrs. Floyd look like? "Writin' down clues?"

"Just making notes of who was here." Greg paused. "Tell me how you spell your last name, Floyd?"

Floyd's face split into a grin, showing Greg the gaps where his front teeth once were. "J-O-N-E-S...it's a tough one to spell, Mr. Reporter. J-O-N-E-S." He slapped Greg's shoulder and staggered off, hiccupping and laughing at his own wit.

~~~~~~~~~~~~~~~~

Pleased at the screaming headlines in the morning's papers, the arsonist was nonetheless annoyed that no mention had been made of the trademark badge.

The arsonist, again careful to leave nothing in the way of fingerprints or clues, bought some cheap notebook paper and wrote a note to the two newspapers, telling them that an important clue was being overlooked by the police. The note jeered at the police and chided them for keeping this kind of information from the press and the public. Horace Parks was not pleased.

~~~~~~~~~~~~~~~~~

Horace Parks had been born and raised in Kittery Point, the seaward side of the Kittery-Portsmouth area. He'd wanted to go into law enforcement ever since he listened to Charlie Chan, Dick Tracy, The Avenger, Sherlock Holmes and Lionel Grant, Ace Detective on the radio. He joined the Kittery police force as a young man, just out of college, married Fanny Michaels, his high-school sweetheart, and raised a family of four boys. Horace rose through the Kittery police ranks and became chief just as the war news was winging throughout the United States. He wanted to enlist, but was informed that, because of his age and the need to keep a responsible police force in the area, he would have to stay stateside and continue to keep the peace. His two eldest boys were fighting in the Far East and he and Fanny got on their knees every night to pray that they would return home safely one day when this was all over and the war was won. These prayers were echoed by most of the parents, wives and children whose loved ones were involved in the war.

His two younger sons wanted to enlist, but were talked into doing valuable war work (working with codes) in a secret division at Pease Air Force Base. Fanny and Horace, in their nightly prayers, asked God to also keep the two younger boys safe and at home.

"I think of Joey and Michael sitting somewhere in a muddy trench and I'd like to throttle the Sherriff's badge killer single-handedly." Horace railed.

"You'll catch him, dear." His wife soothed. "You always do."

~~~~~~~~~~~~~~~~~

In mid-1939, Mary Rose Sabatino left Greenwich, Connecticut, to come to join her Uncle Marco, Aunt Grace and their then nine year-old son, Anton Anderson Sabatino, known to one and all as Andy, in Kittery, Maine. The Sabatinos had moved to Maine to start a gardening and nursery business in the growing little town.

In Greenwich, Mary Rose had apprenticed herself to her cousin Francesca, learning the bakery business. After three years of baking and a disastrous romance with a man who had enlisted in the Army and broke her heart with his cheating and lies, Mary Rose felt it was time to move on. Francesca's own daughter, Lucia, who was two years older than Mary Rose, was now running the business for her mother. Mary Rose, if she ever wished to own her own business, would have to do it somewhere else.

"The man that owns the bakery – Mr. Stupikusky – next to our nursery is sick. He's got no family and he wants to sell the business to someone who wants to continue the bakery. He's Polish…doesn't do Italian stuff, but you can change that. He's got a good following, business is booming up here." Aunt Grace had all of the financial figures. "Before he got sick, he got all new equipment, and the place has a nice apartment upstairs for you and you can also easily rent the area over the big storage room. You could fit four beds up there. Marco and I are contemplating doing the same thing over the back of the nursery shed. With all those workers at the Portsmouth Navy Shipyard, everyone is looking for a place up here. And the extra money helps to pay the rent."

Grace urged Mary Rose. "You gotta get away from Greenwich, honey bun. Get away from where your heart got broken." Mary Rose's dark eyes glistened with unshed tears. Aunt Grace hugged her. "Come on up to Maine." And so, with her little used car, her own savings and a small loan from her mother and father, she did.

She took with her all of the family recipes for crusty bread and crisp rolls; *calzones, biscotti*, Italian butter cookies, fancy pastries and *pizza*. As Aunt Grace had told her, there was little to change at the bakery location. The new Route 95 was being built, connecting Maine to New Hampshire. The bakery and Sabatino's garden shop and nursery were located on Route 1, which was also connected by a bridge to New

Hampshire. "It's a great location," Uncle Marco confided. "You'll make a million dollars."

Cousin Francesca helped as much as possible. "Are there any other bakeries that will compete with you?"

"Mario told me that there aren't any other bakeries in Kittery. Four across the river in New Hampshire…Portsmouth. Two are Kosher. They supply kosher meats and delicatessen stuff to the Jews who live in Portsmouth. They do bake bread, but it is Jewish. Bagels and challah and some rye. Most of the bakeries are in the Islington area. The only one downtown is Liberson's Bakery. It's next to a lot of restaurants…Tedesco's restaurant and meat market on one side and Chang's Chinese on the other. We won't be in competition. There are two others, one near Newington and one near Hampton. Both do American baking. No pizza, no pastries, and no good, hard-crusted breads. *Pah*. I think I can do better than they do." She dimpled. "And I know, I know…I'm going to have to work like a stevedore. But I want to work like a stevedore. It will be good for me to lose myself in the business."

"A name for the store?" Francesca asked. "A good name is important."

"If you don't mind, I'm going to steal your name. I want to call it *'Panis Angelicus,'* just like your store, Cousin Francesca. *'Panis Angelicus of Maine.'* Or maybe I'll anglicize it and call it *'The Bread of Angels.'* Which name is better?"

"The Angels and their bread made me a fortune," Francesca kissed her young cousin, bestowing her blessing on the new endeavor. "Call it whichever you think is best. May it make a fortune for you, too." She made the sign of the cross and kissed Mary Rose on both cheeks.

"What do I have to do to get the rationing board to give me the sugar and butter I need?"

"Go and register as a bakery. That will get you the 'A' rationing stamps." Francesca dusted off her floury hands. "I'll speak with Don Mantaldo."

Don Mantaldo, an elderly Italian man, her friend and sometimes mentor, knew everyone and everything. He never let a small thing like the law interfere with his business or the business of someone he favored. Mary Rose had known Don

Mantaldo since she was a tiny child and Don Mantaldo had dandled her on his knee. He was very fond of her and she knew that he would assist her in any way he could. He was a powerful force, with tentacles everywhere. He'd know someone in the southern Maine area who could help her with any problems she might encounter.

Francesca advised Mary Rose; "You're gonna have to watch the ingredients, though. Even with "A" rations, you might have to modify some of your recipes...use lard and margarine where you can. Maybe find someone with a beehive and use honey instead of refined sugar. Plant yourself a garden so you can have '*scarole*, potatoes and Swiss chard for your *sciacchads*. Make do with what you can."

~~~~~~~~~~~~~~~~~

When Mary Rose cleaned up the bakery, she realized that she would need at least four full time employees to properly run her company. She took out huge advertisements in the local papers, sent her young cousin Andy out with several hundred handbills announcing her grand opening and offering a free loaf of Angel Bread..."Better than cake! Crispy, crunchy crust". ...and had a new sign made.

## *The Bread of Angels*
### Mary Rose Sabatino, Owner

From the day the bakery opened its doors, sending fragrant smells out, customers poured in.

Obviously, she couldn't possibly work alone. It was easy to find herself four additional helpers. Jannus Podalsky, the elderly Polish man who had worked for Mr. Stupikusky, agreed to stay on with her. He'd have to learn her way of doing things, but he'd been baking for at least forty years and might even be able to teach her a thing or two. She was grateful for his expertise, knowledge of customers and his easy-going humor. Agnes Winchell, who lived across the street and whose husband had been killed in the First World

War, would work the counter together with Ursula Bondi, who wanted to work, but not at the Yard. Caledonia Hope, a young colored girl who came into the shop before it opened, was hoping against hope, in a desperate word game involving her surname, that she would be hired. Despite the frantic need for employees, many people would never hire a woman or man of color. But not Mary Rose. "You'll be on time every day? Be willing to learn hard, but satisfying work?"

"I promise that I'll be the best baker you have ever seen. Just give me a chance. Please hire me," Caledonia pleaded.

So Mary Rose did.

In the weeks before *The Bread of Angels* opened its doors, the team baked and practiced, practiced and baked, and all of the neighbors were the happy recipients of successful piles of practice breads, rolls and *biscotti*. Some got the mistakes: the floppy cakes, sullen loaves, leaden *cannolli*, the twelve loaves of Zia Filomande's secret recipe apricot brioche in which Ursula had forgotten to add the sugar. Even the mistakes were eagerly welcomed in this era of rationing.

And from the moment that the doors opened, the bakery was a wild success.

~~~~~~~~~~~~~~~~~

**JULY 19, 1943**
**KITTERY, Maine…Brand new Italian bakery opens on Route One.**

**ROME…Rome is bombarded by the Allies for the first time in the War**

Greg Starr opened the door to the Kittery Police Station. "I've got those pictures developed," he told Chief Parks. Greg handed the Chief a large envelope.

"Lemme see," Chief Parks fanned out the photos. "Hey, Gideon…Aaron…come in here and see who you know."

The three men pored over the photographs. "Here's old Eustace," Aaron pointed, "an' here's Mrs. Monaco. She called in the alarm."

"This is Captain Simeon," Greg said, stabbing his finger, "and then I recognized Nellie Hogan." He flipped to the next picture. "And here's that guy who is at every funeral or time of misery, Jimmy Earnest. Here's Floyd Jones and Fred from the gas station. Charlie Chan...I got a snapshot of him and Fred leaving. He shuffled the rest of the photographs. "I don't know anybody else."

Chief Parks stabbed his finger at one of the pictures. "Here's Mountain Man Aggie and his wife, uh, Mrs. Mountain Man Aggie." He pointed to a couple at the edge of the crowd. The photo was a sharp one, showing the man and woman in full figure. And the man's figure was *more* than full...it was enormous! The man was *huge*, an alp of a human being, from his face, wreathed in folds of suet, to his belly, which pouched out over his pants like fifty pounds of grain in a ten pound sack. His hands and feet were relatively small, his arms like cartoon caricatures of Popeye.

"He's the fattest man I know and she's like a stick. Mountain Man Aggie? Why is he called that? What's his real name?"

"He's called Augustus Charett." Aaron knew everyone and everything. "He was born in York. A widower. Married her...I think her name is Gladys...two years ago. He was always a big man...that's why they nick-named him after Mount Agamenticus. But since he married her...she's supposed to be a fantastic cook...he ballooned up. He not only is as big as a mountain now, he looks like the whole damn mountain range!" He laughed. "They live in Kittery now and my wife tells me she...Mrs. Charett...makes the best damn lemon-meringue pie in the state. Ha! No wonder he's so big." He scrutinized the rest of the photos, writing down everyone else he recognized, then passed them back to the Chief who did the same. Parks called in the rest of his men, asking each of them to name people they knew. In the set of Greg Starr's pictures, there were thirty-seven onlookers at the fire. They identified twenty-four.

"We need about ten copies of these pictures," Parks told Greg Starr. "I want them passed around town and I want each and every face identified, *capeesh?*"

"You think the firebug came to watch?"

"I think he couldn't stay away."

"Are you sure it's a "he"?" Greg was curious. "Maybe it's a woman."

Parks shrugged. "Maybe, but I've never heard of a female arsonist." He tapped his pencil on the table. "And the sheriff's badge...that's a man's thing, don'tcha think?"

"Were there any prints on the badge?"

"Nope. The arsonist is too smart."

"My wife's cousin's next-door neighbor...some Norwegian lady... is one of those professors. She deals with criminals who are insane and I think she's supposed to be a big hoo-ha on people who set fires." Gideon Balfour scratched at his head. "I can ask her if she has any knowledge of a lady firebug, or what she thinks the badge is supposed to convey."

"Great. What the hell. We don't know anything else. We need all the help we can get on this one." Chief Parks sighed. "Nine people dead already and we have no clue at all as to who the hell is doing this."

~~~~~~~~~~~~~~~~~

"We'll be landing in Portsmouth in three days." Carol looked up from the pile of letters she was writing. "How long will we be in port?"

"As of the latest scuttlebutt, two weeks. The old *Bucket* will get some refurbishing, and you and me can refurbish our wardrobes and maybe buy a little bit of lipstick." Michelle turned her hands over and mourned their chapped appearance. "I understand that it's really hard to even buy hand cream."

"And it's supposed to get worse. My mom just wrote that she got yet another new ration book last week."

"What else can they take away? Meat is gone, butter and sugar are gone, shoes are gone...no gasoline, and if you had any, you still couldn't use the car because tires are gone!"

"It is worth it," Eunice stated in a flat, no-nonsense voice. "After all, what are all these men fighting for?"

The women were quiet. Michelle and Carol nodded and went back to writing steamy, encouraging love letters to the fifteen or twenty fighting men who each thought that they were the only one.

~~~~~~~~~~~~~~~~~~

In his cramped stateroom, Alex Patton tried to catch a few hours of much-needed sleep before some other medical crisis called him. Alex was a tall, slender young man, classically handsome, with a quiet demeanor that hid a wildly funny sense of humor. Every nurse on the boat was half in love with him. But Alex was not about to give his heart to anyone, especially during this God-awful War. Sure, he wanted a wife and a family and all that stuff...one of these days anyway. But not just now.

He had been born right in Kittery, and his parents, Julie and Pat, had no idea that their son would soon show up at their doorstep, fresh off his military hospital-ship transport, pleading for a piece of his beloved blueberry pie. Alex grinned as he dreamed of how his mother would shriek when she saw him. His dad, well, he was more reticent. Dad would smile that slow smile that he had, patting him on his back and telling him how glad he was to see him.

In their last letter, Julie and Pat, owners of a boatyard in Elliot, Maine, were doing their part for the War effort. Pat had invented a prototype boat, capable of drawing only three feet of water, that could be used to patrol the eastern coastlines, seeking out enemy submarines or U-boats. He now reported, in a civilian capacity, to the men who ran the security divisions at the Yard. "I'm too blamed old to fight, so they tell me," Pat had written, "but I managed to find something that I can do for the good old US of A."

Julie, too, was doing her bit. Before her marriage, she had been a singer at local churches and choirs. Giving in to patriotism that was spiced with a satisfyingly selfish desire to be a music hall singer and dancer, she had sweet-talked the administration officials at the Connie Bean USO to allow her to put on a show.

So as not to compete with the performers who did the twice-weekly Camp Shows at the USO, Julie, after discussions with her friend and talented singer, Debbie Orloff, had chosen Cole Porter's Broadway classic *Anything Goes* as their first performance.

Julie would most likely play the matronly Mrs. Wadsworth T. Harcourt and Debbie grabbed the part of brassy Reno Sweeney.

Julie wrote to her son: "We had a call for people to join the production. We expected maybe twenty or so. The line went three times around the block! There were hundreds of applicants; singers, dancers, musicians, people to pick our props, do make-up, be ushers...everyone wanted to be a part of the action. It is so gratifying. We begin rehearsals next week...too bad you're not here, darling, you could be Moonface Martin (Ha! Even if you can't sing a note!). The curtain goes up on September third and fourth, and then two more performances on September seventeenth and eighteenth. We have the whole summer to rehearse and won't it be fun!"

Alex turned the page and dreamed of his mother. She was swell. Kind of scatterbrained and funny, nonetheless, she got things done. As soon as the War started and she knew things were going to be tight, she bought flocks of geese, ducks and chickens to supplement their food supply. She had four sheep, none of which she could bring herself to slaughter, and two goats who supplied the Patton family and all of their friends with milk and cheese. In addition, Julie planted a huge Victory Garden and was also occupied with another lady who ran a nursery and plant center. The two of them planned classes to help other local residents start their own gardens. He smiled...his mom was such a character!

He knew that his parents worried and worried. They were uncertain if the Americans could be victorious, especially when some of the misery of the war news trickled to them in radio broadcasts. But Alex wasn't worried at all. He was positive the war would be won by the Americans and their Allies...They were invincible. Alex listened to every scrap of news he could glean and followed the battles and the strategy of the Generals. He decided to leave the practicalities of winning to those who had been chosen to run the war. He'd stick to keeping each and every soldier and sailor who came to him for help alive. Still, he'd be happy when it was all over and he could go home for good.

He was glad about his mother's Victory Garden. Since his final year at med school at Georgetown University, Alex had chosen to eat as a vegetarian. Most of his friends, including the girls, thought he was nuts. But Alex had never given a darn as to what others thought. Like his mother and her sheep, he just didn't want to kill an animal. And after two years as a surgeon in the Army, he never wanted to kill *anyt*hing anymore.

He turned, restless, on the lumpy cot. He was rewarded with a soft swat from the ship's cat, Mystic, who would always be found next to Alex if he could manage. No one exactly knew how Mystic had found nirvana on board the *Bucket,* but, after two days at sea, he had appeared, hungry and thirsty, meowing plaintively and winding himself around Alex's long legs. Despite Alex's protestations of innocence, no one really believed that he hadn't somehow sneaked the coal black cat on board. Mystic was now well-fed (everyone on board gave him treats and snacks) and had worked himself into the crew's life. If anything happened to Mystic, it was widely believed, the ship might just sink into the sea.

Alex wondered if Julie and Pat had sold his old jalopy. With no gas and no tires available, the car might have been sold or donated to the War effort. He shrugged, dislodging Mystic's cozy spot on his shoulder. Whatever.

He sat up, unable to sleep, and tried to catch some music on the radio. Not much luck, mostly static. He picked up his camera and aimed it at Mystic, who was now lying on his back, all four feet in the air. The camera, given to him by his grandfather on his graduation, was one of his most prized possessions. It had accompanied him all over the exotic foreign lands and the sealed canisters of film in his ditty bag, wrapped tightly in cellophane, would show the folks back home some of the horrors and beauty that the War had revealed. The unspeakably loveliness of a Burmese mountaintop, flooded with the early morning sun, the vivid green of the grasses on the beach of Manila, the stark horror of three dead Japs, their bodies being eaten by starving dogs, the heart-wrenching smile on the face of a soldier who had his leg amputated. All these and so much more, would be developed in the little dark room he had built in the basement at home. Home... He shook himself, spilled Mystic off the bed, and went up the ladder to find himself a cup of tea.

~~~~~~~~~~~~~~~~~~

"You've really got it bad for him, don'tcha?" Carol poked Eunice.

"He's the nicest, finest, bravest man I have ever met," Eunice sighed. "And you know, we've met some of the best these past two years.

"How does he feel....I mean, have you ever talked with him about...?"

Eunice shook her head and the scarf that hid the scraggly hair that was just beginning to grow in almost slipped. She hitched it back and re-tied it. "I'm just some nurse to him. He can't see me and even if he could, what would he see in me?" Eunice was pragmatic. She knew what she looked like.

"Where is he winding up? Is he going to be in Portsmouth or Kittery?"

"Nope, worse luck. He's being sent to a hospital in Kansas City."

"Kansas City! Oh, gee, Eunie." Carol was sincere in her sympathy. It was really obvious to all of the nurses that Eunice was deeply in love with the very sick soldier.

His name, on the tag he wore around his neck, was Joseph Martin. Captain Joseph Martin. He was a hero, awaiting three Purple Hearts when he arrived stateside and his name had been submitted for the highest medal of all...the Congressional Medal of Honor. Singlehandedly, he had wiped out an entire company of Germans and rescued nine of his own men...pulling and carrying them to safety...from what would have been torture and then an unspeakable death at the hands of the enemy.

In doing so, he nearly died himself, sustaining horrible injuries, the worst of which were an amputated right foot and a psychosomatic form of blindness. "I think what he saw was so awful that his poor brain just shut it all off. He's afraid of what he'll remember, and so, as our minds can do if necessary, he can't see anything at all." Alex, although not trained in mental illnesses, nonetheless tried to explain. "Maybe he'll never be able to open his eyes and see. Maybe, one day, he'll heal himself within or get a jolt in the head and the gift of sight will just come back to him. Poor bastard. Poor brave bastard."

"I can never remember which one he is," Carol scratched at her newly washed hair. "Is he Joseph Martin or is he Martin Joseph?"

"Funny having two men in the hospital with the same names only twisted around."

"And Joe is so wonderful and the other creep, Marty, is such a horrid man." Eunice made a face.

"Isn't the other one, Marty, scheduled to be billeted in York Hospital? That's right next to Kittery." Carol, who as Head Nurse, always knew everything that went on. "Why did the powers to be send the good one away from Eunice and keep the bad one?"

"Story of my life." Eunice muttered. She got up and put her coffee mug on the tray. "I'm going up to the beds."

Carol watched her go. "She'd be good for him. And he'd be good for her."

"He seems to really enjoy her company," Michelle observed.

"'Course he's blind and Eunice, God love her and certainly I do, isn't the most beautiful woman alive." Carol made a face.

"She's beautiful inside, where it counts," Michelle stuck out her chin.

"Of course she's beautiful inside. She's brave and courageous and a great friend. You can depend on her to the end," Carol agreed. "But will he find her pretty...you know...could he fall for her?"

"If he could see...?" Michelle's green eyes were wicked. She shrugged. "You know, *ma petite*, Eunice could be...she just could be a *leetle* bit more attractive, if she tried. Her hair is growing back nice and curly. Her skin is good. She just needs *Tante* Michelle to give her lessons on make-up...you know...make the best of her features."

Carol nodded. "You and me, Meesh…it will be our job to make her look pretty. We'll be her guardian angels and turn her into a swan."

"Even if we have to hold her down and force her to be pretty!" Michelle laughed.

"OK, she is our project, right?"

"Right!"

Carol stretched, waving her arms high above her head. "I'm going stir crazy. I need to get off this ship…hell, I need to get off *any* ship!"

"We'll have a *luffly* time when we get stateside." Michelle picked up a lurid pink envelope and patted it with a puff of cotton.

"Pee-Yoo! What is that smell?"

"This?" Michelle pretended to be insulted. "This is the perfume that I put onto my letters." She sniffed the envelope and sighed with rapture. "Just think when Louis gets this letter. He will think of me and dream of me."

"He'll probably pass out with the smell!" What is it, anyway?"

"*Nuit d'amor*…Night of Love, what other perfume would I use?" Michelle scribbled her name at the bottom of the letter and then pressed her lipsticked lips to the paper, leaving a deep pink outline of her lips. She sealed the letter and then picked up another sheet of paper out of her letterbox. This sheet was colored pale lavender.

"How many men are you writing to now, you French hussy, you?"

"Seven." Michelle smiled with smugness, arching her dark eyebrows.

"How can you remember what you say to each of them? Suppose you get the letters mixed up?"

"Ah, I send them all the same letter," Michelle giggled. "But I use a different color for each." She counted on her fingers; "Lavender for Johnny in the Marines; pink for Louis, also in the Marines. Pale Green for Richard in the Navy. Richard is in the Far East. Pale blue for Danny. He's in the Navy, too, but he is near Hawaii. White with little French forget-me-nots for…um…

um...ah, Tex who is still stateside in California. He's an Army instructor and ooh-la-la, he is sooo handsome."

"And the other two? You probably can't remember them all!" Carol shook her head in mock despair. "You bad woman, leading them all on."

"They love it. And I know all of their names. The last are flyers. Tony and Sam. Beautiful men, all of them." She smacked a kiss on the bottom of the lavender paper. "They all think I am *tres chic! And* they are all waiting to marry me when this war is over." She batted her long eyelashes over her wicked green eyes.

"And who will you marry?"

Michelle burst out in laughter. "None of them! I will probably marry Joe."

"Joe? You mean there is someone else?"

Michelle bit her lip. She, who was always bubbly and exuberant, suddenly became quiet. "*Oui,* Joe. Joe...I cannot write to Joe right now."

"Why?"

"Alas, Carol, my friend. My darling Joe is in a prison camp. At least I hope he is still in a prison camp."

"I never knew that you had someone that you were serious about," Carol's face was woeful. "You never said anything about Joe."

"I never did, did I? That was because there was nothing to say. His family lives in the immigrant French area near mine and we have been friends since we were children. His family is French, too. Then, just before this damned war started, we began to love one another. He enlisted right away after Pearl Harbor and I finished at nursing school. We wrote to one another every day for a year. Then, just when I was being posted to Egypt, his letters stopped. I was afraid that he had found someone new. But then his mother wrote to me and told me that he had parachuted into enemy territory and been captured by the Japanese." She twirled her chair around. "I have not heard from him since." She unpinned her heavy fall of red-gold hair, curled it with her fingers, and pinned it back up again. "And now, Carol, you know my secret."

Carol ran over to Michelle and hugged her as Alan Bowen, the tall, lanky redheaded orderly, came into the room. "What's up, girls?"

"We're commiserating about the ones who are not with us," Michelle sniffed and touched her eyes.

"I know how ya' feel," Alan sat on top of one of the desks, dangling his feet. "My girl, Clair, misses me something awful."

"And you miss her, too?"

"Naturally," Alan hunched his shoulders. "But she's home and I'm here. We'll be seeing one another in a few days," his handsome face lit up, "when this tub lands in Maine."

"She's from Maine?"

"She is and I am too. Didn'tcha know?"

"Nope. There's a lot that I don't know, Alan." Carol mused.

"How about you?" Alan nudged his chin toward Carol. "You're always flirting with the men. Is anyone waiting for you back home?"

"Sort of." Carol rubbed her chin. "I have a boyfriend. His name is John."

"Oh, yeah?" Alan looked interested. "Where is he fighting?"

"He's stateside. He's a firefighter in Montana. He's exempt because they have such terrible fires in the mountains. John is a supervisor and a trainer and they need him there." She lifted her chin. "He tried to enlist, begged them, but they said that he was more valuable where he is."

"Are you from Montana?" Alan settled in for a good gossip. He'd worked for months with these nurses, but had never shared intimate information. Now, he was curious about their lives.

"Nope. I'm from Massachusetts. Went to nursing school at Burbank Hospital in Fitchburg and then I was sent to Fort Devens. And then, ah, to see the world. So they sent me to the flea pits of Egypt and Libya, and then to the Philippines. All the hot spots!" She laughed and Michelle joined in.

"You forgot to mention the malaria in the jungle of New Hebrides! That was *my* favorite spot!"

"Oooh, the mosquitoes! How could I leave them out. I hated those mosquitoes! *Merde* to them! Ah, back to work!"

She tied on her apron and went into the area of the center of the ship. When it was refurbished as a hospital troop ship, the doughty *Buchanan's* central area, as it was the most stable part of the ship, became the place where the hospital beds housing the sick men were placed.

The large area housed hundreds of the sick and maimed. The ones with the worst injuries were on the right side. Those with serious, but not life-threatening problems were on the left. Joe Martin occupied the third bed in the first row on the right. Martin Joseph was fifth in the row behind him. Far from being a hero, Marty Joseph was one of those men who were despised by all of his fellow men. He'd weaseled out of every work duty he'd been assigned, contracted a virulent case of syphilis, and...it was suspected, but not proven, shot himself in the big toe of his right foot so as to get himself out of the fighting and back to the states. In addition, in the hospital tent outside of Burma, he'd bribed an orderly to bring him booze.

The orderly, a young and ignorant peasant, had mistakenly given him a jug of the alcohol used to clean airplane engines. Marty had guzzled the entire jug before realizing that the ethanol was affecting his eyesight, causing him to be permanently blind in his right eye and temporarily blind in his left. Most of his fellow passengers devoutly wished that he would remain that way. "He'll be less of a son-of-a-bitch, if he can't see," was the prevailing prayer.

The nurses, who were devotedly kind and sympathetic to almost everyone, universally loathed him as much as they universally adored Joe Martin.

"Hello, Eunice." A booming voice greeted her. It was Jack Harrington, the heroic Marine who was being sent stateside to recuperate from the wounds he'd received in defending Chunking. Like Joe Martin, Jack Harrington also had a chest full of medals received for bravery in action and was supposed to be up for the Medal of Honor, too. Although Jack Harrington had never uttered a word about his achievements, the nurses had heard via the scuttlebutt gossip that raced around the ship, that he had personally demolished two Japanese gun batteries and saved ten or more of his own men.

It had also been noted, by the eagle eyes of every nurse and corpsman on board, that Jack and Yashiko Kobiache were falling in love. Yashiko, a slender, dark-haired beauty, had been a nurse on Hawaii when the bombs dropped on Pearl Harbor. She had immediately enlisted, with some difficulty, as she had Japanese blood. Only a sympathetic and understanding Draft Board on Hawaii, knowing of her skills and knowing how badly nurses were needed, managed to make sure that her personnel records stated her background as "Hawaiian" and nothing else.

"Oh, Jack! How are you doing today?" Eunice sat down for a moment at Jack's bedside.

He picked up her hand. "Doing rather well, my little dove. I think that the Dragon Doctor Patten might let me stand up and piss in a day or two."

Eunice laughed. "If anyone can make him let you get up, you can. You'll drive him crazy! I'm sure if you threaten to pee on the floor, he'll be amenable."

"I managed to roll myself over to your young man this morning." Jack motioned his head over to the bed where Joe Martin lay. "We were talking about you."

"You were?" Eunice's bright eyes were wide.

"Yup." Jack's shoulders shook with his own joke. "He's getting better because he wants to see what you look like, you beauty, you."

Eunice blushed. *What a nice little girl she is*, Jack thought. *She'd take good care of Joe. God knows he might need someone like her.*

"I'm going over to see how he's doing," Eunice bent over Jack and kissed his bristly cheek. "Then, I'm going to come back and shave you and give you a nice, soothing bed bath".

"Nothing I'd like better..." Jack sighed and lay back, tired from the conversation. He longed for the day that he'd be recovered. This crappy and complex set of injuries that beset his once-strong young body...well, it sucked!

Eunice poured a cup of coffee, put in some powdered cream and balanced it as she went to the bed of the man she couldn't stop thinking about. "Hi, Joe," Eunice's hand brushed Joe Martin's fair hair. She was almost glad that he was blind so that he couldn't see the tell-tale blush on her cheeks just from being near him. "I brought you some coffee. Here. A few more days and we'll be home."

"Eunice!" He reached a hand out, seeking hers. She put her tiny paw into his huge one and he gripped her hard. "I'm so glad you're here." She carefully helped him to sit up and put the hot mug in his hand. "Eunie, you're the best thing that's happened to me since I went into the Army." He smiled and the area around his sightless eyes crinkled. "You've got to marry me when all of this is over." He joked, and then a sadness enveloped his face. "What the heck am I saying to you, you sweet girl, you? Who'd marry a blind man with one foot?"

"Maybe I would." Eunice sat next to him, stroking his arm. "You're a wonderful man, Joe."

"A blind, footless man," he mumbled.

"Come on, Joe. Stop feeling sorry for yourself." Eunice chided him, trying to keep her tears back. "Let's stop all of this and talk about something else." The nurses had discovered, long before, that the men really didn't want any sign of pity whatsoever. "Kansas City..." Eunice mused. "I've never been to Kansas, have you?"

"No, and I don't want to go to Kansas City!" Joe wasn't having a good day. "I'm a New England fellow."

"Where are you from, Joe? Where were you born?"

"A small town in Connecticut. Called Stony Creek. Nice place, right on Long Island Sound."

"I know where it is!" Eunice smiled. "One of my cousins moved near there and we went on a boat ride to the Thimble Islands. I'm from Greenwich, myself."

"I knew there was some reason, other than your ministering angel hands, that I adored you." Joe was the kind of man who didn't dwell on his misfortunes for long. Already, he'd forgotten his misery...he was laughing and smiling...much more cheerful. Eunice asked him more questions about his youth and family, keeping her conversation light.

As she watched him speak, tears came to her eyes and she blinked them back. This was a *man!* A real, live *man!*

From her Supervisor's desk, Carol watched Eunice. *She's got her heart right splat on her face, the poor darling. She knows he's blind and can't see, but even from over here, I can feel her love. This is a girl who deserves some happiness. We'll dock in a couple of days and she'll never see him again. How the hell can I help her?*

She rubbed the back of her neck. *God, everything I own aches from these Goddam waves, I've been battered from top to bottom, just like this poor mothering ship!* She untied the ribbon that held her long black hair off her face. *Maybe I'll throw caution to the winds and let these guys see my crowning glory! Ha! I've got pretty hair and why shouldn't the boys enjoy me looking my best? Where the heck did I put that lipstick?*

The drawer held a myriad of correspondence, paper clips, rubber bands and odds and ends. Ugh! There was even a half-eaten donut! She opened the second drawer. Forms, forms and more forms. She lifted the stack of paper, and found one lone lipstick rolling around. Fire and Ice. Her favorite color. Holding the papers on her lap, she pursed her lips and painted bright red on her lips. She stuck the tip of her pinky finger into the lipstick and put a dot of color on each of her cheeks. Rubbing it in, she grinned, knowing that she was going to vamp and flirt with each and every wounded man. *I'll brighten up their day!*

She started to push the stack of forms back into the drawer, then looked idly down. The DD 407 Form, listing the medicines that each wounded man was given; the DD 404 Form, outlining the medical records; and the DD 333 Form, showing the final destination of each of the wounded. The final destination of each of the wounded... Hmm? She pulled the DD 333 Form out and read it carefully.

"*Bon jour, mon amie.* Why do you look so...so...?" Michelle sashayed to the chair next to Carol's desk.

"Why do I look so...what?"

"*Tiens*, you look glamorous, that I can plainly see." Michelle's expressive eyes crinkled with appreciation. "You painted hussy, you." Michelle picked up the tube of lipstick. "Some for me, *merci beaucoup*." *I, too, want to look as pretty* as you do." She pursed her generous lips and painted lipstick across them. Pressing them together, she smacked her lips and grinned. "But that is not why you look peculiar." She tipped her head. "You look like a pussy cat with a saucer of cream, *ma petit choux*. What are you up to?"

Carol's dark eyes assumed a wide-eyed expression of innocence. "I just want the boys to see me looking as good as I can. Take your hair out of that bun, Michelle, *ma belle*. Let it ripple down your back. Let's put on some perfume and maybe one of our nicest dresses and do the rounds as if we were famous movie stars."

*"Une bonne idée."* Michelle ripped the pins out of her neat chignon. Her abundant strawberry-blond hair flopped down, running like a silky ribbon to the middle of her back. *"Oooh-la-la, we will drive them crazy!"*

She stood up. "I'm going down to change into something as slinky as I can find." She twitched around, then stopped and turned back. Her cat's eyes narrowed. "But there is still something else, Carol. I have worked with you for years now, in the trenches, in prison, in the sweat of the operating room, in the rain, burying innocent young men. I've watched you seduce a general. I've seen you writing steamy letters to *beaucoup de* soldiers and sailors and even a marine or two. I've held your head as you threw up many times. But this…You are up to something, Carol. Something a *leetle* bit dubious…is that the word? No, not! *D*evious! You are being secretive…*devious!* What is it? What are you planning?"

"Damn you, Michelle. I'd hate to try to fool you…ever!" Carol laughed. "I've just been looking at these lovely forms stacked here in the desk."

"Forms? What forms?"

"These DD 333 Forms."

*"Comment?* DD 333 Forms? What are you *talking* about?"

Carol pulled out two of the forms and tapped them against Michelle's thigh. "These forms are the forms that are stuck on every soldier's bed in those plastic envelopes. Some of the forms have general information about each patient. Some tell the orderlies what's wrong with the patient and what we've done so far to treat them." Her face took on a devilish glee.

"But *these* forms, the DD 333's …*these* forms tell the orderlies and the men who are going to transport them in a couple of days just where each patient is to be sent. Which city, which hospital." She sat back, waiting for Michelle to catch on.

Michelle shrugged. Carol noted that no one shrugged the way Michelle shrugged. It must be something all French women learned from birth. "So"

"Think, you dumb French woman, you! *Think!*"

"So I think. What do I think? Nothing." Michelle shrugged her shoulders again in that typically Gallic way. "What am I missing?"

Carol laughed. "It will be audacious. I'll probably be court-martialed if I get caught, but what the hell. It will be worth it."

"What in the name of *Le Bon Dieu* are you talking about?"

"Think of Eunice…the sweetest and bravest nurse that I know." Michelle nodded, obediently thinking of Eunice. Eunice was wonderful, certainly. And brave beyond anything. The girl was a heroine, naturally. Just before they had boarded the *Bucket,* the company of nurses, orderlies, doctors and their patients had been attacked by a night raid of German planes. Eunice, all by herself, had pulled three helpless and sick men out of a hospital tent that had been hit by one of the firebombs. She had run three times into the flaming tent, humping a man easily twice her size out into the safety of the night air. She had injured herself badly in so doing, and her short, curly reddish hair had caught fire, burning completely off. She was brave and wonderful and Michelle adored her. But what did this have to do with a Navy DD 333 form for transporting the wounded?

"Oh! You are so dense!" Carol threw up her hands. "Here!" She grabbed two of the DD 333's and marched herself, dragging Michelle with her, to the desk at the other side of their office.

She flipped the typewriter open and sat herself on the desk. She threaded one of the forms into the platen. "Go over to Joe Martin's bed and pick up his folder. Then go over to Martin Joseph's bed and get *his* folder." She leaned forward and hissed, "Bring them both here and do not even speak to *anyone at all!*"

"Oh!" Michelle's eyes rolled. "Oh! We are to cheat! Of *course!* What a brilliant plan!"

She drifted into the sickroom and quickly lifted the folders from the beds. As she was stealthy and quiet and as both Joseph and Martin were unable to see anything, she was able to tiptoe back to Carol in a moment.

*"Voila!* Here they are!" She opened Martin Joseph's folder and pulled out the DD 333 Form. "Here! Copy it quickly and change his destination to Kansas City. Quick! Before anyone sees us."

Carol began to type fiercely as Michelle leaned over her shoulder, urging her on. "Good, now do Joe Martin's. Change *his* destination to York Hospital, Maine! No one will remember which man was originally going to which place!"

Carol pounded the keys with fervor and then, finished, ripped the second form out of the typewriter. *Voila* indeed! She scrutinized the new forms, then paused, looking up at Michelle with misery in her eyes. "Oh, nuts! They have to be signed by the doctor! What are we going to do?"

"Poof! Why should this little piece of forgery stop us? After all, we are committing a felony anyway...what is one more crime?" She bent over the forms, her green eyes narrowing as she studied the signatures. "It looks like Captain Hannibal Orth. He has a messy signature. Who is he anyway and how will he ever see these forms? *Pah!* Give me a pen." Michelle sucked in a deep breath, stuck her tongue out, and deftly copied the signature of Captain Hannibal Orth, Physician, USN.

The two girls leapt up and hugged one another. "We'll hang together if we're caught." Michelle laughed, ripped up the two old forms, and inserted the newly forged forms into the folders. "We'll be the prettiest nurses ever hung...hanged? Which is it? No! They'll never catch us!" She sashayed behind the desk. "I'll just nip back and put them on their beds." She waved the folders in the air and tiptoed back into the sick room.

As quiet as she tried to be, Marty Joseph heard the rustle. His nasal whine asked, "Who's here?"

Michelle calmly finished fastening the envelope to the bedstead, then casually picked up the water carafe that stood on Joseph's bedside table. "Just checking to see that you have fresh water, Marty," she cooed.

Joseph waved his arm in the direction of her voice and connected with her arm. His hand fastened on it and he pulled her toward him. "Hey, baby! Which one are you?"

"It's Michelle." Michelle made her words as French as possible. "'Ow are you, *mon ami?*"

"Ah, you little Frenchie! You sexy minx, you. Come here to old Marty and let me give you a big squeeze." He pulled roughly at her, sliding his arm up and, perhaps by accident, but Michelle didn't really think so, brushing his fingers against her breast. "You wanna sit down and fool around?"

"No, Marty. Only see if you need more water." Michelle picked up his hand as if she were touching a tarantula. Holding it with the tips of her fingers, she deposited his hand back on the bed.

"Why donch'a come back later, Michelle," Marty urged in a hoarse, knowing voice. "When they turn down the lights and we can get to know one another better."

"Thanks, but no thanks, Marty." Michelle forced herself to sound light and pleasant. "I'm an engaged girl."

"Ha! I hear you have a fellow in every port! What's one more, right here in front of you?" His arms flailed, trying to find her. "I hear you Frenchies are hot stuff."

"Well...." She didn't know quite what to say. He mustn't have any idea whatsoever, that she had any interest in his destination papers. "Perhaps, when I am not so busy, I can come back and we can talk." She backed away. "Is there anything you need right now? Some coffee? A snack?"

"I need a woman!" Marty laughed coarsely. "A French woman with big tits." Marty sniggered, then wiped his hand across his lips.

*What pig he was. If it were up to me, I'd send him to the North Pole!* Michelle shuddered at his crude sexual innuendoes. "All this French woman is able to offer you is a cup of coffee or a cookie." Michelle laughed and backed further away. "Perhaps I can talk later." Wide-eyed with concern, she sped back to her boss' office.

There, she found Carol pacing back and forth. "What's wrong?"

"Eunice!" Carol cried. "We'll have to tell her what we did."

"Why, for the love of God?"

"Because she already *knows* that Joe isn't going to York. She'll say something if we don't warn her! She'll spoil the whole thing!"

"Hmpf. Leave her to me." Michelle nodded firmly. "I will convince her not to let the two of us be shot in front of a firing squad." Carol laughed. "And besides, if she ever wants to marry this good man, this is her only chance. She loves him. This will give her about three more weeks, while we wait for the ship to be refurbished, to see him and perhaps work her love-light on him. She'll see that what we did was for the best."

"From your mouth to God's ear!" Carol crossed herself with fervor.

~~~~~~~~~~~~~~~~~

That evening, after the patients had been served their supper, the nurses put on an impromptu show for them, also inviting those of the crew of the *Buchanan,* who were off-duty. "Let's give the guys something to remember!"

*"Oooh-la-la!"*

Captain Carol Abbi-Patricks, as head nurse, was the emcee. Dressed in a silk kimono, she started the entertainment by shakily singing *"Don't fence Me In."* Michelle, wearing her best dress and a hat that she'd hastily manufactured from feathers and silks, did a can-can dance, accompanied by Dr. Alex Patten who played an improvised set of drums on pots and pans stolen from the mess hall.

Shy little Eunice, was goaded into participation by the rest of the nurses. "These poor men deserve our best efforts, even if we're not too talented…come on, Eunie; you've got to join in!" Reluctantly, Eunice agreed, but only if she sang with others in a group. She joined Yashiko, Carol and Alan Bowen, singing *"Don't Sit Under the Apple Tree."*

Alex Patten took out his precious camera and went to each patient, taking a photograph so that family back home could see that they were alive and on the way to being healed. "I promise to develop these as soon as I get stateside. I have the addresses you gave me and I'll mail the photographs as soon as I possibly can," he pledged.

Allen Bowen, the husky testosterone-laden corpsman surprised his fellow medics with a dainty tap dance to *"Tiptoe through the Tulips."* He wound his dance up and down the lines of beds, making sure that each patient got a moment or so of his tapping.  His sense of rhythm was so bad that the men nearly fell out of bed with laughter.

Yashiko found enough scarves and beads to make herself a hula costume, and, accompanied by Neil Harmon's banging the beat on a large soup pot, which had also been liberated from under the Mess Cook's nose, she danced barefoot to *"Aloha My Island."*

The entire ensemble wound up the entertainment by singing *"The White Cliffs of Dover"* and then, begged by the wounded men, did an encore. "If all of you will join with us"... of *"God Bless America."*

There were no dry eyes.

# CHAPTER SEVEN

**July 1943 – Russian Army begins offensive and achieves victory in Orel. German attack fails.**

**FROM THE *KITTERY GAZETTE* –**
**Hospital Ship USS *Buchanan* arrives in Portsmouth Harbor…**
**Fifty wounded sent to York Hospital…**

Alex Patten went home, surprising his mother and father. Crying with joy, they welcomed their handsome son, back for a short few weeks, into the bosom of the family. "I can't spend too much time with you, Mom," Alex explained. "I'm on duty and I'm going to be tending those fifty wounded men that we brought here."

"Of course, darling. We understand." Julie ruffled Alex's hair, which seemed to be three shades darker than when he left. She touched Alex's shoulder. He was taller, too. *Strange how he'd changed*, she mused. The boy had really grown, filling out a formerly lanky frame with muscle. *Boy?* She ruefully corrected herself. *He was no boy anymore. He was a man. A full-fledged man.* He was her only chick. *A pretty swell chick,* she thought. He had always been a great son, even though he'd gotten into a few little scrapes now and then. Like the time he'd put the effigy of one hated teacher in the foyer of his high school. The effigy had been surrounded by beer bottles and more than a few girlie magazines and the entire school body had stood around it, laughing. It had been hard to be upset about the prank, as everyone knew that the teacher was a lecher and a drunk.  Even the principal was laughing.

Silly pranks had been eclipsed by Alex raiding his mother's pantry to feed a family in need. "I took your stuff, Mom," he'd explained. "We have so much food and they don't have any. I knew you wouldn't mind at all." He stood there, a gap-toothed smile on his twelve year old face, knowing that she understood.

He'd matured from a caring boy into a caring man and a good listener. Naturally, these were superb attributes for a surgeon, and she *knew* he was a good surgeon. He was clever in his mind and clever with his hands. Hands that saved a lot of lives, she surmised. She wondered about the men he'd been caring for during the past few years. Alex kept his own counsel in the letters he wrote to her during the war. If he stayed true to course, he'd never talk much about what he had seen and done. She worried about him every day, a young man who was often too caring, often attracting needy people who could suck the juices out of him. A mother saw. A mother knew.

Alex hugged his dad, holding on for a long time. Julie watched. *Maybe he'll talk to Pat. Perhaps, as one man to another, he can open up and let the abysmal things...the deaths and the maiming...the rot and stench that had been much of his life these past two years.*

"Say, Dad," Alex began. Julie swallowed. *He's going to open up to Pat. I'll just fade away so that the two can talk...man to man...*Julie turned away, fiddling with the living room curtains.

I've just got to ask...Do you still have that old Ford out in the garage?" There was a gasp from Julie. She simply couldn't help it. The two men turned, open-mouthed, as Julie began to laugh...a loud belly laugh that came right from her heart and soul.

"Honey?" Pat's face was a study in confusion. "Julie? Why are you laughing?"

"What's so funny, Mom?"

Julie laughed harder, then turned away to get her son a piece of home-made apple pie. Maybe she'd put a dollop of vanilla ice cream on top. *Men!*

~~~~~~~~~~~~~~~~~

**JULY 24, 1943 –**
**WAR NEWS: Operation Gomorrah begins.**
British and Canadian aeroplanes bomb the City of Hamburg by night. The American air force supported these efforts, continuing the bombing during the daylight hours. By the end of the operation (November 1943) almost ten thousand tons of ammunition had been dropped on Hamburg, killing more than 30,000 people and destroying nearly 290,000 buildings.

**The Portsmouth News and Bugle: Fifth USO show at Connie Bean tonight!**

Jan's mother helped her into the slinky dress. "Never thought you'd get so much wear out of a dress that barely covers your name and address!" Mrs. Neiman cuffed her daughter, half in jest and half in pride. "You look so beautiful, sugar."

"Thanks, Mom. I can't believe they keep asking me back!" She twisted, turning to see herself from the back in the long mirror that hung on the back of her mother's bedroom door.

"You are always the best thing in the whole show," Mrs. Neiman averred stoutly. She pinned a creamy, fresh gardenia into the roll of Jan's hair and stood back. "Beautiful, just beautiful you are!"

A horn sounded outside. Mrs. Neiman handed Jan a wrap. "Daddy's waiting. Let's go and wow them again, Jan."

# THE USO AT
## THE CONNIE BEAN CENTER

*presents...*

# YOUR SHOW OF SHOWS!

### Saturday Night, July 24, 1943 • Doors Open at 7 PM

## *Starring...*

**Mary Bogucki**, the Polish Nightingale, singing **"I'll Get By"**

**The Cut-Em-Up Barbershop Quartet** featuring
**Jim Van Wart, Ronnie Leard, Leigh Brethauer &
Len Roeber (Mr. Bass Man)**

**Joe Amaral** &his palomino pony, **Diver,** with **Lariat Fantasies**

BACK BECAUSE YOU ASKED!
**Dick & Ursula Bondi** doing the **Peabody!**

**The High Kick Girls**…count them! 24 in all!
Doing fantastic dance routines

**Dan Sargeant, Himself**…the Irish Tenor of the year singing **"Danny
Boy"**

**Mary Jean Labbe** tap dancing on a bucket to
the **Beer Barrel Polka**

Portsmouth's Funniest Comedian…**Dan Birck**

**Mary Ericson,** "the Snake Lady," dances with
her **cobras and deadly black mambas!**

**Missy Hingos,** the Jersey Lily with her rendition of
**"I'll Walk Alone"**

**Stan Sullivan,** singing
**"Praise the Lord and Pass the Ammunition"**

BACK because YOU ASKED FOR THEM!
**The Knickerbocker Brothers, Sam & Eddie**

The **Magic Marimba** of Kathy Maoriana

BACK BY POPULAR DEMAND!
**The Flying Heibels** on their daring trapeze

YOU ASKED FOR HER AGAIN!
**Julie Patten** tap dancing to **"Deep in the Heart of Texas"**!

**Jack the Ventriloquist**
with his wooden-headed friend, **Skippy Boy**

**Magic Tricks** by The Amazing Duo of **Hogan & Annie-Boo**

Exotic Belly Dancing by **Helen Huntress** & her veils of gold!

**The Washington Choir** singing **"Amazing Grace"**

**The Waltz of the Toreadors** as performed by **Bette & Barbara**

**High Wire Wonders** from the **Daring Dingleys,**
**Josh, Jess, James & Conner**

**"Casey At The Bat"** recited by local radio personality **Bob Bossie**

And back by YOUR DEMAND:
**Jan Neiman,** singing **"Takin' a Chance on Love"**!

And our **finale,** with the entire audience invited to join in:
**"God Bless America,"** sung by **Cheryl DeToro,**
**with Rosie Nunn & her all-girl orchestra!**

**Ticket Price: $1.50**
**SERVICE MEN & WOMEN IN UNIFORM**
**ADMITTED FREE**

*Come Early...Bring Your Friends!*

"You've got to come!" Julie, dressed like Broadway's idea of a cowgirl, put her tap shoes into a small suitcase. The suitcase contained her make-up, a towel, and a change of clothing for after the show. "If I'm tap dancing, you are coming!"

Alex moaned. "I don't want any reminders of the war these few weeks. Let me alone! I'm going to stay here and listen to some new jazz records."

"In a pig's eye!" His mother exclaimed. "You've hibernated for three days. Get up off your duff and come out tonight." She turned to Pat, who was waiting to leave. "Right, Pat?"

"Your mother sets a lot of store on you being there to cheer for her," Pat, who usually stayed out of the confrontations between his son and his wife, appealed to Alex. "She'll never shut up about it all unless you're in the audience watching."

Alex groaned. The new Lionel Hampton Trio record was calling to him. And so was his mother. "Ah, what the hell…I mean, heck." He capitulated. His mother was nearer than Lionel. And stronger than Lionel. And louder than Lionel. Lionel could wait until he came home. "I'll come, I'll come."

~~~~~~~~~~~~~~~

At the Portsmouth Naval Prison, supper was over. The inmates who cleaned the tables had finished and gone back to their cells. The cooks were seated at three small tables in the corner of the kitchen, finishing their meal, which was a little bit different from the meal that the run-of-the-mill convict had been served. The convicts got a plate of what was referred to as SOS…shit on a shingle…creamed chipped beef on toast…and the cooks, who considered themselves on a much higher social level than the convicts, ate pork chops and fried potatoes. The three guards, who considered kitchen duty an easy task, were joshing with the cooks, trading cigarettes and randy jokes.

Two of the dishwashers, seeing that the cooks were occupied with their meals, whispered to one another.

"Ya ready?"

"Yup."

"What time izzit?"

The heavier of the two men, a gentleman who was christened Zachary Mullins, but who was known as "Zootz", looked up at the clock on the wall. "Twenny minutes to six."

The thinner man was christened many years ago with hope and joy as Daniel Carlson. Despite the hope, Daniel grossly disappointed his mother and father when he was arrested at age twenty for breaking and entering.

Dan made a gesture with his head to Zootz. "We'll hang around and then, when they tell us to get back, you go to the garbage pails and I'll follow."

"I dunno, Dan Man," Zootz whined. "I donno about the garbage."

"Just do what we planned, you cocksucker. " Dan snarled, glaring at Zootz.     "Don't rat out on me now or I'll kill ya'"

"OK, OK. I'm in." Zootz groaned aloud as one of the kitchen trusties brought him another load of dirty dishes. "I'll never piss you off, Dan Man." Zootz was more frightened of Dan than any prison guard or pile of garbage.

~~~~~~~~~~~~~~

The new Kennebunk Savings Bank, located in Kittery, Maine, had been opened for six months. At 5PM, the officers and the tellers readied themselves…all of them…to go out for a quick supper and then get to the Connie Bean Center to capture good seats at the USO show.

"Everyone ready?" Shelly Richards, the Assistant Branch Manger, checked her watch. "Who is coming? Can we all fit in my car?" Tonight was a cherished night out for Shelly. Her husband, Chris, who worked in an essential job at the Shipyard, was babysitting for Alicia, their little girl. He'd given Shelly a night out with the girls and she couldn't wait to get going.

Hands were raised and Shelly counted off: "One, Julie." Julie Perrault, an attractive brown-haired woman with green eyes, was married to Brian, who also worked an essential war job at the Shipyard. Like Chris Richards, he had agreed to watch little Brianna tonight so that Julie could enjoy the show. "Two, Sally." Sally Leland, a little younger than the rest, was married to Everett, a Marine fighting, Sally thought, some-where in the Philippine Islands. "Three, Michelle." Michelle Johnson was also married to her high school sweetheart, Travis. Like many of the local men, Travis was a pipefitter at the Yard. And like the other good husbands of the women who worked at the bank, he was watching their two girls, Brittany and Katelin so that Michelle could see the show.

"Don't forget me!" Tami Keen, blonde and blue-eyed, called out from her cubbyhole behind the counter. Tammy was one of the single ones, but her boyfriend, Jeff Colburn, received a letter every day from her, mail permitting, on the Merchant Marine ship, some where in the Pacific, on which he was stationed. Tammy, although she flirted with every man who came into the bank, young or old, was faithful to Jeff. She assiduously knitted in her spare time and during her lunch hour, finishing enough scarves and socks to outfit Jeff's entire ship. "After all," she said when one of her friends remarked that she 'talked to everything in pants,' "a girl has to keep her skills honed. Who knows what the future might bring?"

The girls at the bank were especially anxious to see tonight's show. A few of them had attended a previous show and raved about it, but it was primarily that one of their co-workers, Helen Huntress, was actually performing in tonight's show.

"I can't believe that she's going to belly dance!" Tammy exclaimed. "How can she do that kind of thing up on stage and in front of all those men?"

"She *wants* to do it!" Sally laughed. "She just loves having all of them ogle her!"

Julie sighed. "Before I had two kids, I could do a belly dance. Now, well...." she laughed, "I'll save my dancing for Brian."

"Brian would decapitate you if you even thought of sashay-ing around on stage in some scarves."

"Where's Gail?" Tami asked. "She said she was coming."

"She's picking up Cathy French. They'll meet us there."

Armed with the keys, Shelly twisted the lock to the vault, checking to see that all was secured, snapped off the lights, opened the door so that all of them could leave, and then double locked it for the night. "All the money is safe for another night," she intoned, as she did every night when she locked up. "Thank the Lord and pass the ammunition."

"And after the war is over," Tami chorused, "We'll all beeeee freeee!"

~~~~~~~~~~~~~~

"No excuse, you're coming with me," Grace Sabatino gave her niece the ultimatum. "As a matter of fact, the rest of you should come, too. I have plenty of room in the car and the more people I take, the better I feel about using a half gallon of gas and the more money the USO makes. These are wonderful shows and we should all support the war effort and...the best reason of all is to applaud like mad when our own employee and her husband dance. The crowd loved Ursula and Dick and their dancing. They were asked especially to come back tonight...so many people loved their tango."

"I'd go, but...but, you know. Maybe they don't let colored people in," Caledonia mumbled. "I don't want to be embarrassed."

"You're dead wrong, my child. Why they have this wonderful singer, Jan and the tap dancing brothers from Puddleduck...you'll love the whole show." Grace wasn't going to give in to any of them.

"I'm too old to traipse around," Agnes Winchell drew herself up. "I'm going home and read a good book."

"You can read the book tomorrow night. " Grace was firm. "And Jannus, you can ride up front with me."

"I'm not going, Missus," Jannus was respectful, but firm. "I gotta get up to set da bread tomorra." He reached for the broom. "You ladies go and enjoy. I'm gonna sveep up and den drink a glass of vine and go to bed." He pushed at them with the broom. "Maybe I vill go next time. I promise dat I'll try, if I don't have to get up da next morning so early."

Grace sighed. She knew defeat and accepted Jannus's proclamation. If she could bring the ladies, she'd feel she'd done a good deed. Especially Mary Rose. The girl had been moping alone almost every night. Alright that she'd had a difficult romance back in Greenwich, but that was over and done with. She just had to get on with her life. The bakery was doing fine, but Mary Rose... Grace sighed....with all those nice young soldiers and sailors and marines there tonight, surely she might find someone. And, she smirked to herself, when she signed Mary Rose up to be a USO hostess...and maybe they'd take Caledonia, too...there were lots of colored men in the services and they needed colored hostesses to dance with them.... Her round face beamed. Grace loved nothing more than fixing up a nice romance. Or two or three.

~~~~~~~~~~~~~~~

As the crowd at the USO roared their approval at Mary Bogucki's poignant rendition of *I'll Get By...,* a fire was started in a house in the old Puddleduck area of Portsmouth. The houses there were ancient, flimsy and all made of wood with paper stuffed into cracks pretending to be insulation. The arsonist had picked a good target for conflagration.

It was dark. The arsonist had waited...it was just past 8 o'clock...and the lights had been extinguished in the house for a half-hour. The arsonist knew there were two elderly men in the house, and that both of them had, most likely, gone to sleep. *Sleeping the deepest sleep of their lives*, the arsonist chuckled, quietly splashing kerosene around the perimeter of the house, on the porch, around the windows and then emptying the can against the front door.

A match...and then the blaze leapt up, licking at the walls all around the small house, reaching greedily for anything combustible in its way. The arsonist stepped back, face shielded against the flames. Careful to leave no fingerprints, the arsonist threw the tinny sheriff's badge onto the grassy front yard, and then melted back into the shadows to watch the fire engines arrive. The noise the fire engines made was so exciting! And the flames! The arsonist began to pant, exploding with strange desires...then reached a hand to secret places... shivered with a shuddering thrill, gripped in a climax that echoed the screams of the sirens. Then, with a hiss, the arsonist was depleted...satisfied. If there had been anyone to listen, they might have heard the arsonist humming a hymn, *Lead on Kindly Light.*

~~~~~~~~~~~~~~

At intermission, Julie Patten and Brenda Be sat in the hall at a desk conspicuously marked, "JOIN THE USO HOSTESS TEAM! SIGN UP HERE TO HELP!"

Grace Sabatino dragged her niece and Caledonia to the desk. "Good evening, Grace!" Julie called. "How are you enjoying the show?"

"Oh, it's wonderful," Grace gushed with great sincerity. "I'm really looking forward to your performance. I loved it when I was here the last time."

"I'm getting too old to traipse around on stage," Julie laughed. "But it seems like the audience likes to see old ladies out there...reminds them of their mothers, I guess. And who have we here?" Julie asked.

"This is my niece from Connecticut, Julie. Mary Rose Sabatino. She operates a bakery in Kittery."

Julie exclaimed that she had already tasted Mary Rose's products. "I bought a dozen pastries and two loaves of bread." She smacked her lips. "Wonderful stuff." She turned to Caledonia. "And you are...?"

"This is Caledonia Hope. She works at the bakery for Mary Rose. Both of the girls are anxious, with some prodding from me, to be hostesses here."

"Marvelous!" Even Caledonia was convinced of Julie's eagerness. "Young ladies, this is Brenda Be, who is setting up our Arts and Music department."

The girls tried not to stare at Brenda, who was wearing a Viking helmet with horns protruding from each side, smoking a cigar and dressed in what looked like a man's tuxedo. Julie, who was used to Brenda's idiosyncratic ways, continued, not noticing the girls' astonishment at Brenda's clothing and adornment: "We really need junior hostesses. There are so many young men who come here. They want a pretty girl to dance with, to talk to, to play cards with. They're lonely and away from home. You can be their date for the night." She smiled and handed Mary Rose and Caledonia each a sheet of paper. "But only if you obey our rules." She shook her finger at the girls. "You cannot date the men outside of the USO building. You can't give them your telephone number or your address." She grinned, "Even if they are as handsome as Robert Taylor!" She fished in her purse and brought out a pen. "Here. Fill these applications out and bring them to me on Monday night at 6 o'clock." She looked up..."Oh! There's Tricia! Tricia! *Tricia!"*

Tricia Tobey turned at the call. "Hello, Jules. Wonderful show! Can't wait to see you in the next half." Tricia was towing a handsome young man with her. He had light brown floppy hair, wore horn-rimmed spectacles and had an engaging grin. Grace, Mary Rose and Caledonia watched her approach.

"Just the person I wanted to see!" Julie beamed. "Tricia Tobey, this is Grace Sabatino, one of our Senior Hostesses here." The two women shook hands. "And this is Mary Rose, Grace's niece, and her friend, um, what was your name, dear?"

"Caledonia." She laughed. "Difficult to learn, but once you've got it, you'll never forget it."

"Caledonia. Of course." Julie pointed to the application forms. "Caledonia and Mary will be joining us as Junior Hostesses on Monday." She turned back to the two young women. "Tricia has been hostessing for several weeks now. She'll meet you here at 6 PM on Monday and teach you all that you'll need to know. Just bring your completed forms and wear a pretty, but modest, dress. Do your hair in a simple, but pretty style. Wear a little bit of make-up. Wear attractive shoes, but be sure that you can dance in them without breaking your ankle!" There was a loud call for Julie. "Oh, goodness, I have to go. I never even met your young man," she apologized to Tricia and made a moue of disappointment. "After the show! We'll meet again after the show" she cried, as she galloped away.

"Phew! She's a dynamo!" Caledonia was sincere in her admiration and relief that the persons in charge seemed to really want her. "She doesn't seem to care if I'm colored."

"Silly goose," Grace chided her. "We really need you! We need a whole platoon of people of color to entertain the Negro troops." Caledonia nodded, too wise to make any comeback remark.

"Oh, my!" Julie came running back. "I almost forgot! We have several nurses and some male medics who came in on the hospital ship. They'll be here for about three weeks and need places to stay. Can any of you help out? Please, we are desperate for somewhere to *put* them!" She turned at a yell. "Oh, I'm coming, I'm coming! What would you all do if I died?"

"Julie," Grace hollered. "Mario and I can put up two or three men." She turned to Mary Rose. "And can you keep four nurses up in your upstairs room?" Stunned by the swift way her life had changed in fifteen minutes, Mary Rose nodded helplessly. "Good!" Grace ran after Julie to tell her the news.

# CHAPTER NINE

**July 25 – In Italy, the Gran Consiglio del Fascimo withdraws its support of Mussolini; Mussolini is arrested.**

**Portsmouth News and Bugle – Two Convicts Escape from Naval Prison!!!**

They'd nearly suffocated in the garbage. "I puked all over myself! The goddamn men dumped me upside down!" Zootz was nearly crying.

"Shut up, you putz!" Dan swatted Zootz. "We got out! That's all ya' need to dwell on! We got out!"

They were covered with filth; their prison uniforms stained with spoiled food, ketchup and other unspeakable garbage. But they were out! Escaped!

"We escaped from the fucking prison!" Dan exulted. "I can't fucking believe it!" He reached back and helped Zootz as they clambered over the piles of foul-smelling detritus.

The men from the prison had dumped the garbage, as they did every night, onto a tub-like barge that was tied to the pier at the back side of Seavey Island. In the morning hours, another barge from Portsmouth, would pick up the garbage and tow it far out into the Atlantic Ocean and dump it unto the deep.

"Now wadda we gonna do?" Zootz was almost crying with fear and uncertainty. "They're gonna miss us and come to get us!"

"Shut up! Everyone is watching the movie. No one knows we're even missing yet!" Dan had planned carefully. He'd picked Zootz to be his fellow-escapee. Zootz was stupid and cow-like. He'd follow any direction that Dan ordered, never really talk back, and was completely expendable, once they had reached freedom.

"Can you swim?"

"Yeah? So what?"

"See that boat over there?" Dan pointed to a low shape in the water. "We're gonna swim over to it, climb on board, and get ourselves far away from here." He spat in the direction of the prison.

"You'll help me, won'tcha? I don't swim too good."

"I won't let you drown," Dan's mouth stretched into a wolfish grin. "Let's go, *amigo*..." And he dove into the chilly waters of the dark night.

Zootz watched Dan's head break out of the water. Dan waved to him and began to swim towards the boat. Afraid to stay, afraid to go, Zootz dithered for a moment. Dan's head and splashes moved further and further away. "Oh, shit! Here I come!" Clumsy with fright, Zootz jumped in. *Cold? Shit, it was freezing!*

He half-swam, half dog-paddled his way, following the regular splashes that were Dan's kicking feet. His head hit the side of the boat with a thump. He blinked and coughed, trying to stay afloat. Dan's hand reached down and pulled at his hair. "Come on up!" Zootz scrambled as best he could, pulling himself up with clumsy motions, his leg reaching for the top. Dan pulled at him, hauling his dripping weight, until he fell into the bottom of the boat.

Dan was already in the tiny cabin, searching for the keys to start the engine. "Look around and see what's under there..." Dan gestured to the storage bins. "Ah!" His hands heard the jingle of metal. "They always leave the keys on board! Stupid bastards!"

Zootz scrabbled in a lazarette and found some yellow oilskins. "Hey! Look, Dan! We got clothes!" He stripped off the hated prison-striped uniform and stood, stark naked for a moment, letting the chilly night air dry his skinny body. Flailing, as Dan got the engine started and the boat rocked forward, Zootz regained his balance and pulled the stiff overalls on, then put on the jacket. "Hey! Looka me! I'm a fuckin' fisherman!"

"Throw those other oilskins over here!" Dan steered the boat toward the Kittery shore. He stripped off his own uniform and dressed in the foul weather gear. Ceremoniously, he threw his prison clothing overboard and Zootz followed, capering with glee.

"Where we goin'?"

"I'm gonna get away from the barge, go tie up over there and see what else is on the boat." Dan guided the boat toward a dark dock that stuck out in the water. He cut the engine and the boat slid into the dock, bumping against the pilings. Dan slid a rope over the stanchion and tied up. Clumsy, not knowing the right kind of knot, but shrugging... *what the hell does it matter what kind of knot I use?* He gave the rope one extra hitch. *Shit. It had better stay tied.*

Dan opened one of the lazarettes and found it empty except for a dead crab and a coil of line. He opened the second one and discovered a tin box resting on a pile of cloth. Inside was a leather pouch with eight quarters and three dimes. "Eureka. We're rich!"

"We got money?"

"A little.  Enough to start." Dan poked around the cabin, hoping to find better pickings. He found a half pack of damp cigarettes, a tin can with some moldy biscuits in it, and nothing else. Stuffing one of the biscuits in his mouth, Dan turned the key. "We'll go up the coast...maybe to York or Wells...and then we'll see if we can hitch a ride." The key clicked, but the engine was silent. "What the hell?" Dan turned the key again. Nothing. "Shit!"

"They're gonna catch us!" Zootz moaned. "We're sittin' ducks here!"

"Shut up!" Dan snarled. "Maybe I just gotta jiggle something around." He opened the hatch, trying to locate the engine. "Aha!" There, at the bottom, the engine sat, cold and sullen. Dan scratched his head. Shit, how the hell could he get the damn thing started? He didn't know squat about engines, anyway. He shrugged. "Let's see what I can do…"

He squirmed himself down into the tiny space. There was a pile of rags and a toolbox nestled next to the engine. The rags were just rags. The toolbox…"Shit!" Dan stifled his ejaculation. There, underneath a bundle of screwdrivers and spark plugs, sat a small revolver. *Bonanza!*

Dan thought hard. He shielded his discoveries from Zootz' looming face. "Go and re-check the cabin. See if I missed anything," he ordered. Zootz, because he was programmed to be ordered around, obeyed without question.

As Zootz clumped toward the bow of the boat, Dan checked the gun. Three bullets. Enough, if he was clever. And he'd be clever…mighty clever. He put the gun into the capacious pocket of his yellow slicker and then transferred the two longest screwdrivers to the opposite pocket. Wiping his mouth with the back of his hand, he pushed himself back on deck and closed the hatch.

"Nothin' down there." He shrugged, open handed as he met Zootz coming back out of the cabin. "Find anything?"

"Nope." Zootz looked worried. "Can you get us away?"

Dan took the key out, spat on it and tried it again. A click. He tried the key again and when only the click, click, click sounded….He swore in frustration and threw they key into the water.

"Whaja do that for, Dan? Now we'll never get away!" Zootz cried.

"Who's in charge, here?" Dan snarled at Zootz, annoyed and baffled.

From over the water, a siren sounded. They looked up at the outline of the prison. Searchlights probed out suddenly, scoping the waters, sliding up and down in the harbor. Lights came on all over Seavey Island and the relentless siren screamed and screamed. Zootz began to cry, snuffling and knuckling at his eyes. "They're gonna catch us and hang us! We're goners. Goners!"

"Shut up!" Dan spat at him.

"Gee, Dan. You always tell me to shut up." Zootz complained. "Why doncha be nice to me?"

"Cause you're a dope." Dan hollered, beginning to panic. In the distance, boats were being launched into the water. "Shit!"

"Dan!" Zootz almost screamed.

Dan thought hard. What the hell should they do? They couldn't sit here…sooner or later the patrol boats would check every boat. They'd be sitting ducks if they couldn't get away now.

Dan's life, after the six month stretch he'd done for his youthful Breaking and Entering, had spiraled downward. A second B and E found a sympathetic judge willing to let him join the Army instead of going to jail for the obligatory three years second offense. "Maybe the Army will knock some sense into you, young man."

Not really. Dan Carlson's career in the military was a failure from the start. He wasn't a man to recognize authority, even the absolute authority of his Army instructor. In the first three days of boot camp, pissed at being caught cheating in a card game called "Put and Take", Dan picked up a beer bottle, broke it over the edge of the card table, and nearly sliced two of his fellow soldiers to death before he was stopped.

His sentence, five years in the Portsmouth Naval Prison, followed by a Dishonorable Discharge, was greeted by his mother with grief. His father, more pragmatic, dusted his hands of his impenitent son and forbade Dan's mother from ever communicating with him. She was a good mother…she kept on trying…and wrote tirelessly to him for several months, but never included any money in her envelopes. What good was a letter without money?  Dan tore up each and every letter without opening any more of them. After a year, his mother resigned herself to the fact that her son wasn't able to be reformed.

In the Prison, Dan was regarded as 'difficult'. Surly and intractable, he formed no friendships, and barely spoke to any of his fellow inmates. Zootz, marginally intelligent and slavishly devoted to Dan, was one of the few that he tolerated.

The kitchen scrubbing detail, one of the most miserable jobs in the prison, was randomly assigned to those prisoners that the guards liked least. Dan and Zootz were quickly awarded the jobs.

Dan was a miserable, unhappy and mean human being, but he wasn't stupid. He watched for his opportunity, and when he realized just how the garbage left the facility, he decided to try to escape.

And now that he had gotten away, there was no chance that he'd let himself be caught again.

The sirens wailed again. "Get out!" Dan jumped onto the pier. "Let's get the hell outta here." Zootz climbed clumsily onto the dock and followed Dan's dash into the trees and freedom.

~~~~~~~~~~~~~~

Randy Stuart, Portsmouth's Chief of Police, asked for help from Chief Parks.

"They gotta be connected, Horace. Two arsonists right next door to one another? Nah! And the sheriff's badge? Nah! Your guy is travelling over the river to Portsmouth!"

"He's killed a lot of people. Did you get pictures of the crowd?"

"Yeah. I'm glad you suggested it. The guy from the News and Bugle is bringing them over to my office tomorrow morning. Can you meet me there and bring your pictures? We'll compare the onlookers. Maybe we can find a match. If so, that will most likely be our man."

"I'll be there first thing after I meet with this psycho doctor lady."

"Meet with who?"

"She's my deputy's wife's cousin's neighbor's aunt or some such thing.. Some lady from Sweden or Norway. Supposedly, she's an expert on people who set fires. Wrote some paper about their motives and such."

"Yeah?" Randy looked dubious. "Think she can really help?"

"I got nothin' else, Randy. Not one thing."

~~~~~~~~~~~~~~

The bright lights of the Connie Bean Center USO beckoned the sailors, soldiers, marines, and coast guardsmen to the dance.

   Although he'd prefer to spend the night gambling again at the Hess Club for Gentlemen, Seaman Nick Cappiello, three weeks away from shipping out on the submarine *Paragon,* had been so cleaned out by poker players luckier than he, that he'd have to seek much less expensive entertainment this night. Too bad, Nick mused, he'd really liked that short, giggling girl with the dangly earrings. What was her name? Whatever. He had no money to go upstairs with her.  He should have visited with her first, *then* lost the rest of his money!
   Shrugging, always philosophical, Nick checked the contents of his wallet, found enough for a cheap supper, and strolled down State Street to see what was available for a man as poor as himself.  He passed the lights at the USO and paused. There would always be sandwiches and maybe a Coke at the USO…should he stop in?  As he paused on the sidewalk, he was none-too-gently bumped by three marines. "Goin' in, buddy?"
   "Maybe." Nick lit a cigarette. "What's happening in there?"
   "Big dance tonight." The tallest marine grinned. "Starts in a half-hour. You ought 'a put on your dancing shoes. They got a lot of pretty ones in there."
   "Yeah?" Nick offered the marines cigarettes. They cheerfully accepted.
   "Yeah. These are good girls, my man. Not B-girls. No hoochie-koochie with these dolls. You gotta leave them here afterward, but, I'll say, man, they are very nice while the going is good." The marine winked at him. "And everything is free if you're in uniform."
   "My lucky night," Nick brushed his hands down the sides of his dress whites. "I'll be back," Nick gave the men a mock salute and walked toward the other side of the street. There, he found some shops and a few places to eat. No Chang's. His stomach protested.  He'd had chink food last night. Never mind that…what he wanted now was American food, hamburgers, chili, maybe a bowl of stew! He passed Tedesco's Meat Market and stopped. Tedesco's Meat Market…and right next store…*bingo!* Tedesco's Restaurant! In the window was a big, hand-lettered sign:

## Servicemen In Uniform
### SPECIALS

### Stew and Biscuits - 50 cents
### Spicy Chili - 35 cents
### Big Burger/Roll - 40 cents

*I swear, this is an omen*, Nick thought. *Food for less than a buck. I'll have a few bucks left over and I can find a late-night poker game...get my stake back and* then *I can go back to the Hess Palace...visit that little cute short babe or the tall brunette with the tattoo of a rattlesnake on her thigh again.* Salivating for some good red meat, he opened the door to Tedesco's and strolled in, hungry as a horse.

~~~~~~~~~~~~~~

Caledonia met Mary Rose at the door of the USO. "I'm as nervous as a hound dog in an alleyway." She looked at Mary Rose. Mary Rose, tiny and plump, wore the highest heels possible and a peplum dress that emphasized her curves and bosom. "I like your dress." She twirled around. "What do you think? Will I pass muster."

Caledonia wore a slinky lavender rayon dress. Her hair was dressed high on her head in a pompadour. She hoped she looked like Lena Horne. Several soldiers, jousting to get in, stopped and eyed her with appreciation. "They think you look like the cat's pajamas," Mary Rose enthused. "We'll both do fine."

They'd read the rules. Modest in dress and behavior. Give the men your first names only. Do not encourage personal questions. Do not give out your last name, your address or your telephone number. You are here only to dance and talk with these men for this evening. Do not make any dates. You are forbidden, with excommunication from the USO and its delights dangled sternly as a warning, to meet any serviceman afterwards or at any time away from the USO. None. No matter how cute they are!

The main door was guarded by a desk manned by, as their name tags informed, Candace McClosky and Sabina Carter. The two women, both in their mid-forties, somehow embodied a sweet and gentle mother-like face welded to a backbone of steel. "I wouldn't want either of them mad at me!" Mary Rose whispered, *sotto voce*, to Caledonia. Caledonia nodded with earnest solemnity and shivered.

"In a lady-like way, they'd decapitate you!"

Mary Rose and Caledonia were asked for their identification cards, and, upon passing scrutinization, were waved in. "Have a wonderful time, girls. Remember the rules!" They entered the main auditorium and were dazzled by the music and the crowd of servicemen and their beautifully dressed, energetic dancing partners. The band, an all-girl ensemble, dressed in black slacks and white blouses, livened up with red bows, was belting out a peppy rendition of *Little Brown Jug*. Hundreds of men in uniform…some in dazzling Navy whites, some in Marine blues, many in khaki…were jitterbugging with pretty girls.

Along the right side of the hall, a long counter, manned by more matronly women, many wearing the kind of dresses that might be worn to church, and many sporting elegant hats, served up sandwiches, deviled eggs, Jell-o salads, apple and blueberry pie, chocolate cakes, juices, tea and coffee to the long line of hungry servicemen…and even a few servicewomen… that snaked along its length.

At the left side of the hall, dozens of tables were jammed with men in uniform, eating, talking and enjoying the company of the USO volunteers. At the back, longer tables wore a festoon of uniform jackets. The matrons volunteering there manned sewing needles and threads and sewed patches and stripes onto uniforms. Some mended buttons that had fallen off, some hemmed sleeves that didn't fit just right. And in back of the mending area, older women helped young men write letters home to their mothers, fathers and sweethearts.

At the very back was a door that led to a few private rooms, where the most kindly and experienced older USO hostesses assisted problemed young men with personal issues: How should they write a letter telling a former girlfriend that the romance had died a natural death? Should they answer a "Dear John" letter that *they* had received? What should they do if they just found out that their wife (or even worse – a girlfriend) was pregnant?

As the whirl of color and music surrounded them, Mary Rose and Caledonia shrunk back, terrified. "Hi, ladies!" Two blonde girls greeted the newcomers. "You two look as if it's your first night here." The two girls each took an elbow and steered Mary Rose and Caledonia to an empty table.

"I'm Gail Fletcher," the pink cheeked one with the bobbed Dutch-doll hairdo introduced herself…. "And this is Tami Keen". Tami was shorter, her hair done in a Veronica Lake pageboy. "We work at the local bank in Kittery and we've been hostessing here for a few weeks. We're here to help you two get acclimated to this bedlam!"

And acclimated they became! Within the hour, Mary Rose had danced with six men, some of them who danced divinely, and two who stepped on her feet and kicked her ankles. She was dying for a cold drink and a moment off her feet. As the music began, she twisted her head, seeking a moment of respite. The tiny hairs at the back of her neck prickled. She had that curious feeling that someone was staring at her. Her eyes connected to a tall, dark sailor with a forbidding expression on his face, sitting alone at a small table. His stern face split with a grin. *My goodness! He was so handsome! Just like Gary Cooper!* And he waved at her, "You look like a little angel. Come over and keep me in Heaven!"

"Ha!" She gave him her best look. The one she'd practiced in front of her mirror, showing a little bit of sexiness and a little bit of aloofness.

"My heart is beating!" He pretended to clutch at his chest. "You're the most beautiful woman in this place!"

"Ha!" she said again.

"Come and sit with me. You're the one I've seen every night in my dreams. I've been waiting for you!" He winked and her heart beat faster.

"Well…" She pretended reluctance.

"Aw, little one," He put his hands together, as if praying. "You'll break my heart, if we don't get to know one another."

He tipped his head sideways and gave her a pleading look. "I'll go away on my submarine...maybe to some watery grave...and never know the name of the girl of my dreams. You just can't do that to a man in uniform, doncha know? It's against Navy regulations!"

Mary Rose giggled. She was enchanted at his banter. What girl didn't want to be called 'little one'? And, best of all, she could sit down for a few minutes. He half-rose and pulled out a chair for her.

She sat, trying to appear nonchalant, as if she did this sort of thing all the time. "Hi. Glad to sit with you." He was even better up close. Sort of American Indian looking, with an attractively broken nose. "I'm Mary Rose."

"And I'm Nick." He took her tiny hand in his huge one. "You are the cutest thing I've seen tonight."

"Oh, Nick," she giggled. "I've heard that line sixteen times already."

"But those other guys didn't really mean it." His face turned serious. Gary Cooper about to confess his love to Lana Turner. "I mean it, Mary Rose. I've been watching you for a while. You're adorable." He grinned again, "I plan to marry you once this war is over."

"Well!" This was a new line! Her eyes sparkled. "Let me get you a cup of coffee and we can discuss the wedding arrangements."

~~~~~~~~~~~~~~~~~

Caledonia was also having the time of her life. There was a whole group of Negro men here, and very few colored girls to dance with them. That nice Mrs. Carter had intercepted her right at the beginning. "Let me introduce you to this nice gentleman." She skillfully cut out a tall and darkly handsome man in an Army uniform. "Caledonia...meet Marshall Rockwell, PFC. Marshall, this is Caledonia's first night here as a hostess. You've been here for two nights now, and I expect you to take good care of her." She guided them towards the dance floor. "Matter of fact, I hope you'll be very nice to one another tonight. Marshall is shipping out in four days." She shoved them, very gently, into the whirl of dancers.

~~~~~~~~~~~~~~

Some high keening sound woke Jarred Volkmann, the elderly night watchman at the train station. He sat up, rubbing the stubble on his face. *Christ! What was that?* He got to his feet, trying to banish the sleep from his eyes. Hurriedly, he glanced around. Who was out there? It would be his job if they found him sleeping again. He'd been warned sternly. "One more time and you're out, Volkmann! We can't afford to pay you to sleep on the job!"

Fearful, he looked about. The shadows on the platform loomed dark and menacing, but there was no one else there. Jarred turned in a circle, leaning on the bench for support. His foot hit the bottle of rot-gut that he'd been drinking, knocking it over. The bottle clinked down to the floor. *Shit!* He wiped his mouth, feeling the fur...the aftermath of the cheap stuff...that had pooled on his tongue. He bent and picked up the bottle and shook it, listening in the darkness to hear if a drop or two still remained. He tipped the bottle up and a tiny trickle of gin touched the tip of his tongue, a spark of lightning, jolting him into the cold morning. He shuffled over to the trash bin and threw the bottle away, grieving the end of its comfort.

Might as well take a peek around. He'd already forgotten the sound that had awakened him. He picked up the lantern, switched on the mantle, and opened the door.

The wind that blows at four o'clock every morning slugged him. He stopped, hearing a sound again....*What the hell...?* He turned the corner, fearful now...

There were two men bent over a shape leaning against a wagon. The men...one had a bar or a shovel of some sort. The other held a blanket. "Hey!"

Jarred yelled. *"Hey! You!"*

The movement of the men ceased for a moment. They looked up, but Jarred could only see the white blurs of their faces. They were wearing hooded coats, with their chins wrapped high. The men looked at one another, dropped the shape and ran away, their footsteps clattering as they disappeared into the darkness.

Jarred peered into the gloom. The shape moved and groaned. Jarred, squinting his eyes, saw the blur of a body…an arm and then a head. He shuffled forward. "Hey! Who's there?"

"Help me! Help! *Help!*" A thready voice cried out. Jarred came closer, the drink and the darkness making him fearful. It was a woman! A *woman!*

"Help me!" It was a whisper. The arm reached out to him. He crept closer, The arm dropped and Jarred bent to see. A terrible groan seeped out. He stretched his hand out, tentative… The arm flopped down to the ground and he could see now…her head…her pretty face…it was smashed… an oval, oddly shaped and slick with blood and gore.

"Lady?" Jarred stooped, afraid to touch… *"Lady?* Can you hear me?"

Alas, she could not.

~~~~~~~~~~~~~~

Horace Parks and one of his deputies, Aaron Crossfield, met Chief Randy Stuart at the psychology offices at The University of New Hampshire. "We're here to see Inga Hoffman." Horace told the receptionist.

"Doctor Hoffman is in her office. I'll tell her that you are here." The receptionist invited them to sit.

"*Doctor Hoffman?*" Randy's eyebrows asked. Horace shrugged. You never knew what women were up to these days, especially the foreign ones.

The three of them, men of generally high intelligence, were picturing somewhat the same thing. A dumpy woman, probably raised on some foreign farm, attending some far-away university. She'd be round and squat, with hair drawn back in a bun, wearing thick glasses. A dog, really. An intelligent dog.

They all sat up as a tall, willowy woman, wearing a red suit, came into the reception room. Hot Dog! Must be the secretary! The skirt of the suit was short…almost at her knees, and she wore high heeled pumps that were also red. The jacket of the suit flapped open, inviting them to a glimpse of a white silk blouse and the beginning of substantial cleavage. Randy sat up straight, an idiotic gleam in his eyes. "Chief Parks?" The vision spoke. Horace nodded, and, fortunately didn't open his mouth.

The vision put out her hand. "I'm Doctor Hoffman." She smiled and Randy's mouth dropped. "Won't you please follow me to my office?" She turned and they followed, like hungry little puppies sighting a juicy bone, trailing after the back of her red suit skirt.

After introductions, she offered them coffee and they all nodded. Horace, a long and happily-married man, was the first to catch his composure. "Thank you. We'd love coffee." She pressed a button and spoke into a machine. She sat and smiled.

"Well, gentlemen. While we wait for the coffee, let me entertain you with some statistics about people we, in *this* industry, call "torches". Torches are people who just love to set fires. You in the law enforcement business, most likely refer to these people as arsonists." The men nodded as one, entranced by the lovely lilt of her voice.

"The science of psychology treats the arsonist as some-one who is ill. You, of course, consider this person a criminal." She shook her head and her white-blonde hair moved softly around her face. "I will speak to you as a fellow police officer might. The arsonist is usually a man…although women who set fires are gaining percentage-wise in our studies, perhaps as a result of women moving further into a man's realm. For this exercise, let us call your arsonist a man." The three men nodded, already fascinated.

"His reasons for starting fires are many: revenge, alcohol or drugs, political leanings, to conceal another crime…per-haps murder…for gain…perhaps getting insurance money, mental problems resulting in anger, settling a grudge, or frustration with some aspect of his life. Sometimes, it is a case of pyromania…a person who just loves fires and the excite-ment of flames. Sometimes, the arsonist is a fireman himself." She nodded as the men's faces showed disbelief.

"You mean someone can be a person who devotes their life to putting out fires can be the same person who sets the fires?" Chief Stuart goggled.

"Yes. This situation often actually adds to the pyromaniac's excitement. He's in on a secret that no one else knows. It's an added thrill to him."

"How can we tell?" Randy asked. "Are there things that give the arsonist away, if we know where to look?"

Doctor Hoffman shrugged. "Difficult to say. If you saw someone dancing a jig as he gazed at the flames...well..." Her shoulders rose and fell. "I understand, Chief Parks, that your arsonist has left a special calling card at all of the fires."

Horace nodded. "A tin badge...like in a cowboy movie." He mimicked a cowboy drawing a six-shooter and taking aim. "What does that tell you?"

"That you have one that wants publicity. He's playing a game with you. The badge is a hint, somehow, to his identity. It's a toy, but yet a symbol of authority. He's taunting you. This sort of arsonist, deep inside himself, *wants* to be caught."

"Amazing!" Randy was impressed. This doctor was not only beautiful, but she also seemed to have a tremendous amount of knowledge. In a moment of non- sequitur, he wondered if she was married. Randy and his wife had been estranged for months now. She'd tried to understand his job...always working, mentally going over and over the cases that plagued him... He'd tried to reform to her desires for normalcy. To be the kind of man that her father had been. A reliable, stay-at-home fellow, happy with a plate of meat and potatoes set on a starched tablecloth at 6 PM every night and a game of cards or a beer or two with a few friends afterward. He jolted himself back to the present and brought his mind back to the delectable Doctor. "How do you see him? I mean, what makes this person tick?"

"I'd say this was a man who was an under-achiever...maybe holds a menial job...a factory worker or a janitor." Horace reared back. *Who was the guy who was the janitor at the school? Floyd? Floyd Jones? And the other guy...Charlie Chan...he, too, was a janitor or cleaning person at a school, wasn't he?*

"You know someone like this, Chief Parks?" Doctor Hoffman hadn't missed his reaction.

"Yeah. There are two men who have been seen at a couple of the fires. They both work as janitors in the Kittery school system."

"Are they under-achievers?"

Chief Parks chuckled inwardly at the way Inga Hoffman referred to two bums and drunks. "Under-achievers? I guess you could call them that. Neither one ever amounted to much." He stroked his chin. "But I can't say I ever pictured either of them so evil as to kill a dozen or so people...a few of them helpless children."

"This may be his way of announcing to the world that he matters. By being a celebrity of sorts...a notorious celebrity, but someone that gets headlines in the paper...someone who is feared...someone who *matters*. He may be feeling that, by setting the fires, he is important, even if it is in a negative way."

Chief Parks nodded. This woman was clever. "The badge. He...the arsonist...he...I'm just assuming for the record now that it is a man...he wanted the badge acknowledged. He even got in touch with the newspapers to tell them about the badge when I was trying not to let that clue get out. He wanted everyone to know." She nodded, appreciating that he understood.

"How can we catch him?"

She tipped her head, thinking... "Maybe you can interview him. You are most likely going to interview all of the people who watched the fires. Tell them you want their help...maybe they'd seen something that we missed...that sort of thing. In the interview, tell him how clever you think the sheriff's badge arsonist is. Ask him about his childhood...was he abused? Was he a child who was picked on...bullied...by others who were stronger and more popular? Let him tell you about himself. He may slip up and give you ammunition for an arrest."

"Do you think he cares about the people he has murdered?" Randy leaned forward.

"No. They are just objects...pawns, if you will, in his game. He's most likely a kindly person really, weak and craven, trying to please. It is only in his fantasy world, where he and he alone has the power...the power of the match or the gasoline...that the monster within breaks loose."

Deputy Crossfield shivered. "He's got to be a crazy as a loon!"

"In *our* world, yes. He is crazy. But not in his world. In *his* world, he is in control. Whatever it is that guides him, setting these fires makes complete sense to him."

"You say he most likely has a go-nowhere job. Is he dumb? Educated? Stupid?"

"He has some intelligence...may even be very intelligent. You know, all these statistics...they only tell you what a person *might* be like. We get fooled once in a while with all of our statistics." She shrugged, smiling. "He may be hiding how smart he is...not using his brain to capacity, but I do not think that he is stupid or dumb."

Randy bit on his bottom lip. *What the hell*, he thought, *I'll just ask her...*

"Uh, ah, Doctor Hoffman, can we ask you to sit in on some of the interviews? Would you be willing to lend us your expertise?"

"Of course, Chief Stuart," she sent a smile towards him. *My! He was a good-looking one!* Tall and broad shouldered. She liked them built big. Dark, curly hair that tumbled over his forehead, like an unruly schoolboy. And those dark, dark eyes and those spiky eyelashes. Would she like to help him? For sure!

Horace Parks, no one's fool, watched the little play-within-a-play unfolding before him. *They'd make an interesting match*, he thought. *Wait until I tell Fanny all about it!*

"The site of the fire in Portsmouth...it's still cordoned off. Can you visit it with me and give me, um, your impressions of the site?"

"It would be an honor, Chief Stuart. Although I don't own a badge in the shape of a star, I always did hanker to be a detective."

~~~~~~~~~~~~~~~

Doctor Hoffman rode back to the Portsmouth police station with Randy Stuart. 'We'll get the files and then go down to the site of the last fire."

His deputy hailed him as they walked into the station. "Chief, got a body down at the railroad station."

"A body? Any identification?"

"A woman. Head was smashed...looks like they tried to cut her throat, but the watchman got there and interrupted them." The deputy relished telling the grisly details. "She... managed to call out for help, but then she either passed out or died right then.

"Poor woman!" Randy muttered.

"Yeah, well... She...she was dressed like a prossie."

"A prossie?" Doctor Hoffman asked. "What's a prossie?"

The deputy, in his zeal to pass on the grim news, hadn't yet noticed that Randy was accompanied by a woman. "Oh, uh, hello, Ma'am." The deputy shuffled his feet, clearly uncomfortable now.

"She's a doctor," Randy chortled. "She can deal with dead prostitutes."

"Ah! A prostitute!" Doctor Hoffman nodded. "You found a dead prostitute with her head bludgeoned and her throat cut?"

The deputy, now that he noticed Randy's companion, took a moment to admire her red suit and high heels. "Well, not *really* cut off. Whoever it was, tried to maybe cut her throat." The deputy, who had sort of exaggerated the story, backed himself up. It was important now, especially with this lady present, that he report only the facts. "I want to set the facts down correctly." He swallowed hard, embarrassed now that his boss had heard him shooting his mouth off. "Her assailant...or maybe assailants...the watchman said that he thought there were two of them...had hit her, hard enough to crush her skull...then tried to cut her throat, sort of began to saw at it with some kind of hack saw, or some other crude instrument."

"So she was alive when he found her? Did she say anything?"

"She sort of moaned, the watchman said. I think he'd been drinking...reeked of cheap alcohol when he talked to us...so maybe what he told us isn't quite what happened," he shrugged. "The watchman says he got there and the two assailants ran away. The victim moaned 'help' or something like that and then she expired." He was now obviously trying to impress Inga Hoffman with his glib police technical talk.

"What else?" Randy's expression brought him back to reality.

"The watchman said he was doing his rounds. He heard some scuffling sounds and a scream or a moan. He went to investigate and saw two men...he thinks... bending over the woman...she was lying on the ground and at least one of the men, the watchman said, had a knife...or at least he said he saw something metallic glittering."

"Go on..."

"He said that he yelled at them to stop and they ran away, dropping the body. He went over and said that the woman was nearly dead already, with her throat sort of cut, her head sort of smashed and an arm partially severed." He shook with pleasurable horror. "Looks like maybe they were planning to cut her up."

"Great!" Randy moaned. "First an arsonist and now two guys who want to murder prostitutes."

"Prostitutes?" Doctor Hoffman caught the inference. "Are there more than one who have been killed?"

"Nooooo," Randy drew the word out. "But, now that this has happened, I recall that a couple of the street girls have complained that a few of their friends have gone missing. I wonder....?"

"Perhaps some zealot who thinks he has a mission to kill bad women?" Doctor Hoffman suggested.

"Do we know her name?" Randy asked the deputy.

"No. And none of the girls on the street that I've spoken with know who she is." He spread out his hands in frustration.

Randy scratched his head. "We've gotta get to the bottom of this. I'm going to put together a small task force to interview more of the prostitutes to see who else seems to be missing."

"Perhaps I can help you there," Inga offered. "These women interest me, perhaps as much as I am interested in arsonists."

"Perhaps? I'd welcome your help."

"Good. Perhaps we can get somewhere together."

"Perhaps." Randy chuckled and then put his hand on her arm, enjoying the feeling. *Perhaps who knows what you and I may get somewhere together on.* "If you have some time this morning, *perhaps* we can go and visit the arson site and then *perhaps* have a bite to eat before viewing the body." Here was his chance to keep her around. "I could use your opinion...as a psychologist...as to what you might see that I would miss."

"I'm sure you don't miss much," Doctor Hoffman's sky blue eyes were guileless. The deputy looked from Randy to the Doctor and back again, enjoying this tennis match. Wait until the guys hear about the Chief and this goddess!

"I try not to miss anything," Randy rubbed his hands together. "Let's get going, Inga."

*And he's using her first name...the guys are going to love this!* The deputy watched the Chief and the red suit, *and* the red high heels as they went back out of the police station to the scene of the recent fire.

~~~~~~~~~~~~~~~

Grace Sabatino, with the rather reluctant help of her son, Andy, paced out the dimensions of the prototype victory garden. "Mom, do I hafta help? I've got baseball practice today! Joey Hope is coming by in ten minutes and we're gonna' practice."

Normally, Andy loved helping her in anything that had to do with gardening, digging, or eating vegetables. She wondered...he was thirteen, after all...were there a few pretty girls who might be attending baseball practice to watch the boys? Probably. Her son was tall and, barring the slight interlude of adolescent acne and awkwardness, mighty handsome. He was going to be...and it seemed soon...a catch to some local young sweetie-pie.

"Give me a half-hour...at least until Joey gets here... and then you can go off and pitch 'til your heart's content."

Andy knew his mother. She was a stern task master, but always fair. He sighed. "Okey-Doke. What do you want me to do?"

"Hold this string while I pace off twenty feet. Then put this stake in the ground. We're going to make the garden twenty by thirty. A good size for a family of four or six to have fresh vegetables all summer and to put-up tomatoes and pickles and what-not for the rest of the year." She showed Andy the plan she had drawn. "I'm going to use hot-house plants in my garden instead of seeds. I want them to see the plants already up. I want it to be flourishing when everyone comes to see it and hopefully, to buy one just like it…manure and seeds and plants and the raised beds and all. We'll grow tons of food so the men and women overseas can have all the food that they need."

Andy nodded. He and his mother and father listened to the radio every night after supper. They ate in the kitchen now, as the dining room table was now permanently set with a large map of the world. The entire family moved pins and tiny battleships around, visualizing the battles taking place in such far-flung areas as Alexandria, Canterbury, Ruhr and Vichy. It chafed at Marco that the War Department refused to take him as a soldier. "You're needed here," they had ordered. "You're too old to fight now and we need you to grow food and to perform agricultural tasks here."

Annoyed, but happy to do whatever his county needed him to, he was forced to follow the war vicariously.

"OK, Mom. Now what?" Andy had marked the four corners of the plot.

"We'll put up the fence. Let's use a five foot chicken wire all around. Do that and then set two gates, here and here…" she pointed to her plot plan. "After that, you can scadoodle off to play baseball." She ruffled his hair, noting that he was already an inch taller than she was.

"Are other people going to make gardens?"

"We hope so. This garden is going to show people how easy it is to grow vegetables this summer. I'm going to make up packages of seeds and sell them together with the potted plants in the sample garden. I'll be doing a good deed and make some money in the bargain." She bent to bag up the different seeds into small packets. "You'll also be in charge of showing customers just how to set up their gardens." She stood up, groaning as she pressed the kinks out of her back. "But, Andy, darling. You have got to promise me that you'll finish trimming those *buddleias*," Grace pointed to the tall, jagged tops of last year's butterfly bushes. "And the *phyllostachys*…cut them, too. They're messy. The new stalks haven't grown yet…remember that butterfly bushes and the bamboo are late-summer plants. Look at those jagged edges! You only broke them off. Look how sharp they are!" She fingered the tops of some of the stalks, wincing at the sharpness of the strong, rough sticks. "Someone might just trip and fall and one of these would certainly poke their eye out!" She shook her fist at him with mock annoyance. "We'd be sued and lose our home and business!"

Andy sighed. "OK, Ma. I'll do it tomorrow. Right after I get home from the game."

Grace gave him a peck on his cheek. Boyish down was starting to grow, she noted with some surprise. The child would be shaving soon! "All right. But try to get them cut and cut them evenly and cleanly...right down to the ground."

"Sure, Ma. Sure." Andy's mind had already raced ahead to today's fun. The *buddleia* and the black bamboo would wait...and wait...and wait.

Grace watched her son. *He's such a good boy*, she thought. *I love him more than I love anything.* She tipped her head and nodded, thinking. *Yes, I love him even more than Mario.*

The sun shone hot on her head and she bent to pull out two weeds at the side of the raised garden bed. *I couldn't love anyone as much as I love him!*

She thought back to the years of childlessness. Of the sickening grief every month, when her menses came, jeering her with the dark, clumping blood flowing from her insides. *You'll never have a baby! You'll never get pregnant.* And then to that morning, nearly fourteen years ago, when Mina Fiorile had knocked on her door, bearing a priceless gift for them. A tiny, squirming, precious baby boy. A baby to raise as their own!

*Should they tell him now? Was he old enough to understand? Could he comprehend, as a young lad, why a mother would give up her child? Could he understand how much she and Mario loved him?*

*And if they didn't tell him soon, when should they tell him? In a year? Two years? Never?*

*Andy has the right to know the truth,* she acknowledged. *He must be told...but not today...not yet....not just yet.*

Had she known, Andy had known the truth for many years. His cousin Sammy told him.

Every large family has a child like Sammy somewhere in the branches of its tree. Sammy always knew everything. Even as a baby, he was able to ferret out secrets, hiding under tables and around corners to listen to the gossip of the women...pretending to dig a hole in a pile of dirt while listening to the coarse talk of the men, hearing who was not married to who...who was no better than she should be...and, in Andy's situation, who Andy's real mother was. And naturally, with these kinds of knowledge and secrets, Sammy wielded power. It made him feel important, and even better, it yielded him candy bars and quarters when he finally imparted the delicious lore and news to those who had been shut out from information that might be important.

Thus, when Andy was nine and Sammy was fifteen, Sammy, for the trade of Andy's *meccano* set, unopened and new in its box, and fifty cents, had whispered the secret of his birth to Andy. At first, Andy refused to believe it, but Sammy insisted that his source was un-impeachable. "She's your real mother. She got pregnant, and gave the baby to Aunt Grace and Uncle Mario. She wanted to sing, you see, and you...a snotty kid... would have been a drag to her. She couldn't go around to all those opera houses with a baby in a carriage, could she? And your father...well, I hear that he was some kind of detective and that he died when a bad man killed him. That's the truth, Andy. I swear it on my mother's head."

Of course, he knew who his real mother was. He had seen her time and time again, twice on stage at the opera, several times at Grandma Sabatino's house, a few times at family picnics. She was famous. She was a star. She was beautiful. And she *was* his real mother!

And so, Andy knew...and hugged the secret to himself, turning the knowledge over and over. *Did she really give him away? Was she sorry? Did she miss him at all? And what was his father like? Did he know?* It was tough for a boy of nine to carry this burden...wondering....wondering.

*How could she throw me away?*

# CHAPTER TEN

July 28, 1943
**The War: Operation Gomorrah: Payback! The British bomb Hamburg, causing a firestorm that kills 42,000 Germans. Allies cheer.**

The Kennebunk Savings Bank, Kittery, Maine:
"Did Henry come to work last night?" Shelly Richards poked at a wastebasket, still filled with crumpled paper from the previous day's business.

"Doesn't look like it," Sally Leland made a face. "Look at the spittoon." Her face showed disgust. Yuk!"

"He's probably still in bed, sleeping off his night in a bar." Shelly picked up the wastepaper basket and emptied it. "I draw the line at the spittoon," she announced, standing over the offending brass container. "When he shows up, I'll throw the spittoon at his miserable head." She started back to her counter. "Isn't the new girl coming in today?" She made a face. They'd been told that a new employee...a girl from far-off California...would be starting in as a teller this morning.

"Cal-ee-forn-ya!! Sally sashayed, mocking. "I'll bet she's a stuck-up Betty Co-Ed. Blonde and sexy."

"A rich bitch!" Cathy French grimaced. "Probably will think she's too good to work in our little bank."

"Shhh!" Helen warned. "Here she comes!"

A tall, slender girl, wearing a blue and white dotted-swiss blouse over a pencil slim navy skirt opened the door. "Hello!" she called out. "I'm Betty...Betty Cormier, your new teller." She smiled with what seemed like genuine delight. "Glad to meet all of you."

"Hello, Betty," Shelly greeted her. The girls were quick to note Betty's big blue eyes and the fashionable crop of her blonde hair. Her clothes were new and of a style that hadn't quite reached the shores of Kittery, Maine yet. She certainly was a looker.

Helen sneaked an aside to Cathy, "Bet butter doesn't melt in her mouth."

"Meee-ow!" Cathy whispered. "Let's see what Miss California does with the spittoons!"

Shelly had intercepted Helen and Cathy's whispers. *Good idea. Let's see what she does do with those spittoons!*

"How can I get started?" Betty appeared to be anxious to please.

"Well," Shelly's voice pretended reluctance. "It's a miserable job, but our janitor isn't here yet. We've got to clean up the spittoons. Maybe you can take them out back, empty them, rinse them out and replace them."

"Certainly," Betty smiled cheerfully. "Can I put my purse and sweater somewhere and then I'll get right to the spittoons."

Deflated at Betty's cooperation, Helen showed her the cubicle where the girls left their possessions. *Maybe she'll be OK,* Helen thought. *Maybe she's not a snob.* "We were just kidding about emptying the spittoons," Helen muttered, somewhat shamefaced. "That's such an awful job, we'll leave it until Henry gets here."

"Whenever that might be!" Cathy shrugged.

"I'd be glad to empty them," Betty laughed. "I've done worse jobs."

"No. We can't do that to you." Shelly said. "What kind of a welcome would it be?"

"Not the best," Betty chuckled. "But, I've certainly, in my career, given a new teller a terrible job."

"Nope," Shelly looked around. "We're too nice, aren't we, girls?" The other tellers nodded and told Betty that she'd passed their test with flying colors.

"You're too agreeable for us to play a trick like that on you."

"Thanks, girls." Betty grinned. "I think I'm going to like it here." She put her hands on her hips and surveyed the lobby. "This is so different from California. So pleasant and quiet."

Shelly checked the clock on the wall. "Where's Gail?" It was nearly nine-thirty. "She's never late."

"Oh, she's with Tami. They stopped at the Angel's bakery for the cake." Mary Rose's bakery, ever more and more popular, was now such a Kittery fixture that it had its own nickname.

"Cake?"

"Shhh! Don't let Helen hear you! A birthday cake! It's Helen's birthday today!"

~~~~~~~~~~~~~~~

It was a slow morning at the bank. Hardly anyone had come in to make a deposit or cash a check, except six old men each with a savings bond purchase. Each of the six had doddered and lingered, coughed and spit copiously, and the nearly full spittoon near the customer table was filled to the brim with glop. Betty, the new teller, eyed it, truly grateful that she didn't have to deal with that kind of mess and happy that the other girls seemed to be friendly and pleasant.

"Not busy this morning, huh?" Helen remarked. "It's so slow that I might just take this opportunity to dust the tables."

"I'm short. I'll do the bottoms and the legs." Betty grabbed a cloth.

"Great. I'll do the tops." Helen pulled out a can of wax. "California's loss is certainly our gain."

"If it were any less busy, we could all go to sleep." Sally rested her head on her crossed arms. "There's nothing to do!"

*Good*, thought Cathy French. *May it stay this way until after morning break. We can have a nice cup of coffee, sing happy birthday to Helen, and eat our cake in peace.* Idle, stamping duplicate deposit slips and putting them in order, Cathy wondered what kind of cake Tami and Gail would buy. *I love Mary Rose's carrot cake with that two inch crown of cream cheese icing. But then...the deep, dark chocolate cake with its shiny robe of bittersweet ganache...Mmmm.*

The door opened, letting in a shaft of sunshine and breeze. Two men, dressed in fishermen's oilskins, came into the bank. *Odd,* thought Michelle, the teller at the first stanchion, *they've got the hoods of their jackets up. I wonder why on such a pretty day?*

Daniel Carlson answered her unspoken question. "Put your hands up! This is a robbery!"

The six girls, startled and frightened, brought their hands up. *Is this what I left California for?* Betty gasped to herself. *I'm going to be killed!*

"Please...please...don't shoot," Shelly gasped, unable to take her eyes off the gun. "We...we'll...the money. Take the money." The bank's manual stated, on page eleven, "Do not try to bargain or argue with anyone robbing the bank. Give them what they ask for. Do not try to be a hero." Shelly knew the manual by heart. "Take it...whatever you want. Please don't hurt us."

The man with the gun laughed, a nasty sound that ripped Shelly's heart. "Of course, you'll give us the money, sister." He motioned to the second man. "Give him a bag."

Shelly reached into the drawer of her desk. "Careful, now, little lady. Don't try to be a hero." *Just like in the manual*, Shelly found herself thinking. She slowly brought out one of the green transfer bags that the bank used. As she brought it out, she brushed against the safety button that rang the buzzer at the Kittery Police Station's switchboard. *I'm not trying to be a hero,* she rationalized to herself. *Just trying to prevent these bastards from stealing.* Her fright was obvious, as she handed the bag to the man with the gun. He, with a motion of his head, tossed the bag to the second man.

*The first man is tall, a gruff voice, but cultured.* The manual, on page twelve, instructed the bank employees to make mental notes so that they might help the police identify the perpetrators. Cathy French felt strange, as if she were floating. Not really frightened at all, although tall, gruff and cultured was waving a gun around. *He's the boss*, she noted. *The other man is the stooge. Shorter, stouter and he hadn't yet opened his mouth.*

"You want me to take the bag around, Dan?" Short and stouter shuffled forward, the bag in his hand, uncertain as to what he was supposed to do.

"Shut up!" Tall and gruff snapped, turning slightly away, the gun waving in his hand. Out of the corner of her eye, Cathy noted that Shelly was moving toward the safe. *Be careful, Shelly! Be careful!*

Tall and gruff pointed the gun at Shelly. He'd noticed, too. "Stay where you are, sister." He half-turned toward his hench-man. "Just take the bag to blondie here." He gestured with his chin toward Helen Huntress, who stood, hands still in the air, eyes wide. Betty stood next to her, wondering if she might have the courage to try to tackle the shorter man.

"OK, Dan." Short and stouter held out the bag. Tall and gruff made an exasperated sound. *He doesn't want his name spoken!* Cathy thought. *He's getting angry at short and stouter.*

At the Kittery Police Station, six men and Chief Parks jumped into their patrol cars. Sirens wailing, they sped toward the bank.

*It seemed stifling*, Helen thought. *I think I might pass out from fright and the heat. How can I stop them? They'll shoot me for sure...*The second man held out the bag, shaking it, as if he was feeding chickens. Helpless, Helen scooped out all of the bills from her till and placed them in the bag. *I don't want to die!*

"Thanks, lady." The second man made a half-bow and then held his bag out to Julie. She kept her eyes down and pushed a handful of money into the bag. "Thanks to you, lady."

Short and stouter, hefting the bag and grinning at its weight, walked across the lobby to Michelle. "Gimme," he held the bag to her, supplicating, a foolish look on his half-hidden face. Michelle, frightened and nervous, took a handful of bills out of her till. Her hands shook and the money spilled out, over the edge of the bag and fell to the floor in a green and white shower. "Shit!" Short and stouter swore.

Three things happened at once. Short and stouter bent down and knelt on the floor, scooping at the money. At the same time, tall and gruff hollered to him. "Stand up! Tell the bitch to get down and pick up the money!" And the front door of the bank opened.

Later on, Cathy French would say that time stood still. *Like in a movie, you know.* Gail Fletcher and Tami Keen, laughing and joking, carrying a huge white cake box, bumped into one another as they entered the lobby. Michelle, almost as if in a dream, pushed the short and stout man down, kicking at him. The bag of money fell out of his hand. "Hey! Lady! What the hell...?" Short and stouter, encumbered by the bulky and stiff fisherman oilskins, lost his balance and rolled to the ground.

Tall and gruff wavered for a moment. *He doesn't really want to shoot us. He will if he has to, but he wants this to go smoothly.* Shelly Richards watched his face as emotions raced across it. *He doesn't know what to do!*

Michelle kicked again at short and stouter. Betty stepped forward to help her. She scratched at the shorter man's face. Emboldened by Betty's help, Michelle shoved short and stouter, coming between him and the man who held the gun.

The gunman took a step backwards. *It had been going so well. What the hell happened? I gotta kill the bitch!* He aimed at Michelle and pulled the trigger, just as short and stouter reached for Michelle's arm and pulled her down toward him. Even from the floor, he was strong, and she fell on top of him as the bullet sped toward the two of them. "Ooof!" she cried, rolling off the slippery material of the oilskin.

Short and stouter cried out: "Dan! *Dan!*" and collapsed on the floor. All of them...the eight women and the gunman... watched in horror. A gush of bright red blood erupted against the bright yellow.

Panicked now, the gunman yelled: "Bastards! I'll kill you all!" He gulped and tried to grab the bag. Gail yelled some loud scream and shoved him, slamming the cake box against his head. Tami, frantic to help, grabbed the handles of the nearly-full metal spittoon that sat on the floor. She gave a mighty heave and the contents of the spittoon flew into Dan's face. He coughed and choked, trying to get his eyes clear. Tami hefted the now-empty spittoon and and banged the gunman's head with it.

Gail saw the gun waving in the air as Dan tried to regain his balance. She grabbed at the gun, trying to wrench the gun out of his hand, as Tami continued to slam the heavy spittoon into Dan's head. Gobs of sand and mucus, mixed with choco-late cake and dark chocolate *Ganache* frosting, impeded the gunman's ability to fight the women off.

As one, Shelly, Betty and Michelle, grabbed anything they could find. A ruler, a handful of sharp pencils, Michelle's purse, a walking stick that had been left last week by a forgetful customer, and joined into the assault.

Julie Perrault ran to the front door, opened it and began to scream at passers-by. "Help! *Help!* A robbery! Get the *police!*"

It took no more than five minutes for Chief Horace Parks, Deputy Balfour and the rest of the patrolmen to arrive at the bank. They entered, guns raised and ready for action.

It was quiet in the lobby. The eight women stood as they ran in. "They're here," Gail spoke for all of them, pointing to the floor. Horace gaped. Two men lay there, both dressed in yellow fishing outfits. One was obviously dead, judging from the enormous pool of blood around him. The other was trussed up, as Horace later told his wife, Fanny, "like a Goddam Thanksgiving bird. Tied up with extension cords and the rope from the three Venetian blinds from the bank win-dows. You almost felt sorry for the bastard. His face was battered and bruised. The women hit him with their pocket-books, the stapler, a Scotch tape dispenser, their high heeled shoes…Sheesh! I never saw anything like it!"

Gideon Balfour told his wife: "He was one of the escaped prisoners. Daniel Carlson. As dangerous as a pole cat. And these little ladies, why they had him roped and tied like a bawling calf. Best part was, he was covered, just *covered,* with spit and chocolate cake!"

~~~~~~~~~~~~~~

It took a while before Doc Brogden finished with the dead body of Zachary Mullins. While they awaited the men from the Yard, Daniel Carlson was taken to the Kittery Police Station and booked locally for murder and attempted robbery. Sullen, shuffling and swearing, he was then turned over to the en-forcement officers who arrived en masse and took him back to the Naval Prison. The Yard Prison Guards were very happy to have him returned to them and planned something special to mark the occasion.

The body of the weak man formerly known as Zachary Mullins and called Zootz by the few men who bothered to befriend him, as alone and sad in death as he'd been most of his pitiful life, was, late in the afternoon three days later, finally laid to rest in the small cemetery at the edge of the little island in the middle of the Piscataqua Inlet.  His neighbors were sixteen Spanish sailors, captured as prisoners nearly two hundred years ago, who died of influenza before they could be taken off their vessel and brought to the prison for justice.

Greg Starr was called and photographed the body before it was removed. He took a few pictures of Dan Carlson, although Carlson tried mightily to hide his face. He then went to the Kennebunk Bank to interview the women who had foiled the robbery and captured the robbers. Greg took pictures of each of the women and a special picture of all of them holding the spittoon.  He talked to them all at length, enjoying the interview and laughing at the end. His front page story of how an unarmed band of women overcame two desperate criminals was considered a treasure in tongue-in-cheek journalism.

Greg also subsequently learned that the guards at the Naval Prison had been out for several hours after learning of the break-out. The guards were charged with the task of finding and recapturing the escaped prisoners. The erroneous scuttlebutt was that the escaped prisoners had traveled by boat to the *Portsmouth* side of the harbor. "Most likely they're in some bar, somewhere in Portsmouth...we'll find them, never fear!"

Six hours after the botched bank robbery was over, ten or more guards were still looking hard, checking into every gin-mill in town, not leaving each establishment without a drink or two, determined to not miss one. After all, the fugitives might just be at the bar across the street...or the one on Penhallow Road...or the one on the corner of State Street and Library Road.  They'd search and keep searching...have no fear!

~~~~~~~~~~~~~~~

In the early afternoon, Chief Parks, together with both of his deputies, arrived at the bank. The Chief carried a large white box, and Deputy Crossfield hefted a long, shallow container. In the white box sat a large carrot cake with cream cheese icing. The shallower box held two dozen of Mary Rose's finest Italian pastries. "With my thanks," the Chief handed them over. "And a happy birthday to you," he bowed to Helen.

"Thanks, Chief," Gail grinned. "I just hated to see that cake go to waste."

# CHAPTER ELEVEN

**August 3, 1943 – John F. Kennedy's PT 109 is rammed by a destroyer. The Battle of Vella Gulf will defeat a Japanese convoy off Kolombangara.**

Mary Rose had been delighted to share her home with the four nurses from the *Buchanan.* Next door, at the Kittery Nursery and Garden Shop, her Aunt Grace and Uncle Mario cleaned out the second floor store-room to house four medical corpsmen from the *Buchanan,* including Neil Harmon and Alan Bowen and one fledgling doctor from the *SS Sandshark*, a submarine that had pulled into the Yard for some minor repair before being sent back out again.

"Glad to meet you-all," Doctor Hamilton Zapfester, right off his graduation from medical school, greeted his bunkmates.

"Boy, can we use you-all at the hospital!" Alan pumped his hand, mimicking Zapfester's southern accent.

Zapfester, a tall blond drink-of-water from Louisiana, actually said, "Shucks!" and blushed. "I'm so new, I squeak. You fellahs are gonna have to teach me everything you know."

"Don't worry," Neil assured him. "You'll learn really fast!"

Although they were, at first, worried about sharing their homes, both Grace and Mary Rose now felt that they were putting forth extra effort to help enlisted men and women, and besides, the rent money, coming from the War Office, was mighty welcome.

"There's hardly a house in Kittery that doesn't have someone from the Shipyard renting a room or two."

"We're making some money, we're helping the nurses and corpsmen out, and the girls will be good company for me at night."

"Perfect!"

"I've fixed it up as best I could," Mary Rose showed Eunice, Carol, Michelle and Yashiko the long, attic room. "There isn't much privacy for you, but...."

The nurses were thrilled with the huge space. Mary Rose had set the beds far apart, and placed gay curtains made of inexpensive gingham hanging on wooden dowels so as to shield one sleeping area from another. She'd gathered all of her aunt's spare blossoms, and each bed sported a small bedside table with a vase of colorful flowers. With the late-afternoon sunlight streaming through the high clerestory-type windows, the room was a delight. The sweet scents of ripening vegetables, *rosa rugosa* and *buddleia* from the garden center next door made Yashiko suddenly homesick for the flowers of Hawaii. She gulped, missing her grandmother in a way that nearly sent tears to her eyes.

Eunice was more prosaic. "After the tent in the desert and the prison cell in the jungle, this is Paradise!" Eunice hugged Mary Rose. "I wish we could stay here forever." She placed her duffle bag on one of the beds. "This one is mine."

"This is the nicest barracks we've ever been in!" Carol threw her sweater off and bounced on the elderly, but comfortable, bed. "We'll only be here for two more weeks, but we'll remember your hospitality forever!"

In the slightly less beautiful attic next door, over the storage area of the Kittery Garden Center, the two medical corpsmen, Neil Harmon and Alan Bowen, were also testing out the beds. "Thanks, Mrs. Sabatino," Neil grinned, ducking his head in appreciation. "We'll be real comfortable here." He began to unpack the meager contents of his duffle bag, putting a framed photo on the table next to his old metal bed stand.

"Who is that, Neil?" Grace peered at the photo of a red-headed girl, standing on a rocky cliff.

"She's Gerry...Geraldine...she's...well, maybe if this war is ever over..." Neil's young face was pink with effort. "She and I..."

"She's lovely." Grace took pity on him. She turned to Alan. "And where's your bedside photo?"

Alan laughed and reached into his kit. "I do have Clair." He pulled out a snapshot and laid it on the table. "She's sort of waiting for me." He tried to laugh, but the sound stuck in his throat. Grace patted his shoulder. This Goddam war! This Goddam, Goddam war.

"And you, Doctor Zapfester?" Grace turned to the new man.

"Shucks, Ma'am," Hamilton blushed, over-awed at speaking to a woman. "I'm too terrified of women to have a girlfriend!"

"We'll change your attitude," Alan assured him. "We'll have you falling in love in no time. Just wait until you see the girls at the USO! You'll soon be in love with six or seven of them at one time!"

"Well, shucks!" Zapfester's eyes goggled in anticipation. "I cain't wait!"

~~~~~~~~~~~~~~

Inga sat in the lone comfortable chair in one of the back rooms at the Kittery Police Station. On a hard wooden chair, opposite her, sat Portsmouth Chief Randy Stewart, and behind a battered and scarred desk, Horace Parks. There was one empty chair in front of the desk. Horace assembled a stack of files and the photos that Greg Starr had made up for him.

The Kittery Police Station had seen many things since its inception more than three hundred years ago. Pirates who attempted to board frigate ships that sailed into the harbor; the demure farmer's wife, dressed in her blood-stained Sunday-best dress, who walked into the old station, holding a huge knife in her hand and confessing to the butchering of her entire family; the inbred wild men who operated the still up on the top of Mount Agamenticus who massacred the family who operated the competing still on top of Mount Tolivar; the empty-eyed men who tried to hold up the payroll train. Today, the forces of law and order would see if they could discern the internal workings of a man or woman who got his or her jollies burning down houses and roasting the pitiful people who were trapped inside.

"Who's out there?"

Horace flipped open the folder. "First is Jannus Podalsky." Horace pointed to a tall man who stood at the back of the crowd who gaped at the Route 103 tragedy. "Local man, came here from Sweden or Poland. Been here for more than 40 years. No family. Never in any trouble. Worked for the Polack bakery and now works for Mary Rose Sabatino at Bread of Angels."

"Nothing negative at all on him?" Randy looked hard at the grainy photo and the red-circled countenance of Jannus.

"Not a thing." Inga held out her hand and Randy passed the photo to her, hoping that her specialized training might show her something that he wasn't able to see. He watched her as she scrutinized the picture. Today, her hair was pulled up in a simple knot at the back of her head. The style suited her and showed her clean and classic profile to good advantage. She was wearing a dark skirt and a plum-colored sweater with ruffles at the throat and the sleeves. She made Randy's breath catch at the front of his throat. Again, he wondered if she had a husband. He, with all his investigative techniques, couldn't figure out how to ask her.

"A strong face..." Inga mused. 'Shows character."

"Ready for him?" Horace stood up, and at their nods, went to the door, opened it, and asked that Jannus be brought into the room. Inga noted that Jannus was clearly intimidated, worried and upset at his surroundings. He took off the cap that covered his sparse hair and turned it around and around in his thin, work-scarred hands. She scribbled some notes on her pad. Jannus watched her, almost spoke, and then looked down at his bumpy-toed boots.

*I'll try to put him at ease*, Inga thought. After a few simple, non-confrontational, preliminary questions, Inga leaned forward. "Tell me about your childhood, Mr. Podalsky. Were you a happy child?"

Jannus' eyes narrowed and he made a face. "Happy?" His heavily accented voice was incredulous. "*Hap*py?" He gave a short laugh. "Maybe my first five years...dose ver happy. I vas a treasured child, loved by my family and de odders in our village. All children vere loved in our village. And den..." He sighed and his eyes turned inward, remembering unspeakable things. "I vatched my modder being raped by de Army and my fadder vas shot. Da marauders burned our home and da homes of all of my family and neighbors. I vas hidden, wit' two odder children, in a heap of straw in da pigsty." He sniffed. "No, I don't t'ink you could say it vas a happy childhood." He sat back and looked hard at Inga.

"If you t'ink I set dese fires, because my life vas hard, you are wrong. So very wrong." He looked at his hands and twisted them together. "I am a peaceable man. I vant only to be left alone to do my verk and den I go home and haff some beer and bread and cheese. I haff a few good friends, enjoy playing chess...hearing music. I vork hard and am proud of my skills. Mary Rose, little girl dat she is...she's a smart person and a goot boss. She trusts me and I am respected here as a baker. No more and no less." He stood up, his dignity shining around him, bowed to Inga, nodded to the two policemen and left the room.

The three looked at their own hands. "I wanted to ask him if he saw anything that would help us." Horace looked slightly abashed.

"Maybe another time." Randy rubbed his chin. "What do you think?"

"I think he's just what he says he is. A nice, hard-working man. Not our firebug." Horace pounded the table in frustration. "Made me sort of feel bad. Like when my mother made me feel foolish. Inga, what's your opinion?"

"All of my instincts tell me that this is not our culprit." She bit her lip, also feeling as if she'd kicked a helpless puppy. Let's see the next one."

They waded through the bluff heartiness of Captain Simeon, and the shrill outrage of Nellie Hogan. Next on their list was Eustace Barnes.

"Hiya, Chief," Eustace stepped behind the desk and slapped Horace on the shoulder. He brought a whiff of Maine in with him…an effluvium of salt water, stale beer and dusty mule… Randy thought that although Eustace tried to come across as an old, harmless duffer, behind his rheumy eyes was a real anger. He wondered if he was the only one to see this.

"Whatcha' want?" Eustace ambled to the chair and eased himself down, groaning with perhaps arthritic limbs. "Jezebel's outside and she's chompin' to git goin'. We gotta git some old roofin' material up Ogunquit way." He sat, square, knees splayed and his arms folded.

Randy leaned forward. "Want a smoke, Eustace?" He flipped a pack of Lucky Strikes onto the table.

Eustace grunted, "Don't care if I do," and picked them up, flipping out a cigarette, tamping it down and lipping the end. He looked around for a moment, then, with some dignity, took one more cigarette and put that one into his pocket. He took his time, digging into his greasy vest pocket, bringing out a small box of matches.

Inga watched, wondering about this seemingly simple man. Eustace struck a match on the sole of his work boot, lit the cigarette and puffed greedily, settling back again in the chair.

Randy began to ask questions. Where was he on certain days and night? How did he feel about the fires? Eustace replied to all of the questions with ready answers. He'd been here and there…on a few of the dates, he was able to give them a specific…on others, he said simply that who could remember where the hell he was on all those dates. He shook his head, decrying the kind of person who would set a fire, never mind one that killed people.

Inga then asked him about his childhood. Eustace squinted at her. "My *child*hood? What in tarnation does that have ennythin' to do with ennythin'?"

Inga shrugged. "Just routine questions, Mr. Barnes. Simply to give us background information."

His expression let her know clearly how he was thinking. "I wuz born around here, live and work around here, an' I'll die around here one a' these days, lady."

"At the fire…you were at the fire on 103, right?" Eustace nodded. "Did you see anything or talk to anyone who seemed suspicious?" Horace leaned back in his chair. "Do you have any thoughts that could help us here?"

"Nah. I ain't seen nuthin'," Eustace was suddenly restless.

Having no real reason at this point to question him further, Inga gave up gracefully. Eustace stood up with another loud groan, gave them all disgusted looks and ambled out, muttering that some people sure did know how to waste a man's time.

"Was that valuable?" Horace asked. The other shook their heads. "Randy, that was brilliant, to give them a cigarette. We gotta do that with everyone else and see what happens."

"Yeah, but other than knowing that Eustace cadges ciggies and has his own matches, what did we learn?"

"Not much. Let's keep him in the possible category. Who's next out there?"

"Charlie Chan and Jimmy Earnest."

"How about the rest of them?"

"We still have Fred Sullivan, Gladys Charett and her fat husband...what do they call him? Mountain Man Agamenticus. Ha! Some suspects! All from a loony bin!" He pointed his index finger and whirled it in a circle, close to his head. "And then, um," he checked the sheet in front of him, "Uh, Floyd Jones and that other lady, Posey, uh, McCardle. They're the ones who were at three or more of the fires, according to Starr's pictures.

"When are they coming in?"

"Sullivan and Jones will be here tomorrow. We can't seem to get in touch with the McCardle woman. Her neighbor says maybe she's away for a few days, visiting her mother in Bangor or Aroostook County. Somewhere up there. She goes away once in a while, but she doesn't go far or stay long. I'll have one of my men check up north...see if we can find the mamma." He made a note on a pad of paper, checked an entry and informed his co-inquisitors: "The Charetts will be home this afternoon. God forbid that he might miss a meal!"

"OK, um...Charlie first..."

The squat, moon-faced man shuffled into the room. He also seemed nervous, turning his cap around and around in his dirt-encrusted fingers. *Shoot, I'd be nervous, too, if a bunch of cops were interviewing me about arson!* "Sit down, Charlie," Chief Parks tried to set Charlie's mind at ease.

"Thank you, sir." Charlie sat heavily. His eyes darted at Randy and Inga, then flitted at the ceiling, the lamp, the window and back to the chief. No one said anything further for a few moments. Charlie cleared his throat. "Uh, ah….what is this all about?"

"We're speaking with everyone who was at one or more of the fires." Charlie's eyes skittered away from the chief and he bent his head, presumably giving great attention to his shoes. "You were at several of them, Charlie."

"Yeah." He didn't look up.

"Did you, um, ah, see anything at all…anything that might help us catch the sonofabitch who set those fires?" Chief Parks tone was soft, belying the meaning behind his words.

"Nope. I saw there wuz a fire and went to see what was happening. I don't know much more."

"They were horrific, weren't they?" Inga broke into the interrogation.

Charlie looked up at her. Inga thought, *he did look just like that poster of Charlie Chan! Slanty eyes sunk into suety cheeks…his smile was crooked. He certainly looked Chinese!*

"Horrif…horri…they were terrible." Charlie nodded with vigor and his cheeks bounced. Randy noticed that he was sweating slightly.

"What kind of man would set a fire like that? Burn up human beings?" Randy probed. Charlie shrugged. Intellectual questions didn't seem to be of much interest. Randy waited, but Charlie just watched his shoes.

"How about a smoke?" Randy tried his new trick question. Charlie looked up and then his eyes shifted once more around the room. He shrugged and nodded. Randy flipped out his pack of Lucky Strikes again. Charlie scratched at his stringy hair, took the package and delicately extracted one cigarette. He looked at it. Turned it around in his hands.

Inga waited to see what he would do about lighting it. Charlie shifted in his chair and then asked for a light. "I ain't got a match. Anybody got one?"

Randy took a box of matches from his own pocket and tossed it on the table. Charlie bent his head and lit the cigarette, striking the match on the side of the matchbox. He took a deep pull of smoke, sighed and blew the smoke out in one long, cloudy puff. He coughed, wiped his mouth with the back of his hand, and sucked in another lungful of tobacco.

"How long have you been around Portsmouth?" Horace asked casually, crossing one leg over the other and tracing a line along the side of his leather regulation shoe.

"Sheet, Chief...." Charlie caught himself. "Scuse me, ma'am. I mean, you know I was borned here, Chief."

"Here are some pictures," Horace splayed the photographs on the table. "Do you recognize anyone?"

Charlie leaned forward and put a stubby finger here...and here...and there. "Yeah. Here's Ole Eustace...and Mountain Man Aggie and his skinny wife. She's sure a good cook, though. No meat on *her* bones. Ha! Ole Aggie has the most mashed potatoes of anyone I know on his dinner plate, but when it comes to huggin' his old lady, he gets chicken bones - sharp elbows and skinny hips. Ha!" He peered at the photographs, one by one. "An' here's that Polski man that works at the bakery...." Charlie named several more, all of whom had already been identified by the policemen.

"Are you married, Charlie?" Inga asked.

"Me?" Charlie laughed and his Oriental eyes almost disappeared into the suet of his face. "You betcha! Been married nigh on forty-three years." He looked around. "Whut's that got to do with the price of bread and milk?"

"No special reason. I'm just nosey." Inga smiled her best smile to take the sting away. Mollified by her pretty face, Charlie became even more affable. He began to talk about his family, telling the group that his son, Charlie Junior, had a very good job at the hardware store. "They think a lot of him, they do." Inga wondered if Junior also looked oriental. *Did it run in the family? Was there someone who was oriental in Charlie's background? And what did that matter, anyway?*

Horace stood up. "Well, thank you Charlie, for your time. You've been a big help to us." Charlie looked mystified. "You can go now. If you think of anything else that might help us catch this rat, please come back and tell us whatever it is."

"Sure. Sure. Anything I could do ta' help. I'll letcha know." Charlie strolled out, splayfoot as a duck.

"One left." Inga stood up, rolling her shoulders. "I'm exhausted! I didn't realize just how difficult this interrogation is!"

"I'll take you to lunch afterwards," Randy offered, trying to keep his tone casual. "I'll be passing by the University later and I can bring you back there." His glance pleaded with Horace, man to man, to not join them. Horace rubbed his chin and gave Randy a short nod. Who was he to stand in the way of this lovey-dovey sort of stuff?

"Come in, Jimmy." Horace held open the door into the small office. Jimmy Earnest, his chin leading the rest of his whip-thin body, followed. Randy thought that Jimmy's demeanor was somewhat apprehensive. But then again, Randy acknowledged to himself, anyone being talked to in a police station generally had good reason to be apprehensive.

"Good morning, Jimmy...is it Jimmy?" Inga introduced herself as Inga Hoffman and not as Doctor Hoffman. Randy wondered if she felt it might put Jimmy Earnest more at ease. "I'm rather new around here, so I don't know you as well as Chief Parks does." She smiled at him and he nervously grinned back. "I understand you work as a ....?"

"I work at the church, Ma'am." Jimmy's Adam's apple bobbed as he swallowed. "I'm the sexton. I have an important job. I keep the place clean and dig the graves and mow the lawn and all..."

"Pretty important work. I can understand that they rely on you." Inga's eyes were wide. Jimmy nodded.

"And you were at...let's see, three of the fires that have recently been set." Inga relaxed back in her chair. She passed three photographs to Jimmy.

He leaned forward, frowned, and looked carefully at each picture, placing his index finger on his own face in each one. He nodded again. "That's me."

"Tell me, Jimmy, what do you think happened?"

"Some demented maniac set a fire...or maybe multiple fires...more than one fire, that's what happened." Jimmy's face showed his confusion. *What did she mean? What was she asking him?*

"What kind of person set these fires?"

"I certainly don't know. Somebody who had some childhood trauma, perhaps?" He shook his head. "I...just...don't...

don't know...don't know anything." His skinny shoulders bobbed up and down.

"It was very sad, wasn't it?"

"Absolutely. It was horrific."

"Horrific. That's what I thought," Inga made a mental note that Jimmy's vocabulary was certainly above that of the average local.

"Did you see anything suspicious?"

"Not me." He shook his head.

"Did you see anyone who might have acted in a strange way?"

"No." He accompanied his monosyllable with a side to side shake of his head.

"What kind of person would do this?"

"A person who was troubled. A person who had a message for mankind?"

"A message? What kind of message?" Inga leaned forward, genuinely interested in Jimmy's train of thought.

Jimmy shrugged again. "It was a theory of mine."

There was a short silence. Randy moved forward, offering Jimmy a cigarette. The little man shrank back, pushing his hand, palm first, forward. "I never smoke. I work for the church and I am a soldier of the Lord."

"You're a smart man, Jim. Smoking has got to be bad for your health." Chief Parks took a cigarette himself and lit it, watching the smoke rise with the rueful knowledge that he, Chief Horace Parks, certainly, wasn't a soldier of the Lord. Not by any means.

"What else does a soldier of the Lord do or not do?" Inga leaned forward, putting her elbow on the table.

"A soldier of the Lord doesn't drink alcohol. He reads the Bible and listens to the Pastor." Jimmy's thin face bobbed back and forth. "He listens to the Pastor and the Lord."

"Is your Pastor a good man?"

"Oh, yes. He does the work of God."

"Are you a married man, Jim?" Inga asked. "Do you have a family? Children?"

"No, ma'am. I....I live with my father. My mother is dead. She passed twelve years ago." He looked down at his hands, which were tightly clasped on the table top. "I...I'm not much with ladies. I don't socialize much, except for church functions. I work hard, stay home and read my Bible mostly."

*Sounds too fascinating*, Inga mused to herself. *He's a boring little man, isn't he? Boring and insignificant.*

~~~~~~~~~~~~~~

"Maybe we'll have more luck tomorrow. There are still four or five people to interview." Randy's tone was bleak. "Or, rats, it could be someone that we don't recognize…or even someone who just didn't stick around. I mean, just because some arsonists *like* to watch their own fires, doesn't mean that *all* arsonists like to watch." He'd expected more from the interviews.

"It is early days, Randy." She used his first name. He perked up. After a quiet five minutes, she ventured, "I think our arsonist is not married."

"Why do you think that?"

She shrugged. "The statistics say that most arsonists are loners. They need the freedom to be out of the house at unusual hours." She shrugged. "A good wife would notice if her husband kept leaping up and going out in the middle of the night." She looked out of the window as they approached the bridge.

"The bridge is up," Randy pulled into the line of traffic, stopped the car and wound down his window.

Inga followed suit. "This is a beautiful harbor," She gazed at the ships and the piles of sand and gravel that lined the Portsmouth side. "I wish I'd been smart enough to have bought a little house on the harbor."

They talked, enjoying each other's company and the breeze that puffed across the harbor. Finally, the lights changed color and the line of cars began to move again, crossing over into Portsmouth.

"What is the name of this bridge?"

"It's the Sarah Mildred Long Bridge, and it backs up traffic and annoys the locals every half hour when it raises up to let big boats come into the harbor." Normally, Randy counted himself with the annoyed locals, but today, with Inga in the car with him, he was grateful for the few extra minutes of delay.

"I didn't see any big boat? Did I miss it?" She twisted on the seat, trying to see the water below.

Randy laughed and scratched his head. "In the wisdom of our great government, they raise the bridge every half hour whether or not there is a boat coming." He glanced down. Her hand was lying, face up, on the seat between them. Without any further thought, he patted it. "I don't know who made up that rule, but there it is. Up and down, up and down, whether or not it is needed." He chuckled. "Makes me think of a story that one of my elderly neighbors told me. She...Jenny is her name...She's a lovely woman and must have been a knock-out when she was younger. Anyway, when she was a pretty young girl, the boys who operated the bridge would invite the pretty girls to ride up and down on the center section. When the section was up in the air...and it stays up there for about five minutes...the boys would kiss the girls." He laughed. "Maybe that's why they do it whether or not a boat is coming."

"A good story," Inga smiled. "I would like to be one of those pretty girls, being kissed away up in the air." Randy's car left the bridge. She turned back for one last look and sniffed with rapture. "Ah! Smell that beautiful scent of the harbor and the sea. It makes me think of Norway.

"Is Norway like this?"

"Hmmm? Yes, some parts. Many *fjords* and harbors. Many boats. A peaceful land...before this war,"

"Is your family still there?"

"Some of them. When the war broke out, we tried...all of us...to come here where there was relative safety."

"I'm sorry about the ones left behind." He wondered if he should ask her any more about her homeland.

"They are the old ones. It is difficult for them to come here. We are fortunate, however, as most of them live in the mountains, away from the fighting which took place in the harbors, the cities and the coal regions."

"I'm glad that you escaped." He stole a look at her. Her face was drooped downward.

"Yes. I was fortunate." Her voice was a flat, tiny whisper. Behind them, a horn beeped. Traffic moved slowly into Portsmouth. *I wonder what she's not telling me?* Randy pondered.

~~~~~~~~~~~~~~

They parked the car on State Street, a block from the Portsmouth Police Station. On the way, Randy showed Inga the Connie Bean USO Center. "They have quite a fun time there, most nights." He grinned. "Although I am not an enlisted man, as Chief of Police, I can go in and watch the fun and the shows."

"I would adore such a thing." Her face lit up.

"Perhaps I can arrange for you to accompany me one night." She looked up quickly at his face, her eyes alight. "We can go to one of the USO shows."

"What is a USO show?"

"It's a big, vaudeville show...a variety show. Some singers, some dancers...all kinds of entertainment. Jugglers, animal acts...lots of fun...something different every few moments." He scratched his head. "I'll find out when the next one is and perhaps you...you and friends, if you wish...can join me."

"Please. I would like to see this show. *Ingen treff,* we would say in Norwegian."

"Oh, wow!" Randy was impressed. "You can speak Norwegian!"

"Well, of course, Randy, I speak Norwegian!" She began to laugh. "I was *born* in Norway!"

They walked down the cobbled street. "Where would you like to have lunch?" Randy asked.

Inga shrugged. "What is there here?"

He laughed. "Not much in the Norwegian line, I'm afraid."

"We eat many fishes. Herring...smoked chubb...salads... pickles...eggs and meats and cheeses."

"Do you like Chinese food?" She wrinkled her nose.

"Italian food?"

"Like spaghetti?"

"Spaghetti and meatballs."

"Ah! Meatballs. We have them in a cream and dill sauce. *Kjodbulla.*"

"These are in a tomato sauce."

"Let us see…"   They passed Chang's and Tedesco's, turned the corner and saw a small brick building. The sign atop the roof proclaimed: "MARIO's". Randy opened the door for her. "Here we are….I, uh, hope you like it here."

"And why would I not?" She smiled up at him. "I am here with you."

~~~~~~~~~~~~~~~

Alex felt as if he were in some sort of a strange time warp, blending his personal Past with his wartime Present.  The Past was the time so long ago when he was a child…and strangely, the time now…the time carved out of the war… here…the time spent with his parents, at their 200 year-old farmhouse home on Norton Road. His mother's cooking…the blueberry and apple pies she made for him…and then the loving look on her face as she watched him fork them down, often accompanied by a huge scoop of ice cream. His father's camaraderie…the two of them working, sleeves rolled up, hunched over the Ford. He felt as if he were ten years old in this atmosphere…back in the womb of a good, normal family. Folks who always tried to do their best. Generous, fun-loving, intelligent people…Real Americans… How he loved them! All of the people…Americans…his mom and his dad…who couldn't really understand one iota of what had happened to their son since he'd shipped overseas.

He lay under a tree, his mind floating, not quite coherent… lolling in an old striped hammock…the one with the rip right where your rear end sagged…Mystic, the cat from his ship, who had accompanied him onto the land, lay on top of Alex's stomach, his tail lashing back and forth as he thought about leaping off and trying to catch the foolish hen that pecked and squawked under the monkey-puzzle tree.

Alex watched Mystic. In his own mental wanderings, he felt that he could actually understand the cat's thoughts. *Was it worth it to leap down? What would it accomplish? The hen would just run away and the Master would scold him for trying to chase the feathered idiot.* Mystic sighed and batted a paw against Alex's arm.  Alex's laugh was loud and raucous. Who would understand that he *really did* telepath with a cat?

They'd lock him up in the brig if they could know his thoughts. Ha!

He wiggled into a more comfortable position and closed his eyes against the sunlight that slanted through the trees. He drifted off, lulled by the quiet sounds of the country. He slept.

He was hot. Sweating...dripping...skin on fire...it was hard to breathe. The heat slammed down, nearly making his legs buckle. What was *that? In the reeds? Japanese!*

He grabbed for his rifle and pulled it to his shoulder. He heard a scream off to the left. Steady...steady...try to see behind the grasses....*and what was that flash? A gun barrel! He was a* doctor, *for Chrissakes! He was supposed to heal men, not kill them...this was all wrong...all wrong!* He heard the crack of a bullet and leaped for cover! The scream of a jungle beast! Or was it the enemy, screaming to confuse?

The dream skidded into reality. He fell out of the hammock, twisting his leg into a pretzel, thumping his head on the grass of this quiet backyard...this cool, green grass...this safe haven...his parent's home. His eyes, dazed, darted from side to side. *Japanese! No. No!* He was home...here...in Maine... safe. Safe. It was only a dream. A dream. Thanks be. From the ground beside him, Mystic glared, affronted to have been thrown...yes, nearly *thrown* by his master...out of the hammock.

Sheepish, but terrifically glad that no one had witnessed his nightmare...well, perhaps one could call it a day-mare, Alex climbed back into the hammock, but no amount of cajoling would convince Mystic to climb back beside him. The cat, tail straight up, stalked away, annoyed and affronted as only a cat could be.

Alex's mind continued to dart...here...there...And how about those poor bastards...people like Jack Harrington and Joe Martin...real heroes. Guys who lost eyes and limbs and pieces of themselves protecting our country and saving the lives of their fellow soldiers? How did they figure into all of this philosophy? How could a doctor...himself, for instance...hate the war and yet relish the success of patching up these guys? And how could he hate the war and yet scream in delight when he heard of yet another battle won by the allies? It was a screwy world, and he wasn't yet sure how he fit in.

And the dreams!  He sighed. The Present had intruded again. He thought that once he'd gotten off the ship, the dreams might abate. At least until he sailed again…back into the hell that was his war. *If I come through this alive*, he swore to himself, *I'll become a Buddhist. I'll go to Tibet or some place like that. Some place that is safe and calm. I'll learn about peace. I'll never…never let myself be in a war again. Never!*

The little section of his brain…the one that allowed him to mock himself…asked, "And what will you do with this fine education that your parents slaved to give you? Will you throw it all away? All the learning about how to fix broken bones, cure diseases, make a child feel better?" Alex sighed. All of this was crap. The war…the hate…the killings…the atrocities. What was a pacifist doctor doing out there in the Pacific?

"Alex! Alex!" It was his father yelling for him. "Sam-with-the-white-bucks," which was the way his dad referred to Sam Fern, his best buddy, "is here!  He wants to go out with you to the USO dance!"

Alex rolled again out of the hammock, brushed himself off and, as his sense of humor was never too far away, laughed at the absurdities of life. "OK, Dad! I'm coming!" Besides, he was dying for an ice-cold beer.

~~~~~~~~~~~~~~~

They had eaten their spaghetti, served with two meatballs and a basket of crusty bread… "Yeah, the bread is good, huh? We get it from that Angel lady in Kittery. Everyone likes it." They'd laughed at Inga's attempts to wind the strands of the spaghetti around her fork…and enjoyed a jelly glass filled with rough red house wine… "We ain't got a license to serve wine, but we get around the law by giving it away. Yeah, the wine is free." And by the end of the lunch, both Randy and Inga felt loose and free of the worry of catching an arsonist and killer.

"Tell me about yourself," Randy started.

She told him about her life as a youngster in Norway. Her father was a Lutheran minister, her mother, a housewife. She was an only child, much-loved, petted and indulged. She had attended Oslo University and studied criminal psychology. "I was always interested in the crooked people...those with a bent for lawlessness. I always wanted to know what made them leave the road of common sense and take a path into destruction. I might have made a very efficient killer or swindler, if I wasn't so honest."

"I know. Sometimes, I plan how I would rob a bank. How I'd kidnap someone and not get caught." He turned the jelly glass around in his big hands. "One thing I can't figure out how to do is collect the ransom money, though. If I could find a way to do that, I might become a master criminal too."

They both laughed, and then both were silent. He finally asked her if she was married. She sipped the dregs of the wine and peered into the bottom of the glass, as if she didn't really know the answer to his question and sought it in the sludge.

"I was...well, in truth...I am still married. He is a German. Before this trouble started, he was considered a good catch. A Professor of Economics, a serious man, a wealthy man. And so, with the blessings of my father and some doubts from my mother, who saw what I should have seen, I married."

"As the clouds of war gathered, he changed, showing his hatred of those who were defenseless and different. His speech was filled with bile and he became rough and abusive towards me when I demurred to agreeing with much that he espoused. His mask of respectability slipped off and underneath, his real self appeared and I was frightened and worried. I thought that I had to leave him."

"What did you do?"

"I made a huge mistake and told him that I was leaving. He went crazy and said that if I left, he would see to it that the Nazi Regime would take my mother and father.

Randy gaped, seeing this glimpse of life in another country. *This was why we fight for freedom, isn't it? Isn't this was why we're all in this war. Because monsters really do exist.* "He...he...he couldn't do that? Could he?"

"Oh, Randy, you are so innocent. All of you Americans have no idea of what it means to live under a dictator....they can do *any*thing. Anything at all." She put the glass down.

"They can kill you in your home…they can drag you out in the street and beat you senseless…they can rape your mother in front of you and then slit the throat of your father…" She looked at him with wonder. "That is why we fight them or try to run away, hoping to escape such terror. We…my mother and my father, we grabbed everything that we could and we contacted the Resistance Movement. Those people put their own lives on the line for freedom and many of them hang for their efforts." She looked faintly amused. "Do you think we just love war? Ha. We love freedom, and often it is necessary to die for that love." She shrugged. "Ah, well, enough of that. We were lucky. We were smuggled out of the country and we went to England, where we were safe. I never saw Germund again."

"And now? Your parents? Where are they?"

"They stayed in London. They have been bombed, but that is nothing. They are free and cannot be harmed there. Being bombed is nothing. Nothing at all. I chose to come to the United States on a teaching visa. I was placed at the University in New Hampshire." She looked up at him. "And here I am still." She sat back. "My life in seven minutes…and now, my dear Randy, it is your turn."

"It won't even take seven minutes. I was born here, was raised here and joined the police after school. I had a happy childhood and then, like a story in a book, I married the proverbial girl next-door. We are still married…sort of. We have no children. She…well…first, three years ago, I was on a stake-out at a robbery at a fur coat warehouse. I was hit with a stray bullet, and the bullet is close to my brain. They left it there." He rubbed the side of his head. "I can feel it, waiting… waiting…" She frowned and reached her hand out. He took it and held it.

"When the war started, I was not qualified to fight. Because of the bullet. They were afraid….well….anyway, I was then promoted to Chief of Police when Chief Robbie Menson went into the Marines. I guess they felt I could still do the job here."

"And your marriage…?"

"Nancy is a good woman. She wants a family and a yard and a man who comes home every night.  She wants me there on the weekends to cook hot dogs in the back yard. She wants me to be at her mother's house every Sunday to eat her fried chicken. She wants…" He shrugged helplessly. "Ah, well, what she *doesn't* want is a policeman as a husband. A man who is never home. A man who jumps up from the table to go and see how a child got run over. How a dead man was strangled. How to catch a murderer or an arsonist. It…it… we…we just don't think the same or have the same priorities or interests any more. Nancy wants…she…she doesn't even under*stand* the war. She thinks we're being foolish, fighting a war that's across the sea. She…she doesn't…" He sighed. "It isn't anyone's fault. It is just the way it is."

The waiter brought the bill. Randy paid and thanked him with a good tip. They left the restaurant.

"Will I see you again?"

She laughed. "After all of this soul-baring between us? Of course you will! I'll be at Chief Parks' office tomorrow at 10 AM to interview the rest of the suspects, you silly man."

~~~~~~~~~~~~~~

**August 5th, 1943 – Two Solomon Island Coastwatchers, paddling in their dugout canoe, find the crew of PT-109.**

The Thursday night USO dance was crowded. One of the submarines, the *US Catfish,* was going out the next afternoon, and many young men were anxious to have a memorable last night on shore.

At 7 PM, before the night's action started, Brenda Be went to visit Kathie Hess at The Hess Club for Gentlemen. "The girls will be dressed and ready for early visitors, the place will be all lit up, and you can stay as long as you wish," Kathie had told her.

With some nervousness and excitement mingling, Brenda dressed for the occasion. She'd thought a lot about what she should wear. Not men's clothing. No. This wasn't the time to wear a tuxedo or a set of hunting pinks topped off by a derby. No. This was special. She rummaged through her huge and unusual wardrobe. The caftan from the Kasbah in Marrakesh?

She held it up and watched the light glitter on the wild colors and the little pieces of mirror that some foreign lady had painstakingly sewn here and there. No. Too...too... glitzy. Certainly not the tightrope walker's costume that she'd gotten from the last circus that had come to town. No.

Frustrated, throwing garments in piles, she thought about what was paramount in her toilette. A Hat! Her hats were the most important thing she wore. She tore into the closet that held her collection. There were top hats, pith helmets, jockey caps, an aviator's leather flap-eared helmet, cloches, sunbonnets...what? What would be best? She laughed at herself, *worrying my dark, curly hair to a frazzle about what to wear to a whorehouse, for God's sake!*

In the end, she chose her favorite hat. A pinwheel creation in her favorite pinky-blue color. It set off her curly hair and made her look, or so she'd been told, like a movie star. A simple, but ravishingly expensive silk dress, cut low in front to show her admirable bosoms, then close fitting down to within inches of the hem. The hem itself was a marvel of dressmaking brilliance, with a flounce that dipped up and down, emphasizing her slender ankles and her long, long legs. She made a final check in her mirror and was delighted with herself. Hopefully, the Hess brigade of women...she shuddered that she had once called them whores...but...after all...well...she shook her head. Was a whore more appealing if you knew them personally? Or were they still beyond the bounds of society? Anyway, would the girls at The Hess Club think she measured up? Or would they think she was over-dressed and silly. Wondering why she cared *what* they thought, Brenda left the house.

The Club was located on a pleasant, shady street boasting wide sidewalks and stately lamplights. It was an imposing building, four stories high with an ornate porte-cochere and seven marble steps that led to a small veranda and the front door. Brenda thought it might have been an old sea-captain's residence in the heady days of robber-barons and no income taxes.

She felt right at home and pleased that she'd chosen to wear what she was wearing. And, to judge from the grin on Kathie's face when she entered The Club and the admiring glances on the face of the colored maid who admitted her, she'd chosen well. "Well! We are delighted to see you, Brenda. Sandra, this is Brenda Be. Brenda, this is Sandra, who has been my right-hand woman for more years that we both want to remember." The two women shook hands. Sandra was also dressed beautifully, in an attractive mauve dress, accentuated with tiny pearls at the collar and cuffs. "Come into the lounge and meet a few of my ladies and some of our early guests."

The lounge was huge...the entire length of the house, and furnished in tasteful luxury. There were six women and five men there. She recognized one of the men as a bank president, and one as a mover-and-shaker in railroads, but made no comment about knowing them or their professions when she was introduced. The women were all striking...lovely, beautifully dressed, cultured and witty. The men were all imposing. Their very stances screamed money and power. Had she not known exactly what The Club was, Benda might have thought herself in the mansion of some wealthy merchant or captain of industry in any cosmopolitan city.

With a cocktail in her hand, Kathie guided Brenda on what she called "the grand tour". On the ground floor, in addition to the lounge, "where the gentlemen can get acquainted", there was a large gaming room with tables set for card games. In addition, there were three smaller rooms where gentlemen could have privacy, if they wished. There was a dining room. "This is always set every night with a cold collation...salmon, a baron of beef, fresh-cooked turkey and a large ham...the gentlemen often wish to take a break from gambling and have a plate of food, or perhaps have their girls make sandwiches that they can eat while they're playing cards." Kathie explained.

"The kitchens are downstairs, along with the laundry rooms..." She laughed. "You have no idea of how many tablecloths, napkins, sheets and pillowcases we go through every night!" She winked at Brenda, a slow, easy wink accentuating her remark about the sheets and pillowcases. "Sarah and her husband, Samuel, live down here with her sister, Gloria. They take care of the house for me."

"Everything is beautiful!" Brenda exclaimed with unstinting enthusiasm. "Can I, um...go...upstairs?" She blushed becomingly and Kathie laughed again.

"Certainly! I want to show you the naughty places!"

The second and third floors housed each girl's chamber. The bedrooms were large, high-ceilinged rooms, each with a sumptuous bathroom, each decorated in a different manner. "I let the girls, within reason, choose their own furnishings and decorate their rooms as they wish." She knocked at a door, listened for a moment, and then opened it. "Come and see Jocelyn's room. She's downstairs now, so I don't think she'll mind."

The room was furnished with breathtaking antiques and what looked like valuable original art work, and featured, as an eye-grabbing focal point, a huge, four-poster bed festooned with draperies. The color scheme was pale green and grey. "Any museum or expensive hotel would scream to have this room!" Brenda gasped.

"And now, come and see the bath..." Kathie held the door. Brenda peeped into a marble room with a sunken tub. A dove-grey Recamier posed under a crystal chandelier and piles of silken towels were heaped here and there. The air pulsed with a subtle perfume that somehow, very delicately, reeked of forbidden sex.

"Son-of-a-gun!" Brenda's mouth was open. "This is magnificent! Are all the rooms like this?"

"Jocelyn has been with me for more than ten years. She's finagled the best of the rooms, but they are all beautiful, if not quite like this one. The gentlemen pay huge sums of money to be able to gamble in peace and quiet. The Club rakes off a percentage of every hand played, and I get a cut of every girl's wages for the use of these rooms. The girls are paid handsomely, and they also receive many gifts...jewels, furs, bank accounts...from their favorites. Many of them, as I told you, have a child, or even two, most of them fathered by the men who visit our establishment. The children board and attend the private school on the next street. It's a good arrangement for me, for the children and for the girls."

"I'm very impressed." Brenda and Kathie walked out of the room. Brenda looked back, noting the large oil painting over the fireplace. "I like that painting."

"You ought to!" Kathie chuckled. "Jocelyn has marvelous taste in art. It's an original Totman. Her last semi-permanent friend bought it for her when he moved back to Europe."

"I'm flabbergasted!"

The ladies walked down the stairs. Brenda thought of how it might be if she joined this establishment. She imagined herself flirting and finding a man she approved of....then walking with him up these stairs. Maybe into the sunken tub filled with bubbles. Kathie watched the expressions flitting across Brenda's face and laughed again, knowing full well what Brenda was thinking.

"You could always try it for a few nights."

"Hmmm. Maybe I will!"

~~~~~~~~~~~~~~~~

At the USO, the girls from the Kennebunk Bank, considered genuine local home-town heroines, manned a booth selling war bonds. Everyone at the dance had heard of their bravery, and business was brisk.

"Come on, sailor…give us a donation and I'll give you a big kiss!" Tami Keen flirted with a young blonde sailor, sporting his first mustache and looking fresh off the farm in Kankakee, Illinois.

The sailor gulped, looked back at the six men with him, hooting and urging him on…"Huh!" He gulped. "I…I… Well, sure!" The sailor dug into a pocket and pulled out a dollar. "Is this enough?"

"You don't want to rob the child of his last dollar, you trollop, you," Helen Huntress, chided. "If she doesn't kiss you for the dollar, I will, you handsome lad, you!" Helen leaned over the table, lips pursed.

"Hey! He's mine!" Tami grabbed the dollar, then grabbed the wide, white collar of the Navy blouse, pulled the astonished sailor halfway across the table, and bussed him hard. The sailor broke the kiss, looking stunned.

"Holy smoke!" He gaped. "Holy Joe Smoke! I can die right now!"

His buddy pushed him aside, grabbing Helen's hand. "Here's my dollar, Blondie. Pucker up for all the men from Poughkeepsie!"

Cathy French waved to the third man in line. "My lips are free! I mean, they're free for kissing, but the kissing part will cost you one dollar!" Three soldiers waved dollar bills at her.

It was Betty's first night at the USO. She'd never heard of an effort like this in California. This was *fun!* She hoped that neither of the two boyfriends that she regularly wrote enthralling letters to, one in Africa fighting and one flying a bomber, got word that she was dancing and having a ball entertaining lots more servicemen.

"Men! Try a California kiss!" She called out, waving her hand in the air.

"Never mind California kisses...come over here and try good old Maine lips!" Helen leaned over the counter and beckoned.

Gail Fletcher loved the idea of the kissing. She leaned forward, big blue eyes flashing, lips pursed..."Who's next? Come on, kisses...All-American kisses...nice enough for you to remember when you're stuck in a foxhole! Come on, boys! Only one dollar!"

Helen switched from a sailor's lips to those of a waiting Marine. "If Ken catches you smooching these guys, he's gonna kill you!" She pretended to put a gun to Gail's head, reminding her of her stalwart boy-friend who did hush-hush war work at the Shipyard. "You better hope he never hears about how patriotic you are tonight!"

Nick Cappiello, looking in vain for Mary Rose, sauntered up to the Kennebunk Bank table. The poker tables and the acey-deucy games had been very good to Nick tonight, and he was once more flush with moolah. He waved a twenty dollar bill overhead. "Here's my proposition, ladies!" he hollered. "I've got a twenty dollar bill here! One kiss from each of you..." He counted "...three, four, five...seven. No, eight." He winked at Gail. "I almost missed you, darling. Eight of you... eight kisses and you get the twenty... Whaddaya say, ladies?" He grinned as the bank ladies shrieked their acceptance. He stood, his hands on his hips, bent down to accept their kisses...Helen first, then Gail, then Sally, then Julie, Betty, Cathy, Michelle and when he kissed Tami, the last banking heroine, he lifted her high in the air and held her there, in a lip-lock that raised whistles and cheers all over the hall.

Grinning, his hands pumped up above his head, Nick ceremoniously gave Tami his money, then bowed to the crowd and the men lining up, jostling one another to kiss the

Kennebunk Bank heroines.  At that moment, he noticed Mary Rose at the back of the throng. She watched him for a moment, then turned and melted away. His eyes widened. *Oh shit!*

~~~~~~~~~~~~~~

As Rosie Nunn's all-girl orchestra finished playing a tango, Brenda came in, remarking to herself the difference between this location with its cute and perky All-American girls, and the lush glamour and exotic promiscuity that she had just witnessed. She shrugged. That was what was wonderful about the good old US of A! You can do pretty much what you want to do. She stood at the door, and several people rushed up to tell her how much they loved her hat and dress. She grinned and said she'd just been to a tea party at a special venue. There! That would make everyone wonder!

She was swept up in the music and her own patriotism, and even danced three jitterbugs with one sailor and two marines. What a night!  After the third dance, she thankfully sat at the Senior Hostess table with Sabina Carter and Jacquie Small.

"Are we going to allow that Hess Club woman to have a gambling night?" Sabina leaned close so that no one could hear her question.

"Why not?" Jacquie shrugged. "They want to do their part for the war effort and they certainly will pull in a ton of money."

Sabina made a face. "Well," she said slowly. "It goes against everything my minister might think, but….well, what the heck."

Brenda studied Sabina as she stood to answer an enlisted man's question. Hmmm? Sabina was putting on a bit of weight, wasn't she? Or was she simply wearing a rather unbecoming dress? She turned to ask Jackie if she'd noticed, but was interrupted by a young sailor asking her to dance. "You see, Ma'am," the sailor cajoled, "I'm leaving on a big boat tomorrow and may never dance again!"

~~~~~~~~~~~~~~

Brenda's request for approval of a Hess Club for Gentlemen's Gambling Night caused no end of a stir. Many on the committee nearly had fits; some almost foamed at the mouth; others merely shook their head, stamped their feet and refused to consider such a thing.

"But, it is for the *war!*" Brenda appealed. "They're going to donate every penny of the proceeds...and I think there will be enormous proceeds...to the York Hospital's wounded veterans' ward." She stood up, beseeching the group.

"Money is money, no matter where it comes from!"

"But this money is earned from *sin!*" The middle-aged woman who always wore the rose-patterned kerchief wailed. "We can't let women like that," she nearly spit out that last word... "be a part of our organization!"

"They really don't want to be part of our organization!" Brenda cut in. "They simply want to hold a fund-raising event and donate the profits to the war effort. They were nice enough," she stopped for a moment and saw the flint-eyed stares directed at her. She sucked in her breath and plowed on. "They were nice enough to want to participate in helping our injured men and women. This is a way that they can do it. We can't turn down a large sum of money that we need...the hospital needs...so badly." She turned in a circle, her hands out and open in supplication. "Doctor Eneman from York Hospital told me that this money will supply prostheses for men who have lost a leg or an arm. It will enable a dying man to send for his wife or mother to come to his bedside and visit him one last time." She peeped at the crowd. A few of the people were softening, perhaps thinking of a loved one or the men and women who were maimed. *Good, I just may be able to swing opinion my way!*

Grace Sabatino stood to join Brenda. "Do you think the war is only won with money that has no taint? Ha! Think of the gamblers who donate to the effort. Think of the men who give up drinking and use that money to buy war bonds. If your son were dying if he didn't get medicine, would you care where that medicine came from?" Grace cleverly directed that question right to rose-patterned-kerchief. The woman opened her mouth, thought better of it, and slowly shrugged, capitulating.

   Candace McClosky, who had originally not been in favor of the gambling night, stood up. *Rats!* Brenda thought. *She's going to put the ki-bosh on it!*

   "You all know that I had spoken against letting Hess House...Hess Club...whatever they call it...you know what I mean," She blushed, a little out of her depth. "Anyway, The Hess Club... be a part of our war effort," She put her hand up to the back of her neck, massaging the vulnerable little spot in nervousness. "But I've searched inside myself. I remember Sabina asking us if we are fighting among ourselves or are we fighting Hitler?" Mary nodded, slowly, and then nodded again. "Well, I think I was wrong and Sabina was right. *All* Americans are in this fight and *all* Americans can help. What does it matter if you are someone who...who...who has a different way of helping? What does it matter if you're a bad mother, or a mean father? What does it matter if you are an atheist, or that you vote differently from me?" She stood tall. "It doesn't matter...not at all! We are all...no matter who we are or what we think about some things...all fighting together. Fighting against Hitler! And whatever money The Hess Club can give us to help those poor, injured men...why, I think we should give them a big cheer." She sat down, looking defiant.

   Brenda sensed that the moment had come. She struck. "I propose that we permit The Hess Club to hold a gambling night. We...the USO Committee...will not directly be involved with this evening of entertainment, but we will graciously thank our benefactors. Right, ladies and gentlemen?"

   Rose-patterned kerchief threw up her hands in defeat. "I don't approve, but...if it helps our men and women....well...I guess..." She sat down, gnawing at a knuckle.

   Julie Patten hammered on the table. "Fine! The proposal is passed and approved." She leaned both hands on the table. With great sincerity, she addressed the group: "The most unusual people can have great strengths. As Sabina and Jacquie have said, 'we don't have to agree with everything they might do'...." A murmur rose above the crowd.... "But, after all is said and done, a good thing will be the result of this fund-raiser." She smiled at Brenda. "And thank-you to Brenda Be for seeing potential where others might not. Let's see how this all goes."

~~~~~~~~~~~~~~

**August 6, 1943 – The US Army drives the Japanese out of
Munda Airfield on New Georgia.**

Kathie Hess spent several hundred dollars advertising
Gambling Night at The Hess Club for Men, printing flyers
passed out by young boys on street corners, taking full-page
advertisements in the local newspapers and plastering every
telephone pole with a poster. To the amazement of the hoi-
polloi, tickets were one-hundred dollars, and that entitled a
man to enter her establishment, kibitz with Kathie and her girls
and partake of a buffet supper. To play black-jack, poker,
pinochle or acey-deucy cost one hundred dollars per game.
To play Twenty-One or Baccarat cost two hundred. Huge
amounts of money were asked for, and evidentially, gladly
paid. Champagne or mixed drinks were extra, and the attend-
ees were told to expect several extra games of chance and
opportunities to donate even more money to York Hospital.
Every cent raised would be going to the Hospital. The Hess
Club would absorb all of the expenses entailed with the night.
No expenses would be taken out of the proceeds. For some
reason, this little bit of charity seemed to soften the most
hardened opponent.

Brenda wondered to herself if the monies the girls might
earn...upstairs...would also be donated, or would the girls
keep their hard-earned dollars. But she was the only one
knowledgeable and curious enough to probe this particular
situation.

Three days before the event, all tables were completely
sold out. "If half of them come, I think we'll be packed like
sardines!"

In delighted joy, Kathie and Brenda screamed at one
another and danced like two maniacs.

"We did it! We did it!"

~~~~~~~~~~~~~~

The Hess Club Gambling Night was a huge success. Many ordinary wealthy customers, without benefit of reservations, took the opportunity to attend, dropping hundred dollar bills like cheap leaflets. A few notable civic leaders from the Portsmouth area also attended, telling themselves that, after all, this was a charitable event, when, in fact, they were simply dying for an excuse to breach the polished glass doors and see just what the inside of a fancy house looked like. There, and lavishly entertained by Kathie and her girls, some of the most cultured and beautiful women they had ever met, these civic leaders decided that The Hess Club wasn't such a bad place after all.

Kathie came to Brenda's office at the USO the next morning, almost hysterical with excitement. In her hands, she held a leather pouch. "Here!" She whooped, opening up the pouch and upending it over Brenda's desk.   Hundreds and thousands of dollars cascaded over the desk. Bill after bill after bill floated down, to nestle in a gorgeous green heap.

"Thirteen thousand, seven hundred sixty dollars!" Kathie screamed, pushing both hands into the pile and tossing the money upward.

"Son of a *bitch!*" Brenda was nearly pole-axed with amazement.

"Son of a bitch is right, my friend! Son of a bitch is *right!*"

~~~~~~~~~~~~~~~

In the war ward at York Hospital, the news about the windfall from the gambling night was greeted with cheers and delight.  "Now, Jack," Dr. Jonathan Eneman, York's doctor who specialized in treating difficult trauma, announced to Jack Harrington. "I've already ordered the machine that's going to fix you up so that you can walk in a straight line." He patted Jack's twisted left leg. "You're screwy enough. We can at least fix this part of you."

In the next bed, Joe Martin listened in his dark cocoon of blindness. He wondered if there was anything...perhaps some new miraculous machine... that might make a whole man out of him. He didn't want sympathy...no. He didn't want charity...no. He just wanted to be able to somehow earn a living. The Japs hadn't made him cry. Not even when he saw six of his men bayoneted in front of him. Not when he hopelessly dragged the burning bodies of two of his best friends out of a straw hut engulfed with flames. He didn't cry when they cut off his foot and part of his leg, nor when he found that when he opened his eyes, no matter how he strained to see some flicker of light, there was only inky blackness. But today, hearing that there was a machine of some sort that would help Jack get better, his tears ran warm. He rolled his head into the pillow so that no one would see and note his weakness.

But Eunice, approaching his bed, noticed. She wondered what she should do. How should this be handled? Her rubber soled shoes made no noise as she stopped, thought how much she loved him, and then silently backed away, leaving him at least some dignity.

Two others noticed Joe's silent distress. One was Jack Harrington, who had become Joe's best pal in the weeks that they had traveled together from the bloody and chaotic war fields, to the desperate hours at the field hospitals, the choppy sea crossing under Doctor Alex Patten's tender and anxious care, to the clean, bright sickroom of York Hospital and the dedicated people who tried to put their bodies and lives back together again.

Jack had watched the little nurse with the short, curly hair and the anxious eyes fall in love with Joe Martin, one of the bravest and most honorable men that Jack had ever known. And, in his years of service with the US Marines, Jack had met hundreds of the finest. He'd noted that Joe had come to depend more and more on Eunice's touch and laugh. He saw Joe's ears practically bend over when he heard her step or her voice. He saw Joe's face light up when Eunice touched his hair or his arm, and he saw how Joe fought hard against the love that was so obvious to anyone who looked at the two of them.

And the hospital ship was nearly done with its re-fitting. It would be leaving Portsmouth in a week's time to return to the war theater, somewhere, to pick up the pieces of hundreds of more soldiers and sailors and marines whose bodies had been ripped apart by the horrors of war. *And Eunice, together with my little darling Yashiko, and those two pips, Carol and Michelle and that good doctor Alex and the two hard-working corpsmen would all sail away too. Christ! I'll miss them all!*

*Don't make this big mistake, Joe. Don't shut her out because you think she feels sorry for you. Don't turn away because you think you'll be a drag on her, my friend. She loves you, Joe…not your foot, not your eyes. She loves your soul, old friend. Don't shut her away.* Naturally, because he was a tactful man, he beamed this advice – hopefully – through the atmosphere. Hopefully, Joe, attuned to seeking things beyond what his eyes could not see, might catch some of this advice. Hopefully.

The other person who watched was Doctor Jon Eneman. His clever, aesthetic face was lined with sympathy. Jon's eyes met Jack's, and the two men, without speaking, formed a bond that was set in cement to fix the lives of these two people. Somehow. Somehow.

He walked heavily, hoping Joe would hear his tread, to Joe's bedside. "Hey, Joe. I've got great news for you."

"Yeah? I sure could use a bit of good news." Joe's eyes were dry now. He was back in control.

"We've just about finished your new foot." Jon patted Joe's shoulder. "It's just getting its final coat of shellac. It's just adorable and you're going to love it." He chuckled. "It even has toes on it! I think we'll try it on this afternoon and maybe get you up on it tomorrow morning."

Joe's face was stoic. "I'm grateful, Doc. I'll try anything to get myself up and out of here, although, even if the foot works, what the hell am I going to do with myself? Make baskets by touch?"

*Let's nip this right in the bud.* Jon Eneman had handled worse before. "Stop with the sorry stuff, Joe. Save your energy for swearing when we finally get you up and the stump hurts like hell. I don't have time to worry about you and your career in the hereafter. My job is to get you as well as possible. When we're finished with that, then you can piss and moan."

Joe had the grace to look abashed. "I never meant to piss and moan and feel sorry for myself, Doc. Honest." He dipped

his head down and rubbed the sockets of his sightless eyes.
"I should be ashamed of myself."

"Ah, Joe. Don't take this huge job all at once. Let's fix the
leg and foot. Let's get you running around here, chasing the
nurses, and then we can hope that your eyesight might clear
itself up by itself. There's really nothing physically wrong with
your eyes, Joe. No damage that we can see. It's just that your
poor eyes have seen more than they can cope with. They
need a bit of a rest." He rubbed Joe's neck. "I'll be back in an
hour or two. In that time, I want you to think of a good name
for your new body part." Joe's mouth flapped open. "I find that
the guys who give the part a name, love it and cuddle it to their
hearts, do the best." He laughed. "You lie back and think of a
nice name and I'll be back in about two hours."

Eunice had returned to hear the last part of Doctor
Eneman's conversation. She stood by Joe's head until he
sensed her presence. *She smells so good*, he thought. *She
smells like fresh air and a field of flowers. My Eunice. Ah, God
give me strength!* "Eunie?"

"Hi, Joe." She wondered why he wasn't able to feel the
blaze of love from her heart. "I hear you're going to have to get
up off your duff. Great! I intend to make you work like a galley
slave. I want you playing tennis with me and dancing a
jitterbug before we sail back in a week or so." She patted his
hand. "Here's a Coke for you. I put lots and lots of ice in it, just
like you like it." She rattled the glass. "Here," she handed the
glass to him and their hands touched. Joe thought he'd
collapse with want, feeling the two senses…one of a warm
hand, and one of an ice-cold glass. She was wonderful…the
nicest, friendliest, funniest, kindest woman he'd ever met. He
knew she was beautiful. Everyone told him so, describing her
as slender and petite. Her hair, which had been singed off
when she went into rescue the patients in the burning tents,
was growing in with curly red-gold ringlets. He'd been told that
her eyes were grey-green, direct and honest, with flecks of
humor and deep patience. He was in love.

*I can never say anything. She's nice to me. It's her job.
She's a good nurse and she sees me as a pitiful patient,
helpless and unable to manage. God forbid that she knows*

*how I adore her! Please, God! Never let her guess how much I want her!*

"I hear you're thinking up a name for your new leg and foot. Any ideas yet?" He voice was light and cheerful.

"How about 'stumpy'? He forced a chuckle.

If he could see, he'd have seen her short, upturned nose wrinkle. "No…that's too morbid. You need something…more original…."

"I'll have to think on it." He gulped the Coke, nearly swallowing the entire glass. It felt fizzy and cold as it traveled down his tight throat. "Goodness me!" He held up the glass. "I do love ice! You know, Eunie. When I was in the jungle, and it was so damn hot that my skin was burning and my throat was dry as dust…parched…I just wanted a glass…and it had to be a glass…filled with ice cubes and Coke. I dreamed of it." He finished the Coke. "And now, I can have as much as I want." He laughed. "And I want it all!" She joined him, chuckling, and then sat down by his side and shared the latest war news with him.

# CHAPTER TWELVE

**August 6, 1943 – The Allies take Catania, Sicily and prepare to run the Axis completely out of Sicily.**

It was funny, Mary Rose mused, but with all the hoo-ha about rationing, all the newspapers and posters and difficulties, she had no problem at all getting sugar and butter and flour for baking. Perhaps it was with the help of sweet old Don Mantaldo, her family's great friend and man who was able to fix or arrange almost anything. *He's always been sweet to me...to all of our family...but I think he could be a savage enemy. I've even heard that he's had men killed...men who crossed him or tried to cheat him...I wonder if that's true?*

Perhaps his amazing Italian touch, and his fierce reputation if things didn't go well, was able to reach all the way up to Maine to influence those who were in charge of passing out rationing points to those who were involved in commercial baking. "Be sure that Mary Rose Sabatino gets all the sugar and butter and flour that she needs! Otherwise, I will shoot your kneecaps off!" She giggled at the thought, but knew, from her family's stories, that Don Mantaldo wouldn't hesitate to threaten someone, just like that!

Or perhaps all bakeries were able to get the supplies they needed? Whatever, she shrugged, dusting the flour from her hands. *Whatever angel up on high is watching over me and my bakery...thank you!* She giggled, wondering if the name of her bakery had anything to do with her own Guardian Angel keeping her well-supplied.

This afternoon, she was going over to South Street in Portsmouth to assist another bakery that was in a temporary quandary. Bertha Abbott, the Jewish lady who ran Liberson's Jewish Bakery, had fallen down the cellar steps and broken her arm. Her sister, who lived in Boston, was coming up to help out, but couldn't get there for a day or two. Bertha begged Mary Rose to help her. She was desperate for someone experienced to give her two days of assistance.

"Can you come?" Bertha's voice sounded frail and anxious.

"Of course." Mary Rose assured her, thanking her stars and her personal Guardian Angel again that The Bread of Angels was running so well. Jannus did all of the night work, mixing and preparing the batters and dough, then proofing and setting all of the loaves and cakes. Ursula appeared in the early morning to ice and decorate. At 8 AM. Mary Rose and Caledonia took over the back of the business, leaving Ursula to wait on early-morning customers. Agnes Winchell arrived later in the day and Jannus then went home to sleep a well-deserved sleep.

"What time do you need me?" Mary Rose asked Bertha.

"If you can arrive at 7 AM, it would be a great joy to me. I have enough helpers to get through the night. It will only be for the two days." Already, her voice sounded stronger with the knowledge that Mary Rose would be there.

"Do you have any specials?" Bertha understood the lingo. 'Specials' were generally cakes...birthday cakes, anniversary cakes...those confections that were made to order and generally took a great deal of time to ice and decorate.

"Three." She sounded guilty. "Two birthdays and a Bar-Mitzvah...Can you cope?"

"Certainly." Mary Rose sighed with relief. It might have been worse. "Anything special on them?"

"I've written it all down. Made you a sketch of each top. Nothing out of the ordinary except the Bar Mitzvah wants an airplane theme. I have a nice little war plane model and some fake trees and it should be easy." She ended the call professing her undying gratitude. "I'll come and help you some time. You never know."

"I hope it never happens, Bertha. I look forward to a little bit of change. It will be fun."

"From your mouth to God's ear." Bertha hung up.

~~~~~~~~~~~~~~~~

The rehearsals for the USO's production of *Anything Goes* took place almost every night at the high school auditorium. Julie was in charge. She had originally thought of playing a part herself. She just loved all of the songs, but alas, being in the play and directing the play simply couldn't be done by one person. Sighing, she relinquished the lead to Debbie Orloff, her friend who sang, Julie wryly admitted, much better than she.

Mario Sabatino had surprised everyone, especially his wife, Grace, when he trotted over to the tryouts and sang, as his audition, a very bawdy version of *Bell-Bottom Trousers*. Everyone watching laughed themselves sick. Julie and her assistant, Bonnie Dridi were ecstatic in their effusive praise. "You're going to play Moonface Martin," Julie told him. "You're our guy!"

The musical, *Anything Goes*, was collaboration between Cole Porter and P.G. Wodehouse, told the musical tale of a ship, the *S. S. American*, sailing from New York to England. Julie had thought it was appropriate that a show about a ship would be shown to a town that wallowed in boats.

She re-read the *Anything Goes* Description: The passengers are a very unusual bunch. Included among them are a sexy nightclub singer (Reno Sweeny) and her troupe of chorus girls, a gangster (Moonface Martin, who is Public Enemy Number 13, but who wishes hopelessly that he might be promoted upward to Public Enemy Number 1), a wealthy debutante and her mother (Hope and Evangeline Harcourt), a snobby New York businessman (Elisha Whitney) and his stowaway assistant (Billy Crocker).

The story has changed and changed again over the years, but basically tells the audience that Hope is Billy's long-lost love. Unfortunately, she is now engaged to Lord Evelyn Oak-leigh, an uptight Englishman. After a series of comedic mix-ups and glorious songs, Billy manages to win back Hope's love. Billy's glamorous friend, Reno, manages to seduce and win Lord Evelyn's heart.  The hysterical play bounces to its finish, while dancing and carousing, Moonface manages to evade the law and Hope's mother strives to keep her social status.

Julie hoped and prayed, every six or seven minutes of her waking hours, that everyone involved would learn their lines and songs and that she wouldn't die of anxiety before the opening in September. "Relax, babe," Pat rubbed her back. "It will be just fine. Just fine. But Pat, Julie mourned to herself, wasn't involved in the production.

"You don't have any idea, Pat! Any idea at all, of the mishaps...the things that could go wrong! Debbie could get laryngitis!  Mario might forget his lines! No one would buy the tickets! The USO might burn down! Anything! Anything could happen!"

~~~~~~~~~~~~~~~

**August, 1943 – The Nazis carry out a ruthless and relentless pillage on the resources of the Ukraine, forcing the people of the Russian villages into slave labor, compelling them to gather in the rich harvest and then sending the entire yield to Germany. Deprived of their food, the Russians began to starve.**

Randy picked up Doctor Hinkle's autopsy report. "What's up?" His young deputy, Mike Perkins, asked.

"If you cut through the medical jargon, a woman, perhaps twenty one or twenty-two years old, had her throat cut so severely that she died instantaneously, or nearly instanta-neously, from loss of blood.  She was, we believe a prostitute by the way she was dressed and the rubbers and money in her handbag, but no one on the street seems to know her name or has any knowledge about her."

"Gee whiz," Mike breathed. "Do you have any idea of who killed her?"

"Nope. The old watchman heard noises and saw two people run away, but he was so befuddled with booze that he doesn't remember anything else."

"Gee whiz."

"Yeah. Gee whiz is right. Mike, I want you to gather a few of the ladies of the night and talk with them." He laughed at Mike's expression. "Yup, Mike, you're getting the best job today. I understand that a few of the girls have either gone missing, or moved away, or who-knows-what. We need to look into this and you'll be my chief prostitute investigator, OK?"

Mike stood up and saluted his chief. "Yessir! Gee whiz!"

~~~~~~~~~~~~~~~

They gathered around the wheelchair. He'd been able to swing himself out of the hospital bed, holding hard onto the strong arms of Alan and Neil, feeling his way, desperate and anxious to seat himself into the wheelchair without falling on the floor. There in the chair, sweat sprang to his face and he gulped in huge breaths, steeling himself for the ordeal that awaited him. Eunice and Michelle stood by his side, ready to dispense medical care or just to cheer him on, whatever was necessary and needed. The two women locked eyes. *God help Joe!*

Doctor Eneman and Doctor Patten came in, wheeling a table on which a draped shape rested. "My new foot?" Joe asked, with a smile.

"Your new foot." Jon Eneman patted the sheet and then whipped it off. "If you could see it, it would look mighty hand-some to you. Wanna feel it?"

"I want to meet it," Joe laughed. "You told me to name the foot. Well, Eunie and I spent about two hours with Bartlett's Familiar Quotations.,"

"Huh?" Alex Patten's eyes were wide. "Who?"

"Tell them, Eunice," Joe turned his sightless eyes towards her. Eunice chuckled softly.

"First, we tried lots of names…silly names, body-part names, and then, I had a brainstorm and thought of quota-tions. I ran to the office and borrowed Jud Knox's Bartlett's.

It's a book that's a compilation of lots of famous quotations. We looked up the word 'foot' and then read all of the quotations that were pertinent." She grinned and took Joe's hand.

"While you two talk, we'll fit your quotation onto your leg," Alex picked up the prosthesis, and bent to begin buckling it onto the stump of Joe's leg. "Just relax Joe. Don't worry this time about doing anything or even trying to help." Deftly, he unbuckled the straps.

Alan crouched down to help. "Tell us how you picked the right name, Joe."

"Well, we perused the book and then chose five quotations that seemed to suit the occasion." Joe began to tell the story, enjoying his audience's rapt attention. He barely seemed to notice that Jon and Alex were on the floor, strapping his leg and prosthesis together.

"Here are the four runners-up..." he looked towards Eunice. "Eunice, tell them. I can't quite remember..." His face was turned towards hers. If one didn't know, one might think that he was looking right at her.

"It might have been Quintus, from Quintus Ennius, who said, 'No one regards what is at his feet; we all gaze at the stars.'"

"Quintus, hey. I like Quintus," Alan slapped Joe's shoulder. "What's next?"

"The second one was Zapata...from Emilio Zapata, the famous Mexican, I think. He said, 'It is better to die on your feet than live on your knees.' Joe liked that one, but I thought it was rather defeatist." She began to giggle helplessly.

"Get it?" Joe asked, laughing. "De-feet-ist?"   Everyone groaned.

"The third," Eunice managed to stop giggling, "was Robert, from Robert Trail Spence Lowell of Boston, Massachusetts. He talked about a spider: "To get up on its feet and fly, it stretches out its feet...', but again, that wasn't the right one... too many feet there." She touched Joe's shoulder and they both chuckled. "Joe and I had a grand time doing this. We laughed for hours."

"OK,  OK." Joe held out his hands in front of him. The doctors had finished and the prosthesis was buckled on. The prosthesis was the best that the hospital had ever made. If one squinted one's eye, or looked at Joe from twenty feet away, one might not notice that his leg and foot was anything but perfect.

"The runner-up. So to speak, was Titus, from Titus Livicus. Old Titus almost won. He said: 'You cannot put the same shoe on every foot." She looked around. "What do you think?"

"Good one, but what's the winner?" Neil and Alan slipped their strong arms under Joe's and hauled him up on his feet. Or on his foot and the prosthesis.

"The winner and champion, my good and great friends," Joe announced, "is the great and profound Plutarch, who said so many wonderful things. This here foot is named for him now." He bent and patted the artificial limb. "I name thee Plutarch, for Plutarch once said, 'An old doting friend, with one foot already in the grave.' "

There was silence marred only by someone sucking in his or her breath sharply. "That's the ticket, Joe." Michelle held one hand out to him. Eunice took his other hand. "Come one step forward and let Plutarch meet two bee-yoo-ti-ful women. Two women who love you and him dearly."

And with the aid of Alan and Neil, with Alex Patten holding hard to Joe's backside, Joe and Plutarch took a step. A halting step, a step that nearly buckled, but…a step.

Joe was sweating with effort. His lip was nearly bitten through with his determination not to groan or cry out. His once-strong body was trembling, fighting to keep itself upright. *I must not cry. God, please, God, if you ever loved your servant, Joseph Martin, please let me not cry!*

"Great, Joe!" Alex nodded to his two corpsmen and, with ease, they swiveled Joe around so that his weight was on his one good foot. "Now sit back down on the bed, Joe. You've done marvelously today."

Joe held hard onto Michelle and Eunice's hands. He felt the wetness of their tears on his skin. "No!" He called out. "One more step. Plutarch is a stern task master. One more step, please."

And so, the brave man managed …somehow…to take one step further along his long, difficult road to recovery.

~~~~~~~~~~~~~~~

"Andrea! I must speak to you!" Candace McClosky, the USO committee chairwoman in charge of Junior Hostesses, put out her hand as a group of giggling girls entered the USO building. "Please come with me."

Andrea gulped, stopping abruptly just beyond the door. Her friends, bumped against her as they rushed in, stopping only to show their identification cards to the three women who checked incomers at the door. "What's the matter, Andrea?"

Andrea already knew what the matter was, and quaked. "Of course, Mrs. McClosky." Mrs. McClosky's corseted hips turned as she beckoned Andrea into the small office just off the entryway. Andrea glumly followed. *Rats! She'd been caught!*

"Please close the door, Andrea." Mrs. McClosky seated herself behind the desk and motioned Andrea to sit in the small chair. She looked hard at the young girl in front of her. She certainly was pretty, with dark hair curled into a soft pompadour. Her lipstick was painted on heavily, Mrs. McClosky noted, tsking to herself, and she looked like she wore heavy eye shadow. Not really becoming in such a young girl. No matter. No matter at all.

Andrea shifted in the uncomfortable chair with nervous apprehension. *Did the old bat really know anything? Had someone told on her?*

"Do you know why I have called you in here?"

Andrea squirmed. Should she try to lie her way out of this? "Um, no, Mrs. McClosky. I don't know what you mean." She bit at her bottom lip, opened her eyes wide and tried to look as innocent as she possibly could.

Candace McClosky had seen better innocent looks. She was no one's fool. Why did these girls think they could get away with this?

"Andrea. You were reported to me by several people. You have broken one of our most important rules."

Andrea jumped up, stung. "The rules are stupid!"

"They are not stupid. They are in place to protect you, to protect the USO and to protect the members of our Armed

Services. You know the rules. You broke them. Please hand over your identification badge." She held out her hand. "You can no longer be a junior hostess volunteer and can no longer come into the USO." Her hand was steady.

Andrea stomped her foot. "You...who do you think you are? You...you old bat! Just wait until my father hears about this! He'll....he'll...." She took the badge out of her pocket and flung it onto the desk. "You wait!" Tears of anger spurted from her eyes and the carefully applied make-up streaked and smudged on her face. "I'll fix you! You'd better watch out!" She turned and ran out of the office, slamming the door on her way.

Candace let out a sigh and slumped back in her chair. It could have been worse. Silly little flibberty-gibbet. She knew the rules. Knew what the punishment was. Junior hostesses were forbidden to date servicemen after USO hours. They were not to even tell the men where they lived, nor to meet them anywhere outside of the USO building. It was for their own safety. A man in uniform, going off to some foreign destination might tell a young girl anything...anything at all, even a pack of lies. Some men...well, they'd read the reports...some of them played on a teenager's innocence, leading the inexperienced girls into situations that could lead to tragedy. She shook her head in sorrow. Girls had been raped, injured and, in two cases in Florida, even murdered. Andrea was a bit too mature for her age. Too easy and too anxious to try to please men. The reports about her had come from several different sources, and each of them involved a different man. Silly girl. Constance got up, shut off the lights, and went back into the hall.

"Everything go all right?" Sabina Carter had been worried. She knew that Andrea had a temper and also was over-doted on by her father. "I saw her stomp out of here."

Constance placed Andrea's identification badge into the lock-box that sat on the table. "I think it went as well as it could. She never even asked me what the problem was. She never even offered any kind of excuse or explanation."

"It's a tough rule. Sometimes, I'm tempted to look the other way if the girl and the soldier seem to have made a real friendship and seem to truly care for one another."

"I know. It's hard on them. If the relationship is one based on mutual love and respect, well, then they can write to one another until such time as he gets leave. That way, the family and the girl can get to know the boy in time. I'm sure there have been many marriages that ultimately occur from these USO dances, but Andrea and her boyfriends aren't going to be sashaying up any aisle under my command!"

"If she keeps up her boy-crazy ways, she'll wind up in a real pickle. Her daddy gives her too much freedom and too much money and too little love and never pays her any real attention." Sabina nodded, envisioning some future misery for Andrea. "She needs some restraint."

"She needs a good whack across her bottom." Candace sat down and looked back at the gyrating and whirling dancers, doing a lively jitterbug out on the dance floor. "I'm glad she's not our responsibility any longer."

"Think her daddy will come and complain? Think she'll come back and try to burn down the building?" Sabina's worries were half in jest.

"No. I think he knows her. Poor child."

# CHAPTER THIRTEEN

**August 1943 – Determined Yugoslav patriots refuse to surrender to Nazis.**

They questioned the remaining suspects. "First the Charetts, Gladys and Augustus, also known as Mountain Man Aggie, then Posey McCardle, if she's back from wherever she was, then Fred Sullivan, and last, Floyd Jones."

"Were you able to find McCardle's mother up in Bangor?"

"Nope. We don't know Posey's maiden name. We tried Bangor and the whole of Aroostook County. We're interviewing a few of her neighbors again to see if anyone has any further information."

Horace sighed. "Who said detective work is exciting?"

"Not me," Randy agreed. "Slogging, repetitious stuff. Ah, well. Send in the clowns."

The Charetts came in together and sat side by side. Gladys, as thin as a stick of peppermint, and Aggie, as fat as a man could be.

"We asked you to come here to see if you can be of any help to us," Chief Parks began. "You were both at...oh, at least three of the fires...and we were hoping that together, you might have noticed someone who acted suspiciously... or maybe you saw something that we missed...?"

Gladys shrugged. She was attractive in a haggard, nervous way, with a luxurious mane of thick, glossy brown hair, worn pulled back in a heavy bun. Inga studied her, wondering at the marriage of two such differing people. Gladys' hands were beautiful, small and white and her fingers tipped with pale pink nails. The only jarring note came when she opened her mouth to speak. Her teeth were all crooked, stained and unsightly. Other than that, she was nearly perfect.

Her feet were dainty and shod in grey leather pumps. She was dressed neatly, almost elegantly in one of the smartest-looking house dresses Inga had ever seen. *She must have been beautiful when she was young, and maybe her teeth were better then. She's certainly very attractive now, except for those unfortunate teeth. Why didn't she go to a good dentist? What did she see in this lump of a husband?*

"We were passing the fires and saw the fire engines."

"I just like to watch when there's a fire," Augustus piped up. For such a huge man, his voice was high and twitty, like that of a bird.

"How did you feel?" Randy addressed his question to Augustus.

"Feel?"

"Mmmm." Randy nodded in encouragement. "Were you frightened or worried?"

Augustus tried to twist in his chair, attempting to look at his wife. The chair creaked in worried protest as more than three hundred pounds pressed against its slats and armrests. "Me? Worried. No." Horace saw sweat spring out on his forehead. Good grief! The man was enormous, with wobbly fat cheeks and an unhealthy red, blotchy complexion. Horace thought back. Aggie had never been this fat. Matter of fact, he'd been tall...always tall, but rather lean before his marriage. Can't be good for his heart, could it? All this lard to carry around?

"Of course, we felt very badly for those people trapped inside." Gladys tched, making a clicking sound of disapproval. "Poor things." Augustus nodded and even that small effort made the sweat pop out again.

Randy took out his cigarette pack and offered it first to Gladys and then to Augustus. Both refused. "We don't smoke," Gladys answered for the two of them.

"Well, we'd like you to go over each incident again. Talk to one another and see if you might have noticed something or someone…maybe, if you try hard, you might recall something that could assist us in catching this murderer."

"Murderer! My! I hadn't thought about it that way." Gladys stirred in her chair.

"Mmmm," Horace shook his head from side to side. "A sad and terrible thing. Imagine being trapped in all that flame and not being able to get out." Augustus again wiggled in his chair, shaking his massive head from side to side. *I wonder if the chair is going to break apart, right in front of us!*

With elaborate casualness, Horace asked, "How long have you two been married now? Two years? More? I know you're a local man, Augustus, but you, Mrs. Charett…where are you from?"

'We've been married for two and a half years," Gladys smiled affectionately at her husband. "We met at a grange meeting in South Paris. That's were I lived before."

"You born in South Paris?"

She suddenly looked uncomfortable. "No. No. I was born in Bangor. My mother and father were farmers up there. I married a man from South Paris. He…um…he, um…died a few years back and I was a widow. He worked in the chair factory."

Augustus grinned. Inga thought that his red, round face looked even more terrifying when he grinned. Almost as if it might explode. "I went to that grange meeting and ate her lemon meringue pie." He rubbed his prodigious belly. "My! Oh, my! That pie was the best thing I ever tasted." He grinned even more widely. "I ate the whole danged pie, all by myself and then I said: 'I gotta meet the lady who baked that pie!'" He reached out a pudgy hand toward Gladys and she smiled fondly at him. "Gladys is the best cook in the entire world!"

"Are you a good cook, Mrs. Charett?" Inga asked her. "What are your specialties?"

"Oh, I love to cook and Aggie simply loves to eat." She reached over and patted his arm. "My best dishes are dessert things…pies and cakes and cream buns."

"Oho! And don't you forget to tell them about your mashed potatoes. Why she makes the best mashed potatoes in the world, I tell you. Mmmm-mmmm!"

"I adore potatoes...what is your secret?"

Augustus' face seemed to gleam even more than before. "She puts heaps of butter and cream in them. Oh, boy!" His piggy sunk-in eyes glistened with the memory. "And her biscuits. Oh, Lordy, can she make good food!"

Randy and Horace glanced at one another. Inga seemed to be straying from arson to recipes. *Wonder why she's pursuing this line...?*

"I'd love to get some of your recipes, if you share them with strangers..." Inga leaned forward, her hands clasped.

"Why, I'd be honored. Just stop by anytime...you know where we live...right across the street from Frisbee's store... I'll copy out some of my favorites for you." She gave Inga a critical look. "Maybe you can put a little meat on your bones yourself if you try a few desserts now and then."

The Charetts left the office, Gladys leading and Augustus turning sideways so that he could get himself through the door.

The three investigators looked at each other and then burst into laughter. "My goodness! He is so *fat!* Does she stuff him like a Christmas goose?"

"He's almost splitting out of his skin! I'll bet she feeds him pork chops and gravy and those mashed potatoes for breakfast."

"And don't forget those biscuits!" Chief Parks groaned. "He's gonna die of a heart attack soon."

"Why do they call him Mountain Man Aggie?"

"You don't know your Maine geography, Inga. Mount Agamenticus, sometimes called Mount Aggie by the locals, is the highest peak around here. The biggest mountain. He used to be called Augustus...just Augustus. But since he ballooned up to be as big as a mountain, his nickname has evolved to refer to his immense size." They all laughed again. Mountain Man Aggie was such a funny name, but, they all reflected, also very suitable for such a huge mountain of a man.

Inga stopped laughing and looked thoughtful. "I wonder how the first Mr. Gladys died?"

"From a heart attack?" Randy was still guffawing. "A mashed-potato induced hearty attack?"

Inga shrugged. "Maybe he was insured for a lot of money? Maybe she marries them, feeds them to overflowing and then they die, leaving her a rich widow...?"

"Maybe that's not so funny, Inga. It's a little problem in the middle of this big problem. I think I'll set my deputy to do some investigating a few things up South Paris way. He's got an aunt that lives up there. She'll know any scuttlebutt.

"Death by overfeeding. Is there a law against that?" Inga asked.

"Seems like there ought to be, doesn't it?"

"Ooof! What a silly conversation we are all having here! Death by overfeeding! How droll How...shall I say....how American!"

~~~~~~~~~~~~~~

Joe worked hard. He quickly learned how to buckle Plutarch onto his stump, using his fingers and their new agility. It wasn't complicated. It just hurt like hell. It hurt when Plutarch was attached, it hurt when he tried to put his weight on Plutarch, and the stump ached and throbbed even after the implement was removed. Joe accepted the pain stoically. He'd conquer this, just as he'd conquered everything else in his life. Somehow.

Doctor Patten recommended that the prosthesis be used for an hour every morning and for an hour every afternoon. "Take it slow, Joe. The stump is still a bit raw and it will take a while for the callus to form. When it does, some of the pain will abate. Don't rush it."

Joe immediately put Plutarch back on after a half-hour of rest. Jack Harrington managed to stumble over to his bedside and cheered him on. "You're quite a man, Joe, my friend. You'll lick this thing yet."

Unknown to Joe, Eunice and Alan watched from the other side of the room. "He shouldn't rush this," Alan stepped forward to urge Joe to use moderation. "He's gonna mess himself up." Eunice put her hand out and stopped Alan.

"Let him decide what he wants to do himself. He's a big boy. He can make up his own mind about how much pain he can take."

Alan opened his mouth to disagree, then looked down at Eunice's face, naked in its feelings. He shrugged and closed his mouth. *What can you do with two people who are in love?* He asked himself. *Nothing.* He answered. He stepped away. The guy with the amputated arm was calling to him.

As Eunice watched, Joe pushed himself up, holding onto the rail of the bed and the back of his wheelchair. *His arms! Look at the muscles in his arms! How can he summon such strength?* She almost stepped forward to help him, but made herself stay back, biting at her lips in anxiety. She saw Jack Harrington also watching from the other side of the room. Jack made a face at her, then made an A-OK sign.

Joe reached out, grabbing hard at the rail. It was very hard, Eunice realized. He couldn't see the rail...couldn't see how far it extended. Yet, he couldn't let go to feel ahead of the grip that he had. He needed both hands to keep himself upright. She wanted more than anything to help him, and she knew enough, both as a nurse and as a woman in love, that to help him would ruin everything. She stayed where she was.

Joe shuffled his good leg forward, then hitched his hip up to move Plutarch. It was his undoing. He lost his precarious balance; wind-milled his arms for a moment, then crashed onto the floor. Eunice heard the loud, involuntary groan. A groan that came up from the depths of Joe's soul. She started forward and bent to him.

"Nice going, Plutarch," she tried to say the right thing. "Let's get you back up."

Joe's voice was harsh. "Leave me alone, Goddamit!"

*"Joe!"* She felt as if he'd slapped her.

"Get out of here, Eunice. I don't want you around."

"Joe! You're hurt and you need help."

"Get out! I mean it! I don't need your sympathy or your pity. Get away from me!"

Eunice slowly stood up, dropping her hands to her side. She gulped back her tears. Joe scrabbled on the ground, trying to fix the prosthesis, which had moved slightly from its fixed position of his stump. He was breathing heavily, trying to gather some of his composure, trying to keep some dignity. What he really wanted to do, however, was lie on the floor and howl. Howl his frustration, his despair, his helplessness.

Eunice bent back down, her face was inches from Joe's. She spoke in a whisper, so that no one but Joe could hear her. The whisper was a whiplash, aimed straight at Joe. "*Stop it*! Stop feeling so damn sorry for yourself! You're alive. You can laugh and cry and eventually, you'll be able to walk and get around like anyone else. So you can't see...who cares? Get over your self-pity! I'm tired of tiptoeing around your feelings...trying to watch every word I say so that I don't make you upset." Her voice rose higher and higher. Joe's eyes, so sightless, were wide open in astonishment. Was this really Eunice yelling at him? Eunice? His little mouse?

"Eunie," he croaked. "Eunie."

He heard her suck in her breath and begin to sob. "Eunice, forgive me." He scrabbled on the floor, trying to right himself. He heard footsteps and the sound of tapping. A strong arm, attached to a scratchy uniform, reached down to help.

Eunice looked up, gasping in astonishment at what she'd said and done. "Oh! Oh!"

"Let me give you a hand, soldier." The hand gripped him and pulled him up to a sitting position. Out of the corner of her eye, Eunice could see Alex Patten standing quietly behind them, watching.

"Who are you?" Joe's composure was returning. "What are you...?"

"I'm Admiral George Wood, Retired. I was last on a ship in World War One, so you know I am a very old sea-dog." The Admiral's voice was easy. "I'm here to talk with you about coming to work with me."

"Work?" Joe's voice was broken. "I can't see, Admiral Wood. How the hell...how...how can I work with you at any-thing?"

"You can manage the job I have in mind. I want you to be a teacher, Joe."

"A *teacher*? Are you nuts?" Joe's voice went up an octave.

The Admiral's voice was calm. "Oh, many people who teach are blind. It doesn't seem to be a problem to them. You can learn your way around the classroom. You'll learn to read Braille. You'll be a fine teacher."

"A *teacher*?" Joe was incredulous. "Me?" The Admiral heaved Joe up, as if he were a kitten, and set him at the foot of the bed. "Here's the rail of the bed." He positioned Joe's hands there. "Hold on tight and move your bad leg...that's right." He called back. "Alex! Come and fix the damn prosthesis, will you?"

Alex moved quickly, twisting the straps and buckles so that Plutarch once more held Joe's stump firmly. "How's that, Joe?"

"Its fine," Joe muttered, remembering what a scene he and Eunice had played out in front of everyone. "Fine."

"Good," Admiral Wood's voice boomed out. "Now get yourself back into your wheelchair or your bed so that we can talk. I need you and your skills right away. Most of the teachers... the men anyway...here in York have been conscripted. And a lot of the women are now doing war work. We need some good teachers and we need them now. I heard you have a good knowledge of *Bartlett's Famous Quotations*. Good! You can use that to start your classes. You'll be teaching boys and girls who are thirteen to fifteen. They'll love looking up quotations and if you run out of things to do, you can show them how you put your leg and foot on and off." He patted Joe's shoulder. "Now, where do you want to perch yourself while we talk?"

"In the wheelchair," Joe mumbled, astonished at what had happened in such a short period of time. "But, Sir...I can't *see! I'm blind!* You just don't *understand!* I can't....I never could..." Joe's sightless eyes zigzagged frantically, seeing nothing but his own frustration. "You can't hope to understand." Eunice took a step forward. But Doctor Patten motioned her back. Wide-eyed, she waited.

"Why can't I understand, son?" Admiral Wood's voice was soft.

"You're not blind!"

"What makes you think that?"

Joe's face crumpled. His sightless eyes glazed and his mouth dropped open in a caricature of a man who has been kicked. "You...? You...?" His head swiveled frantically, seeking the Admiral.

"I've been blind for more than twenty years, Joe. I lost my sight in France...I was on shore leave. We figured we were safe, but they tossed one of those mustard gas things at us.

Burned my skin and affected my eyes." He harrumphed and patted Joe's shoulder.

Joe's brain was churning. He opened his mouth, but couldn't think of one thing to utter. Admiral Wood seemed to understand. "My eyes were gone. I understand what you're going through, my lad. I went through it too. I was married, with two children, and I wondered how I could manage. I simply could not see how I could be a father, a husband, a sailor or a man anymore. I pretended that I was coping. Put a jolly face on, told everyone that I was going to be just fine. I fooled the Navy pill rollers, fooled the nurses, fooled almost everyone."

Joe found his voice. "What did you do?"

"Well, I figured that I was so smart. Smarter than anyone else. Ha! I began to save the pain pills they were giving me. Tucked them away, one by one. I planned, as soon as I collected enough of them, to swallow them all and kill myself. I figured that I was no good to anyone and that everyone would be better off without me. Hell, my wife was still beautiful... she'd find herself another husband in a heartbeat. My kids...well, they'd cope better with me gone than with me, a dumb palooka, stumbling around and helpless. I didn't know what else to do and coiling my lines seemed the best way out." He stopped for a moment and all, except for Joe, saw his grin.

"'Course I was feeling so sorry for myself, I wasn't thinking straight. I'd forgotten my wife and her female intuition." His voice was sheepish. *"She* knew. *Oh,* yes, she knew. She knew me inside and outside and upside down. She took one look at me that afternoon and nearly throttled me." He turned his head and waved his hand toward the group around Joe's wheelchair. "You, the young lady nurse. When you ripped into him...you kinda reminded me of my wife that day. Whew!" He wiped imaginary sweat from his brow. "She began soft, calling me every scurvy name. She escalated, little by little, reminding me of our life together and our love, dropping little pot shots at me about the kids, about my mother, about what a man I once was, before I got soft in the head with self-pity." He shook his head. "Ha! By the time she was at the end of her rant, she was screaming at me and we'd attracted the attention of several dozen very interested spectators. She turned me, and properly so, into jelly." He reached behind him, feeling for the edge of Joe's bed. He eased himself down.

Joe thought that if he'd been a dog, his ears would be pricked up. *I can hear what he's doing. I hear the slight shuffle of his feet, the touch of his hand on the sheets, the sound of him sitting down, and then, the little sigh of relief that escapes from his mouth as he takes the weight off his feet. He's older, this Admiral. I can hear it in his voice, and he gave me some clues when he talked about the old war. Maybe my ears will listen more. Maybe they can help me to cope. Maybe this is how I start this new life that I'm going to have.*

~~~~~~~~~~~~~~~

# THE USO AT
## THE CONNIE BEAN CENTER

*Presents*

# ANYTHING GOES

A musical comedy with Lyrics and Music by Cole Porter
Book by Guy Bolton, P.G. Wodehouse, Howard Lindsay & Russel Crouse

**FRIDAY and SATURDAY NIGHTS: September 3, 4, 17 and 18, 1943**

Tap your toes and sing along to such favorites as *I Get A Kick Out Of You, You're The Top, Friendship, Anything goes, It's DeLovely* and *Blow, Gabriel, Blow!*

### CAST

| | |
|---|---|
| Bonnie LaTour | Mary Jean Labbe |
| The Purser | Frank Accurso |
| The Captain | Burgess LeMonte |
| Sailor Luke/Sailor John | Dan Sargeant/Philip Perri |
| Reno Sweeney | Debbie Orloff |
| Hope Harcourt | Alexis Stein |
| Mrs. Wadsworth T. Harcourt | Lucy Daniel |
| Lord Evelyn Oakleigh | David Labbe |
| Elisha Whitney | Russell Merritt |
| Billy Croker | Alan Leone |
| Moonface Martin | Mario Sabatino |
| The Steward | Murphy Bush |
| Ling/Ching | Ruby Stevens/Maggie McCurdy |

Reno's Angels: Ursula Bondi, Helen Huntress, Michelle Johnson, Tami Keen, Cathy French, Gail Fletcher, Shirley DeToro, Mary Ann Caporale, Fedelia Loparco, Alice Wolfert., Ginny Vought, Harriet Grannick

DIRECTED BY: Julie Patten and Debbie Orloff
ASSISTANT DIRECTOR: Bonnie Dridi
SET DESIGN PRODUCED BY: Brenda Be

## Tickets on Sale at the Connie Bean Center USO
## $2.00/ticket
## Servicemen in Uniform $1.00/ticket

The hotly-contested slots for the musical had been filled and the cast was working nearly every night, rehearsing and rehearsing, listening to Julie's suggestions and Bonnie's criticisms. Tempers flared, shouting matches erupted and then, they all managed to laugh and rehearse some more.

The orchestra from Portsmouth High School, under the direction of Gerald Mack, accompanied them. "Those kids are really good!" Julie enthused. "I don't think the Philadelphia Philharmonic could do as well."

Brenda, with the assistance of the Portsmouth High School Art and Theater Departments, had constructed sets, gathered costumes, and practiced make-up. Brenda felt that the original show at Radio City Music Hall…"or wherever they played in New York"… hadn't been as professional.

They all discovered that Rabbi Fish had been hiding his show business talents under a bushel, or, in his case, under the yarmulke he wore on his curly hair.

"I had no idea that you had studied tap dancing!" Julie was astonished. "You're like…like…Fred Astaire!"

"Oh, I can do a mean time step," Rabbi Fish blushed. "Everyone is so talented and so eager. It's easy to teach them the dances and all." He hummed a few bars of "Let's Fall in Love" and did a jazzy time step ending in a kneel with hands thrown out wide. "Ta-DA!"

"Please, Mother of Mary," Bonnie Dridi prayed aloud. "Let at least a hundred people show up!"

Tickets – all of them – for the three hundred chairs that they could cram into the auditorium each night – were completely sold out for all performances in one week.

"We should'a charged three dollars!" Bonnie moaned. "We could'a made a lot more money!"

"Be happy that all the tickets are sold," Debbie Orloff scolded. "This might have been a disaster, if no one came."

"They'll be fighting for seats, "Bonnie averred stoutly. "Everyone will be here!"

~~~~~~~~~~~~~~~~~

"Are you nervous?" Grace asked Mario. "Will you forget your lines up there on that stage?" She, herself, could not even *think* of standing up on stage under the spotlight, never-mind singing and dancing and capering around.

"I'm fine." He laughed and rumpled her hair. "Maybe I'll give up my life as a gardener and nurseryman and run off to find my fame and fortune on Broadway."

"You'd better run very fast!" She kissed him and prayed that he wouldn't throw up in front of the audience.

*"Friendship! Friendship! Just a perfect blend-ship..."* Mario warbled, doing a buck-and-wing step. *"Ta-da-ta-dat!"*

~~~~~~~~~~~~~~~~~

Posey McCardle's whereabouts were still a mystery. "She never goes anywhere," her next-door neighbor averred, beginning to worry. "I hope she isn't sick or anything."

Chief Parks himself had enough to worry about. "If she doesn't rise up from wherever she's gone to by the week's end, we'll start to worry. Until then, let's just suppose she's taken a slow boat to China. Who's still out there this afternoon?"

Randy looked at his list. "Floyd Jones, janitor at the Shapleigh School and Fred Sullivan, the guy who pumps gas at the Esso station."

"Bring 'em in one at a time. Let's start with Jones."

Floyd Jones, wearing a greasy cap on his sparse hair, was a man who appeared as if he had just arisen from his slumbers, slouched in and took a seat without being asked. He slid the cap off and placed it on his lap, straightening it carefully. "Afternoon, gentlemen, and you, too, lady."

Chief Parks introduced him to Randy and Inga. Jones was affable, nodding and grinning. "How can I he'p you all with these terrible fires?"

Right to the point, huh. "There was a reporter and photographer at all of the fires..." Inga began...

"Yeah. Efficient young pup." Jones nodded in approval. "Spelled my name right an' all. I cut the article out and sent it to my brother in Florida."

"We're asking all of the onlookers that we know to help us," Inga continued. "Is there anything you noticed or anyone you saw who was acting strangely?"

"Shoot, Missus," Floyd nodded to her. "Them fires were raging. All of the people there...why, their eyes were glued to the houses."

"Nothing that you noticed that could help us?"

Floyd shrugged. "I saw a few people I knew. But they were watchin' the fire, just like me." He sat back and folded his hands. Inga noted that his hands were calloused and his nails were dirty. *Well, what do you expect?* She asked herself. *He works with his hands, cleaning up a school. Of course his hands are dirty!*

She didn't know what else to ask him and turned towards Randy. Randy offered him a cigarette. Floyd, just like Eustace, took two cigarettes, putting one into his pocket. He took out a large, nickel Zippo lighter and lit up. He pulled the heavy glass ashtray closer and puffed away, making some rings and watching Inga's fascination with them.

"Ya' like the smoke rings. It's easy to do. I'll show ya' if ya' want."

Inga laughed and shook her head, declining. Despite trying to stay non-judgmental, she found herself sort of liking this man. Astonishing.

"Are you married, Floyd?" She asked him.

"Ya! Married for forty-seven years. Five kids. Six grandbabies. I'm gonna retire next year and I think I'll go nuts with being bored. I mean, how much fishin' can you do? I tried to enlist again, but they threw me out. 'Yer too damned old,' they tole me." He looked disgusted. "I could'a done somethin', ya know. Taught some of them youngsters how to shoot...whatever. I'm still man enough to take a pot shot at one of them Heinies."

Randy stood up and shook Floyd's hand. "If you think of anything that might help us, please get in contact with Chief Parks."

Floyd walked out and Inga tried not to laugh. "He walks like a duck!"

"Ah, but did that duck light some fires...that is the question?"

Inga bit her lips and Randy thought that she bit her lips like no-one he'd ever seen before. "No," She shook her head. "He's too...too...ordinary."

Horace groaned and scratched his belly. "I'm tired of these interviews. I have no idea whatsoever if any of these people are anything but nosey and curious. Hell's bells, if I see a fire, I stop to look. Why did I ever think that stopping might be a crime?" He rubbed his chin. "You know, usually, I can tell if a man is lying. I've spent more years than I can remember studying human nature and doing interviews to catch liars. I watch their eyes, their facial expressions, their hands..."

"The hands are good indicators, always," Inga interjected. "Also feet. Did any of these people jiggle their feet?"

"Not that I can recall," Horace thought back. "One left, huh, and then just that lady who isn't home yet." He stood up for a moment and twisted his torso, first to the right and then to the left. "Let's finish up here. Who is left?"

"Fred Sullivan. Pumps gas at the Esso station in Kittery Point. Used to be the janitor at one of the Kittery schools. Kind of hefty with reddish hair. Limps."

"Let's get this over."

Had they not known that Fred Sullivan worked at the Esso station, they would have been so informed by the blue uniform shirt that he wore. Over the left pocket, in flowing white embroidery, the name *Fred* appeared. Underneath *Fred*, the words **Kittery Point Esso** were printed, but not in such elegant script.

Fred himself also walked like a duck, (*what is it with these people walking with their feet splayed out?* Inga wondered) with his feet, clad in heavy black work boots, turned out. He had a slight limp, favoring his left leg, which made his walk even more peculiar. Inga wondered if that was the way walking was taught in the United States. *Funny way to walk*, she thought. Then, as she scrutinized Fred, she decided that he *was* a rather peculiar-looking person. He was perhaps sixty or sixty-five years old, much too old to be in the Army. His face was round and pudding-like, with snapping dark eyes sunk into the folds of his cheekbones. He appeared nervous and his dark eyes shifted around the office, restless and settling nowhere. His hair was thick and bushy, fox-red in color, and he wore thick horned-rimmed glasses. His shoulders were rounded and powerful and his arms hung down on his sides...

*long arms for such short legs. He walks like a duck and moves like a chimpanzee.* He sat down at their request and immediately began to bite his fingernails. Inga noticed that they were unsightly...bitten to the quick. What was left of his nails was grimy and his hands were black with grease.

"What?" he said to her with surprising truculence, as he realized she was looking at his hands. "What's the matter? Never seen workingman hands before, lady?"

"I, uh..." Inga was discomfited. She hadn't meant to make him feel as if she were judging him and his state of neatness or, as it was, messiness. "I didn't mean...."

"Cut it out, Fred." Horace jumped in. "The lady is a doctor. She's here to help us find a killer. She's a professor, too and she's trained to notice things. Your hands are a mess...why didn't you have the decency to wash up before you came here?" Horace had done battle with the Freds of this world, and usually came out on top.

Fred blustered. "Hey, man! I didn't mean nuthin'. I was just...ya know...sometimes people think if you work with cars and car grease that you're a slob. I ain't no slob." He smiled with ingratiation at the three of them, but they all saw that the smile didn't reach his obelisk eyes. "I should'a washed my hands. I'm sorry." He raised his arm in the air and sniffed at his underarm. "I should'a taken a bath, too. I smell like grease and sweat."

Horace made a motion. "Forget all that, Fred. This is serious business here. We noticed that you, and quite a few others, were at two or more of the fires." Fred began to rear up from his seat, his black eyes angry. Horace held his hand up, as if to stop him. "And don't get up on that high horse again. No one is accusing you or any of them of anything. We just hope that you'll be able to help us out."

"Whaddaya mean?"

"Maybe you noticed someone who was acting suspicious...maybe someone who smelled of kerosene...we are trying to stop this person." Horace got up and walked around his desk. "Maybe you can assist us." He moved in front of Fred's chair and perched his backside on the desk top.

Somewhat mollified, Fred shrugged. "I didn't see anyone... I mean I saw a lot of people. Heck, there was Eustace

and Nellie and Big Aggie and…I donno…lots of others there."
He peered up at Horace from under thick, reddish brows.
"Didja ask them if they saw anything?"

"You're our next-to-the last interview. We've talked to them
all except, um, what's her name? Ah, yes, Posey McCardle.
Do you know her?"

Fred inserted his index finger into his ear and twisted it
around. Inga tried to look away. "Posey? Funny name, huh. I
don't know any Posey." He took his finger out of his ear,
inspected it, and then wiped it on his sleeve. Inga swallowed
thickly.

"Care for a Camel, Fred?" Randy leaned forward with the
pack of cigarettes.

"Don't care if I do…" Fred took the pack and tipped out
three cigarettes, stuck two in his shirt pocket. He patted his
pants, looking for a light… "Thought I had my lighter…" he
muttered. Randy passed the box of matches to him. He lit the
Camel, drew in a lungful of smoke, and then put the matchbox
into his pocket, too. Randy's eyes met Inga's and they shared
a silent moment of amusement.

"I'm a busy man." Fred jiggled on the seat. "What else do
ya' want to ask?"

"Chief? Any further questions?" Randy shook his head.
Horace pushed himself off the desktop. "Thank you, Fred. We
appreciate your time and please, if you think of
anything…anything at all that might help us, kindly stop into
the station to let us know."

"Sure. Sure." Fred's look was one of annoyance. "I'll do my
duty like a good soldier. You kin bet on that." He limped out,
giving them all one glance of mild malevolence as he shut the
door.

"Whew! Nice customer!" Randy's eyebrows climbed.

"Made me want to brush my teeth!" Inga joked. In truth, the
man had made her nervous. *I'd be afraid to meet him on a
street on a dark night. He'd scare me,* she thought. *Not a
duck, not a chimpanzee…maybe an alligator. Ungainly, lurch-
ing and dangerous if you turn your back.*

~~~~~~~~~~~~~~~~~~

Mike Perkins waited until nine in the evening to look for streetwalkers to interview. Mike was a relatively young man, and often looked at with suspicion, as he wasn't in military uniform. "Had tuberculosis when I was young," he told everyone. "My chest...they won't take me." It rankled him that he wasn't fighting. And yet, he was glad that he was safe here in the good old US of A. His job as a policeman was a relatively easy one. His doctor had insisted that he only be put on light-duty assignments, and Perkins was generally to be found on traffic duty or walking the beat.

Randy felt sorry for Mike. He understood what it felt like to not be a part of the war effort when one's outside appearance looked fit and normal. *I'm always explaining and explaining to people why I'm not in uniform. I'm sure that Mike is sick and tired of those disdainful looks and questioning glance, too.*

Mike stood on the platform at the Railroad Station. He watched as several women gathered, just before the evening train came in carrying uniformed personnel. He approached a group of three.

"Excuse me, ladies." He tapped the blonde on her shoulder. She jumped, took one look at Mike and groaned.

"Oh, jeez! It's a cop!" She was wearing a thin purple dress of some flimsy rayon material. She clutched her arms around herself. "I ain't doin' nothin' wrong, here. I'm waiting for my brother. He's comin' in for a visit."

The two women with her stepped back, trying to melt away. Mike waved his hand. "I'm not bothering you ladies. Yes, I am a policeman, but I'm not interested in what all of you are doing here. Honest."

The blonde peered closely at Mike's clean-shaven cheeks. *He's just a kid. Can I believe him that he's not gonna arrest me?* Mike's hands went up, palms out. "Honest, girls. I'm here to ask some questions about...well, about your friends or... um, other...the other girls. The ones who are missing.... We think one of you was murdered this week. Do you know anything about it?"

The three girls looked at one another. Mike noted the fear in their eyes.

*Can't be easy,* he thought, *being a prostitute and being questioned in any way, shape or form by a cop!*

He took a package of Lucky Strike Greens out of his pocket and offered it around, trying to ease their tensions. "Here, have a smoke. I just want to talk, girls. Honest." Two of the girls took cigarettes, and Mike lit them up.

"OK, I guess you know that a woman…a young woman… was killed here at the railroad station a few nights ago. She was dressed as if she was on the game," he managed to look as awkward as he felt, and the three women smiled at his discomfort. "She had no identification. only a pocketbook with some cigarettes and a packet of rubbers." Mike blushed. *Rubbers! Here I am, talking to a bunch of hookers about rubbers!* The blonde prostitute grinned, taking pity on him. She patted him on his arm and murmured something soothing. Mike relaxed and continued. "She was maybe twenty-two or so, dark hair, long and in a page-boy, dark eyes, slender build. She was wearing a pink sweater and a black skirt. Black high heels. She had a charm bracelet on her wrist. Six charms…an angel, a shamrock, a cross, a bird, a dollar sign and a round medallion with the letter 'L' on it. She had a long scar on her left arm and the doctor tells us that she'd had at least one abortion. Do any of you know who she was?"

The older of them, the peroxide blonde, narrowed her eyes. "I seen her around. She was new to the area. I think I heard someone call her Lena, or somethin' like that."

Mike was delighted. This was more than they knew. "Did she have any friends?"

"I donno." Blondie shrugged. "I just seen her around."

"She was eating at Tedesco's last week. She was with a mark. He was a sailor, I think," the shortest girl offered. "But I'm not sure she's the right person. Do you have, um, a picher of her?"

"I'll get one." There was a hoot from the engine of the incoming train. The three women looked at each other, nervous that Mike would keep them from earning their night's wages. "Look, Mike offered, "Let me get a picture and I'll bring it here tomorrow night."

"Ain't no train comin' in tomorrow."

"Where and when can I meet you then?"

"How about Tedesco's later tonight. Maybe around two."

"I usually am sleeping," Mike grinned. "Gotta get my beauty sleep, you know. But this is important. If someone killed one of the girls, we want to find out who. No matter who she was or what she does for a living," He smiled gently. "We want to catch these murderers."

With a lascivious giggle, the blonde reached up and stroked Mike's cheek. He jerked his head back, embarrassed. The blonde, enjoying his discomfort, reached up and kissed his cheek. "Baby, you are so cute, ya' know? You be at Tedesco's later and we'll all show you how much we appreciate you takin' such a *personal* interest in this case. We'll ask around, too. See if any other *ladies* have seen anything or know more about Lena, if that's who she is." The other girls giggled, blew kisses and waved to him as the train pulled in.

He watched them as they worked the crowd of servicemen. Within seconds, each of them had latched onto a uniform, and in moments, they and their new partners for the hour or so had vanished into the night.

~~~~~~~~~~~~~~~~~

He went to the station and got out the photos of the dead girl, including a blown-up one of the bracelet. The photos were grisly and it was difficult to find one that showed her face without showing the brutal damage that had been inflicted on her neck. He shrugged. These girls knew the streets. They weren't delicate hot-house daisies. A little gore wasn't going to bother them much.

He showed up at Tedesco's a little after midnight. There were two women sitting in a booth. Both appeared to be street girls. They were eating and watched him with wary eyes. None of his girls were there yet. He was hungry, sat at a table for four near the booth and asked for a cup of coffee and a menu.

The waiter, a fat man with a small toothbrush mustache, gave him a suspicious look. "Menu? We ain't got a menu. What we got is listed there." He gestured to a blackboard propped against the cash register. "We've got stew...great stew and you better be happy with it 'cause stew is hard to find, ya know, buddy."

"What else?" Mike's stomach roiled against stew at this hour.

"We got chili, hot dogs and chili *and* hot dogs," the waiter guffawed at his own joke. "We got sausages and beans an' grilled cheese sangwiches." He stood, waiting.

"That's it?"

"Yeah." The man gave out an impatient sound. "If ya want Chink food, go down the street. If ya want Wop food, go down the street." He shifted his feet. "Well? Whatcha want?"

"Bring me a grilled cheese on rye. And a pickle on the side." The man gave a brief nod and went into the back of the restaurant. Mike shifted in his seat, aware that the two women were obviously talking about him. He took out a copy of today's News and Bugle and lit up a cigarette.

The sandwich arrived. It looked worse than he thought it might, but he was hungry and began to eat. He wondered if the waiter had maybe spit on the cheese before he grilled it.

The door opened and Blondie came in. She saw Mike and grinned at him, blowing him a kiss. He blushed again and stood, holding a chair for her. Wide-eyed, she sat. "Hey, hey! You got good manners, sweetie pie." She sat down and whooshed out her breath. "Whoooo! I'm pooped!" Mike wondered if he ought to make some sort of comment. Nah.

"I brought some of the pictures for you to look at," he pulled out the photos. "They're pretty ugly. Are you sure you want to look at them?" He held them down on the table.

"Sweetie pie, I've seen it all. What makes ya' think I ain't seen dead people before?"

"You have? Where?"

"Ah, my father throttled my mother when I was nine years old. He was comin' for me next, but my brother Jimmy... Jimmy was eleven at the time...Jimmy hit him with a broom. My father was so surprised that he was stunned for a minnit. That gave Jimmy time to hit him again...and then again...until he beat my father to death too."

"Gee whiz!"

"Yeah, gee whiz. That's what I said, too." She laughed, not unkindly. "If you came from where I came from...the streets of Dorchester...you'd never be surprised at anything."

"What happened? I mean, what happened to you and Jimmy?"

"We wound up, together with my baby sister, Orna...we were all taken into the orphanage. They didn't charge Jimmy with anything after they heard what happened. They said he was just trying to protect Orna and me...and after all," she shrugged with the weight of the world on her shoulders, "he was."

"So you grew up in an orphanage," Mike thought of his own upbringing, with two loving parents who took care of him and adored him. "What was it like?"

"Jimmy ran away after a week. I tried to stay. I wanted to help Orna. But she got adopted. They...the nice people who came to orphanages to take babies home...they always took the cute blonde, blue-eyed babies. And Orna sure was a cutie. They never even looked at older girls like me, and boys like Jimmy were only picked to work for somebody who had a farm and no one to do the crap work."

Mike was flabbergasted at this glimpse into another kind of life. "So what did you do?"

"I tried, as I toldja', to stay. But they had this manager-guy there. Randy, his name was and he sure was just like his name!" She chuckled at her joke. "He was the kind that would stick his hand up your skirt and accidentally bump into your bazookas. A real prince. Anyway, I tole him if he touched me again, that I'd kill him."

"And then...?" Mike leaned over the table and touched her hand. *Golly,* he thought, *I don't even know what her name is!"*

"He tried to kiss me and grab me down there. I kicked him down there and he punched me." She looked down at the table as the waiter shuffled over and asked what she wanted. "I'll have franks and beans," she told him. "An' a cup of what you call coffee." He made a rude gesture and went away.

"I don't know why we eat here. Place is like a dump. I got sick the other night when I ate their damn stew. I think they use cat meat in it." She waved to the two women in the booth. "I think that's how they get so much meat when rationing is in force."

"Please....I don't even know your name...what is it?"

"Wanda. Wanda Farr." She looked at him with guileless blue eyes and burst into a guffaw at his astonished expression. "You baby, you. You ain't got any idea of the big, bad world out there, do you?"

"I thought I did. I thought I knew about what happens." Mike shrugged. "But, obviously, I am sadly lacking."

She laughed again. "Oh, you sweetie pie. You innocent child!"

"What happened to the man, Wanda." He tried out the name she gave him. He knew that it wasn't the name she'd been born with.

"Oh, he had an accident." She waved her hands in the air. "Whoops! He slipped on the stairs and broke his neck." She grinned at him. "The poor man just up and died. Do you believe me?"

"Did you...I mean....did you..., well, *did* you?"

"Me? Do you really wanna know if I pushed the bastard down the stairs?"

"Well, *did* you?"

"Oh, really, now. Would I...a little girl...do that?" She winked...a big, outrageous wink. "Yeah. I pushed him." She turned as the waiter placed her food and coffee in front of her. "Thanks, Al."

Mike's mouth fell open and he snapped it closed. *Could she have really killed a man? Could she?* He watched her take a huge bite of hot dog, chew it and swallow, her long-nailed hands holding the bun tightly. *Yeah. I think she could have done it easily.*

He was going to tell her, but at that moment, the other two girls came clacking noisily into the restaurant. Both looked exhausted, with blue-black circles under their eyes. "Hey, Wanda." They greeted her. "Hey, cop." They greeted him. The two girls in the booth overheard their greeting and snapped to attention.

"Ladies," Mike was relived that they had come in and interrupted. He really didn't want Wanda to confess anything to him. He might have to report it.

"Their names are Sharon...she's the tall one...and Patty...the half-pint." Wanda waved them to the table. Al, the waiter, appeared. Both girls ordered stew.

Mike placed the photos on the table, one by one. As hardened as these women were, they blinked back, looking at the ravaged corpse that had once been a vivacious young woman.

"Christ!" Patty gasped. "Somebody sure took that quiff for a ride! Her neck is sawed right through!" She looked up. "Is it that Lena?"

Wanda shrugged. "I think so." She took two of the pictures over to the booth and showed them to the girls there. They pointed to the bracelet and nodded.

Wanda beckoned Mike to come over. He was introduced, with a great deal of friendly joshing, to Magda and Sophie, two Polish girls. "Magda and Sophie think that's what her name was. They remember the bracelet."

Magda spoke. "She was new around here. Maybe been here for a week or so. I think she came in on a train from Chicago." She shrugged. "I don't know anything else."

"Was she living anywhere?" Magda shrugged again. "Who knows where anyone lives. A room, if you can afford it…then another room. We don't keep address books on ourselves."

"Anything else you can tell me about her?" Both girls shook their heads. Mike tried again. "Please ask around. We want to find her killers."

"How about Big Bess?" The girl named Sophie asked. "She ain't around any more, either."

"Who is Big Bess?"

"She was one of us. A big, jolly girl. Always laughing, always eating. She had a lot of meat on her bones…almost fat, ya know. Big legs, big maracas. The men loved her. She just upped and disappeared too." Wanda nodded and frowned thoughtfully.

"And there was that other girl…the one who could, what's the word, tie herself up in…" She snapped her finger. "A contortioner! A circus freak kind of woman! The johns just love contortionists! And dwarfs. For some reason, men just wanna be with a dwarf." She shrugged. "Who is to say? Anyway…the contortionist woman…don't remember her name…she was always here or at the Wop's after work. Loved to eat spaghetti. She ain't around anymore. What was her name?"

"Something exotic. Zenobia? Zeena? Something like that."

"Do any of you know these ladies' last names? Where they stayed? Where they came from?"

All of the girls shook their heads. "No, sweetie pie," Wanda answered for all of them. "We girls…us women of the night…we don't ask too many questions about one another. We're all the same…sad stories and we're now on the game.

We just know each other by our first name, or whatever name we're introduced by. That's enough for us. We don't really want to know anything more."

Mike thanked them and again, asked them to be on the lookout for anything that might help. He left his telephone number with all of them and assured them that he would keep an eye out for them and try to help them if they ran afoul of the law. "I won't let anyone hassle you. You're helping me and I promise to help you all I can." He called the waiter and paid all of their checks and left a minimum tip. *I would have done better, but he was a surly bastard*, Mike summed it up.

Wanda walked to the door with him. "You a cherry, Mike?"

"Huh?"

"You ever had a woman?" She ran her fingernail up his sleeve and he shivered. *Who the hell thought a prostitute would excite me like this?* Despite himself, he felt the pressure of an erection building. He blushed as she came closer and felt it too. "Nah. You're too much of a sweetie pie to have ever been naughty, right?"

"I, uh...I..." His voice was stuck.

"I'd be happy to, um..." she grinned and then licked her lips. "Give you a treat. You'll enjoy it, I promise. And I won't tell anyone." She winked at him, reached down and squeezed him. He gasped with shame and lust. *Should I? Who would know? Could I? She was a whore, for goodness sake!"*

"And there'd be no charge." She stroked him through his pants and he almost died. "No? Well," she relented. "Maybe next time." She winked at him and once again, stroked his soft cheek before she went back inside. He stood there for a moment, watching them all burst into laughter.

He stumbled back to the station, wondering if he'd been a chump or a wise man.

# CHAPTER FOURTEEN

**August 1943 – American soldiers and British volunteers on holiday gathered the largest harvest in Britain's history, thereby insuring food for the troops and civilians in the coming year.**

It was fun to work for Bertha, Mary Rose thought. Liberson's Bakery was laid out differently, and she had to watch what she was doing to be sure that she didn't violate any of the Jewish dietary laws, but all-in-all, it was interesting and a good learning experience. *I'll be all set if someone orders bagels or bialys, she mused. And that bar mitzvah cake, the customer was so pleased with it! I'd never mentioned that I decorated it. Let Bertha take all the credit.*

"The building was really old," Mary Rose told Uncle Mario. "That part of Portsmouth goes way back to the days of sailing ships. The buildings are old brick and cold as a tomb. I had to go down to her cellar several times. What a creepy place! All drippy with moisture and cobwebs." She shuddered. "I was actually frightened when I was down there. Seemed like there were shadows and sounds."

"Who-hoo-hoo" Mario groaned theatrically. "Maybe there are ghosts in those old cellars."

"I swear, I heard groans and screams," Mary Rose shivered again. "Odd sounds. It was, um, well, *though*tful, to be down there. Like that Christmas Carol…you know, locked in a stone-cold tomb!"

"Brrr!" Mario made a face and hooked his hands into talons, hoping that he looked like a scary ghost.

Mary Rose laughed at him. "You don't look scary! You look like Moonface Martin, Public Enemy Number Thirteen!"

~~~~~~~~~~~~~

At York Hospital, Jack Harrington's injuries were mending rapidly. Although he'd never be able to go back into battle, his steps were firmer and the dizziness and vertigo that had accompanied him since he'd been wounded, had dissipated. Naturally, a great component in his recovery was attributed to Yashiko Kobiache's tender and effective ministrations.

"Here are my mother and father to visit you, Jack," she told him one day. "They now live nearby. When the roundup came for *Nisi*, they pretended to be full-blooded Hawaiians and went to the Eastern states, where there was not so much prejudice." Jack stood up carefully, holding onto his cane, as Yashiko's parents bowed their way through the ward to the spot by the window where he liked to sit, watching the lobster boats in York Harbor.

They greeted one another and Jack noted the way that Yashiko's parents watched him. *Perhaps they are wondering if a white man can love their daughter in the way that they'd hoped.* He wanted very much to assure them that he could…and more…but the time was too early. He merely held Yashiko's hand for a moment longer than necessary, and saw that Mrs. Kobiache had certainly noticed. She shyly glanced at him and gave him the smallest of nods. He grinned and his heart expanded. *Perhaps it would be all right. Perhaps.*

When they had lived in Hawaii, and before the war had broken out, Mr. Kobiache had been employed by Hawaii's biggest sports retail store, *Aloha.*

"I have now a new job, here in Maine in Freeport," he pointed north, "perhaps one half hour away from here, in a big new store called by the name of L.L. Bean."

"That's a funny name." Jack was determined to be as polite and interested in anything any of the Kobiaches were up to. "What do they sell there?"

"They sell boots, mostly. Leather boots that are guaranteed to be waterproof and also guaranteed never to wear out." Mr. Kobiache stuck out his foot. On it was a high-topped boot with a rubberized bottom and a leather top. "Right now, the company is making these kinds of boots for the soldiers who are fighting in the Pacific, to keep their feet dry in the mud." He waggled his foot. "They are sending all the boots to the Army. When the war is over, they will again make these boots for those who hunt or hike in the mountains. This company, named for Mr. L.L. Bean, who works in the shop right next to his lowest employee, also plans to sell hunting and fishing clothing and equipment. Mr. Bean, whom I think is a smart and frugal man, thinks that when the war is over, the soldiers will come home and want to fish and to hunt and do peaceful things. He thinks the company will thrive."

"And what do you think?" Jack had a reason for asking.

"I will follow Mr. Bean. I think he will lead me in the right direction."

"And what is it that you do there, Mr. Kobiache?"

"I am his man who pays the bills." Mr. Kobiache bowed toward Jack. "He calls me his Money Man. He says that I am inscrutable. I think he means that as a compliment." His eyes twinkled.

~~~~~~~~~~~~~

At the other side of the ward, Joe Martin was progressing over the torture of walking with his prosthesis, Plutarch. Since his outburst and tumble, and with the encouragement of all who cared for him and the assistance of Admiral Wood, Joe was now working one day a week at the York High School.

He taught English, and had been given carte-blanche for the time being, to teach it any way he saw fit. He had two classes, eight girls and six boys in each class. In the older group, the children were fourteen and fifteen years old and in the younger class, the children were thirteen years old. All of the boys were jumping out of their skins to get into the war.

They felt that Joe was a hero…someone they could look up to… and the classes, each of which ran for two hours were lively and informational. The girls all thought that Joe was the dreamiest, handsomest man they had ever seen.

"He's like a movie star! Like Lionel Barrymore or Robert Taylor. Remember, in *Dark Victory* how Robert lost his sight and then it was all fixed up when a new medicine was discovered? Remember how he looked when he opened his eyes…ohmygoodness! I was crying and praying! And then he saw Mary Astor for the first time! I thought I'd die! Ohmygoodness!"

"I know! I dream of him. I want to be a nurse now, so that I can help soldiers who are blind!"

"I'd dedicate my life to him!"

Little did these teenaged girls know that there was a real nurse who also dreamed those kind of dreams about Joe. But, somehow, even in the best of her dreams, Eunice never really believed that Joe would ever be able to see. And that he'd never marry her or even declare any feelings for her as long as he was blind. And then, in the early dark hours before the dawn, Eunice faced that fact that Joe thought …in his inability to see anything … that she was pretty. And if he ever was able to see, he'd be so disappointed in the way she really looked that he'd never be able to hide his thoughts.

*He'd be polite, oh yes. He'd never actually say anything, but I'd see it in his eyes, should he be able to see me, that I wasn't…quite…what he thought I'd be. He'd let me down easy-like, but he'd turn his attention to someone who was really beautiful, like Carol or Michelle or those other nurses that I see making goo-goo eyes at him, even though he can't see them.*

And, as the dawn broke and she wearily climbed out of her bed, she wiped the tears away. It would never do to have anyone…*any*one…know what she was feeling.

~~~~~~~~~~~~~~

At the Yard, Trisha and Scott were bound together by many things; their pride in the submarines that came down the ways of the Shipyard, faster and faster, each week breaking a new efficiency record, seeing President Roosevelt and shaking his hand when he visited the Yard to praise all of the workers, and their growing feelings for one another.

In late 1943, the Shipyard workers were justified in their pride. Submarines were being churned out there faster than at any other shipyard in the United States. The subs and their crews were more comfortable and rested than any other crews, thanks in whole to Trisha's innovative ideas for making the common, cooking and sleeping areas of her subs better and better. Her efforts won her a special commendation, which pleased her mightily. Her pleasure and pride in the commendation was heightened with the knowledge that the request for the commendation had been sent to the President directly by the men of the crews of the submarines she had designed.

There was the *S. S. Balao*. She conducted ten war patrols in the Pacific and sank over 32,000 tons of Japanese shipping, and received nine battle stars. And the *S. S. Pintado*, named for a Spanish mackerel, and guided by Chief-of-the-Boat, Gary Hildreth, which sank six Japanese ships with six torpedoes in one day. Or the *S.S. Pollack*, which conducted eleven patrols and received ten battle stars. Or the *USS Sand Lance*. The *Sand Lance* also sent six torpedoes speeding toward six Japanese boats and also sank all of them, then spent the next sixteen hours dodging barrages of more than 100 depth charges. Or the *USS Ronquil*, who, during her fourth patrol, rescued ten aviators from certain death in the choppy seas.

Indeed, these were worrisome days. The war was raging, but Trisha and Scott were certain that the Allies would prevail, and prevail, in part, because of the work done in the Kittery and Portsmouth area by the men and women who worked at the Portsmouth Naval Shipyard.

Trisha had taught Scott the pleasure of long-distance running. Every chance they got, they'd take Hannah, who by now had grown to be a huge, larruping dog, and run from Trisha's house to Seapoint Beach. If the day was fine and they felt ambitious, they'd continue, down through the marshes, past Eustace's shack and the ruins of the burned out dwelling, to the edge of the wall that looked out over the ocean. There, they'd rest, Trisha and Scott sitting on the wall, and Hannah, her tongue hanging out, all drinking cold water in small sips, resting for the return journey.

"I like to think that one day, we'll be sitting here and we'll see one of our submarines come steaming home."

"Wouldn't that be marvelous! Oh, Scott, do you think this war will ever be over?"

"Of course! We're winning, little by little."

"I worry so. What if we don't win?"

"We will, honey. We will." *And when we do, my darling,* he whispered inside his head, *you and I will be able to get married and live happily, in peace. Forevermore.*

They sat on the wall, holding hands, until Hannah began to frisk around, biting at their hands, raring to be running again. "Ok, Hannah-boo, let's go!" Tricia jumped up, held her hand out to Scott, and then they were all off, flying down the marshy path toward Eustace's shack. "Let's stop and talk with Eustace," she yelled and Scott, breathing in the strange manner advocated by Mrs. Genevra Davis, nodded without speaking.

There was no wagon outside Eustace's shack and the place looked lonely and empty. The wind had picked up and seemed to burn through the shabby edifice, making a mournful whistle. "Guess he's not here," Scott said.

'We'll stop and see him next time," Tricia was dancing up and down, trotting in place, keeping her pace and heart-rate going. "Let's go home and take a hot bath. Mrs. Genevra Davis suggests a hot bath after strenuous exercise."

Scott wiggled his ears and grinned lasciviously. "Sure 'nuf!" and they ran on, Hannah's tail, thick and strong, doing circles in the air.

~~~~~~~~~~~~~

Randy, dragging the still sleepy Mike, drove over to Kittery. "Got your message, Horace. What happened?"

"Another fire. Come on." They joined Aaron waiting in the police car. "The fire's at one of the stores in Kittery Foreside. We got lucky this time. A neighbor smelled smoke and called the fire department. Those guys are good. They hustled right over and were able to put out the blaze before it did too much damage. No one hurt or killed."

"Was there a badge left at the scene?"

"We'll see." They pulled up to a small commercial area with buildings stacked against one another. The still-smoldering building was at the end, just off the cliff that dropped to the Piscataqua Harbor. The night was lit up with the acetylene lamps on the fire truck, some torches and the still-bright embers of the conflagration.

"Hey! Chief O'Brien!" Horace yelled at a tall, yellow-slickered man, holding the end of a hose. "Hey!" O'Brien turned and waved, then handed the hose to one of the firemen. He came over, wet and disheveled, his grin a slash of white teeth in his grimed face.

"Nice of you to drop in, Horace." He doffed his helmet. "Where the hell were you when the fun was going on?'"

"What happened?"

"We got a call. Lady smelled smoke. I understand that she was the local busybody. Thank the Lord for busybodies…she saved the lives of the two men who were asleep in the first floor apartment."

"Set by our torch?"

"Yeah. His style was everywhere. Kerosene splashed on the foundation and one of my men found this on the concrete walk." He handed over the tin star, wrapped in a waxed paper bag. "We didn't touch it. Man must think he's Hopalong Cassidy, what?"

"He usually wipes any prints off, but…maybe this time he forgot. Thanks, Chief. We sure got lucky this time." Horace hefted the bag. "I wonder if this…nobody hurt or killed… will make him angry."

"What do you think he'll do now?" Randy shook his head, surveying the devastation. "Lucky…shoot…you were *really* lucky! Look how close all of these buildings are. If that fire had burned a little more, it would have jumped right along. Maybe burned down the whole block.'

"I think our man…or woman….will be mighty annoyed." Horace rubbed his face. "Mighty annoyed."

~~~~~~~~~~~~~~

The night train pulled out of the station, after dropping off sixty-seven sailors. There to meet them was a bus that was going directly to the Shipyard, and thirty prostitutes who hoped that the submariners might take a little detour *before* going back to the Yard. They'd try their best, anyway.

The girls surveyed the group, picked out their marks, gathered them up and, two by two, began to walk away from the station towards the town and the rooms that they used by the hour. The crowd began to disperse until the station was nearly deserted, except for one buxom street girl, who had haggled too long with her would-be customer. They'd been unable to come to terms and he finally stomped away, thinking that he'd save his energy and money for the pool hall instead of a quick bonk.

She looked around at the empty platform. Empty, it suddenly frightened her. Dark shadows loomed and shapes of carriages and carts took on a sinister meaning. *Could someone be lurking behind that cart? Did that shadow move?*
Scared and nervous, she clutched her cardigan close to her and started to walk quickly back to where the crowds would give her the illusion of safety.

There was a noise, a sound of muffled footsteps. She called out, "Who is there? Who is it?" Her voice was thready and high with fright.

Behind the large cart, two men stood, waiting patiently until she passed the end of the lighted area. She'd be around the corner in a moment. Her footsteps clicked closer and closer. One of the men took a rope from his pocket. The other held a glittering knife. The footsteps were almost upon them...

"Hey! Hey, cutie!" A slurred voice called out. "Whatcha doon? You all alone?" She looked over her shoulder and saw a sailor, weaving towards her, waving his duffle bag. "I forgot my stuff and came back!" he announced cheerfully. "Had a quick beer and forgot to get my things!" He lurched toward her. "How 'bout you an' me, cutie. We go have a little fun, huh?"

He was already drunk, she figured. It wouldn't take too long. She turned away from the dark shadows of the cart, wheeling to link her arm with the sailor's. "Sure, honey-man. I was waiting for you."

"An' I was waitin' for *you!*" He laughed loudly and allowed her to guide him back to her room and the transient delights of her soft, warm bed and her soft, warm body.

The dark shadows were angry. The night and a drunken sailor had snatched their prey away from them. Annoyed beyond belief and worried at what their boss would say about the mishap, they slunk back from whence they came.

~~~~~~~~~~~~~

"She's not just some street girl, she's a respected member of The Hess Club!" Kathie was almost in tears, worried and distraught. "You've got to do something about this!" She pounded her fist on Randy's desk. "I heard that prostitutes have been going missing from around town. I heard that one woman was found dead at the railroad station. I'm worried sick about where Gloria-Ann has disappeared to...she'd *never* go anywhere and leave her little girl behind! Never!"

Randy assured Kathie that they would put all of their energies on the case. "Can you tell me about her? Describe her and tell me what she was wearing?

"She's about thirty. Very beautiful with long, dark hair. She wears it very straight, down over her shoulders, sort of like Myrna Loy. She has a pale complexion and green eyes. Slender. She went to the railroad station to meet her sister, Patricia. Patricia was coming for a visit on the ten o'clock train in from Boston. Gloria-Ann was wearing a violet colored suit, with a darker purple scarf. She had purple high heels on, and carried a purple handbag. Here..." Kathie delved into her own handbag and pulled out a photo. "Here is a recent picture of her."

Randy took the photo and looked at a beautiful woman, dressed in an obviously expensive gown, standing in front of an ornate fireplace in a museum or mansion. "She is lovely," he said. "Where was this taken?"

"At the Club." Randy had never been into the Club. *Never been, but today, I'll be doing an investigation in a fancy whorehouse. This job never fails to amaze me.*

"Tell me more. How long has she worked for you? Where did she come from and does she have...oh, yes, you said she has a sister and a daughter....tell me more..."

"Her name...well, the name she said was hers...is Gloria-Ann St. Claire. I have no idea of whether that's her real name or not. You'll have to ask her sister. Her sister's name is Patricia Fundy, but I think the sister is married. Gloria-Ann came to me from another house in Baltimore. I think she'd been there for a few years. She wanted to move closer to her sister. Her sister lives just outside of Boston. She's been with me since....oh, maybe 1933 or 1934. She's reliable, honest, sensible, well-liked by the customers and the other girls. About 4 years ago, she had a baby. The baby, Shirley, resides at the school that I own...a boarding school here in Portsmouth." Randy raised his eyebrows. He thought he was well-informed about the goings-on in the city, but this was news to him. *What school?*

"That little girl is the love of her life. Gloria-Ann would never leave her alone for a moment! Something bad has happened!" Kathie twisted her hands together. "I know it in my bones!"

Randy handed the photo to the desk sergeant and asked him to make copies and pass them around. "I'm going to The Hess Club with Mrs. Hess." He ushered Kathie out to the very interested stare of every single person in the police station.

He was stunned at the magnificence of the Club. Patricia was seated in the dining room, with a cup of coffee at her side. She was agitated, worried and nervous. He watched her for a moment. Patricia Fundy was a tall and statuesque woman in her late thirties. She was very attractive, but just missed being as beautiful as her sister. Her hair, too, was long and dark, but she wore it upswept. "I'm worried, Chief Stuart. You don't know my sister. She's....well, you don't want to judge her by her profession. Underneath all of that, she's a good woman and she loves little Shirley more than the life itself."

"Is St. Claire your sister's real name?"

"No. She changed her name because she thought St. Claire sounded more refined."

"More refined than what?"

She gave him an amused look. "More refined than Klopberger."

"Hmmm. I can see that." Randy allowed himself to smile. "Can we go to visit the little girl? Perhaps her mother told her something about where she could be..."

Kathie walked with them down the street and turned the corner, then went two blocks south to a large white edifice, surrounded by a high iron fence. A discreet sign told them that this was the premises of The Portsmouth Academy for Children. A Private School. Admittance by Appointment Only.

Kathie rang the bell and then opened the door herself. They were in a spacious lobby. Two staircases ran up, one at each side of the end of the hall. There was the smell of chalk and good cooking. From behind the closed doors, Randy could hear the voices of children, some singing, and some chanting lessons.

An attractive woman, wearing a business-suit, greeted them. "Nancy, this is Police Chief Stuart...Chief Stuart, this is Nancy Grossman, who runs this school with her husband, John." Randy shook Mrs. Grossman's hand and received a pleasant and professional smile in return. *She's already heard the news,* Randy thought. *She's been waiting for us.*

"Nancy, you already know Patricia, Gloria-Ann's sister." The two women nodded to one another.

"Any news?" Nancy asked. The trio shook their heads in unison. "Oh, dear. I was hoping that something would have come up..." She sighed. "Come into my office and we can talk there. John is bringing us some coffee." She led them to a sunny and spacious room at the front of the hall. The room was decorated with children's drawings and colorful cut-outs of butterflies, birds and animals. *If I had any kids, this would be a great place to send them,* Randy mused. *I wonder how much they charge to have a child attend this little school building?*

"Is this school expensive?" He just had to ask. Kathie and Mrs Grossman looked at him.

"Is that something you need to know for this investigation?" Kathie's voice was cold.

"Nope." Randy grinned. "I'm just a nosey man. One never knows what's valuable information and what's fluff. But, If I wonder, I've just gotta ask." His cheery answer took the venom out of the question. Kathie shrugged. What did it matter what he asked? The important thing was to find Gloria-Ann and quickly.

Kathie relented. "It is very expensive. We have twenty-two pupils and run classes from childhood to eighth grade. Some of the pupils are the children of my employees. Some are from families in and around the Portsmouth area. John and Nancy are extremely qualified teachers – they are also very successful publishers of books – we are very fortunate to have them working with our children – *and* we have a list of private families who are extremely anxious to get their children into this school."

"Is it a day school?"

"No. The children board here. It is convenient for my employees and very convenient for the ambassadorial families...the government families from foreign soil...who leave their children in our care."

*I have been put in my place,* Randy realized. *Ambassadorial!*

"I see."

The door opened and a large, affable man wheeled in a trolley with the implements for a lavish morning repast. Randy was introduced to John Grossman and liked what he saw. These kids were being very well taken care of. Certainly, there was a lavish amount of money being spent here, but, obviously, it was being spent well. He wondered what he might have done differently with his life had he been taught at a school like this. *I might have been President*, he laughed to himself. *Nah, who wants to be President? The life of a Chief of Police was easy compared to what poor old Mr. Roosevelt had to deal with. Less stress, more fun.*

After a quick cup of coffee, Randy asked to speak with Shirley St. Claire. "You can stay with her," he turned to Patricia. "And you, too, Mrs. Grossman. I promise not to upset the child."

"Come with me." Nancy rose.

Kathie said she'd wait there with John. "You don't need poor Shirley all crowded with grownups."

The child was a tiny wisp. Blue-black hair, curly as a little lamb, dark eyes. *She'll be a beauty, like her mother,* Randy observed. *I wonder who the Daddy is? Should I ask?*

Patricia hugged the little girl and Shirley returned the hug. Obviously, Auntie Patricia was someone who visited often. Patricia asked a few questions, but the little girl had no knowledge at all of where her mother might be. Patricia patted Shirley's head and kissed her, then Nancy Grossman led the child back to her classroom.

"Is there any significance in who the girl's father is? I ask," Randy put up his hand before Patricia objected, "because it may have some bearing on Gloria-Ann's disappearance." He shrugged. "Maybe a vendetta against the father. Maybe abduction for money. We just need to know everything. Nothing that isn't directly meaningful to the case will ever be publicized. I promise you."

Patricia sighed. "Well," she drew the word out. "It might have some bearing, although I don't really see…" She rubbed her chin and then nodded her head, coming to realize that all avenues had to be explored. "Her father is a banker and financier in Boston. His name is John Peabody, and yes, he is married and has a family that knows nothing at all about Shirley, Gloria-Ann or anything like that. He has been, uh, a friend, uh, of Gloria-Ann's for several years now. He knows that he has a daughter. He has provided for her for the rest of her life. For her education, for her perhaps setting up a business and purchasing a home. He is very, very wealthy and is very, very generous, both to Shirley and Gloria-Ann. Maybe it is because he cannot be…cannot ever be…publicly in their lives. He's a man who has both business and personal dealings with senators and corporate presidents. He sits on the boards of many corporations and hospitals. He is generous, as I said, extremely generous and supports them fully, but I don't think, apart from myself and my husband and Kathie Hess, that anyone else knows of the relationship. Not even the Grossmans have any knowledge of this. I just don't see how..." She bit her lip. "But if it helps to get Gloria-Ann back....well. Now you know."

*Now I know. But what do I know? Nothing at all, that's what.*

~~~~~~~~~~~~~~

The USO Victory Gardens were springing up all over the seacoast region. People were putting them in their backyards, their side yards and even in their front yards. Schoolchildren dug gardens on the sunny side of the schoolyard, businesses donated a patch of land to their employees, and the employees grew corn and tomatoes and some of the unusual vegetables that Mario and Grace Sabatino suggested. The Sabatino's garden shop was constantly crowded with customers buying vegetable plants, talking knowledgeably about seed selection and manure, and seeking advice. The Sabatinos coffers were bulging with the fruit of their vegetables, as Mario was wont to say several times a day, making sure you understood the cleverness of his pun.

The whole community supported the gardens. The elderly commandeered plots in some parks, mimicking England's allotments, places that they could walk to, spend a few hours tilling their crops, then sit on an old chair and talk to one another. About the good old days and who was where overseas. America was at war, growing vegetables.

The only unhappy member of the Sabatino family was Andy. All this vegetable growing, not to mention bundling up the lumber for raised beds, the fencing and the plants themselves...all this work cut radically into his baseball time. The only good thing, Andy grumbled to himself, was that he was so busy that his mother forgot to yell at him for not cutting the *buddleias* and the old, sharp canes.

~~~~~~~~~~~~~~

Brenda's success in starting a jazz band had reached the ears of Commander George Ragusa, the man who was at the head of the Portsmouth Naval Prison. He asked her, together with Scott Wanner, to meet him at the prison. "I want to talk to you about starting some programs with some of the more progressive prisons. The ones who agree with me that some prisoners can be rehabilitated. They've told me that there are a lot of prisoners who are, or want to be, musicians who love Jazz, and also a group of avid chess players. I want you two to give me three hours once a week to help these prisoners get ready for their transitions back to Navy life."

"How will jazz help them?" Brenda didn't really want to give up one night a week.

"And what will chess do to make them better?" Scott felt that he was involved enough with the Shipyard. His nights were precious.

"Anything that they get themselves interested in can build character...give them something to think about other than work duty and sitting in their cells. These are my best prisoners, many of them in here because of some quirk of circumstance. All of them are up for review for a release back into the Navy. This would erase the record of their imprisonment and give them a good chance to go back to defending our country, and maybe an extra boost to their morale ... they'd have something to brag about...when they are finally out. What do you say?"

Brenda looked at Scott, who shrugged. "What else can I say? You'll probably put me in the brig if I don't agree. All right. I'll try."

The prisoners, sixteen of them, named their jazz band "Brenda's Beboppers." Scott's chess players, twelve of them, ranged from beginners to a few who could whip Scott's own chess-playing efforts blindfolded.

Brenda called all of her friends and begged for the donation of used instruments. "These fellows have no resources. We need a few trumpets, maybe a set of drums, and any kind of wind instruments you can find in your attics. You can also just give me a donation, but I'd rather have the instruments. Even if we had the money, musical instruments are in very short supply, as the war has taken all of the brass and chromium that's available. Your money can buy them uniforms, though...Come on, dig deep and outfit my band!"

The band practiced with Brenda on Tuesday nights. It was supposed to be for three hours, but, with the cooperation of

Commander Ragusa, the sessions often stretched until mid-night.  Paul Krueger, on trombone, in prison for running an illegal gambling ring, was loud in his praise of Brenda. "She's taught me a lot. She's a real go-getter. Never let's me slack for one moment.  I never thought I'd be interested in jazz again, but now, I think I'll take some lessons after I get out. Maybe get a job with a band at night." He laughed. "For now, I'm behaving myself, trying hard to rack up all the points and stars that I need to get out of here. I've learned my lesson and I bless Brenda and Commander Ragusa for giving me back my life."

The jazz band had been given a very unusual offer...Brenda had convinced the powers-to-be to let them play in the upcoming USO Show. Brenda swore that she'd watch them like a hawk. "They'll never let me down, I know these guys." She swore.

"Brenda's all right," the men agreed. "We wouldn't mess around with her. And we won't take advantage of being out for the night. Shit! We're all less than a few month's away from being able to get back in the fighting. Every man here wants to beat those Krauts and Japs. No one is going to mess up this opportunity."

"I sure hope I'm not going to be sorry," the Warden prayed. "I'll lose every medal I have if they mess up."

"We'll be good!" The men chorused. Brenda cemented their promise by kissing the Warden on his cheek. The men howled their approval and Warden Ragusa blushed and won-dered if he'd mention the kiss to his wife.

Two of Scott's pupils had asked to enter the New England Chess Competition, which was to be held in mid-September in Providence, Rhode Island. These two men, Nick Catanzaro and Lloyd Williams, were three months away from release, barring any unfortunate incidents. Commander Ragusa was hopeful that he could get permission to let them attend the tournament. He didn't hold out much hope that they would qualify, but he thought that the trip, escorted by one of his Lieutenants, would be good for prison morale.

~~~~~~~~~~~~~~~

# THE USO AT
## THE CONNIE BEAN CENTER

*presents*

# YOUR SHOW OF SHOWS!
### Saturday Night, August 27, 1943 · Doors Open at 7 PM

## *Starring...*

**Mary Bogucki**, back by your demand, singing **"How High The Moon"**

**The Flying Heibels** on their daring trapeze!
See **Christa** do her **blindfolded triple!**

**Tony & Suzie Stevens** juggle with **knives & hatchets!**

**Louie the Talking Dog** with his mistress, **Debbie**

**Mischievous songs** about the war, sung by **Alice Wolfert**

**Bette Burbank** on the bagpipes, blasting out
*Donald, Where's Yer Trousers?*

**Jill Jackson** & her astounding Weimaraner, **Libby**

**Lasso tricks** on horseback, starring
**Mary Jane Burke** & her palomino, **Jackson**

**Lucien Skip** plays the noseaphone – hear him do **"Swannee River"**

**Mad Madeline Monaco** & her fabulous **balloons.**

**Barbara Naylor** plays her harmonica doing *The Too Fat Polka*

**Lia Venedictou & Finlay Anderson** do **Scottish Sword Dancing!**

Back AGAIN...**Mary Ericson**, Snake Charmer,
with her **Cobras & Asps!**

Back by popular acclaim, **Jan Neiman** sings **"As Time Goes By"**

# INTERMISSION – Buy your War Bonds NOW!

**Jacoba Goldman, Dennis & Mary Molchan** – our artists will do **Caricatures** of you during **Intermission!**

**The Jazz Band** known as **Brenda's Beboppers** plays *Sleepy Lagoon*

**Onstage Magic** with **Terese Menard** & her white rabbits

**Soft shoe tap** dance with **Fran Lefavour** to
*"Deep in the Heart of Texas"*

**The Balcony Scene** from **Romeo & Juliet**
with **Dave & Mary Jean Labbe**

**Mario Sabatino** singing **"Bell Bottom Trousers"**

**Barbara Connolly** & her talking dog, **Bailey**

**Buck "The Strongman" Frederick** astounds you
with his **Feats of Strength**

**Jim & Debbie Munson** sing *"Smoke Gets In Your Eyes"*

**Ventriloquist Leann Moccia** & her little friend **Mister President**

**The Southworths…Oriental Acrobats from Shanghai**

**Banjo melodies & Barbershop Music by Rick & Mary Rogot**

**Contortionist Peggy Grimes** twist herself into a **pretzel!**

## And a special event...
**Antonina Sabatino,** beloved opera star of **WORLD WIDE FAME,**
will thrill us with operatic arias from
**Madam Butterfly, La Traviata, Tosca & La Bohème**

## Admission: $2.00 for this special show
## Servicemen & women in uniform FREE

# Don't miss this show!

Grace Sabatino didn't know whether to jump up and down with delight or to scream and cry with despair. Most people would have been thrilled to be offered a free concert for the USO show. A free concert starring one of the most famous opera stars in the whole world – Antonina Sabatino! Adored by opera fans everywhere! Lauded and applauded at The St. Petersburg Opera House, The Vienna Opera House, Glynde-bourne, The Royal Opera House, La Fenice, The Grand Theater, Komishe Opera Berlin, and La Scala, not to mention her home theater, The Metropolitan Opera. Antonina! Here in the Connie Bean USO Center!

*I ought to be in seventh heaven*, Grace anguished. *But here I am, shaking and terrified that she'll ruin everything! Everything!*

The letter had arrived the night before:

My dearest cousins Mario and Grace:
I have a few weeks of resting from singing. I would love to come to   Maine to see you two and visit with Andy and also see young Mary Rose and her new bakery endeavor. I under-stand that Andy is growing up to be a fine young man.
My mother tells me that you are involved with raising funds for the USO and for the service-men who have been injured fighting. I would be delighted to sing some arias in one of your *programmes* and help with the war effort. Per-haps people there will pay a handsome sum to hear me sing.
I hope I can stay with you at your home, but if it is inconvenient, we ... my accompanist, Giorgio Vasileff, will be with me...can reserve some accommodations at a hotel in Portsmouth.
I will arrive on .........

Grace read the letter and clutched at her throat. *Antonina! Here! And she wanted to see Andy! Oh sweet Mary, Jesus and Joseph! What shall I do?*

She showed Mario the letter. He shrugged. "It had to happen sooner or later, Grace, my sweet. She's seen him three or four times already and nothing has happened."

"Yes, but he was a baby! He was six years old!"

Mario shrugged. "What can happen? She won't tell him anything. She promised, like we promised, to keep the secret. She has no desire to let him know anything."

Grace began to pace up and down. Mario watched her. He had heard of the saying, 'wringing her hands' and now, he saw that the saying was truthful. Grace's hands were twisted together so tightly that he thought that blood might begin to drip from them. "Relax, *cara*. It will be fine."

"Should we tell him ourselves?" Her face was anguished. "Should we have told him from the beginning?"

Mario shrugged again. "He'll have to know one of these days. Maybe this is the time."

"What will he think of us? Lying...living a lie all these years?" She began to cry, great, hopeless sobs of despair. "I love him so much, Mario. I can't bear it if he...if he..."

Mario reached for her and enfolded her into his arms. "Shhh, shhh, little one. It will all be fine. It will all be fine."

# CHAPTER FIFTEEN

AUGUST 23, 1943 – Berlin sustains smashing air attack. The Bomber Command of the R.A.F. smashed Berlin in the heaviest and most concentrated attack the capital of Germany has ever experienced. 700 planes took part and dropped 1,700 tons of bombs in 50 minutes, causing enormous devastation.

Mary Rose had been tickled pink when the four nurses moved into her house. For all of the closeness and love between her cousins Mario and Grace, they were older than she. They were married and had Andy and, although she adored them unconditionally, there was an age gap. She'd made many friends in Kittery and Kittery Point, but none of them were her own age, or, if some of the people she met were her age, their friendships never really became as close as she would have liked.

But the four nurses...they were all within a two or three year range, and she adored all of them from the moment they met. They'd giggled and talked, sharing experiences and laughter, and Mary Rose was nearly desolate that the *SS Buchanan* was scheduled to sail away again in a week or so.

One of the best parts about being friends with Yashiko, Carol, Eunice and Michelle was the discovery that Eunie had been born and raised in the same town! "We're both from Greenwich! Imagine that!"

They had both graduated from Greenwich High School, but there were three years that separated them, and they hadn't really known one another, although Eunice had known two of Mary Rose's cousins. "There are so many of you Sabatinos in town! Of course, I know your cousins Anita and Ricky! What a hoot!"

Eunice had then gone on to nursing school at The Greenwich Hospital. Mary Rose had attended the *Cordon Blu* Academy in New York City. "We must have passed each other a million times! Isn't this exciting?"

"I'm going to miss you all like crazy when you leave," Mary Rose cried. "Who am I going to *talk* to?"

"We're going to miss you, too, *cherie,*" Michelle threw her arms in the air. "Where will we find such comfortable beds again?"

Although she loved all of them, Eunice was the one she felt closest to. Maybe because they were from the same town. Maybe because they both had curly hair. Maybe because...well, who knew? Mary Rose just felt...*warm*est...to Eunie. And the feeling seemed to be reciprocal.

They talked about it one night when the others had fallen asleep. "Want a cup of hot chocolate?"

"Can't you sleep either?"

"I'm so worried about Joe," Eunice confided. "He's nice to me, but he keeps his distance."

"He probably doesn't want you to feel sorry for him." Mary Rose sympathized.

"I don't feel *sorry* for him!" Eunice wailed. "I love him!"

She poured her heart out. "I love him! He's the finest man I've ever known. He's trying hard to cope with his blindness and his foot. I can't imagine how difficult it's got to be for him. He...I..." She tried to blink back her tears. "I think he likes me," she sniffed. "But I wonder if he'd love me if he could see me." She couldn't contain her emotions and burst into sobs. "I never said this to any of the girls...I just...I..."

"What do you mean?" Mary Rose hugged her hard. "Why wouldn't he be in love with you?"

"Be...because..." Eunice mopped at her eyes. "I'm...I'm not pretty. I'm so pla-ain!" Mary Rose opened her mouth to give denial, but realized that Eunice wasn't just looking for sympathy. She honestly felt that she was plain.

"I understand," Mary Rose muttered slowly. "I'm plain, too." Eunice looked up quickly, opened her own mouth and then shut it.

"You know my family," Mary Rose began. "So many cousins...the girls are all beautiful. They're vivacious and gorgeous and they all attract men like a peony attracts bees." She sat down, her hands hanging in her lap. "I was always popular, you know. I always had lots of friends...both boys and girls. I even always had dates for parties and dances. But they were all boys who were *friends*. Not boy-friends. I was kind of a tom-boy. Good old Little Mary Rose. Up until then, no one ever said he loved me or made me feel...you know...special." Her round, earnest face was doleful. "Oh, I know I look OK, but not *pretty."* Eunice nodded. She understood. Oh, *how* she understood. "Look at me," Mary Rose stood up. "I'm overweight. Too fat. Too short. They always called my 'Little Mary Rose', like I was some kind of joke. They all love me, my family. But they never saw me as beautiful, or even pretty. I was always good old Little Mary Rose. Like a dog to be petted. Always the sister. Never the princess."

Eunice looked critically at Mary Rose. She saw a small girl, curvy and cute, with curly dark-reddish hair, a good complexion, a slightly turned-up nose and a wide smile. Why wouldn't a boy be attracted to her? "You're not a raving beauty, Mary Rose," she admitted. "And neither am I! I'm not even what one would call pretty. Interesting, maybe. Intelligent. A good person to talk to...that's me. But you? You're not the dog's dinner, either. You're cute. That's what you are. Cute."

"I don't want to be cute!" Mary Rose wailed. "Cute is what the puppy dog is! I want Nick to think..."

"Nick? Who is Nick?"

Mary Rose sighed with dejection. "He's a man I met and danced with. I thought we had something special, but then... He was at the USO...and we had such a wonderful time...and

then I went back and hoped he'd be there...and he was..."
She stopped and sighed.

"So what was wrong? Didn't he ask you to dance again?"

"No." She looked down at the floor. "He was kissing all
those girls from the bank. They were selling kisses. I wouldn't
dare do anything like that. They were so pretty and free and
funny and cheerful. Selling kisses! I...I just... He...Nick, he
looked over at me and I couldn't laugh or joke about it. I...I
walked away."

"And then what happened?"

She shrugged. "Nothing. I walked away. I didn't look back.
I can't play those kind of games. Especially with a man in
uniform."

"Why not?"

"I have a terrible secret."

"Oh, no!"

Mary Rose's foot ground into the carpet. "I never told anyone this. Before I came up here...*why* I came up here."

"You can tell me. I'll never say anything. Cross my heart."
Eunice made the sign of the cross over her left breast.

Mary Rose sighed again. "Well...maybe I *should* talk
about it. I made a fool of myself when I was home. I...I met
this man. He...he was in the Army. I'd gone to Radio City
Music Hall with my cousin Dorothy..."

"I think I know her. Doesn't she work at the library?"

"Yes, that's Dee. She's a few years older than me. Anyway, we went to see *Now, Voyager*," Mary Rose chuckled. "I
pretended I was Bette Davis for days!" She smote her brow
dramatically. "Anyway, while we were in line, there were two
soldiers in back of us. They started to talk to us, and before
we got to the ticket booth, I was smitten by the taller one. His
name was Kurt Dunleavy, and he said he came from New
Jersey. He said he was single and he said he was studying to
be an engineer. Lies...all lies, but I didn't know it at the time.
I believed every word he said."

"Why wouldn't you?" Eunice shrugged, leaning forward,
elbows on her knees.

"You're right. I had no reason, not then, anyway. Dee sort
of latched onto the other soldier. After all, we'd been told to be
nice to all the men in uniform."

"And if I remember Dee, wasn't she sort of nice to men even if they weren't in uniform?" The girls laughed.

"That's Dee. Love them and leave them. But that wasn't me...no, I'd never had anyone who romanced me the way Kurt did. From the moment we got into the movie...they sat with us, naturally, and he held my hand. I thought I was going to burst with pride and delight. Then we went out to Lindy's for champagne and cheesecake.

"I thought I was in heaven. He was so good-looking. Tall and blond, with a little dimple in his chin. He was gorgeous. He talked and said all the right things...how he fell for me in the wink of his eye...how I was the girl he was looking for all his life...and then, he said he was going into battle, leaving for the Pacific Theater in a couple of weeks after his training was complete. He said he wanted to spend all of his time with me. And that was just fine with me. I was delirious with happiness."

"What went wrong? When did you realize that he wasn't...?"

Mary Rose flapped her hand. "Not until much, much later. Not 'til it was too late. Not until...well, he came on the train back to Greenwich with us. His friend, I think his name was George, said he couldn't take Dee back, but she didn't care. She wasn't really interested in him. So Kurt rode back with us, walked with us back to my house, came in and met my mother and father, and then, after a cup of coffee and some conversation, walked himself back to the train station and took the train back to New York. Let me tell you, I was so impressed!"

"What did you mother and father think?"

"My mother was snookered, too. My father...well, he seemed reserved. Didn't say too much. I should have been more perceptive, but, hey, I was already in love. I thought he was a combination of Alan Ladd, John Wayne and Robert Taylor all rolled into one.

"He came back the next day. We spent every waking minute together and he told me that he loved me and that we'd be married once he was out of the service. I was so starry-eyed. We talked about babies...even named our first boy and our first girl..." She ducked her head. "I was so naïve. I believed everything. He told me all about his family. How his father was the mayor of the town he was from and his mother was wonderful and he'd already written to them and told them all about me. He said they couldn't wait to meet their new daughter-in-law to be." Eunice sucked in her breath at the perfidy.

"And then," Mary Rose hung her head, "He...we...well, I wanted to. It wasn't just him. We went to New York and spent the night together." Eunice's mouth gaped. Mary Rose ducked her head. "I have no real excuse. I was simply in love. I would have done anything for him." She laughed, a funny kind of laugh. "As a matter of fact, I *did* do something for him. He said that he wanted to buy me a ring, but that all of his money had been stolen at Fort Dix. I assured him that I didn't need a ring. He said he really wanted to get me one. I think he said that he'd feel so proud to know that his ring was on my finger while he was fighting the Japs."

"Did you give him money?"

Mary Rose nodded. "You can see why I never told anybody any of this. I am so ashamed."

"Ashamed? You didn't do anything that I wouldn't have done! If Joe asked me to stand on my head, or to give him a night of love, or give him a million dollars or die for him, I would. I would in a moment." Eunice nodded with understanding. "You were duped!"

"He said he'd seen a ring that was fit for his queen. That was me....his queen. Ha! Some queen. Queen of the idiots! The ring was an expensive one, but he wouldn't be happy unless I had a big ring. He also said that his mother was sending me a necklace that had been his grandmother's. I was...well, I was delighted. I practically begged him to take six hundred dollars from me for the ring."

"Six hundred *dollars!* Gol-lee!"

"I know. I was a dumb Dora, wasn't I?"

"What happened then?"

"Oh, first, I have to confess that I lied to my mother and father. They never would have let me go to New York with Kurt overnight. So I lied and said that I was going to an event at my *Cordon Blu* School. I said that it would be over so late that I was going to stay with my friend Sheila. I think my father saw through my lie, but he only looked hard at me. I felt like a rat, but I wanted so badly to be with Kurt. "

"How was it?" Eunice face yearned. "I mean…you know…. was it…was it like they say? Fireworks and all that?"

"Yes. I have to say it was. I adored him and he was a skilled lover. He gave me my money's worth." Her face was downcast. "Maybe not six hundred dollar's worth, but that was afterward. He hooked me well and good."

"Did you mother and father know that you lent him money?"

"No. Kurt convinced me that it would be our secret until he could send me the money back. My mother didn't see why we had to get engaged so fast. My father just looked angry, but he didn't interfere. Later on…well, let me tell you the rest…"

"He had to go back to Fort Dix and he said his outfit was shipping out in a week. He promised to write…and he did. He sent me a letter every day, with poetry and songs and wonderful promises about how our life together would be. And then he came to see me one last time and my father stepped into the situation."

"What happened?" Eunice was enthralled.

"Unknown to me, Daddy talked with our Police Chief. Chief Emerson. Chief Emerson knew someone who knew someone who was a big hoo-ha out at Fort Dix. He asked this person to investigate Kurt and report back to him. Daddy told Chief Emerson that he had suspicions from the start. Daddy told me afterwards; 'I didn't like his eyes, honey. They were shifty.' Daddy was so kind to me. I was crying and he was hugging me. 'You were so happy, though, I didn't want to stomp on your bubble. I was sick at night. I just knew there was something wrong with this guy.'"

"Wow."

"Yeah. Wow. I was such a dope! Anyway, when Kurt came to see me for the last time, Daddy was waiting on the porch for him. He said he wanted to speak with him. I thought…silly, stupid me…that Daddy wanted to know about his prospects and all that. I didn't know what he was going to do."

"What did he say?" Eunice was squirming with curiosity.

"He told me that he had some papers in his hand. The papers were Kurt's enlistment papers and all of his documentation. 'I see that you have been married, Kurt,' he accused him. 'I see that you are *still* married.' He said that Kurt was dumbfounded that he knew. *'And* you have two children.'"

"Oh, noooo! Children!"

"And that wasn't the worst." Mary Rose's round little face looked glum. "He'd been arrested for trying to romance another girl and he'd embezzled money, or extorted money from her, too. He was exempt from the Army because he had two children. Actually, Daddy suspected that was *why* he had two children....so he could stay out of combat..."

"The rat!" Eunice's voice was warm with sympathy.

"The Judge gave him two choices. He could go to jail for two years or, even though he had two children, he could go into the Army. He chose the Army. Told the Judge that he'd be better off away from his wife and kids."

"What a creep!"

"My father told him that he wanted to punch him in the face, but that it wasn't worth the effort. 'You've hurt my daughter, and I cannot forgive you. I have spoken with your Commander and the Army will be dealing with you when you go back to Fort Dix.'"

"What happened then?"

"I never saw him again. My father came in and told me that Kurt had left. I was astonished. 'Sit down, Mary Rose.' 'Carina,' he called to my mother, 'come here, too. Both of you.' He patted the sofa and I sat down next to him. I figured that this was going to be awful, whatever it was. 'I want to talk very seriously with you. I have something to tell you.'"

"Oh, Mary Rose! I am so sorry! What an awful thing to happen to you." Eunice came over and hugged her. "Your heart must have been broken."

"It was. I cried for three days, and then, well, after a time, I recovered. It took a long time and I thought I'd never want to see a man in uniform again. My cousin Grace thought it might be a good thing for me to get away. Maybe see some new part of the country, maybe forget what a chump I had been. Everyone was so nice to me. No one made me feel too stupid, but I *had* been stupid. And I knew it, no matter how nice everyone was."

"You were lucky, you know..."

"I *was* lucky. Stupid, but lucky. I might have given him more money... I could have been caught and had a baby...I...well, I was lucky."

"Did you...I mean, I'm just nosey but, did you..."

"Tell my mother and father about making love and lying to them? Tell them I gave him six hundred dollars?"

"Well, did you?" Eunice bounced on her chair.

"Are you crazy? Tell them? *Never!*"

Eunice began to laugh. "You are the limit!" Mary Rose began to laugh with her.

"I guess hearts heal, no matter what happens to them."

"I hope so..." Eunice's voice was small. "I don't think my heart is going to be the same...ever...after I leave here and leave Joe."

"Oh, honey! Something will happen! I have my cousin Grace and all of my aunts and uncles praying for you."

"With all of your relatives, if that doesn't do it, nothing will. Now, one more thing while we're having all of these girl chats, what about this Nick fellow?"

"I met him and we danced all night and we seemed to really like one another. It was all so wonderful... And then there was this kissing thing. There he was picking up some beautiful bank girl...lifting her up in the air and smooching her in front of everyone! I just...I just walked away. I think he called my name, but I just couldn't look back."

Eunice thought hard. "You ought to give him another chance. How the heck was he to know that you had a terrible time with a man in uniform?"

Mary Rose had the sense to look ashamed. "You're right. How could he know about my foolish love affair? I'd be mortified if he *did* know!"

"All right, how about you and I go to the USO tonight? I usually go to see Joe, but maybe it would be a good thing if I skipped a night. Perhaps he has to get used to me not always being there, and perhaps I have to get used to leaving him.

After all, I do have to leave him in a week or so." Eunice's face was dejected.

"Are you sure?"

Eunice nodded, her face doleful, but determined. "There's no happy ending for me here. He'll go one way and I'll go back to the hospital ship. I'll probably never come back to this area again. He'll meet someone nice and pretty and...and well...what can I do?"

Mary Rose wanted to tell her that it would all be fine in the end. But how could it be fine in the end? Eunice would have to leave. Joe would stay. They'd most likely never see one another again. She shook her head. What else could they do? Nothing. This was war and this was how it was.

# CHAPTER SIXTEEN

**August 23, 1943 – The people of Berlin get a taste of their own medicine. Berliners, for the first time, suffer the effects of the terrible bombings that they had inflicted for so long on others. The Allies rejoice.**

Randy and Horace met to talk about the missing prostitutes and the arson investigation. "We've spent hundreds of hours interviewing people, house-to-house near each fire, all of the people who live nearby to the railroad station, checked records and alibis. We've come up with nothing. Nothing at all. Most of the people in the photographs were just curious. They have no reason that we can see to burn down houses. Oh, there are a few that we're watching, but by and large, I think we're whistling up the wrong rope." Horace mourned. "We've got nothing."

"We've been patrolling the railroad station each night." Randy offered. "We'll see if anyone is lurking around. The girls on the streets assure me that they have warned each other about being alone. They're staying in twos and threes and making sure that no one lingers at the station." He laughed. "I think we put a crimp in their bargaining power. Now, instead of waiting to see if a better fish comes along, the girls are going back with the first man who asks them!"

"Far be it for me and crime to bite into their love life!"

"Better a cheap screw than being dead or missing. What are we doing about Gloria-Ann St, Clair?"

"Nothing. There's nothing to even think about doing." He shrugged with helplessness. "She's vanished off the face of the earth."

"Did you go over to The Hess Club to, um, investigate?"

Randy grinned a lascivious grin. "You bet! Probably my only chance to linger around expensive sex-for-hire. My goodness, those women are beautiful!"

"I wonder if they're worth it?"

"I hear that a few of them are," Randy winked, "but shoot, on my salary, I can't even afford to shake their hand!"

Horace guffawed, "Most likely best for you."

"So you say." Randy muttered. "Just once...just once..." He brightened. "She...the St. Clair woman...she had a sunken bathtub in her room."

"No! A bathtub?" Horace's face crinkled up. "I wonder....gee, whiz! A bathtub!"

"Yeah. I woke up last night thinking about it all. A bathtub. A beautiful whore, bubbles and me. I had a hard-on that wouldn't go away for hours!"

"Well, we can knock Mountain Man Aggie off our list of suspects, anyway," Horace told him.

"How come?"

"On the night of the fire in the Kittery Foreside, he was in the hospital." Horace grinned and finished. "He had a heart attack from eating too much rich food!"

"My goodness! I told'ja. She's trying to kill him with mashed potatoes and whipped cream." He smacked his head. "Hey, I did ask my deputy to ask his aunt to find out about his wife and what happened to the husband she had before Augustus...I should be hearing soon."

"You really think she's feeding him to death?" Horace gave him a dubious look.

"Why not? It beats strangling!"

"Just takes a little longer, that's all. Anyway, Aggie is doing well and should be out of the hospital in a day or so."

"Maybe they put him on a restricted diet at the hospital. That should put a crimp in his old lady's claim on his insurance!" Laughing, the two men went into Chang's to have lunch.

~~~~~~~~~~~~~~

**August 1943 – The Lindy Hop is no longer the most popular dance step. Jitterbugging, with its vigorous athletic movements, has taken first place.**

Grace watched Andy as he helped a new customer purchase an entire Victory Garden Kit. He was a born salesman, her Andy. Could sell ice to the Eskimos. He could operate the store nearly as well as she. My son.

She sighed. And rubbed her forehead as the headache pain which had been affecting her ever since she'd received Antonina's letter, pounded at her temples. This situation. It had to be faced. Antonina would be here in a few short days. What were they going to do?

"Andy?" Maybe she should just tell him.

"What, Ma?"

"Oh, nothing, sweetie. That was a good sale you made."

"Yeah, Ma."

"The Victory Garden things are almost sold out. It's time to start picking squash and tomatoes. Putting them up. I'm doing a demonstration at the USO in three days, showing the women how to preserve the bounty of their gardens. Canning tomatoes, tomato sauce, ketchup, chutney, preserving berries, making jellies and jams." She stood up, groaning with the aches in her back and hands. "Lots of work to be done here."

"Lots of work by me, you mean." Andy grimaced. "Good thing you have a strong son, huh, Mom?"

"A very good thing that he's so strong." She reached up...my goodness, Andy was growing by inches every single day! He'd be well over six feet tall when he was grown.

Tall...like his father had been, so she'd heard. She'd never seen Anderson, but Mina had told her that he'd been tall and well-built. "Handsome...oh, so distinguished looking. A gentleman." Mina had sighed. "Too bad things worked out like they did, but...if they hadn't, you'd never have had your own Andy. So maybe God works in ways we have no knowledge of...bad things turn into good things. Maybe better, maybe worse..." The little midwife had flashed her wicked grin at Grace. "And in your case, the best thing of all, right?"

"Right." Grace clasped her hands over her heart. "The very best thing of all."

She gave Andy a smacking kiss. He laughed and went back out into the sunshine to check out the zucchini. Zucchini! If there ever was a vegetable that never stopped producing...it was zucchini!

She watched him as he counted the zucchini he could see. And there were always dozens more, hidden under the broad leaves. Lots and lots of zucchini. She sighed. Maybe she wouldn't say anything until after...long after...Maybe she would wait. *Mario and I can do this better if we do it together. Oh, Lord! Help me to get through this and not alienate my darling son.*

~~~~~~~~~~~~~~

"I hope she'll be there," Nick gulped down a beer. "She's a very nice girl and I think I made her angry last week."

"How'd you do that?" His bar companion, Jessie LaRue, a tall-gangly man from Texas, signaled the bartender for another round.

"Oh, these girls were selling kisses and I bought a whole bunch."

"Who wouldn't?" Jessie raised his glass.

"Well, I was smooching this babe and I looked around and there was Mary Rose, gaping at me as if I'd shot her mother."

"Is she important to you?"

"She could be. She could be."

"Well, then git over to the USO and find her. Git down on your knees and apologize. Sheet! If she's worth hangin' on to, hang on to her!"

Nick nodded. Sage advice. Sage advice, indeed.

~~~~~~~~~~~~~~

"Droshka, my beauty, my love. Why do we have to travel to the North Pole to see your cousins?"

"Don't be foolish, Giorgio. We are going to New Hampshire and to Maine. They are side by side, separated by a river and they are two of the forty-eight United States. You're being silly." She sipped the glass of wine that he had placed on the table for her. "Sometimes, I get lonely for my dear family. I grew up with Mario and Grace and am special to their son, Andy. From time to time, I wish to see them."

"And do we have to sing for them, too?"

"You are being a bear, my sweet. Try to be more accommodating and less grumpy. We do not have to sing for them, we *want* to sing for them. This concert is for the war effort. I will help them bring in a lot of money. And, it will be excellent press for both me and you. You can say how you are supporting the men and women in uniform. Some newspaper will pick up the piece and send it to Russia and your whole family will be proud of you."

"Humpf. My whole family is proud of me only when I send money home to them." He picked up his own glass of wine and watched her. Lovely. Just lovely. Ah, well, if she wanted to go to the moon, he would go, just to be with her and hold her hand...to kiss her little foot....she was his goddess and he would do anything she asked. But where *was* New Hampshire anyway? Where was Maine? Somewhere near the North Pole, he was sure. He wondered, *did they have vodka there? Or should I bring my own?*

She watched him sip his wine. So handsome. So talented and so dense. She shrugged mentally. *I wonder what he'd think if he knew why I really insist on going to Kittery. What would he think of me? Would he care that I had a son and abandoned him when Anderson died? Would he think less of me? Or, as Giorgio is one of the most self-absorbed men that I have ever been with, would he think more of me? I won't tell him anything, she decided. There is no need for anyone to know what folly I perpetrated in my own self-absorption so many years ago. The secret is safe. I will just kiss him and hug him as if he were a favorite nephew or cousin. Give him some money. And then, when I have sung for my supper, I will leave him to the two people who love him even more than I do. But it might have been so different. Ah, well. My son. My son. If you knew, would you understand and forgive me?*

~~~~~~~~~~~~~~

Caledonia met Eunice and Mary Rose on the steps of the Connie Bean Center. "Hey, you two!"

"Hi, Cal!" The three of them hurried in, drawn by the music and the noise. A record was blaring: *"I got a girl, in Kalama-zoo-zoo-zoo…"*

"Good evening, girls," Father Nick and Sabina Carter manned the desk tonight. The three echoed a greeting and were duly passed in.

"I got a long letter from Marshall today," Caledonia confided happily. "He sends his greetings."

"Where is he stationed?" Eunice asked. She'd really liked Marshall Rockwell and hoped he wasn't being shot at in some foxhole. She was the only one of the three of them that had ever seen action. She wasn't about to mention the horrors to Mary Rose or Caledonia. Enough time for them to learn about them.

"He's a Seabee. I think he's in or near Hawaii, or some island out there. He keeps talking some nonsense about ukuleles and hula dancing. I think the words are supposed to be hints. A few things he wrote have been crossed out, so I suppose, wherever he is, it is being censored."

"Send my best to him. By the time he gets the letter, who knows? I might be out there with him, dancing a hula." Eunice looked for a vacant table. She saw Doctor Patten sitting at a table for four. He was the only man there...sitting with him, hanging on to every word he said, were three young hostesses. She grinned. Alex was really hot stuff for the girls. She wondered if any of the girls knew he was going to be sailing out of their lives in a week or two.

Before they could sit down, Mary Rose felt a tingle...a vibration in her heart. He was here! His hand touched her elbow. "Hello, Mary Rose. We have some unfinished business, don't we?" The music had changed. The Ink Spots were crooning, *"Don't Get Around Much Anymore."*

Nick took her onto the dance floor and held her close while he sang in her ear, *"Heard they crowded the floor....couldn't bear it without you..."* His voice was soft. He pulled back and looked down at her. "That was how it was last week. I was here and you left. I couldn't bear it without you. The place wasn't any fun without you. I guess you've gotten into my blood, Mary Rose. How can we deal with this?"

She looked up at him. *Was this just like the time before? Was he conning me?* He winked and twirled her around, letting her out, and pulling her back. *I feel bereft when he twirls me away. I feel happy when I'm back in his arms. Like I came home. Is this for real?*

The music stopped and all of the couples clapped and began to talk. Nick and Mary Rose stood still, clasped together and looked at one another. *I think it is real,* she thought. *I think it is all OK.*

He led her to a small table. "I made you angry, didn't I? You were disappointed with me." He picked up her hand. "I should have been smarter. I was just...I don't know...it seemed like fun to join in the kissing game. I'd hit the cards for a lot of money and felt like a king when I threw a twenty onto the table." He bit his lip and gave her a rueful look. "Dumb, huh?"

"You weren't dumb. You were having fun and being generous. It was me that was the problem. I was just being, well...I was jealous. I saw you kissing those girls and laughing and joking. I wondered if I could sell kisses and kiss a man and not be serious. Just kiss for fun." Her eyes looked down at the tabletop. "I don't know how to kiss for fun..."

He sighed. "Well, Little One, quite soon I am going to kiss *you.*" Startled, her eyes flew to his. Her heart started to thump at the thought of him kissing her. A hot feeling blazed up from her innards. She was sure everyone in the place could see her feelings written on her face. Nick smiled gently and said, "And the kiss will not be for fun. It will be for real. Forever and ever real." His face was sincere and his eyes filled with honest emotion. She gulped. It *is* OK.

~~~~~~~~~~~~~~~

From the table across the floor, Eunice and Caledonia watched them. "Is he the one?" Cal asked.

"I think so." Eunice's expression grew fierce. "He'd *better* be true!"

"What if they really fall in love," Caledonia asked. "She can't see him away from here. He can't go to her house. It's against the rules. You can only write to one another, like Marshall and I are doing. I wanted more than anything to go out with him. Go to supper. Go to the movies. Go to the park and talk. But, the rules! You can't do it and keep on being a hostess here."

"So what did you do?"

"It wasn't so bad for Marshall and me. He shipped out a few days after we met. We really liked one another, but it was nearly impossible for us to sneak off and meet, even if we wanted to. I mean, sure, I wanted to, but I also wanted my family to be proud of me as a USO hostess. You know, the colored people have been kicked around so much, when we get an opportunity to show that we're just like anyone else, we've got to do it right. Or even better than right. I represent my whole race while I'm here. It's a heavy load to carry. Always thinking of how I'll be seen." She sighed. "Crimps my style sometimes! I *have* to be good."

"I never thought about that," Eunice touched her hand. "You poor kid!"

"Oh, I don't feel sorry for myself, or anything like that. Actually, it made it easier for Marshall and me. We just followed the rules. We know that we like each other. We're getting to know one another through our letters and when he gets back, then we'll begin to date and see if this is permanent."

"When is Nick shipping out?"

"I think his sub gets launched this week. There's a trial run, or so I hear, and then a week later, he'll be gone."

As they peeked at Mary Rose, they saw her reach out and stroke the side of Nick's face. He captured her hand and kissed the palm. Embarrassed to be peeking at such a personal scene, the girls looked away. "Can she just keep seeing him here every night? Will it be enough?"

Caledonia shrugged. "It's for them to work out. Hell's bells, I can't be the Momma for everybody!"

She gazed around the floor. "There's that handsome doctor from the ship. She jutted her chin out toward Alex Patten's table. " All the girls think he's the bee's knees."

"He's pretty handsome. He's as nice as he is handsome, and a very clever and brave doctor. I'm always impressed when I watch him operating or listen to him talking to a soldier who has lost a limb. There are a lot of men that would have died without his skills."

Caledonia twisted around. "I was looking at Mrs. Carter. She's putting on a lot of weight." She pointed back to the reception desk. "She's busting out of her dress."

"She probably spends so much time here that she nibbles on all those great desserts. If I ate here all the time, I'd look like a blimp."

Their conversation was brought to a screaming halt as two soldiers came to the table. The shorter one, a Negro, bowed to Caledonia, and the taller one held his hand out to Eunice. Caledonia stood up. In her high heels, she was a full head taller than her dancing partner. Laughing, she followed him... the Queen Mary following a tugboat...onto the floor.

~~~~~~~~~~~~~~~

"What is it about you that makes me tongue-tied. I want to tell you what's in my heart, but I can't get the words out." Nick smiled across the table.

"Before you tell me sweet things, please tell me more about yourself." Mary Rose, although she was sure that Nick was sincere, wanted to know more about him. She was sure that he was being truthful....pretty sure, anyway.

Taking her at her own words, Nick began to tell her his history. "I was born in Springdale, Connecticut...." He started.

"Springdale! I was born in Greenwich!"

"Really? Amazing! Hi, neighbor!"

"Isn't that funny?"

"I might have run into you anywhere!"

"Well, you've run into me here."

"And it was my best day. Anyway, I'm the oldest of three boys. We're known as the Three Cappiello Terrors. My parents came to the U.S. from Italy. My dad is a carpenter, and my brothers and I are also builders by trade. We build houses, and until Der Fuhrer and Germany screwed up our lives, we had a good business going. My two younger brothers are married. I figured, what the hell, I'll join up and they can stay home and keep the business running while I keep the Japs running." They both laughed.

It was Nick's turn to look down at the tabletop. "I had a girlfriend. I figured we'd get married one of these days and I even asked her to get married before I left for boot camp. She laughed at me and told me, 'Why should I tie myself down? You could get killed and then what would I have left?' Well, Jeez, after she said that, I said to her that we...well, I said some rotten things to her. I was hurt and upset, but then, after I went home, I felt better. She really wasn't the woman I wanted to spend my life with. She was selfish and a bitch." He grinned and she noted that one of his front teeth was slightly crooked. It made her want to touch him, but she clasped her hands tightly and concentrated on his lips. "Hell, I deserved better than her!" He leaned back and his eyes met hers again.

"To cement my decision that she wasn't right for me, she called me up the next day. She says she changed her mind.

She *will* marry me right away. She told me that her girlfriend told her that if I died and we'd been married, that she'd get my allotment and a lump sum in life insurance. She came right out and told me that she'd heard about some women who are called Allotment Annies. They marry a lot of men, and then, if one or two of them die, they just sit around and collect the money. She warned me that if she and I got married, I'd have to sign over my life insurance to her and then maybe, if she had time, she'd write to me. What do you think of that? Now I was a valuable asset to her!" He laughed. "I told her to get lost. And wasn't I right? Here I am with you, and I hope you don't want to marry me right away for my allotment. Do you?"

"Maybe not right away." She giggled. "Just sign over those insurance papers and then we can get hitched."

He gaped at her and then realized that she was making a joke. He pulled her to her feet and hugged her. "Mary Rose, you *are* the woman for me!"

They danced and talked and talked and talked, saying all those silly and wonderful things that new sweethearts do when they explore the former lives of the one they love. What do you like best about me? What is your favorite thing to eat? Do you really like me? How much? What are your dreams like? When can we see each other again?

And this was a problem. Mary Rose had to tell Nick about the rules. "I can't really go out on a date or see you away from the USO."

"What a load of crap! These are stupid rules!"

"I know, I know. Maybe we can....well, let me think about it and ask the other girls what they would do. I don't want to get myself or you into any trouble, but, oh, Nick...I *do* want to see you." Her heart was in her eyes.

"And honey-sweet, I want to see you, too. And alone. Not here with all these people around us. We've gotta figure something out."

"Well, I'll be here tomorrow night. We can see if we can finagle something. There has to be *some* way..."

The lights blinked twice, signaling the end of the evening. "We've got five more minutes together. At least we can walk out together, can't we?" Nick pleaded. "And maybe have two minutes alone. Then I can go back to my lonely bunk and dream of you all night." He grinned and winked. "I'll pretend my pillow is you and hold it close."

"Oh, Nick!" Her cry was a wail. "What are we going to do?"

"Hi, you two. Time to go." Eunice waved to Caledonia. "See you tomorrow!"

"We're just going." Mary Rose stood up. Nick took her hand. Eunice stood back and let them go out together. She was bumped by Alex Patten.

"Hey, Nurse Eunie. Having fun?"

"Hey, you! I was watching you tonight with your harem. We're going to start calling you the Doctor of Love!"

Alex laughed. "They're all nice girls. A little too young for an old goat like me, but nice, nonetheless. Thank God my mother wasn't here tonight."

"Why? I like your mother."

"I adore my mother. But she is always trying to marry me off to any girl who talks to me. Are all mothers like that?"

Eunice shrugged. "Not my mother, when she was alive. She never thought much of me. She always acted surprised when I did something right." Eunice laughed, but Alex got a glimpse of some long-standing sorrow. "She was always as-tonished that any boy *talked* to me, never mind thinking that anyone was going to marry me!"

"Mothers!" They both laughed and went out of the door into the night. Alex greeted Mary Rose and was introduced to Nick. The men talked for a few moments...war talk, of course...and then Nick quickly kissed Mary Rose's cheek and went down the street.

"Nice fellow," Alex commented. "Not that it's my business, but is this serious?"

"Not that it is your business, but maybe." Mary Rose laughed. The girls went to Mary Rose's dilapidated car, and Alex drove himself home to read before he fell asleep, with Mystic's purr keeping him company.

The girls chatted about this and that. "Did I ever tell you about my gift?" Mary Rose asked. Eunice shook her head.

"What gift?"

"Well, in my family, some women, and I am one of them, have a special gift."

"For what?"

"For seeing things about women who are going to have a baby. My cousin Mina is sort of a well-known good witch in Greenwich..."

"Mina Fiorile? The lady that owns the dream shop on Greenwich Avenue? She's your cousin? Why am I so surprised? Golly, Mary Rose, you're related to everyone from Greenwich!"

"How do you know Mina?" Mary Rose was astonished.

"Well, I've been in her shop. It's a fabulous place. But even more than that, when I was a little girl, there was a murder in town and two little girls were missing and I helped...and Mina helped...to solve the mysteries."

"You're kidding me? I never knew that!"

"An altar boy was murdered. I was a classmate of his and I was, well, not to be modest, very helpful in solving it. I also helped them to find these two little girls who had run away from their father. He was a hateful man. The police department gave me a nice medal and I think Mina got one, too. She could sort of see into the future and she...I don't know...she could see what no one else could see..."

"Well, she and my mother were cousins, and I think I have a bit of her power."

"You do? I know what she was able to do, so why should I doubt you? What can you see these days? How much you adore Nick?" She giggled and Mary Rose blushed.

"I can see that you are going to be trouble!" Mary Rose joked. "Seriously, I can see things about babies. I could see, tonight, that Sabina Carter is going to have a baby. I think it will be a boy, and she's almost ready to have it."

"What! You're crazy! Sabina Carter is old! Much too old to have a baby! She's just putting on weight. Cal and I were talking about it. She needs to go up one size on her dresses."

"Nosiree. She's going to have a baby boy. Mark my words." Mary Rose took both hands off the steering wheel and waved them in the air. "I prophesize…me, Mary Rose Sabatino… who is from a long line of good witch women…*stregas*, we are called in Italian….is right on this. Mrs. Carter, whatever age she is, is having a baby and I don't think she even knows she's going to have one."

"My goodness! Are you sure?" Eunice just couldn't comprehend. "I think you're crazy!"

"You'll see. I'll be proven right and you'll have to bow down to my witchy ways!"

"Let's make a bet. I'll bet you … um, I'll bet you, let's see…ten dollars that she's not pregnant."

"Ten dollars! Is that all? I'll bet you a *hundred* dollars that she is!" Mary Rose nodded her head for emphasis.

"A *hundred* dollars! Whew. That's too steep for me. Ten bucks. OK?"

"Ten bucks it is." They rode for a few moments in silence, each thinking of how they were going to surprise the other and win the bet.

Mary Rose broke the silence. "How can Nick and I see one another away from the USO and not get caught or not get disciplined? I just *have* to be alone with him!"

"Are you sure he's the one? Remember what happened with that Kurt creep? You barely know Nick."

"I know. I know. I shouldn't have told you about Kurt….now I sound stupid saying that Nick is the one."

"Well, if you think he's true and real…."

"I do. But I can't even see him except in the USO room with seven hundred other people around. "I've got to be alone with him before he ships out."

"Well…" Eunice drew the word out. "What would happen if you just happened to go to the movies and he happened to go to the movies?"

"Sounds fine. As long as no one sees us there together."

"Someone will always see you, that's the rule of trying to be sneaky." Eunice spoke from experience. "Whenever I've tried to do something slightly awful, everyone in the world finds out."

"What else can we do?"

"Could he come to your house?"

"I guess he could..." Mary Rose got a mental image of Nick in her kitchen. No one else was there...just the two of them..." She squirmed on the car seat. "Do you think I'd be crazy to do that?"

"You're an adult. The worst that would happen is that you'd be dropped from the USO."

"And my cousin would be ashamed for me. And my customers would know. And Nick's commander would know." She was silent for a moment. "There's a lot at risk here."

"Why don't you see him tomorrow night at the USO for now? Let me think about it. I'll talk with Michelle and Carol. They are the most...well, they can get around any regulation, and they *always* get away with the most atrocious things." She thought about the way that Carol and Michelle had manipulated the forms that sent Joe to Kittery and that odious Martin Joseph to Kansas... "If the two of them can't figure out how you and Nick can be alone, no one can."

And with that to hang her hopes on, Mary Rose had no choice but to slide into bed and hug her pillow, pretending that it was Nick.

~~~~~~~~~~~~~~

"Andy! Your cousin Antonina is coming for a visit. Isn't that nice?" Grace and Mario had decided that they would approach the matter step-by-step. This...the telling to him that she was coming...was step number one.

Andy looked up from his cornflakes. "It will be good to see her. Mike told me that she's going to sing at your USO. Opera songs, right?"

"Right. She's going to stay here and use the guest room. She's bringing some piano player and he'll bunk up with Neil and Alan."

"Great. Can I come to the show and hear her sing?" Andy's voice was casual, but inside, he was quaking. *His mother was coming! His real mother! Would she...?*

"Sure." Grace's voice was casual, too. But inside, her stomach was churning.

Trying to put some normalcy in her voice, she changed the subject. "I want you to clean up those butterfly bushes."

"I will. I promise."

"You know, there was a story when I was young…" Andy drank his milk and leaned forward. He loved to hear his mother tell stories about when she was young. "You know, my mother and father came from Sicily, not from the upper part of Italy like Mario's family?" Andy nodded. Italy sounded marvelous, but *Sicily!* It was dark with intrigue!

"Well, the butterfly bushes made me remember the story of the Widow Maker…*la vedova.*"

"*La vedova.*" He liked the sound of it. "What does that mean?"

"It means the widow. And the butterfly bushes, *la buddleia*, was always known as the widow-maker bush."

"Go on, Mom!"

"Well, *La vedova*…the lady, not the bush, was a lady that lived in our village. The rumor was that she had been married several times…and each time, her husband was killed!" Andy's eyes goggled. "She was called *La Vedova*. Everyone just referred to her as The Widow. She was middle-aged, but very pretty in a sharp way. Her husbands had all been wealthy men. All their wealth came to her when they died, so she was a widow of large substance. She had several suitors, all men of wealth. All very willing to marry her, even if all of her former husbands had passed away in the same way."

"What way?"

"First, I must tell you that she had beautiful gardens," Grace knew how to spin out a story. "Her gardens were renowned for the beauty of their butterfly bushes. She had them in all shades of purple and blue, white and yellow, and even a few that were dark…almost black." Grace made the last word hiss.

"The black *buddleias* were the rarest of rare. They were huge bushes, larger than a man, and the canes were thick and, when they had dried, as strong and as tough as a sword."

Andy's eyes were wide. "Like the ones in our yard?"

"Worse. Much worse." Grace's hands showed how big and how sharp the stems of the black *buddleias* were. "Ouch!" she cried, pretending to be stabbed by one.

"Each of her husbands had been out in the garden at night. *La Vedova* told the *polizia* the same thing each time: 'My husband,' she said. Naturally she was speaking in Italian, you understand?" Andy nodded, mesmerized by the story.

"She said to them, 'I asked him'…whatever that husband's name was…'I asked him to pick me some black butterfly flowers – they're my favorites. He went out into the garden. It was dark. Perhaps he stumbled. I do not really know. I waited and waited but he didn't come back. I called my servant and he went out into the garden to look. *Ai! Ai!* There he was… dead! Stabbed in the heart by the sharp sticks of last year's butterfly bushes!'" Grace stopped then and looked at Andy. She raised her eyebrows, as if asking him what he thought.

"Aww! How could the police believe that?"

"What? What could they say? She stayed in the house. The servants confirmed it. She stayed in the house. How could she have done anything?"

"Maybe one of her trusted servants pushed him." Andy was thoughtful. "But when it happened over and over again….weren't they suspicious?"

"Perhaps, but what could they do? She was rich and respected. No one could accuse her of anything except liking black butterfly bushes, could they?"

Andy got up and took his bowl and glass to the sink. "Is that really a true story, Mom?"

"My son, my heart. Would your mother lie to you?"

~~~~~~~~~~~~~~

August 15 – 20, 1943 – Allies advance in the Pacific! The island of Kiska in the North Pacific was retaken by United States and Canadian troops. In the South Pacific, the Allies are making good progress in New Guinea. The Allied superiority in the air smashed the vital airport in Lae so badly that the Japanese were never able to make use of it.

**August 23 – 30, 1943 – Germans retreat along the entire Russian Front! Russian families are able to return home again.**

She was ashamed of herself. There was no excuse for the way she'd been slacking off her running. Mrs. Genevra Davis would be shaking her head and tsk-tsk-tsking at the way she'd almost forgotten the disciplines of running.

Ah, but…she could excuse herself somewhat. She'd been working so hard…three more submarines with interiors designed by her had been launched in the last two weeks….

The accolades had been heart-warming. The men and women at the Yard, not to mention all of the officers, were always popping into her office, or waylaying her on the floor of the site, all of them vociferous in their compliments and admiration. She had been a bit…well, maybe she'd call herself a little bit complacent. *I almost know what they're going to say. They thank me and compliment me and make me blush and stammer. Still, I know that I've done a good job... the men down there in the subs are more comfortable, better rested, happier, and thus, they are better able to fight the stinking enemy!* She tied her sneakers. *And I'd better stop congratulating myself! My head is going to be so big that I won't be able to stuff it into the day room of the next sub! The subs look great. My ideas are great. But it is the entire team that gets the subs built. The men and women who rivet and paint and scrape and weld…they're the ones who should be getting the compliments.*

She vowed to be more humble. She was a decent girl and never forgot to say thank you…she always complimented all of her fellow workers…even the ones who swept the floors and manned the coffee wagons. But, it couldn't hurt to be even nicer to all of them. *Their* wonderful work made *her* work easy.

And then there was Scott. She bent from the waist and did her warm-up exercises. She'd been so busy with work and with Scott, that her vow to run every day had been cast down by the wayside. Scott's prison chess team had been given the almost-unheard of permission to attend the chess tournament. He'd been spending every free evening coaching them. Sometimes, she'd tag along. Her chess was abysmal, but the men always were happy to have her join them. "You're our good luck mascot," Nick Catanzaro assured her. "If you are around, I play chess like some Russian genius."

How could she let them down?

But this afternoon, her body felt heavy and lumpy. "I've got to get out and run. I need the exercise. I *crave* the exercise!"

Scott had laughed and patted her on the shoulder. "OK, Atalanta," Scott joked. "You run and I'll teach chess, but next time, we'll run together."

" Atalanta, huh! Wasn't she the one who chased after those golden apples?"

"Yup. Fooled by...what was his name, anyway? The one who loved her so much?"

"Hippo...? Hippo-something-or-other," She chewed her lip, trying to remember what Mr. Estes had drummed into their heads in High School Mythology Class. "Hippomanes! He was the one who figured out how to beat her!"

Scott bent and kissed her temple. "That's the man! And...I do believe, he married her in the end."

She looked up at him and smiled. "I do believe he did." He patted her rear end fondly and she marveled that their relationship was proceeding so well. "I'll see you later, you Greek goddess, you. I'll bring a few golden apples and we'll play a game or two."

And here she was, dressed for running and ready to go. Hannah, sensing a possible outing, frisked and barked at her heels. "All right, hound. You can come!" She clipped the lightweight lead onto Hannah's collar. "It's getting late and I would welcome company, even if it is from a dog."

It was getting late. Trisha's mother leaned out of the doorway. "Why don't you stay home and relax? It's too late to go traipsing around. With all those women going missing and the fires, you can't be too careful, honey. Run in the morning," she admonished.

"I'll be back before dark," Trisha twisted her shoulders, loosening up her weary muscles. "And I have Hannah to protect me."

"That dog will lick any assailant to death!" Mrs. Tobey began to bring in the sheets and pillowcases that were hanging on the clothesline. "Be careful, dear."

"I will. Goodbye, Mom."

And she was off, starting slowly, as Mrs. Davis advised, picking up her pace after a mile. *I'll just jog down past Seapoint, over to Eustace's shack, and then I'll run back.* "Is that OK with you, Hannah?" she asked the dog out loud.

Hannah's enthusiastic bark was answer enough.

# CHAPTER
# SEVENTEEN

**August 1943 – Germans boast that no one can conquer their fortifications and defenses on the coast of the Atlantic and the Mediterranean.**

She jogged to Seapoint Beach, meeting three dogs and four walkers on the way. Hannah growled and barked, clearly annoyed at being confined to the leash. Trish finally relented, once they were clear of the area where other dogs might be, unclipping the lead and putting it into her pocket. Hannah went mad with delight, chasing her tail and running ahead, stopping and falling to the sand, rolling over and over.

Laughing at the dog's antics, Trisha began to jog faster, timing her steps to *"Blow, Gabriel, Blow!"* Everyone in town knew the lyrics to the songs from the upcoming *Anything Goes* production. *"I've been a sinner, I've been a scamp, but now I'm ready to trim my lamp, so blow, Gabriel, blow!"*

The sun slid behind a bank of clouds and the air became slightly cooler. Tricia was glad that she'd tied a light sweater around her waist. *I'll jog to Eustace's, then stop and put the sweater on. Wonder if he and Jezebel are home...Brrr. It's really getting chilly!*

She rounded the corner by the stand of poplar trees. Their paper leaves rustled in the increasing wind. Eustace's shack was in sight. No wagon. No sign of anyone around. She stopped, grateful for the pause. *I'm in worse shape than I thought! I've gotta start jogging on a more regular basis. I'm not getting any younger!*

She slid the sweater on, grateful for the warmth. The sky had turned that grey-green color signaling an upcoming storm. Despite the sweater, Trisha found that she was shivering. There was an eerie feeling...*the barometer must be falling...Yikes! Next thing you know, I'll be getting the heebie-jeebies and seeing ghosts!*

She turned to call Hannah, wanting the company of the gregarious pup. There was no sign of the dog. "Hannah! Here, Hannah!" she called, cupping her hands. *Where the heck is she? Bad pup!* "Hannah! Come here!"

Suddenly nervous, she turned in a full circle. Night was falling fast. She hadn't realized how late it was. She stopped and listened carefully...*was that a dog howling? Crying?* "Hannah!" she cried again, a sharp desperation sounding in her call.

A rustle from the clump of grasses to her right... "Hannah?"

She jumped, her heart thumping. What made her think that there was someone behind the clump of grass? "Who is it? Who's there?" Her voice was a near-scream.

The wind answered and the clouds obscured the sunset. Her nervousness turned to something more...she began to be frightened. Was anyone out there? Was there someone who might hurt her? "Hannah!" She screamed, suddenly terrified. *"Hannah!"*

The bushes rattled, their dried pods making a lonely sound. She gasped and began to run, panicked by, she hoped and prayed, her own over-vivid imagination. She plunged past Eustace's house, her feet out of control, seeking only to get home and get to safety. The echo of her footsteps pounded in her brain, pushing out any song that might have lingered there.

A touch on the back of her leg made her scream! She twisted and nearly fell on top of Hannah. The dog whined and wheeked, nosing into her, close up against her, fearful of her own canine shadows and animal instinct fright. Hannah stopped suddenly and barked, her nose pointed toward the back of Eustace's barn. She growled and her fur stood on end. She barked again, but backed up fast, hard against Trisha's leg.

"What are you afraid of? What's out there, Hannah, girl?" Trisha whispered, holding onto to the ruff around Hannah's neck. She wound the leash out, and clipped it to Hannah's collar. Hannah strained, pulling toward the shadows, and she began to bark again...sharp, staccato barks of fear, interspersed by low growls. Hannah's front foot pawed the sand, and Trisha moaned with trepidation. She jerked Hannah's leash and began to run again, trying to listen between her own harsh breathing. Was there anything behind her? Was someone chasing her?

She caromed past Seapoint and scrambled onto the road toward home. "Hey, Trish!" Someone called to her. She peered through the dusk. Who was that?

"Trish? Is that you runnin' around like a Red Injun?"

Eustace! Thank God! She saw the wagon and the comfort of Jezebel's furry bulk.

She stopped, her heart still pounding. She could smell her own sweat. The scent of fear and dread. It had its own acrid odor, unfamiliar to her.

"Eustace!" She called, now feeling foolish for her fright.

"Hey, Trisha! It's almost dark out here! You better getcher tail home!"

"I will, Eustace. You bet I will!"

~~~~~~~~~~~~~~

"There will be a real need for help once this war is over," Admiral Wood confided. His driver was escorting him and Joe to Joe's history and quotation classes. "There will be thousands and thousands of men, many whole in body, but perhaps bruised in mind; some damaged beyond our ability to help them; some who needs prostheses, like you and Plutarch; many who are whole in body and mind but who need financial help..." He sat back, envisioning the needy army that would return. "We'll win this war, man. There is no question.

The tide is turning and the Japs and the Krauts are running scared."

"The returning soldiers will get married to their sweethearts who have been waiting for them. They'll meet the children who were born while they were away. They'll need inexpensive housing and have to learn a trade that can be used in peacetime. And then, like you, Joe, there will be so many who need medical help. And even worse, there will be some who need help for the injuries of their minds."

"How can I help you help them?" Joe was anxious. *Seems like the lad has gotten over his self-absorption,* the Admiral mused. *Good thing, too. Too much feeling sorry for oneself can mar one's life.*

The Admiral grunted. "I'm working on legislation that will get things going. Even now, before the end of the war, we need funding for men like you." He slapped Joe's arm, missing by several inches. "You're going to be my poster boy for all of this. We'll have you down in Washington talking to Congress and maybe even the President. Show 'em all what a real hero is like."

"I don't think I want to be put on display," Joe demurred. "I just want to get on with my life as best I can, not paraded around like a pet monkey for people to gape at."

"It wouldn't be like that, Joe. I promise you. Think of the swell fellows you could help." The Admiral sensed he had said enough for now. "Gonna marry that cute little nurse?" Admiral Wood felt that, as a man of many years, he was eligible to ask.

Joe shook his head. "I can't ask Eunice to ruin her life by carrying along a crock like me. She's got the world on a string. What would she want with me?"

"She could do a lot worse, Joe. You're a remarkable young man. Any lady would be happy to have you spend some time with her."

Joe shook his head again, forgetting that the Admiral couldn't see him. "I don't know....I don't think so."

~~~~~~~~~~~~~~

The car stopped and the driver opened the door. "Here we are, sir."

Glad to end this much-too-personal conversation, Joe said goodbye and eased himself out of the back seat, balancing himself carefully on Plutarch's metal and rubber strength. He turned, sensing the wind and the sounds that echoed back from the school's brick sides.

He'd practiced learning directions, using every sense that he still had. The school was that way. Using his white cane, he tapped along the grass verge, heading toward the sidewalk. When he felt the concrete beneath the tip of the cane, he knew just where to go. Sixty-three steps to get to the front stoop. Up four steps, holding onto the hand rail. Open the door. Door closing behind him... thunk.

Seven steps into the lobby, remembering the sound that his cane tip made on the shiny (and slippery) marble floor. Joe *knew* that the floors were slippery. He'd fallen the second time that he walked on them. But he'd learned, as he would learn many things. *When you cannot see, you learn a lot of things,* he thought to himself. Turn right at the corridor. Know you are at the beginning of the corridor by the echoing sound the tunnel-like corridor made. Twenty-seven paces. Stop. Two steps to the right and touch the wall and then the wood of the classroom door. Feel for the handle. Open the door.

"Good morning, Captain Martin!" His class greeted him.

"Good morning, class." Time to teach these wonderful kids. Sixteen steps to the front of the classroom, touching the wall with his right hand to help him. Turn left, three steps to the desk. "Let's hear who is here today."

The children knew what to do. Starting at the front, they called off their names, loud and clear. "Stanley Sullivan."

"Bob Goldman."

"Karen Lium."

"Barbara Armitage." And so on...

~~~~~~~~~~~~~~~

**August 1943 – Americans grew enough fresh vegetables in their Victory Gardens to provide the entire army with produce to see them through the year's end. The Ball Jar Company, makers of the glass jars used to "put-up" produce and safely process the gardens' bounty, was working 'round the clock to keep up with housewives' demand for canning jars, lids and seals.**

"Aunt Sallie-Mae told us the entire story. At one time, it was the talk of South Paris." Randy regaled Horace and Inga with his story. "She came to South Paris, a widow. She'd been married to a man named Ferlin Woolworth. He was from The County. Matter of fact, they both were born in Aroostook County." Randy sat down, taking the time to spin out his story. "Woolworth was a heavy-set man…a farmer with a big and prosperous farm. She was already well-known as a good cook, winning prizes from the grange halls and county fairs for her pies and cakes. She fed him like a hog going to slaughter, so the tale goes. Aunt Sallie-Mae said she knew the woman who lived on the next farm. The woman told Sallie-Mae that Ferlin blew up like a school kid's balloon. He was nearly four hundred pounds when he died. They'd been married for two years. No kids. Heart attack. Right!  She got everything, including his life insurance, which then was worth five thousand dollars. Sold the farm for a good price and moved to South Paris".

"Son-of-a-gun" Horace breathed.

"Yup." Randy sat down to tell the rest. "She met a man named Zachary Soames. He was a Maine State Legislator, representing Oxford County. A large man, not fat, mind you, but sturdy. She fed him up, alright. Fed him into an early grave again. Another heart attack, another grieving young widow, disconsolate because her man was gone." He grinned at the expressions on Inga's and Horace's faces.

"She really did feed them to death!" Inga was flummoxed. "I never really thought…"

"How could you prove it?" Horace was thinking. "She fed them well, they ate." He threw out his hands. "Was that her fault?"

"Well," Randy continued, "everybody in town called her the 'pie widow'. Naturally, they didn't say it to her face, but they all felt that she'd certainly been instrumental in stuffing her husbands to death."

"Did the police look into it? Did they have any suspicions?" Horace asked.

"Nope." Randy laughed. "Remember, there were two different towns. Two different places. People just thought she had bad luck with her husbands." His audience was gaping. "Then, though, she almost overplayed her hand. She stayed in South Paris. Soames was rich, but he didn't have a house or a farm. Only seven thousand in life insurance. She got the insurance money. Some of the neighbors, then, they started to talk and whisper a little bit more. Somebody knew somebody from up in the County. Somebody began to speculate. The woman from the farm where she was a bride came to South Paris. There was more talk. Wasn't anything that anyone could do. After all, a lot of people thought she was a wonderful wife to feed her husbands so well." He laughed. 'And then she went and married another man."

"Another one?" Inga could not contain her incredulity. "She killed more than three men?"

"Well, Inga, killed is a mighty strong word. We know that three of her husbands died. Three that we know of. This one, the third one...his name was Hiram Gull. He died after three years of marriage. Oh, by the way, he was the town undertaker." Randy began to laugh. "It isn't funny, really, but..." He nearly choked on his chuckles. "And he died at the pie judging contest...he was one of the judges and they had just awarded a blue ribbon to Gladys for her lemon meringue pie!" He nearly fell off his chair with mirth. "And there was ole Augustus, ignoring the corpulent body of Hiram Gull, lickin' up pie and looking with goo-goo eyes at his future missus. "

"I can't believe no one looked into this?" Horace stood up. "Why didn't the police...?"

"What could they do?" Randy turned to him. "What can you do?"

"I'm going to warn Augustus. He should know what has happened." Horace jumped to the telephone.

"Wait up, wait up," Randy put up his hand. "He loves her! He adores her! You're not going to make any impression at all on him. He thinks the sun rises and sets on her pie!" Inga began to giggle, thinking of the entire scenario.

"He'll listen to me!" Horace began to bluff..."He'll...he'll..." He sat down, rubbing his chin. "Shoot, Randy...you're right. What did she do but make them happy."

"Fat and happy," Inga concurred. "She's found the perfect crime."

"Nonetheless," Horace slapped his hand down hard. "I'm going to the hospital to see him in a day or two...and if I can manage, I'll slip something into the conversation...and sort of warn him....I won't say she's hell bent on blowing him up with apple pie, but I'll make some kind of hint. Maybe she'll listen if she knows we suspect her...." His voice trailed off as he thought of just how he was going to plead his case. "I'll say something." He slapped his hand on the desk. "Something!"

~~~~~~~~~~~~~~~~

She expected Antonina and her accompanist in the morning. The best sheets were on the bed, there were fresh flowers waiting to be picked for the crystal vases, she'd prepared all of her best recipes and had steeled herself for the worst ordeal that she could ever have.

**AUGUST 26, 1943 – Sir Winston Churchill spoke to the World: "Now those who sowed the wind are reaping the whirlwind. There is no halting at this point. There will be no pause in our journey. We must go on."**

At supper, the night before the USO show, Grace made her mind up to talk with Andy. There was no holding back now. The time had come to speak. If only she knew what to say and how to say it. Why had they waited so long? During the meal, she barely spoke, barely ate. "Are you feeling OK,

Mom?" Andy watched as she picked up a forkful of ravioli, and then put it down again. "Aren't you hungry?"

Andy himself had eaten one plateful already, plus a large dish of sautéed broccoli raab, and was halfway into his second helping. He certainly had no problems with his appetite. Mario wasn't there. He was at the high school gym in Portsmouth rehearsing and re-rehearsing *Anything Goes.* Grace blinked. It was up to her alone.

"I'm fine, Andy," she started. "Just not very hungry, I guess." She opened her mouth. *Here goes.*

There was the fusillade sound of a car horn, beeping and beeping a greeting. Andy leaped up from the table and ran outside. "Hey!" he yelled, "Its Cousin Antonina and her piano fellow!"

Grace sagged at her chair. Too late. Too late.

~~~~~~~~~~~~~~~

The desk sergeant at the Portsmouth Police Station was intrigued by the woman who stopped and asked to speak with Patrolman Mike Perkins. He eyed her with the experience of twenty and more years…she was a hooker if he'd ever seen one. Pretty, in a coarse sort of way. One of those jolly kinds. Peroxide blonde, cupid's bow red lips. A few pounds heavier than she should be. Bet she was a scrumptious armful. Tasty.

"He's not here. Can I take a message?" He tried to look avuncular. Maybe she'd tell him why she was there.

"Just tell him that Wanda Farr…he'll know…tell him Wanda will be at Tedesco's tonight at about two. Tell him I have a little bit of information for him." She winked at the sergeant. He raised his bushy eyebrows. Tasty, indeed.

"I'll leave a note for him and if I see him, I'll tell him that you're waiting for him." He leaned over the desk and scrutinized her. "He'll be happy that you were asking for him." He winked at her.

"Don't get any big ideas, copper," she waggled her finger at him. "Just tell'em that I'll see him later." She sashayed out of the station house and he watched the mesmerizing twin globes of her haunches with amused eyes. Little Mikey, huh? Little Mikey was in deep, deep waters here. She could swallow him up in one gulp. He laughed as he recalled his own youth and the women that had asked for *him,* back in those carefree and heady days at the station desk.

~~~~~~~~~~~~~~~

Grace and Andy drove to the USO show rehearsal with Antonina and Giorgio. Andy was impressed with Giorgio's automobile, a cream-colored Cadillac with all of the trimmings. Giorgio promised, if the concert went well and he was in a good mood, to let Andy drive it around the fields at the back of the garden center. Andy was in seventh-heaven. The prospect of driving the car was so thrilling that he barely remembered that his beautiful cousin was, in truth, the mother who had deserted him.

But Grace hadn't forgotten.

At the Connie Bean Center, the rehearsal had just begun. Mary Bogucki was finished with her song and the Flying Heibels were in the middle of their trapeze program when Grace, Andy, Giorgio and Antonina came into the room. Christa Heibel, the star of their act, who did a triple summersault, blindfolded, had just completed her leap. Even though it was a rehearsal, everyone watching her gasped. The trapeze riggings were at least thirty feet in the air with no netting below.

"I don't see how she does it," Mary Bogucki muttered to Jan Neiman. "Jumping off the little tiny bar and praying that she'll get caught by Charlie!"

"I sure wouldn't mind Charlie catching me." Jan eyed Charlie's muscles. "I'd fall into his arms any time."

"Fat chance you or I have! He's got eyes...and arms...for Christa and nobody else."

As the Bondi's whirled around the stage performing their waltz, there was a loud bark from Louie, the talking dog, who was waiting in the wings with Debbie Higgins. Louie barked again and Jackson, the horse, who had just clip-clopped up to the stage, neighed. The animals' greetings alerted the band.

Rosie Nunn, noticing Antonina, and sensing her fame, stopped in the middle of the Bondi's music. Dick and Ursula were suspended in a graceful dip. "It's Antonina Sabatino!" Ursula whispered. "She's here!"

"Hey!" Christa hollered as she finished coiling the ropes which helped her to descend from her aerial perch. "Are you that really famous singer?"

Antonina laughed and the entire ensemble...those on stage...those backstage, and those waiting for their turn... began to clap. Antonina bowed and threw a charming smile and wave to all. Clearly, she was a star of the first magnitude. An *artiste.* Jan Neiman, waiting to sing her song, sighed. How could she go up on the stage and embarrass herself when this woman...this opera star...was here?

And this was where Antonina shone. She'd been there herself...the young and untried singer, waiting for her own chance...watching those who were more famous than she. She'd sat in the audience, watching and glorying in their talents, wondering...unsure of herself...could she sing like they could? And she remembered that feeling. She was a star, yes...now. But she had walked in their footsteps...and remembered.

And thus, she sat herself down and watched...cheered loudly for the talking dog, laughed at the songs of Alice Wolfert, gaped at the lasso tricks, and clapped enthusiastically for Lucien Skip, the noseaphone artist.

And then Jan Neiman got up, shaky and nervous, to sing *"As Time Goes By."*

Antonina leaned forward, as if not to miss one phrase of the song. When Jan finished, Antonina leaped out of her seat, clapping wildly, obviously and honestly delighting in Jan's rendition. "Oh, my dear!" Antonina had cried. "You are wonderful! Your voice is so smooth...like velvet!" She clasped Jan to her bosom, "If you can come to New York, please, Jan. Come and see me. I will see...I know some people in jazz clubs there. I will promise...promise! I *will* get you a job there! You *will* be a success. I know it! You are so talented!" And everyone in the hall knew that she was sincere and genuinely impressed.

Jan nearly sobbed in happiness. "Thank you, Miss Sabatino! Thank you! I am so honored." *Wait until Momma hears! Just wait until she hears that Antonina Sabatino told me that I would be a success!*

As the group broke for a five minute interval between the acts, people clustered around Antonina. "Like bees around honey," Grace said, holding her hands to her breast. "She shines, doesn't she? Really shines!"

Giorgio nodded. "She is a real star. She is a lady, and an angel and she is kind and sweet to everyone. I am proud to be with her." His eyes were glued to Antonina and Grace could see the love that was in them. She wondered if the feeling was mutual.

*He adores her. Everyone adores he*r. She turned to Andy. "Your cousin is very special, Andy. She's really famous and very special. Her audiences adore her."

Andy's smile almost broke her heart. "She's really pretty, isn't she, Mom? I remember her singing. I was just a kid then, but I remember that she sure did have a set of pipes." He grinned and put his hand over hers. "She's almost as pretty as you are, Mom. But not quite." Grace bit her lips, trying not to cry.

There was no way that she could be at two rehearsals at the same time, thus, being selfish for once, Julie had turned over the *Anything Goes* rehearsal to Bonnie. The show was in one week and there was still a lot of work to do. But there was no way that Julie was going to miss meeting Antonina Sabatino.

She spoke to Giorgio, who nodded and went to the piano that was at the edge of the stage. Julie clapped her hands loudly and hollered that everyone should settle down. "We're going to let our diva have her rehearsal now. We're being very selfish, all of us here. We want to hear you sing! So…If that is all right with you, Antonina?"

"Oh, certainly." Antonina jumped up. "I am at your beck and call, Julie. Whatever is best for you, I am happy to do it, as long as the wonderful entertainers in Act II don't mind?" She turned, questioning…and everyone in the second half of the show assured her, loudly and emphatically, that they, too, wanted to see her perform.

"If you are all sure," Antonina was gracious. "We are all in this performance together. After all, this is for our men and women who are fighting for our freedom. Nothing is too much trouble if it helps them." She went to the microphone at the center of the stage and waited until everyone had quieted. Then, she introduced Giorgio. He stood and took a bow. With a nod, she then launched, without fanfare, into one aria after another, singing without effort, her voice soaring. There were tears and gasps from the audience of fellow performers. They were spellbound.

Afterward, she spoke with Julie for a few moments, then sat quietly while the second act went through its paces, clapping and laughing and cheering as each act performed.

Her compliments to all were sincere. Each performer felt a hundred feet tall. After all, hadn't they performed with one of the greats of the operatic stage? And hadn't she told them that they were marvelous?

Brenda's jazz group came in for some special accolades from Antonina. "I had heard what you had done, Brenda. Teaching these men how to play jazz together and giving them hope for their future. You are to be applauded, and I, as a longtime sinner," she grinned, making Brenda wonder at what she had sinned, "applaud you and the men, loud and clear." She'd spoken to each member of the Beboppers, promising them that, when the war was over and they had redeemed themselves, she would personally be on the look-out for jazz bands who might hire them all.

"What a wonderful person!" Brenda was nearly speechless in her reverence for Antonina. "She's...she's super!"

And in her sincere praise of Brenda, Antonina hadn't noticed anything peculiar about what Brenda was wearing. After all, she *was* theater, and theatrical folk were always dressed in costumes and unusual clothing. The fact that Brenda was wearing a pin-striped three-piece suit that looked suspiciously like a man's suit, festooned with a paisley foulard tie, and topped with a straw boater hat, went unnoticed. The rest of the audience, however, were buzzing with gossip about Brenda's clothing.

"And now," Antonina told them, "I am going home to be with my wonderful family. My cousins Grace and Mario...and Mary Rose and my darling little Andy. I will be here tomorrow night, ready to make music with all of you. And then, my dear new friends, as we stage folk say, may we all break our legs!"

~~~~~~~~~~~~~~~

Mike sat at the same table again, eating the grilled cheese. The way it tasted, it might have been the same grilled cheese, just scraped off his plate from a few days ago and reheated. *What crap this place served! Why the heck did anyone eat here?*

She came in alone at a few minutes before two. *She looks tired,* Mike thought. Then, *shit, you'd be tired if you did what she does every night.* He half rose to offer her a seat. "Hey, Mike! You are a true gentleman. No one ever gets up for me. Thanks!" Her face lost some of its fatigue.

"What will you have?" He asked.

She shook her head. "Nothing. I'm too tired to eat, and the food here...yuk." She sat down and stretched, trying to ease the weariness from her shoulders.

"I've got some news for you. About Lena. That is her name. I found a girl who knew her. Was in Newport last year with her. She tells me that she was known as Lena LaRue." She made a face. "Of course, that isn't her real name, but it's more than you knew before." Mike nodded, happy with any information at all. This case was going nowhere unless they got a lucky break.

"She was with some sailor in Newport, and he came up here and shipped out on a submarine. I hear that Lena followed him and then decided that the pickings were good up here and stayed." Wanda spread her hands out. "But that's it. That's all I know."

Mike pushed his plate away, untouched. *That way, they can serve it back to me a third time when I come in again.* "Thank you, Wanda. It's more than we had before. I want this monster caught. I know Lena is the only dead body we have, but there are other women who have gone missing. I don't know what happened to them, but I'm determined to get to the bottom of it and make it stop. You girls have enough problems without worrying if someone is going to behead you."

Wanda smiled at him. "Mike," she put her hand on his knee. "You really are a sweet man. I like you a lot. Come with me. I want to show you my appreciation." She got up and pulled at his arm.

Wondering if he was losing his mind, Mike stood up. He shrugged. "What the hell." He took Wanda's arm with a gentle touch. Together, not really seen by anyone except the surly waiter, they walked out into the warm, sticky darkness of the early, early morning.

# CHAPTER EIGHTEEN

**August 28, 1943 – King Boris III of Bulgaria dies under peculiar circumstances. His 6 year-old son, Simon, ascends to the throne.**

**August 29, 1943 – Germany dissolves the Danish Government after it refuses to deal with a wave of strikes and disturbances.**

There was standing room only at the USO show. There were a number of VIP seats in the first and second rows. Alden Be came to Portsmouth to see what his beloved mother had done with her jazz group. Alden and Brenda sat together, and each was as proud as could be. Brenda was decked out in a theatrical costume looking as if it came from a rendition of *Carry Me Back To Old Virginny*. The dress, adorned with tulle flounces, was topped by an enormous cartwheel hat. The *dernier cri* touch was added with a parasol, decorated with bows that matched the tulle flounces. Alden, who obviously took his sartorial splendor from his mother's side, was wearing outfit suitable for striding the dunes of the Sahara. A pith helmet topped his desert whites, complete with puttees and a swagger stick. Many in the audience gasped and craned their heads to better gape at them. Both Brenda and Alden reveled in the attention.

The Sabatino family, as relatives of Antonina, also sat in the honored seats. Doctor Alex Patten, together with most of the nurses and doctors with whom he had sailed, and some of those he now worked with at York Hospital, also had special seating. The President of York Hospital, Jud Knox, also joined the medical group, and he was suitably honored at the end, when the dazzling total of the show's monetary take was revealed.

Admiral Wood, his wife Ardenia, Eunice, Joe, Yashiko and Jack Harrington also occupied the front row seats. The Admiral was to be lauded by Julie at the end if the intermission for his work with the injured servicemen. Jack and Joe had warned him that if he mentioned them at all, they would stumble up the aisles. "If you don't want the spectacle of a blind and a lame man jerking around, then don't even think of talking about us!" Jack had warned him. Knowing these two modest men well, Admiral Wood believed every word they threatened, and never mentioned them at all when he got to talk.

Neil Harmon came with his girlfriend, Gerry, and Alan Bowen held hands with his sweetheart, Clair. The two girls had met in Portland and driven down together to be with their boyfriends and see the show as an added treat.

The USO Committee were seated in a two-row grouping at the right side of the room, with Julie Patten at the last chair, so that she could pop up and down and greet the throng and make introductions. Rabbi Joel Fish led the Pledge of Allegiance, and Father Nick Calabro guided audience in prayer, praying primarily for the troops and for the peaceful and quick end to the war. His fervent "Amen!" was echoed loudly.

Those who sat in the less-prestigious seats enjoyed the performances as much or possibly more than the VIPs. Portsmouth's Police Chief, Randy Stuart, was accompanied by Doctor Inga Hoffman. Mary Rose was supposed to sit up front with the rest of the Sabatino cousins, but a quick whisper in her ear by Nick Cappiello convinced her to sit in the fifth row with him. The other young USO hostesses sat in a group, the hostesses interspersed with the servicemen that they liked and danced with. Jan Neiman's mother and father sat together, beaming at everyone, so proud of their daughter and her upcoming performance. After all, Jan had been asked...nay... begged...to perform in this, the third of the USO shows and the famous opera singer had *promised* Jan that she would try to find her a job singing in New York. Why wouldn't they be proud?

At the back of the auditorium, Kathie Hess and five of her girls sat. "We'll just stay here in the back, sort of inconspicuous," Kathie whispered. "Don't want to rock too many boats too fast. Everyone has been so nice to me since we had the gambling night, I don't want to be pushy."

Kathie wore one of her least ostentatious outfits, a mauve dress, trimmed in purple ribbon. Her girls were also dressed in muted colors with minimal decoration. Still, despite their caution, there wasn't a show-go-er who didn't goggle at them. If Kathie had been paying attention, she would have laughed and realized that no matter how inconspicuous they tried to be, everyone was going to gape at them anyway.

~~~~~~~~~~~~~~~~

On the way home, Andy rode in the front of the Cadillac with his cousin Antonina and her accompanist, Giorgio. "I'm gonna take you out in the car tomorrow," Giorgio whispered. "I'll take you to a big field and let you drive, OK?" With stars in his eyes, Andy nodded fervently. *What a night!*

In the back seat, Grace and Mario, who had run over to the USO from his rehearsals of *Anything Goes* in time to catch the last few acts and to hear Antonina sing, were huddled together, their hands clasped, wondering just what might happen. To tell the truth, Grace was wondering what was going to happen. Mario, who had been enchanted with Leann and her little puppet, was imagining a career on stage as a ventriloquist.

Antonina pulled Andy over to her side of the front seat. She was surprised at how tall he had become. "I still think of you as a little boy, Andy. Obviously, you are becoming a man now. You are big and tall." Andy grinned, pleased at the obvious compliment.

*He looks so much like Anderson*, Antonina nearly cried out. *His height and his broad shoulders. He will be a handsome young man soon. As handsome a man as his father had been. Girls will flock to him. Should I say anything to him? Is it better to let the secret stay a secret? Oh, Anderson, if only you hadn't died! How things would have been!*

And then, because Antonina tried hard to always be honest with herself, even if it was to her own detriment, she wryly admitted, *If you had lived, Caro, things would have become, perhaps, difficult. Our love might not have stood the test of the tug of war between your career, my career and a child who needed two unselfish parents. Andy seems extremely happy and well-adjusted. Grace and Mario adore him.* She tucked her arm through Andy's and kissed him…a loud and friendly smack…on his cheek. *It is better, much better, this way.*

*She's so beautiful, and boy, can she sing*, Andy thought, as he smelled Antonina's exotic perfume. *I wonder if she'll ever tell me that she's my real mother? I wonder what all the kids would think if they knew that my real mother is a famous star.* He wiggled free of Antonina's embrace and turned around to face the back seat.

"Hi, Mom!" His voice, sometimes squeaky and sometimes a newly-found bass, caressed Grace's heart. "What did you like best?"

"I enjoyed that Shakespeare scene; *Romeo, Romeo, wherefore art thou, Romeo?* How about you?"

"Shakespeare is so yucky, Mom. I liked the horse and the cowgirl best. Maybe I'll go to Wyoming when I get older. Become a cowboy."

He blushed, wondering why everyone laughed.

After, they all sat around the dining room table, sipping *Limoncello* in tiny, chilled glasses, while Antonina told stories of her operatic adventures. Slowly, Andy's head began to droop and soon he shuffled off to bed. Giorgio yawned, too. "It has been a long day. I will go to my own bed now."

Mario took him up to the dormitory where Doctor Hamilton Zapfester had given up his cot to the guest. Zapfester, who had been on duty at York Hospital's Emergency Room that night, was curled up on the floor in an old Army sleeping bag, fast asleep.

Giorgio pretended gratitude at the loan of the cot. In truth, he was used to sleeping in luxury, curled up on a soft and luxurious mattress, coiled against Antonina's silky body. *This cot and this dormitory...poof! Sleeping in a room with four other men! Horrible for a man of my sophistication. Horrible.* Nonetheless, he brushed his teeth in the basin, climbed under the covers and fell asleep in three minutes.

Andy's dreams were disturbing, waking him with their strangeness. He was on a stage, dressed in some Shakespearian costume, trying to sing. His mother was in the front row of the audience and Antonina sat next to her. Both of them had their arms out to him, begging him to come to them. "Come to me, Andy!" Grace called.

"No! You are my son! Come to *me!*" Antonina begged.

Andy tried to sing to both of them. He opened his mouth, but instead of singing, birds flew out of his open lips. He spit out the birds and the feathers and when he looked at his two mothers, there were two monsters in their chairs. Each of the monsters tried to claw and grab at him. He woke up, his heart pounding, sweat dripping from his body.

"Whew!" He said aloud. "What a killer-diller dream! I wonder what it all means?" He drank a huge glass of cold water, padded to the toilet, and then jumped back into bed, covering his head to protect himself from further nightmares. In the morning, he was gritty-eyed and disheveled. He could only remember the monster dream, but he knew that during the entire night, demons had plagued his sleep.

He stood up, a tall, thin man-child, not quite able to understand what had happened in his earliest life, not understanding what was going on now. He vowed that he would try to put the whole matter out of his head. "I'm not gonna let myself have those kind of dreams any more! She's leaving this afternoon. Then things will get back to normal."

~~~~~~~~~~~~~~~

At two o'clock, Mary Rose drove her little car stealthily back into her yard. She'd been with Nick. She took off her shoes and tip-toed into her bedroom, her heart beating hard, half from the evening's splendor and half from fear that she'd be discovered.

Upstairs in the ladies' dormitory, Eunice heard her footsteps. She smiled, hoping that Mary Rose and Nick had had a wonderful time together and delighted that they seemed to have gotten away with flouting the USO rules. She turned over, buried her head in her pillow and went back to sleep, dreaming that she and Joe might one day spend such an evening together, too.

~~~~~~~~~~~~~~~~

In the early morning hours, Scrappy, a small, white dog of indeterminate parentage, cried to his mistress that his bladder was filled to overflowing. His mistress, Jana Ciboroski, grunted, trying to pretend that Scrappy's whines hadn't penetrated her slumber. Maybe Scrappy would forget about his bladder and go back to sleep. No such luck. Scrappy, nearly frantic, scratched at Jana's hand.

"OK, OK." Jana groaned, sitting up. Scrappy, understanding that he was nearly at his goal, began to dance around, yipping and yapping.

Jana put a raincoat over her striped cotton pajamas, thrust her feet into her old gardening boots, and clipped the lead onto Scrappy's collar. She shuffled out, still half-asleep, to the small park that fronted her house. Scrappy, nearly bursting, pulled hard on the leash. Ah! There! He cocked his leg against a tree, blissful at the stream that gushed out of him. All that a doggie could wish for!

Jana patted the dog's fur. "Good dog. Good Scrappy." She turned, pulling on the leash, hoping to sneak back into the warm cocoon of her bed for one more hour of solid sleep before her alarm clock buzzed.

Scrappy had his own mindset about following her. He jerked at the leash, whining and crying, pulling hard. "What's up, boy?"

Scrappy's paws scrabbled hard, pulling her toward a clump of evergreens in the center of the park. Jana shrugged. *Let the dog have his way,* she conceded. *Maybe he still has to do his number two. Oh well, let him. If I take him back now, he'll just pester me to go out again in ten minutes.*

Scrappy's pull was insistent. He dragged her to the trees and scurried himself into the overhanging branches. Willy-nilly, Jana let herself be dragged under the greenery. Scrappy stopped suddenly and began to howl, a high, keening sound that made Jana's hair stand on end. Jana noticed a peculiar smell...a zoo-ish smell, like the monkey house... The dog began to dig, throwing dirt up in the air. Jana bent down... there was a large lump...she bent further and put out her hand. The lump...the lump...it felt rough, like fur...like....and the smell was stronger... acrid...a bitter, metallic smell...

"Oh! Oh, God!" Jana screamed. It was a *head!* The head of a *mon*ster! With ears! Huge ears! What? What? It was...."Oh, *God!*"

Someone screamed, high and keening and then she realized that the sounds were issuing out of her own mouth. She backed away, stumbling over her dog, falling backwards, flat on her back. Another dog walker, over on the verge of the grass, saw her fall and he ran over to help. She scudded backwards, as far away as she could, from the unspeakable lump under the trees.

"Please, God! Help me! *Help* me!"

~~~~~~~~~~~~~~~

Chief Horace Parks tried again to get in touch with Posey McCardle. Her door was still locked and there was no sign of life at her house. Again, her neighbors stated that she hadn't been seen in a few weeks. "Sometimes she goes to her sister's house in Belfast," one woman mentioned.

*Sister...mother...where was the damn woman?*

"What's her sister's name?"

"I have no idea, sir." The neighbor shrugged. "I keep to my own business."

*If everyone kept to their own business, we'd never solve any crimes*, Horace muttered to himself. He wondered if he should try breaking in to Posey's house. *And what reason would you use, dummy? You have no cause to suspect her of anything?* The Chief spoke to himself. *I'll wait another couple of days and see if she shows up.*

He drove to the police station, feeling grumpy and disturbed. *When was luck going to come my way? When will this arsonist make a mistake so that I can put a stop to these awful murders?* As he backed himself out of his car, Gideon Balfour came running to him, half-alarmed, half-laughing.

"Get back in the car! We've got the head of a monster to investigate!"

"The *what?*"

"I swear, Chief, that's what the call-in said. 'Come as fast as you can. There is a monster's head in the trees!'"

Parks swung the car around and they roared off, sirens howling. "The call said that it was at Lyons Park. It was a woman that called. Left her name...a Jana Cibr...something." Gideon tried to read the scrap of paper in his hands. "She was screaming about the ears, the ears....." He rolled down the window to let the morning breeze cool the steamy interior of the elderly police car. "What the hell are the ears of a monster?"

Horace allowed himself a shrug. "Things are getting screwy, aren't they?" He rubbed the sweat off his glistening brow. "It's gonna be a hot one." The car skidded to a stop at the edge of the small park area. There were two cars already pulled up and a knot of people and dogs milling around in the middle.

"All right!" Gideon stepped forward. "What's going on here?"

A young girl, dressed in a raincoat over her pajamas, looked up. "My dog and I...we came here and he... Scrappy...he went into the trees. Maybe he smelled something. I went after him and there was this big thing...hairy and with long ears...a head...the head of some kind of a monster!" She held her hands out in front of her, as if to shove the apparition away.

A man backed out from the clump of trees as Horace and Gideon trotted towards them. "It's not a monster, sir." The man's face was ashen. "It's a mule's head and the head of a bearded old man. The heads have been cut off and are just sitting there, under those trees." The man gulped and swallowed, then turned, ran towards a bush, and vomited into it.

Horace walked carefully. If there were decapitated heads lying in the forest, they weren't going anywhere. Any head, ears or no ears, cut off its body would clearly be dead. No need to rush. He stopped, holding his hand out so that Gideon didn't trample the grass any more than it was already trampled. "Let's try not to gum up the scene of the crime. Call Doc Brogden, call that photographer from the paper, and get three or four men here with the crime scene kits. Maybe there are some clues and we don't want to disturb any evidence."

Gideon ran to the car to call back to the station. The man who had vomited, looking sheepish and wiping his mouth, stood up. At Horace's inquiring look, he nodded. "I'm all right now. Just seeing that...Sheesh! Did a job on those two donuts that I ate. I'm Caleb Samuels. I work at the Yard. Anything I can do to help you?"

"You can keep everyone away. Did you go into the woods, Caleb?"

Caleb nodded. "See anything?"

"The head of some kind of horse or donkey. Flies all over it...must have been there for a while, 'cause I could smell it. And then, I stepped a few more paces in and saw the old man's head. I didn't touch anything, didn't move anything. He was dead, no doubt about that!" Caleb shivered. "I backed out and saw you and then...well..."

"Well done. Now, you stand right here and don't let anyone or anything come any closer. My team will be here soon and we'll rope off the area, but if you can help out until then, I'd be very grateful." Caleb nodded and took a stance, as if defying anyone to try to come any closer. No one in the group huddled together had any intention of coming any closer. They had seen enough.

Horace took a moment to cement the scene in his memory. Green, grassy parkland, with a few dogs and dog walkers. A clump of trees in the middle. If there were any footprints, he didn't see them. He stepped forward, slowly, step by step, his head swiveling as his eyes raked the ground for any clues. Nothing that he could see. He stepped forward again...then again...then again, until he was at the edge of the trees. He peered ahead and on the ground, he could see the brown and black thing...it did look like the head of a monster...a monster with a long head, big teeth and long ears. Or, instead of a monster, maybe a donkey's head or horse's head. No, not a horse...ears too long. A mule. A *mule! Shit!* Jezebel! *Eustace's mule! Could it be...?*

His curiosity peaking, his adrenalin surging, he stepped closer, careful to give a wide berth to the horrible apparition of the mule's head. *Mule? Donkey? Was there a difference?* It shimmered in the dappled light...almost seemed to move, neighing up and down. Ugh! It was the Goddam flies that made it seem to move. They covered the head, buzzing and beating their blue-black wings...raising up in the air and then settling back down to eat...to eat... Horace's own stomach, somewhat used to fending off terrible things after so many years in the police business, gave a lurch. He swallowed hard and breathed through his mouth, praying that he'd keep the bacon and eggs Fanny had cooked him for breakfast down where they belonged. He'd always had a nervous stomach when he saw the grisly remains of a murder. He focused on the tops of the trees until the nausea settled itself down, and then stepped closer to the other mutilated head.

*Shit!* No question at all. It *was* poor Eustace Barnes. His head lay propped up against the stump of an evergreen tree, face to the sky, sightless eyes looking into the sun. Horace came closer, gagging slightly.

The cut at Eustace's severed neck was clean. Perhaps someone had used a scalpel or a very sharp knife. Even with a professional instrument, it was a difficult job to saw off someone's head neatly and cleanly. Whoever did this was either a butcher or a surgeon... someone strong and used to cutting up bodies. He paused, wondering who the hell would do something like this and why... and where were the rest of the two bodies? Why cut off the heads?

His face was sad. Old Eustace was sometimes a pain in his rear end, a crabby old man who probably broke the law as often as he could. Nothing major, most likely getting drunk now and then, perhaps some petty thieving, trespassing and it was a well-known aggravation that Eustace never paid for a license for his wagon, nor ever paid taxes. He was a mean old drunk, when he was in his cups. Picked fights, maybe threw garbage on the porches of those that he disliked. Might have stolen a chicken or two from some henhouses. Yet, Eustace was also well-known for bringing food to a family or two who were on hard times. He'd dropped off a rusty tricycle to the orphans' home in Portsmouth. He had his good side. Some said that he couldn't be trusted around little girls, but Horace had never received a real complaint along those lines.

He bent, peering at what was left of a long and colorful life. A man with scraggly grey hair, blue eyes, now opaque and milky in death, bad teeth showing in a rictus of his former sardonic smile, bristly grey stubble on a slightly pudgy, double chin... *Talk to me, Eustace! Tell me who did this to you!* The dull eyes never moved. Never sparked. Never conveyed anything.

Ah, whatever secrets Eustace knew...how his last moments on Earth had been...the stories that had been so freely told over and over in local bars...his hopes and dreams...all of that was gone. Eustace would never tell anyone anything any more. Horace hoped that Doc Brogdon would be able to winkle out some kind of information or clues from the autopsy of the severed head.

There was minimal bleeding, leading Horace to think that the murders had occurred elsewhere. *Why drag the heads here?* He walked around Eustace's skull to the other side of the wooded area. There! At the opposite edge...Drag marks...and a parade of insects feeding on the dark, sticky substance that led to a deeper copse of vegetation. There was a pool of dried blood, or what seemed to be dried blood...a puddle, perhaps two feet around. A veritable swimming pool for the flies and insects that had and were still feeding there. Tiny footprints of some forest creatures had also fortified themselves on the blood of Eustace and what seemed to be his mule, Jezebel. Horace tiptoed backwards, not wanting to disturb the scene any more than he already had.

Good! Here was Doc Brogden and his assistant Audrey, gloved and wearing white coats, and the rest of his team. "Hey, Doc."

"Christ! Whatcha got here?"

"Eustace Barnes' head. His mule's head. A mess." Horace's voice was shaky. "Poor bastards. Not even an animal should die like this!"

"Hmm." Doc bent to the mule's head. "Mule. A mule. Why decapitate an animal?"

"Why decapitate Eustace? And where's the rest of the bodies?"

"If we knew that, we might know who dunnit." Doc flapped his hands, sending clouds of buzzing insects up in the air. "Well, for the official dénouement, I declare that this here mule and this here man are stone cold dead in the market."

Like many men who see what no man should see, Bert Brogdon tried, sometimes clumsily, to inject some humor into an intolerable situation. He stood up, grunting. "Get your pictures and get your evidence, and then we'll take these...these..." – he spread his hands out – "...these poor things away to see what we can see. Humpf! This is a new one for me...fifty years of cut-em-up, but this is the first time I'll be doing an autopsy on a mule!"

"Mule's head, Doc," Audrey corrected him. "Only the head. Where's the rest of the animal? Where's the rest of Eustace?"

"There are some things only the Shadow knows." Horace backed away, swallowing his bile and leaving the grisly objects to the ministrations of his crime scene team.

~~~~~~~~~~~~~~~

Horace finished up the morning with a working lunch, sharing roast beef sandwiches slathered with mustard with Inga and Randy. "We're trying to ascertain if Eustace had any relatives. No one seems to know. I'm going over to his shack now, to riffle through heaps of junk, and maybe there will be some clue there as to what might'a happened and why. Maybe we'll find a long-lost son or daughter." He shrugged and swigged down the rest of his coffee.

"Can I tag along?" Inga asked. "I think I'd be a good detective. I adore snooping around in other people's medicine cabinets and making conclusions about their lives from what's on the shelves."

*Why not?* Horace said he'd be glad of the company.

"I'll come along, too," Randy offered. "I always wondered what he had stashed in that old dilapidation that he lived in. It's a wonder that the place is still upright."

Gideon Balfour knocked at the door. "We've found the wagon. It was set on fire with kerosene. Over at the beach, near Seapoint. Nothing much left of it, just a burned hulk of wheels and scrap."

"Kerosene?" Randy mused. "Think there's some connection with our arsonist?" He scratched his chin, cocking his head.

"Nothing would surprise me today," Horace shrugged. "Who the hell can say?"

"Is there anything else on the list of people who were at the fires?" Inga leaned forward and took another pickle out of the Mason jar.

"Nothing at all. We've sort of cleared a few of them. Augustus and Gladys Charett are in the clear. Nellie Hogan," he began to count on his fingers. "Captain Simeon seems OK, Jannus Podalsky, Eustace, obviously…although, I can't really count him out. He might have set the fires. Might have nothing at all to do with him being murdered."

"Really? You think he might be the arsonist?" Inga's eyes were wide with astonishment. "I mean, he's been *killed!*"

Horace shrugged. "Maybe…I just am keeping my options open. If we get a fire tonight, well, then I'll take Eustace off my suspect list. If the fires stop right now…well, then I'll move him up to the top of the list." He patted Inga's hand. "Ya just never know until it's all over. Stranger things have happened, Doc. Much stranger things."

"So, who is still on your suspect list?"

"Charlie Chan. Floyd Jones. Fred from the Esso station. Jimmy Earnest. And…oh, yes. We still haven't been able to find that Posey lady. So she's still there."

"Do you think it's one of them, then?"

"Who the hell knows?"

"As you so succinctly said, 'Only the Shadow knows!' "

~~~~~~~~~~~~~~

"Come on, kid," Giorgio gently shook Andy's warm body. "Hop out of your bed now. We have some driving to do, you and me."

"Huh!" Andy sat up, his hair spiked from the tussles with his pillow and his dreams. "Give me two shakes of a lamb's tail! I'll be right down!"

~~~~~~~~~~~~~~

When Grace learned that Andy was being given a treat, she went into the shop to handle the customers. Antonina, coffee cup in hand, trailed her. "I want to see what you do here. How you work."

"You can watch me, but put down that cup and help. I need you to bring all of those cartons up here." She pointed to a pallet stacked with cardboard boxes. "We're going to sell all of those Mason jars today."

"All those?" Antonina was astonished. "Who will buy all of them?"

"Everybody who has tomatoes and zucchini growing all over their gardens. They'll have so much that they've got to buy mason jars so that they can preserve the bounty. We're going to make a lot of money today!" Grace turned to greet her first customers of the morning.

~~~~~~~~~~~~~~

"This afternoon? You need me now?" Mary Rose groaned.

The telephone call was from a hysterical Bertha Abbot. "I'm in the hospital! My appendix! Please, Mary Rose! I beg you. My cousin will be here tomorrow. Just this afternoon and evening...*please!*"

How could she work for Bertha? Tonight was supposed to be saved for Nick! How could she be at Bertha's bakery and miss seeing Nick! His ship was going out in a few days. She might never see him again! Every moment together was precious for the two of them. Oh, no! She *had* to be with Nick!

She'd just have to say no. There was no *way* that she would miss even an hour of time with Nick. No. It was that simple.

She opened her mouth… "Of course, Bertha. I'll help you out. I'll be there at three and stay as long as needed." She found herself astonished at the words pouring out. "You relax now and do just what the doctors tell you to do. I'll take care of everything. Lie back now and get better."

"May blessings pour upon you," Bertha was crying with gratitude. "You are a true friend, Mary Rose. I will say a special prayer that you will be granted your heart's desire. Such a *mitzvah* you are giving to me. Thank you. Thank you." She hung up, sobbing half with anxiety and fear over what was to come and half with relief at the knowledge that her beloved bakery would be in good hands.

"Are you ready now?" The starched nurse came to her bedside, holding a hypodermic needle aloft. "All your troubles settled?"

"I have a wonderful friend," Bertha held her arm out. The nurse skillfully slipped the needle into her vein. "I can now close my eyes and let you and Doctor Sowerby take care of me. My anxieties are gone. I can relax…relax…re…" Her eyes fluttered shut.

The nurse checked her pulse, nodded in satisfaction and, grunting, pushed the bed out into the hallway. It was always best for a patient to go into surgery in a happy mood. It boded well for the best recovery. *How nice that she has someone she can rely on.* "Coming, Doctor! Here we are…all ready for you."

~~~~~~~~~~~~~~~

"I can't seem to locate Nick," Mary Rose almost shook Eunice off her feet. "I've left messages at his dormitory, but he hasn't been back to get them. He's expecting me to be at the USO at seven." She blushed. "We were planning…we thought…we…" She bit her lip, refusing to even *look* at Eunice in her consternation and confusion.

"What? What were you two up to?" Eunice's eyes danced with curiosity.

"Well, we were going to casually leave the USO. Maybe five minutes apart. I thought…we thought…well, we were going to come back here." She bit her lip. "Now, I can't ....oh, *why* did her appendix have to pop out tonight?" Mary Rose wailed. "It has spoiled *everything*! This is the only night that he's not on duty until he leaves! If I don't see him tonight...why, we may never get to see one another again until after the war is over!" Her panic was palpable.

Eunice patted her shoulder. "Don't get yourself upset. This can all be worked out. Give me the telephone numbers and I'll find Nick somehow and give him your message. You want to meet him later. Maybe at ten o'clock." She thought for a moment. "Gee, that's cutting it fine. The USO closes at ten!"

"What else can I doooooo?" Mary Rose's agitation made her voice squeak. "He'll think...he'll think I changed my mind."

"I'll get in touch with him one way or another. I'll go to the USO and find him myself. I'll explain everything. He'll find you, never fear. Love will make everything come out OK. You two were made for one another! No one and nothing, not even her blasted appendix, is going to screw up your night together."

"Oh, Eunice. I'll die if we can't be together! I'll just die!"

"Don't panic, Mary Rose. It will be fine. Just fine."

# CHAPTER NINETEEN

**End of August 1943 – Heinrich Himmler is named Reich Minister of the Interior by Hitler.**

**Allies prepare for invasion of mainland Italy.**

He finally called back. "What do you mean; you have to work at the Jewish bakery?" He was incredulous. "This is maybe our last night to see one another! I need you with *me*, Mary Rose! Not at some bakery selling bagels!"

"I can't…I just have to…oh, Nick! We'll be together! It just will be a little later than I anticipated." Her voice caught on a sob of frustration.

"I can't believe you!" His own disappointment made him careless. He *loved* her. He just *had* to see her tonight! If his ship sailed and he hadn't told her how much he loved her….oh, shit! Shit! Shit! Shit! He tried once more. "Mary Rose, call this lady back. Tell her you just can't be there!"

"I can't call her, Nick! She's in the hospital!"

"Well, just leave a message. Close the Goddam bakery for the day! Everyone will live without their bagels! I've just got to see you, baby. I need you and if you love me, you'll put me first and not some woman that you barely know!" His voice

was harsh.   Frustration and desire warred with good judg-
ment. "Who do you care about? Me or that Jewish lady?"

"Nick! You're not being fair!" Stung, she began to get
angry. If Nick had known Mary Rose's father, he'd have been
warned that she had a terrible temper under certain conditions. As a matter of fact, he would have told Nick that she
could be positively pig-headed. But, alas for these two youngsters, Mary Rose's family wasn't around.

"I can't believe this!" Nick, too, had a temper. "You've got
to chose. Me or her!"

"You are being pig-headed!" Mary Rose was losing her
ability to think straight.

*"Me? Me? I'm* being pig-headed?" His voice rose to a
shout. "You're the one who is being pig-headed!"

Ah, the tempestuousness of young lovers.

"You don't love me! How could you love me and talk to me
like this?" The tempo accelerated.

"You don't love *me!* How can you pass up the opportunity
to see me one last time? I might never come *back!"* Ah, the
ultimate guilt-provoking, but too often true, threat.

Unable to breathe, unable to speak, Mary Rose felt her
world fall apart.

Unable to take back his words, Nick felt *his* world fall apart.

"I…I…you…" She tried to bring the falling-apart together.
Had it not been war time, had they been together a bit more,
had they weathered an argument or two or made love to one
another, perhaps it would have worked.

"Mary Rose…." He tried to gather himself, knowing that he
was making the biggest mistake of his life, but unable to stop.
"Mary Rose….I…I'm…" The apology choked him. Mary Rose's
mother might have told him to just tell her that he loved her
and that all would be fine. But she wasn't there to help out.

The silence stretched on and on. Finally, knowing that she
was going to start sobbing and not wanting him to know that
she was going to start sobbing, and not knowing what else to
do, she gently hung up.

"Son of a bitch!" Nick was stung. "She hung up on me!"

~~~~~~~~~~~~~~

**End of August, 1943 – The theater-going public in New York City nearly danced out of Rogers and Hammerstein's *Oklahoma* singing "...*People will say we're in love...*"**

"Andy?" *Was this the right time?*

"Hi, Cousin Antonina."

"Andy, come and sit with me...I want to talk with you..." *Should I talk with him about this? Should I wait until Grace and Mario tell him?*

Warily, he sat next to her. *She's so pretty, with her long, pale brown hair and her beautiful grey eyes.* His eyes were the same color, but, somehow, they looked ordinary on him and pretty on her. He knew nothing about her and the secrets of her own birth. How could he know that she, too, had been born out of wedlock, the child of a man who adored her mother? How could he know that *her* mother had also done what she thought best, letting Antonina grow up thinking that another man was her father? *What is she going to say to me?*

"I want to tell you a story," she began, picking her words carefully. "It's the story of a young girl who had a dilemma. A problem. She was very young and very inexperienced in solving a problem like this. She had just suffered a cruel blow, a very sad and terrible thing. It made this problem nearly insurmountable to her."

"Was this young girl you?" Andy turned to her with the blunt honesty of youth.

"Yes, Andy. It was me. Let me start at the beginning. You, too, are very young, Andy. I hope you will hear this story and let it rest in your mind. Later, take this story out and taste it again, when you are a little older and maybe a little more able to comprehend that people are never perfect. Not me, not your parents, not you. We all make awful mistakes in our lives. We rush, unheeding, into things. We're greedy and selfish and want to be happy. Sometimes, we make others very unhappy in our selfishness."

"I don't understand..." He squirmed, uncomfortable. *I don't think she knows that I already know what she's trying to tell me. Maybe I should let her know...make it easier...* In his youth and own inexperience, he didn't, however, know what to say to her.

"Let me try to tell you... I was very young. I had always wanted to be an opera singer. I lived and breathed opera. Practiced every day, every moment. Dreamed of my future. Hoped and prayed that I would succeed and be famous and be able to make people happy with my gift. My voice. It was my passion. My reason for living." She bit her lip, remembering.

"By a curious and terrible circumstance, I was given the opportunity to sing at the Metropolitan Opera. I was an immediate success. I became an opera star. A good and dear friend told me that being an opera star was a wonderful thing, but that I would have to give up being a normal woman. A woman who might have lived a normal life with a husband and children. She told me that I couldn't be both. That one day, I'd have to choose my path and stick to it. The other path would not be open to me."

He nodded, uncertain.

"I met a man...a wonderful man...and I fell in love with him. He fell in love with me. We were deliriously happy. I was singing and I was becoming more and more famous. I was also determined to marry this man. In my youth and foolishness and optimism, I thought I could have everything and not pay the price."

"The price?" He really didn't understand her story or it's moral.

"Yes. When you want something with all your heart, sometimes you get it. But there is always a price to pay." Her face was sad with dark shadows in her eyes.

Unbidden, he thought that the shadows reached down into her soul. With a child's innocence, he saw with truth.

"I became pregnant. I was ecstatic. Now my cup ran over with joy. I had my career, I had my beloved, and now, we were about to have a child." She turned to him. "Are you understanding me so far?"

"I think so."

"Good," she smiled at him; the dimples in her cheeks making him yearn for something. "You are an intelligent boy, Andy. This will all make sense to you one day." She sighed and continued; "But I was beginning to be worried. How could I be a famous star, moving from place to place, giving my soul to my audience....for to be a truly great opera singer, I *had* to give my soul...and my heart...every night... to my audience... Otherwise, I could not be great or successful. The audience would know that what was coming out of me wasn't real. They, an audience, *know*. They *feel*...they demand it all from you." She was silent for a moment, reliving her memories.

"How could I do it all? How could I cut myself up? All of me to the audiences, all of me to my beloved, all of me to my child?" She shook her head. "I would have been cheating everyone that way. I began to worry more and more. I didn't know what to do." Her eyes were downcast.

"And then, a solution came my way. A terrible, terrible solution. I told you, Andy, when you want something badly enough, sometimes you get it. And then, you cannot believe that you ever wanted it...but you have it."

He shook his head. "I...I really don't understand, Cousin Antonina."

"How could you? Just listen to me and have some pity on me, my darling boy." She raised her eyes to him and in their depths, he saw her agony and sorrow.

"My beloved...his name was Anderson...Anderson Von Vogel, and he was the Chief of Detectives in New York City. A wonderful man, Andy. A wonderful person. You would have adored him, Andy." She touched Andy's cheek with her finger and then looked down. "One day, Anderson was murdered as he tried to save my life. Poof! In an instant, he was gone. Dead."

He gaped at her, never expecting this...

"And I was alone with the baby yet-to-be-born."

"Was I that baby?" He was blunt. "I know...I have known for years... that you are my real mother."

"How could you know this?" She gasped, stunned. "It was a sworn *secret*!"

Andy was torn. He wanted to laugh...and he wanted to weep. "Cousin Sammy told me. He always knew all the secrets. He told me when I was just a kid."

She laughed. "Cousin *Sammy*. That little sneak! He *knew*! All these years, I kept this secret locked in my heart. All these years, it caused me to cry. And Cousin Sammy knew all the time!" She turned and hugged him. "Oh, Andy! Can you ever forgive me? I didn't know what else to do. I loved you so, even before you were born. But I didn't know how to cope with you. I knew I couldn't be a good enough mother, and so, I gave you up. Your parents...are such good people. They yearned... *yearned* for a baby. And so, we gave each other what we felt we wanted. Your mother and father took you to their hearts. They adored you and loved you from the moment they saw you. No mother and father could have loved their own child more than they loved you. I know, because I watched and my heart broke, but I was happy that you were happy. And you were! They loved you better than I could have."

"I think...I think I can understand." He took her hand in his and she felt a thrill better than a million people applauding. "When Sammy told me, I was too young to even know what the heck he was talking about. It sat inside me, and I think I just grew more and more to understand what it must have been like. I love you, Cousin Antonina. But, I love my mother and father more."

"I understand, Andy. *They* are your real parents. I was simply the package that let them be your parents. That's not the right word..." She was emotional and confused, with tears dripping down her cheeks. "You...you are my secret treasure, but *she* is your mother and Mario is your father. For real."

"Tell me the rest."

"We made a bargain. I could see you whenever I wished. They would always keep me informed of everything you did, but I couldn't interfere with your upbringing. We all agreed that one day you'd be told. Today was the day I thought it would be all right to tell you." She began to laugh again, a little wildly. "But, son-of-a-gun, Cousin Sammy beat me to it!"

Grace found them, sitting on the wall in the sunshine, their arms wrapped around one another, their laughter bubbling out, perhaps a little hysterically.

"Come here, Mom," Andy opened his arms further. "We have quite a story to tell you!"

~~~~~~~~~~~~~~~~

"Their necks were severed by some sort of very sharp instrument," Doc Brogdon reported. "Maybe a scalpel, but I don't think so. The cuts are too broad. Not fine enough. I think it was some kind of specialized knife…like a boning knife or a large filleting knife. A professional knife, whatever it was. Not some butter knife from a kitchen."

"Maybe a fisherman's knife?" Horace asked.

Doc nodded. "Could be. Or a butcher, or a hunter. Whoever did this, knew something about anatomy. Might have been a medical person, or even an undertaker. This assailant knew just how to cut a head off. And how to cut the mule's head, too. This is specialized knowledge. You might think cutting off someone's head is an easy thing. But, *noooo.*" He shook his massive head. "The neck muscles are strong and difficult to sever. They were put there by God to protect the throat, the body's breathing apparatus, the carotid artery… God wanted it to be hard to chop off a head. He made it tough. *This* person has thwarted God. And by everything that we hold dear, we must help to catch and punish this bastard."

~~~~~~~~~~~~~~~~

Moving slowly, like a carnival automaton, she waited on customers all afternoon. She gave out bagels and bialys and poppy seed cakes. She made change, greeted people and bade them have a good evening. She smiled and spoke and made no mistakes at all. But, if you had quizzed her on what had transpired during the day, she would not have been able to remember a single thing.

And on the base, he walked and marched and did the tasks that he was assigned to do. He joked and laughed with his friends and comrades, saluted the brass, ate what was put in front of him in the mess. He'd performed to perfection, even earning a thumbs-up from the difficult-to-please Commandant, but if you had asked him what had gone on during his day, he wouldn't have been able to tell you what he had done.

The two of them, sick in love, and too pig-headed to understand that to love is to give as well as to take. It was a sad thing to see, if anyone had noticed. Two people in utter misery, longing for one another, and not knowing what to do about it all.

*I'll call the base. Ask to speak with him. Say that it's a family emergency.* She nearly picked up the telephone, but didn't.

*I can go off base tonight. I'll go to the bakery. Find it somehow. I'll grovel on my knees to her.* He almost walked off the Shipyard without permission, but didn't.

*I'll just shut the shop up. He was right. He means more to me than anything. I was a bitch and I deserve everything I get. I may never see him again. Ever! Ever!*

*I might get shipped out and never see her again. She'll forget me. How can I live without her?*

*He could be killed. His ship might be torpedoed. He could die without me ever having the chance to apologize. Tell him how much I adore him. Oh, Mary Rose, you stupid, stupid girl! To let a man like Nick go!*

*I want to be with her the rest of my dumb, stupid life! How could I start such a silly argument? She's a girl in a million, ready to help out someone in a pickle...not just a person in a pickle, but a woman who was sick! In an emergency! And I made her feel bad. I'm such an idiot! Not fit to touch the hem of her dress.* He felt sick. His stomach was roiling and he didn't know what to do. Maybe, just maybe, he'd talk to the Chaplain. He could use some advice.

~~~~~~~~~~~~~~~

Fanny Parks stuck her head into her husband's office. He looked up, astonished. It wasn't often that Fanny invaded his work domain. "Hey, cookie! What are you doing down here?"

She waved a white box at him. I was at the hospital today. My turn to volunteer."

"Yeah? And?" She'd been volunteering at York Hospital now for more than ten years.

"And." She smiled at him. "And...for the first time in our married life together...I know about someone dying that you don't know yet." Horace reared back. He knew his wife well. Her face held a mixture of glee and sadness. What did she know? Who died? *Damned if I'm going to ask her.*

She sat down and opened the box. In it were three jelly donuts, a specialty of the York Hospital lunchroom. She handed him one and picked one up herself. She settled back into the chair, milking the situation for all it was worth. She took a huge bite and jelly squirted all over her fingers. She laughed at herself and licked the jelly off her fingers, enjoying his annoyance at her silence. *It must be killing him! He's going crazy, not knowing what I know!*

Horace and Fanny had been very happily married a long, long time. He stuck his tongue out at her and grabbed a donut. "Good donut," he said, munching. *Damned if I'm going to beg her to tell me who died!*

Fanny finished her donut and wiped her hands on a paper napkin. "I'll leave the last one for you," She stood up.

"Siddown! All right, you wench. You win. Who died?"

She came around to his chair and bent to kiss his cheek. "Well, I was just leaving the hospital when the ambulance came roaring in. Naturally, me being a curious person..."

"Nosey, you mean."

"Some might call it nosey. I prefer to think that I am curious." She ruffled his hair. "If you want to know the rest of the story, you're going to have to be nice to me."

"I'm always nice to you, my darling. Now tell me, who the hell died?"

She took pity on him. "Gladys Charett."

His jaw dropped. "Mrs. Man Mountain Aga*ment*icus? She *died?*"

Fanny nodded. "I shouldn't be enjoying this. It's sad, really. The poor, poor lady. But isn't it weird? We all thought that *he* was going to die from a heart attack, and here she beat him to it."

"She died of a *heart* attack? No way!"

"No." Fanny was genuinely sorry. "She fell."

"Fell? How?"

"Sue, the nurse at the Emergency Room told me that Gladys had been in the kitchen and had tried to get up on a step ladder to get something off a top shelf. Her heel caught on a rung and she fell. Her neck was broken." Fanny's generally sunny nature failed her. "I feel bad that I am joking about this…I shouldn't be making fun of her or making light of her death, but, oh, Horace…she was baking Augustus a lemon meringue pie!"

~~~~~~~~~~~~~~~~

The hours dragged by. There hadn't been a customer since six o'clock. The bakery was supposed to stay open until nine. If she locked the door quickly, right at nine, could she then run over to the USO and maybe find Nick waiting for her? Would he be there? Would this miserable day ever end?

She tried to pass the time doing some cleaning…re-arranging the bread, the bagels and the *rugelach*. She counted the money in the till and wrote up the deposit slip to be taken to the bank tomorrow. She swept the floor once again, this time making sure that every single corner was bereft of crumbs.

The clock said eight-thirty. She peered outside at the night sidewalks. There were people scurrying by, soldiers and sailors stopping into the nearby restaurants. A few bar girls, linked arm-in-arm with their evening's income, sauntered along the street, but no one, not one single person, seemed to be determined to buy a loaf of pumpernickel bread.

At six minutes to nine, she decided to close up. She pulled down the shade on the front door and turned the sign around to CLOSED. She checked herself in the mirror that decorated the wall. *I look like a wreck. Bags and shadows under my eyes. Horrible. I look horrible!*

She began the process of officially shutting down the shop. The breads and the cookies, the bagels and the bialys could stay where they were, clean and dry in their bins and on their shelves. The cakes, the cream buns and the pies had to be refrigerated so that they wouldn't spoil. She took a large tray and began the tedious process of bringing all of them down the narrow steps to the area in the cavernous basement where the refrigerator resided, humming along.

The stairs were steep. Even without the heavy load of pies, it was treacherous going. With the load of pies, she had to balance the heavy tray with one hand, and brace herself along the banister with the other hand. "Uuuuf!" she groaned, almost slipping on the next-to-the bottom step.

The basement, as she had noted that last time she had been in it, was filled with gloom. It was festooned with cobwebs that caught in her hair, chilly, and dank. She shivered. *Best get this job done fast and get the heck out of here! Oh, Nick, darling, Nick. Please be at the USO waiting for me!*

Using both hands now, she walked through the room that was used to bake the bread. She set the tray down on a table and opened the old wooden door that led even further into the basement's abyss, into the back room where the refrigeration sat. If the baking room exuded gloom, *this* room was even worse.

*I feel like I'm going into a crypt! How does Bertha go into this horror every day? Why doesn't she light the place better? Clean it up so that it doesn't feel so awful?*

She pushed the door open and, with her hip helping, manhandled the tray through. She began to whistle, trying to make herself feel more cheerful. *"Oh, Johnny, oh, Johnny, how you can love...."*

The big door swung shut behind her, taking half of the light. *This place is giving me the heebie-jeebies. Stop it, Mary Rose!* She admonished herself.

She put the tray down on a dusty table and, with both hands, pulled open the huge freezer door. *What was that?*

"Hello?" She called out. "Is anyone here?" The hum of the refrigeration unit answered her.

She shrugged, trying hard to shake her nervousness. She began to put the pies on the lower shelf. There! She'd heard it again...a chopping noise, as if someone was cutting up wood with an ax. She stood still once more, trying to figure out where the sound was coming from. There! Again, she heard the noises. They were muffled, but nonetheless, a rhythmic chopping noise was coming from the back wall. And then....a high, keening sound...some sort of machinery?

Curious now, nearly forgetting her fright at the morbid atmosphere, Mary Rose came out of the freezer box. The noise was louder out here...a locomotive screeching along? What *was* it?

She stepped to the bricks of the far wall. It was loudest here. She leaned forward and put her ear to the wall. The buzzing sound was very loud now. She patted the wall. Solid brick, probably two hundred years old. *Could ghosts be here? You dumb woman, you,* she scolded herself. *There are no ghosts! Yeah? Well then who was making that noise? Who was scaring the bejeesus out of me? How come those little hairs on the back of my neck are standing on end?*

Her palms, running along the bricks, touched a different surface. "It's a door!" She was so astonished that she spoke aloud. *No one to hear me anyway, just the spooks and the goblin and the dead people on the other side of the wall.*

Her intrigue beat out her fright. In the darkness behind the freezer, she felt along the wood of the door, seeking a handle or a knob. There! A handle...a lock... She wiggled herself further into the narrow space. The sound was louder here. Screeching, strident. A buzzsaw? Some machinery? What *was* it?

She wiggled in further, then managed to half-turn herself so she could stoop and put her eye to the keyhole.

She blinked, trying to see. But the keyhole was blocked with the dust, dirt and debris of a hundred or more years. She couldn't see anything at all. She maneuvered herself closer and her foot hit something that made a metallic noise. She almost decapitated herself bending down...*there! There!* A little closer. She could touch it with her fingertips, but couldn't quite pick it up....ah! OK. *Careful, careful, don't drop it now!* She felt its contours in her hand. It was a key! A big, heavy key. Was this the key to the door?

She backed herself out of the tiny space, stood up straight, putting her hand against the small of her back, easing the kinks. The key winked in the dim glow from the light bulb strung up overhead. She wiped it off. It was made of brass, or some kind of non-tarnishable metal. Ornate, with a big loop at the top.

The whining noise stopped. In the silence, she thought she heard voices. She leaned her ear again against the bricks, but whatever was being said was swallowed up buy the thickness of the wall.

Undaunted, she looked around for some sort of tool. A screwdriver or a thin, but sturdy stick. Where? Where? She ran back into the baking room and found a stack of narrow, thick skewers. Not knowing that these skewers were used every day to hold stacks of bagels, not really caring *what* they were used for, Mary Rose was elated. *The very thing!* She'd be able to pry the dirt out of the keyhole with one of these!

She wiggled again into the opening behind the freezer, stooped, and began to winkle-out the dirt that was stuck in the keyhole. As she pried at it, the buzzing noise started up again. She thought she heard a man's voice shout, "Be careful!"

A chunk of dirt flew out, followed by another. There! She put her finger into the keyhole and with her nail, scooped out more…whatever it was…filth?…dirt? Dead spiders?

She bent again and this time was rewarded by a beam of light coming through the keyhole. The buzzing was louder now.…keening and whining. She squinted and looked ….

The sound of the saw masked her gasp of horror.

~~~~~~~~~~~~~~

**August 1943 – Round the clock bombing of Germany begins.**

**August 1943 – Hans and Sophie Scholl publish and distribute anti-Nazi pamphlets in Munich. They are caught and executed.**

He didn't care if they court-martialed him. What would it matter? Nick paced the floor of his bunk-room. It had been a mistake to talk with the Chaplain. The Padre had betrayed him and his confidences. Told on him to Admiral Wither's staff. Warned him about trying to see his girl.

"You're leaving in a day or two, Cappiello. You know that you are strictly forbidden to see those USO canteen girls! They'll be chastised and you'd be chastised."

"But, Chaplain! She's my sweetheart! I plan on *marrying* this woman! For Christ's sake…oh, I'm sorry, Chaplain…but …but, if I went off base tonight and met a bar girl, you wouldn't care at all. If I paid for a whore, you'd just pat me on the head and tell me to use a rubber so that I didn't get VD!" Nick shook his head in disgust. "Nobody would care if I left here tonight and got blind drunk on the street! Went to that fancy cat house! Nobody would give a....give a...darn." His voice trailed off lamely.

The Chaplain smiled with sympathy. "I understand your frustration."

"No you don't! I confide in you and you...you...!" Nick's voice rose. His frustration rose even higher. "I'll just walk out of here and you can't stop me! I have leave tonight and I'm going!"

"Cappiello, you already told me that you were going to meet this girl. She sounds like a wonderful girl, but the rules for the USO girls are the rules. Now that I know what your plans would have been, I'm telling you that you can't go out."

Nick was seething, but this was getting him nowhere. Every time he tried to explain, he got further and further into the morass of military rules and laws and bumped against the equally as frustrating complications with the USO rules.

He slumped his body into submissiveness. "OK. OK." He pretended to capitulate. "I'll stay here like a good little boy. I'll try to talk with her tomorrow."

The Chaplain smiled. *See? It isn't hard to reason with these young boys, fresh off the farm or just out of high school. You just have to be firm. Explain to them with short sentences that they'd understand. Tell them that you know what they're going through, and then be sure that they cannot get around the rules. Simple.*

He watched Nick walk back to the barracks. *The boy understands now. Simple. He just needed me to talk to. Man to man.*

# CHAPTER
# TWENTY

**1943 – The Mills Brothers rendition of "Paper Doll" holds the
Number One position on Your Hit Parade for twelve weeks.**

Through the narrow aperture, her eye saw an abattoir of
blood and horror. A cellar, the twin of the one she was in...
*next door? What was next door?*

A wooden trestle table with the body of some grotesque
creature strapped to it. Three people...*three men,* she
thought...*dressed in what had formerly been white overalls,
now spattered and smeared with guts and body fluids, wearing some sort of rubberized aprons...what in God's heaven
was this glimpse of Hell?*

Her eyes strained to see more, even as her stomach
heaved its disgust at what she *was* seeing. Another person,
this time it was a woman...a fat, hefty woman with her
hair...blonde hair...braided in heavy coils on her head. Her
face was sweaty, her eyes...even from this tiny glimpse...
glittered with a mad fervor.

She...the lady butcher, held a long, sharp knife. With it,
she was skinning the fur...fur? Whatever she was doing, she
was stripping the skin from the creature. Mary Rose's mind

simply stopped working. She couldn't comprehend this...so she just watched, numb with horror.

She startled as the machine started up again. The high keening scream of machinery. The men adjusted goggles onto their faces, *who were they? Who were these monsters who covered up their eyes and obliterated their features?* The men shouted to one another over the whine of the saw. The table moved slowly as the men held the huge, shapeless body, directing it toward the gleaming teeth of the round saw at the end of the table.

*Ohgodohgodohgod!*

*Zzzzzz!* The saw whined as it bit into the carcass. The saw screamed and bits of blood and sinew and bone flew into the air, droplets of flesh hanging for a nanosecond, turned the room into a chamber of unspeakable gore. A large slice of flesh peeled off, and one of the men picked it up and brought it to a table, almost out of Mary Rose's sight.

Almost. She swiveled her eye. The man took a huge glittering knife, its shiny surface already marred by smears of blood, and began to fillet the chunk of flesh, carving the bones away, then chopping the meat into dripping chunks.

*Suitable for stew!* She gasped, almost out loud. This was the cellar of the butcher shop next door! *Tedesco's!*

*Zzzzzz!* The saw's music rang out again, slicing into the bones and spewing out another enormous slab of gore. She gagged, then covered her mouth so no one could hear her. *If they caught me seeing them...they'd put me on that table, too! Oh my god! What shall I do?*

One of the men moved out of sight, then back into sight, coming close to the other side of the door with the keyhole. Unable to help herself, Mary Rose shrank back, huddling herself against the machinery that kept the refrigeration going. *They can't possibly know I'm here. They can't possibly see me or hear me...can they?*

The man returned carrying ... *Ohgod,oh no! ... No! How much can I take here, God? How much that is inconceivable are you going to let me see?* Mary Rose buried her head down in her chest, huddling as best she could into a fetal position, closing her eyes so that the storm of tears flowed down her cheeks. So that her sobs were stifled. So that her soul had some rest from the awful things before it.

It was as if she simply had no will of her own. She looked back out of the keyhole. She *had* to watch. *Had* to see. It was a human body...an elderly, wrinkled, hefty human body. With dispassion brought on by her overloaded capability to see and process that which was inhuman, she noted with clinical indifference that the body, like the animal, had no head. Simply arms and legs, hands and feet, connected by a fish-belly-white torso. In some recess of her brain...a recess that normally processed things that were amusing and funny, she was able to make a joke. The body was a heavy one. It would make a great stew.

Afterwards, she thought she must have fainted. She didn't remember the saw screeching, didn't remember the bones cracking and the blood and body fragments blowing into the air. Didn't remember the lady and one of the other men wrapping up the chunks of flesh into small parcels of perhaps a pound or two each. But somewhere, deep down in the part of her brain where darkness dwells, the images were burned.

When she came to her senses again and looked through the keyhole, the room had been cleaned and rearranged. There was only one person there now. The man carried several white paper-wrapped packages. His apron, unlike the ones worn by the rest of the men, was clean. He put the packages in a basket, and hefted the basket. He looked around, perhaps to check that all had been cleansed, then put out the light and closed the door.

*Just like somebody's dad, going out shopping for the family's meat ration for the week,* Mary Rose nearly laughed out loud in her hysteria. Only the steaks and chops and ground hamburger will be of some animal and some old man. *If I begin to laugh out loud, I'll never be able to stop.*

*What have I just seen here? Was it simply some butchers cutting up animals to make dog meat? Is that how they prepare dog meat?*

*But Tedesco's is a* butcher *shop, not an animal meat shop. They don't sell meat for animals, they sell meat to people who take it home and consume it. They sell chili and stew and hamburgers to* people. *Human beings. What is it all about? Are they selling people to people?*

She shivered, worried that she was going mad. *Should I go to the police? What should I tell them? They would think I was crazy. And maybe I am.*

She stayed, crouched and dazed, for what seemed like hours. Had she really seen a murder? Had she really seen an animal chopped into steaks? A man ground into hamburger?

Only one way to be sure. She checked the keyhole again and saw a dark and silent room, cleaned of everything that might give its secrets away. She hefted the key in her hand and put it into the keyhole. Click, it turned, as sweetly as the day it had been fitted. She pushed at the door. It moved slightly, but then stopped, most likely impeded by something on the other side. She pushed harder and felt the heaviness behind it slide…a shhh-ing noise. Maybe a pile of boxes? She pushed it open enough to slide herself through. She crouched then, listening hard. All was silent.

She stepped into the room and looked back. Yes, there had been a pile of boxes stacked against the door on that side, effectively hiding the keyhole to a casual observer.

She came in further, squinting to see in the darkness. She felt the table, its top still damp from the cleansing. She touched the hard steel of the smooth conveyor leading toward the wicked blade of the buzzsaw. Her fingers touched the edges of the saw…short, vicious tips, capable of chewing through meat and bones and gristle. Capable of slicing through the horse or whatever it had been. Capable of eating through a man's torso, hips and ribs. She shuddered, almost beyond horror. But not quite.

She tip-toed to the door on the opposite wall and listened….not a sound. The door had no keyhole, nor any aperture. She knelt on the now-swept floor, putting her face on the ground, trying to see if the bottom of the door might allow her to see to the other side. If so, there was just blackness. She could see no light at all. She stood, trying to decide what to do. *Shoot, I'm here now. I may as well see all there is to see. Then, I'll go straight to the police. This is really no place for me.*

She opened the door.

~~~~~~~~~~~~~~~

**1943 – Notre Dame wins the College Football Championship**

**In 1943, the Indianapolis 500 was not held because of the severity of the war, nor was the US Golf Open.**

Nick walked out of the Yard, waving to the guards in the sentry box. Just a sailor going on leave. That's all. He walked along Route 103 and quickly hitched a ride into Portsmouth from a friendly oil truck driver. He'd thought his solitary exit was more prudent than riding to the USO with the rest of his group in the Navy bus. After all, he *did* have leave that night. There was no reason that he had to stay at the base. He'd been cautiously warned by the Chaplain not to pursue Mary Rose, but no one had actually *ordered* him to stay put.

He shrugged as he slid out of the oil truck's passenger seat, thanked the driver again, and walked into the USO. Shit, if they caught him and screamed at him, so what? He was leaving to fight the Japs in a few days. What could be worse?

He saw Eunice sitting at a table with three USO girls and Doctor Patten. He beckoned to her. "Where's Mary Rose?" His eyes searched the tables and the dance floor.

"Oh, Nick! I'm so glad to see you. She's been trying to reach you. She's not here yet," Eunice was uneasy. It upset her to know that Mary Rose and Nick had quarreled. "She was supposed to be here a half-hour ago. Maybe they got busy at the Jewish bakery." Her clear, fine eyes drilled into Nick's. To Nick, Eunice's thoughts were as clear as if she'd had them written on her forehead: *Why did you argue with her? You know what kind of a girl she is! She could never let anyone down, not even the lady at the bakery!*

Nick shuffled his feet. He answered Eunice's thoughts out loud: "I know. I'm an idiot! Here we have only tonight and I go and pick a fight with her. I should be hung by the neck."

"Mmmm," Eunice's grimace showed that she might likely enjoy pulling on the rope. "Well, she should be along any minute. I'll watch out for her, too." She turned and sat back down at her table. Alex Patten leaned forward, probably asking her what was going on. Eunice shook her head and then looked over to Nick. She gave him a lop-sided smile.

Nick rubbed his chin. What should he do? Wait, go back to the Yard, or maybe trot over to the bakery to intercept her if she was still at work. *I'll walk over. If she's not there, I'll come back here. She ought to be here by then. If she isn't, I'll assume that she's gone home. I'll ask Doc Patten to drive me over.*

An uneasiness sat on his broad shoulders. He went out of the USO and scanned the crowd at the sidewalk, praying that he'd see her face. No.

The uneasiness increased. Where the hell was she? He began to walk towards Liberson's Bakery, then, for whatever reason, he began to run.

~~~~~~~~~~~~~~~

It took a few moments for her eyes to become adjusted to the darkness. She was in a large room…perhaps a storage room. All along one wall sat the whiteness of a line of refrigerators, and at the corner, a large stainless-steel door announced the entry to a walk-in freezer. She opened one of the refrigerator doors. The little light inside the door went on, showing her the contents. It was filled with vegetables. Carrots and lettuce and onions. She'd been holding her breath. But it was only carrots and celery.

She opened a second door. The refrigerator was stacked with dozens and dozens of small parcels, each wrapped in white butcher paper. They were similar to the ones she'd seen one of the men wrapping. She picked up one and read the black-penciled label: **3 lbs. Chopped Meat.**

*Chopped what kind of meat,* she wondered. *Horse? Man? Woman? Cat? Dog?*

She shut the door and went to the huge walk-in. She tried the door, but it seemed to be locked. Frustrated, she looked for a key, feeling along the floor and then on the ledge above the door. Nothing. She tried again to open it. In her intense frustration, she didn't hear the other door, the one that led to the upstairs butcher shop, open. She didn't hear the muffled footsteps of the two men who burst into the room, flicking on the light.

"Vell, vell," one of the said, freezing the marrow in Mary Rose's bones. "Vat haff vee here?"

"A liddle girly." The other, armed with a heavy cudgel, waved it in the air, threatening her.

She backed up, trying to distance herself, her eyes bugged out with fright. *Can I run? Can I slide by them to the door? Can I run back into the other room and get out the way I came in?*

It was as if she'd shouted her thoughts aloud. "No, missy. Don't even t'ink of running away." The man with the cudgel came closer, holding the weapon aloft. She shrank into a small ball. *They are going to kill me! They are going to kill me and then make me into a roast beef!*

She screamed as the cudgel came down toward her head and shoulder. Twisting like a cat, she pushed at him and scrambled away. *I'm free! I'm free!*

She grabbed at the handle of the back door and pulled. And then, the cudgel smashed again on her head and she slumped to the floor.

The man came closer. "She's out cold," he remarked, as casually as if she'd been a mosquito. "Let's get her tied up and into the other room. Call Al and let him know that we had a visitor. Meanwhile, I'll get her ready to be taken care of permanently."

"Vat the hell vas she do-ink down here?" The taller man asked in his German accent. "How did anyvun get in?"

"Who knows and who cares?" The cudgel man shrugged. "We'll just make her disappear."

"Yeah, but suppose somebody knew she vas coming here?" The taller man scratched his head. "Al's gonna vant to know vhat's the story."

Cudgel shrugged again. "Sure, sure. I'll tie her up and then we can wait and see what to do." He grinned. "Al will get her to talk. She'll tell us whatever we want to know when he saws off her fingers, one by one."

~~~~~~~~~~~~~~~

The lights at the bakery were off. The door was locked and the CLOSED sign dangled in the window. Frustrated and now worried, Nick started to bang on the door. *She might still be there. Maybe in the back.*

He rattled the doorknob and called her name. Loud, and then louder. The silence of the night answered.

He stood, hands on his hips, wondering what the hell he should do now. Shrugging, unable to think of anything else, he turned to go back to the USO.

~~~~~~~~~~~~~~~

The bright lights hurt her eyes. She tried to turn her head away, but she couldn't. A stab of terror shafted through her as she remembered. She shuddered as a new voice assailed her: "Ah, you vake up now! Goot. Goot. I vant you to be avake. I haff questions to ask of you."

She turned her head and a shaft of pain shot though it. But no pain could be as bad as the pain that was in her brain. *These men are going to chop me up. They are going to run me through that machine and make me into sausages! God, help me, help me, help me.*

She was lying on the stainless steel table, her arms trussed tightly. Her legs tied, but not as tightly as her arms. *Can I wiggle my feet loose,* she wondered? *Maybe kick them and run?*

The cudgel man was standing near her head, holding the heavy club. He waved it, menacing, at her head. She winced, anticipating the blow, but the man just grinned at her, terrifying her even more, if possible. The other man, the taller one, was not in the room, she noted.

*I can't get out of this,* she was proud of herself for not screaming and pleading with them. *I am doomed. Unless the Germans decide to bomb Portsmouth right now and the bomb falls on Tedesco's Butcher Shop and restaurant, I am going to die in a few moments.* She forced herself to look away from the gleaming blade of the buzzsaw. *I'll think of my family. I love them and they'll miss me forever. They probably won't ever know what happened to me, but they'll never stop wondering and looking for me. I'll see them in Heaven and I can tell them then. And Nick...I'm sorry, Nick, that I quarreled with you. We would have made a very good match, me and you...together. I hope you don't think I ran away from you, Nick. I pray that you understand that I love you and will always love you.* A tear dripped on her cheek.

"You cry, liddle lady. Goot. You should cry." Al Tedesco fiddled with the buttons of the saw. "If you didn't cry by yourself, I vould have helped you to cry." His smile was tender.

Mary Rose thought that she could not be more afraid. But she was.

"How did you find my liddle place down here, heh?"

*I'm not going to say anything to him. If I start to talk, I'll begin to really cry, and he's not going to get that satisfaction. Please, God. Make me strong. Let me stay strong, no matter what they do to me. I'm going to be dead in a few minutes, so that will be that. I can't be more dead than dead, so I will just let them kill me.*

"You must answer me, liddle lady. Who are you and vhy are you here?"

Mary Rose closed her eyes.

"Oho! You t'ink you are brave, heh? Vee shall see." He flipped on the switch, and the buzzsaw's blade began to turn. The muscles in Mary Rose's stomach clamped, in a spasm of terror. "I t'ink ve vill start wit' you liddle fingers." He moved her, shoving her around, so that her right hand was closest to the whirring saw blade. *God make me strong.*

"Ach!" Al said. "Ve need butcher paper." *He's starting to talk more and more German,* Mary Rose noted in some far-off compartment of her brain. "Go upstairs and get some of der paper." He jerked his thumb toward the door. "Get some rope unt ein elmer..."

Cudgel nodded and waved the weapon around one more time. *Is he trying to frighten me?* Mary Rose chuckled to herself in a macabre joke. *How could I be more frightened than I already am? If I were any more afraid, I would die from fright!*

Cudgel waved the stick again, put it down on the table and went out of the room.

Al came closer to her. "You are a pretty one, *mein leiben.* I could make love to one such as you." He traced a pudgy finger along her jaw line. She turned her head as best she could. He grabbed her hair and jerked her head back, making her eyes tear with pain. "You are a spitfire, nein? I luff liddle spitfires." He put his hand on her breast. It was useless to try to wiggle away. He held it there for a moment, then began to stroke her, his hand going around her breast and then his finger plucking at her nipple. Mary Rose bit at her lip, as hard as she could, causing her lip to begin to bleed. *I will not think of what he is doing. I will not!*

"I vill first cut your fingers, one by one...den, perhaps your arm...you vill scream and scream....ach! and vell you should scream. I t'ink it vill hurt you a lot. You can make it easy on yourself, *leibling.* All you haff to do is tell me about how you got here and den promise to neffer tell. Den, I vill let you go."

*Sure you will.*

"No. You choose to be silent? Ach! Den it vill be terrible for you." He calmly took his hand off her breast and moved it to her thighs. *I'm glad that I put slacks on today*, Mary Rose thought inanely. *This way, he won't be able to shove his fat hand under my dress.* Somehow, it mattered terribly to her.

There was a crash behind them. The door flew open, banging itself against the wall as Nick came through. "Nick!" Mary Rose cried out. He had a huge bread knife in his hand. "Be careful, Nick!" She screamed.

"You bastard!" Nick's teeth were drawn back in a feral smile. He looks like a wolf, Mary Rose thought. Her head hurt dreadfully and waves of dizziness threatened to engulf her into blackness. Muzzily, she thought: *I hope Nick can kill him. I hope Nick gets away.*

Al grabbed for the cudgel. Mary Rose saw him reach for it and, with some unknown strength, kicked at it, knocking it to the floor.

Nick stabbed at Al, cutting his upper arm with the sharp knife. Al gasped and clutched at his arm, backing away. Nick, seeing an advantage, crowded up to Al, swinging the knife in a crazy, demented way. The knife nicked Al's face, drawing more blood. Mary Rose wanted to cheer.

Al kicked out with his foot, knocking the knife out of Nick's hand. He lunged hard at Nick and the two of them fell to the floor, now slippery with Al's blood.

They fought like two tigers, kicking and punching, biting and gouging. Grunts and half-words punctuated their efforts, compounded by the whine of the buzzsaw blade, hungry with nothing to eat, nothing feeding its relentless maw.

From Mary Rose's perch, she couldn't see who was winning. *Please, God, you've been so good to me by sending Nick. Don't spoil it by letting him die, too. I don't mind dying, God. Honest. Just let Nick be OK.*

Al got to his feet, clawing at the leg of the table. He kicked at Nick's head.

Nick grabbed his foot and pulled, toppling Al over again. Nick then stood up, heaving with effort. "Are you all right?" he screamed at Mary Rose. He reached over and shut off the saw. In the silence, the two men's labored breathing sounded louder than the noise of the saw.

"Look out!" She saw Al launch a body block to Nick, pinning him on the table, inches away from Mary Rose's foot. Nick twisted and clawed at Al's overalls. With some superhuman effort, he pulled Al up against him, and tried to gauge Al's eyeballs out. Al twisted himself, trying to get away from Nick's fingers.

Mary Rose pushed her head up. She saw that Al's back was up against the now-still saw blade. With every ounce of effort that she possessed, she wiggled her foot to the side of the saw. With the edge of her foot, she punched at the button that switched the saw back on.

# CHAPTER
# TWENTY-ONE

**September 3, 1943 – 4th year of war opens as Allies begin the invasion of Italy, taking one of the riskiest moves of the war. They are completely successful, securing a beachhead in Salerno and Sicily.**

**September 3, 1943 – The Allies move into Europe, turning the tide of war.**

"I don't know whether to court martial you or to kiss you!" Admiral Withers leaned into Nick's face. Nick swallowed, but, to his credit, didn't say a word.

"Look at you!" The Admiral waved his hand. "You look like shit!"

Nick grinned. He had a concussion, three ribs were broken, a tooth knocked out, a black eye and it took five stitches to close the rip in his cheek. He felt wonderful.

The Admiral glared for a moment, then relaxed. Grinning back at Nick, he swatted him on his shoulder, causing Nick to grimace in pain. "Shit, Cappiello. I guess you're a hero." He waved to the other people in the room. "These good citizens seem to think you've done well."

From their chairs, Police Chiefs Horace Parks and Randy Stuart smiled, broad, happy grins and gave Nick their thumb's up. Mary Rose, her own head wrapped in bandages from the concussion she had suffered, almost cried with relief and happiness. She was so damned proud of Nick!

"They figure that Al Tedesco, his wife and his crew, most likely murdered fifty or more people."

"And one mule," Mary Rose added. "Don't forget Jezebel, poor thing."

"And one mule." The Admiral sighed. "One mule."

He rounded back at Nick, seeming to swell up to six times his size. "And, Cappiello, you're so beat up that you can't possibly go with your group overseas this week." He glared at Nick again. "We've got to keep you here and coddle you for a few weeks until you heal..." He shook his fist at Nick, but couldn't manage to keep up his stern demeanor. "You son-of-a-gun...you hero, you...Don't think you're getting out of battle. You're going to be air-lifted across the ocean and you'll meet up with your fellow sailors and submarine in Italy. They're going to need you and your hard head to fight for us."

Nick stood up and saluted smartly, only wincing slightly as his hand touched his forehead. "Yessir! To tell you the truth, Admiral, after that taste of fighting, I can't wait to get into battle."

"You're a good man, Cappiello. A hard-headed wop, but a good man. Use these two or three weeks wisely. Get yourself better and in shape to fight, and give this lovely woman of yours something to remember you by."

Mary Rose's eyebrows climbed. *What the heck did the Admiral mean by* that?

There was a knock at the door and a clerk entered. He handed the Admiral a piece of paper. "This note is for Chief Stuart, Sir. It's from his Deputy."

Admiral Withers handed the note to Randy. He tore it open and read it. "Good news, Sir. Two of the men involved, Henry Tedesco, Al's nephew, and Arnold Leach, have sung their brains out. They've confessed to luring women at the railroad station, killing them and then chopping their bodies up and selling the meat in the butcher shop, as well as preparing stew and hamburger from the meat."

Nick made a retching sound.

"And not only that," Randy continued, a huge grin stretching around his face. "We've found out that Al Tedesco has been using an alias. His real name is Adolph Klemperer. Henry's real name is Heinrich Klemperer, and Arnold Leach's name is Vilhelm Klink."

"So they're all German!"

"Yup. Even the missus...she was christened..." He peered at the paper in his hand... "Girta von Lein before she married old Adolph." He began to laugh. "Klemperer and Klink insist that the entire scheme was the brainchild of our lovely Girta."

"No! A woman!"

"Some woman!" Horace shook his head. "Imagine! Here in downtown Portsmouth, people like Girta and Adolph! It's like some kind of movie!"

"Adolph! My least favorite name these days!" Admiral Withers slapped his head.

"And they also sold their stew meat and roasts to other restaurants in town."

This time, Admiral Withers jumped up and made the retching sound. "Which restaurants?"

"Almost all of them."

Randy looked stunned. "All of them? I mean, I ate downtown. I probably ate...I ate..." He choked on his words, thinking back. "I ate..."

Nick coughed and wiped bile away from his mouth. "I *ate* the stew there! I *ate*...!"

Randy scratched the top of his head. "Hell, most of Portsmouth has either eaten at Tedesco's or bought their meat... sheesh, wait until this gets out!"

"I guess this is the end of Tedesco's" Horace shook his head. "I always hated even going by there. Never knew why. The people of Portsmouth are going to go crazy when they know what happened."

"Yuk!" The Admiral said. "Imagine all of the people who ate....."

"Most of the men at the Yard," the clerk piped up. "Nearly everyone ate downtown." He looked sick. "I mean, I thought that Al Tedesco was from Switzerland. He told everyone that he came here from Switzerland. Who the heck would have known that he was a German?"

"Why didn't you know he was a German?" Mary Rose asked. Her face held a curious expression .

"What do you mean?" Horace turned to her. "Why would we know? He lied and said he was from Switzerland. He changed his name to fool everyone."

"Do any of you speak Italian here?" She seemed to be bursting with her own personal joke.

All of the men, including Nick, shook their heads.

"Nick?" She questioned him. "You're Italian, right?"

"Yeah, honey, but I don't speak it. My mother wanted us all to speak English. Why?"

"Because the word 'Tedesco' in Italian..." she paused for effect.... "means 'German.' That's why."

~~~~~~~~~~~~~~~~

Greg Starr's exclusive article was read by every single human being over the age of eleven in New Hampshire and in Maine. The Associated Press picked up the story of the murders and the cannibalism and ran Greg's story nation-wide. It was the talk of nearly every American citizen for weeks. Sales of meat at local butcher shops all over the country dropped significantly and police in all jurisdictions began to test the meat at every restaurant and butcher shop. The meat tested in the Portsmouth restaurants was not hu-man, as far as the laboratories could tell. "Means that all of it was already sold and eaten," Randy muttered.

In six isolated cases, interspersed here and there across the country, the meat tested turned out to be animal flesh. These shops and restaurants were closed immediately, with criminal charges filed. No other instances of murder and cannibalism were found, but two meat markets, one in Kanka-kee, Illinois and one in Yuma, Arizona, closed their doors in the middle of the night and destroyed all of the meat in stock before the police arrived.

"Makes you wonder," was Greg's comment.

The Tedescos and their employees were all charged with many counts of First Degree Murder, as well as Kidnapping and other assorted less serious charges. "They'll likely all be executed and good riddance to them all," was Fanny Park's succinct comment. "Sick bastards!"

~~~~~~~~~~~~~~~~

"Mario, you're going to drive me *pazzo!*" Grace pushed at her husband. "Go out into the garden! Go out into the shop! Get out of my hair!"

Unable to stop fretting, Mario wandered disconsolately around the Victory Garden's fence. He noted, with pride, the burgeoning zucchini, the red globes of the ripening tomatoes, the sheen on the eggplants and the lush greenery of the Swiss chard. But his mind was really elsewhere. *I hope I don't forget my lines, he worried. I hope I don't trip when I dance. I pray that I don't make a fool of myself! Oh, why, oh why did I ever try out for this play? Why did I think that I could be funny?*

At five o'clock, Grace took pity on him. "I made you some nice chicken soup with *pastina.* Light on your stomach, but nourishing. Come in and eat, my darling man and then I'll drive you into Portsmouth."

Mario allowed himself to be pushed to the table. "Break a leg, Dad." Andy cheered him on. "We'll be in the third row. Don't worry, we'll clap for you even if you mess up!"

Mario stared at his only son, the darling of his life and heart. "Up yours, kiddo!" was Mario's answer. He got up from the table, feeling much better.

"Let's go, Grace," he called. "I don't want to be late." Marveling at men and their funny ways, Grace started up the car.

~~~~~~~~~~~~~~~~

Mary Rose planned the party carefully. "I'm going to have a little get-together to say good-bye to the nurses and the doctors who are leaving next week. Can you come?" Mary Rose was ebullient nowadays. She seemed to have completely forgotten her grisly ordeal. *Nick and I are together. We love each other. That's all that is important.*

"Who are you inviting other than us?" Eunice was trying to keep up her spirits. She *wanted* to get back to her ship. She *wanted* to be back in action and perform the duties that she had enlisted to do. She *did* want to do all these things. Of course, she did. She was a combat nurse. It was what she was trained for. But to leave Joe behind. *That,* she didn't want to do.

"Well, all of you," Mary Rose ticked off the names on her fingers: You, Yashiko, Michelle, Carol, Alex, Alan, Neil and Hamilton. That's nine. I'm ten and Nick is eleven." She grinned, happy that Nick was still with her. Even if he was leaving in a week or so. Their romance, after their grotesque ordeal, was proceeding along a rosy path. "Uh, Gerry and Clair. Um, I invited Caledonia and she's bringing a guest." She put her hand up, "Don't ask me if he's in the service or not. I don't want to know if she's breaking any of the USO rules, and I don't care!"

"Thirteen," Eunice kept count. "Who else?"

"Dick and Ursula Bondi...that's fifteen. Joe, of course and Jack Harrington. Admiral and Mrs. Wood and Doctor Eneman and his wife...Aunt Grace and Uncle Mario...Alex Patten's mother and father...that's oh, maybe twenty six or so...oh, and a couple of others, let's say thirty in all."

"Should be great. I'm really going to miss all of you," Eunice looked as if she might cry. "This is going to be the worst week of my life!"

Mary Rose hugged her. "Don't give up the ship, as some famous man said. I was going to cry myself to sleep for a month over Nick's departure, and now, we have a week left. You never know..." She held up a finger. "You never know."

"With my luck, I'll never see Joe again." Eunice was determined not to look on any bright side.

"Wait a minute!" Mary Rose jumped up. "Let's see if I'm really the woman I think I am." She left the room for a moment or two and returned, carrying a small, leather box.

She set the box on the table. Eunice began to shiver. "It's getting chilly in here," she muttered. "Maybe I should get a sweater." She started to rise as Mary Rose opened the box. A puff of smoke or vapor arose and hung in the air, smelling like some exotic wood. "Maybe I'll just sit down." As if pulled back, Eunice sat herself, unable to take her eyes off the box.

"Give me a moment now." Mary Rose reached into the box and brought out a cloth pouch. Eunice was silent, her eyes now riveted on the pouch. She wondered if there was an electrical storm approaching...the air seemed to pulse with some energy...she shivered and leaned forward...

Mary Rose laid the pouch in the exact middle of the table. It rested there for a moment, and then, as if by some external energy, the sides of the pouch petalled open, one by one, reminding Eunice of a pink peony at full bloom. The spicy scent changed and now the room smelled like flowers. Inside the pouch, in a heap on the exact middle of the table, was a pile of stones and bones, a feather, a red jewel, and what looked like a mummified paw from some small forest animal.

"Can I touch the stones?" Eunice heard her own voice coming from some far-away place.

"If you want to. Which one do you want to touch?" Mary Rose's voice was hypnotic, sing-song, and seemed to come from within Eunice's own head, too.

"This one." Eunice pointed to a roughly heart-shaped pale pink stone. The pinkness of the stone was bisected by a streak of pure white. Mary Rose nodded her permission and Eunice picked the stone up. It seemed warm in her hand, almost soft and her palm felt a faint pulse. "The stone is alive!" she exclaimed. "It's moving in my hand."

"Maybe," Mary Rose's voice came now from far away. "Let me move these things." Her hand dipped into the pile, turning one stone over, dropping one on top of another. The feather was stroked with the animal paw. She turned the animal paw so that its palm was cupped upwards, then slowly, muttering to herself, she put the red jewel into the cupped paw. There was a clash of thunder outside and Eunice saw a flash of lightning at the window. Inside, the light was dim and the room now smelled like a new-mown meadow.

The girls sat, silent and unmoving for what seemed like a long time. Then, with a sigh, Mary Rose held her hand out, palm up. Eunice placed the pink rock in Mary Rose's hand. The room seemed to brighten and the storm outside, if indeed there really had been a storm, receded.

Mary Rose gathered all of the bits and pieces, re-wrapped them in the cloth, put the cloth back in the leather box, closed it, and got up to return it to her room. Eunice sat....*I'm not breathing at all. What's going on?*...until Mary Rose returned.

Eunice sat up. The spell seemed to be broken. "What was all that?"

"Well, you know I told you about Cousin Mina and her powers. I told you how she sort of gathers her forces around her? Well, I think I have...I think I can...I thought I might try to see if I could...sort of see..."

"See into the future?" Eunice was skeptical, but she had heard, back in Greenwich, that Mina Fiorile *did* have certain powers, not to be scoffed at.

"Sort of....it isn't like fortune telling or stuff like that....It's really hard to explain...let me see..." She put her fingers to her temples and pressed.

Eunice sat still. Mary Rose closed her eyes and swayed rhythmically...Eunice nearly started to giggle. This was silly! People, especially someone as ordinary as Mary Rose... couldn't see into the future! No one had magical powers!

She opened her mouth to tell Mary Rose to stop, but her tongue felt heavy and the words would not come out. Eunice shivered. She felt hot...then cold...then hot again. The air felt heavy.

She jumped as Mary Rose began to speak: "Flames and fire. Hot! Hot!" Mary Rose's voice seemed to be coming from far away. Her words had a peculiar sound. First a whisper and then a hiss.

Eunice thought that the room had darkened and that it had begun to storm. She heard the rumble of thunder and then a spark of lightening. Worried, she looked up at Mary Rose's face. Her eyes were still closed...she seemed to be in a trance. She spoke again, this time her words were in a sing-song cadence. "Sometimes you get what you wish for, but it isn't the way you think... His veil...his veil...gone... gone...the flames...*the flames!*" Her voice rose to almost a scream and Eunice jumped back.

Mary Rose's eyes snapped open and she slumped down in her chair. "I...I...what did I say?" Mary Rose blinked, uncertain. "Did I say 'fire'?

"You said flames and fire." Eunice's face was scrunched up. "Did you see something? A fire?"

"I don't know. I can't remember. I was afraid, though. Very afraid. " She shivered. "A boy...a baby boy..." She shook her head, trying to understand and remember.

Eunice peered at her. "Are you making all of this up?" She shook her head. "No. You wouldn't do that kind of thing."

"No. I don't think....I don't remember..." Mary Rose's face was worried and drawn. "I thought I could...I never dreamed that..."

"Are you trying to fool me?" Eunice was still skeptical.

Mary Rose shrugged. "I can't explain it. I wonder what it all means?"

"If you don't know, I sure don't!"

"Girls!" Cousin Grace's voice yelled. "Let's get going or we won't get good seats!"

The two girls looked at one another, then, simultaneously, shrugged.  At Grace's second call, Mary Rose and Eunice tumbled down the stairs to Grace's car. Eunice noted that the day was bright and sunny. Had she just imagined a storm? Lightning and thunder?

~~~~~~~~~~~~~~~~

"Do you mind if I sit and take the tickets?" Sabina Carter's face was shiny with sweat.

*She looks ill,* Julie noted. "Sure. You take tickets. I'll greet everyone. I'll save you a seat up front and when everyone is in, just make sure the doors are shut and creep down to the front row."

"It will go well. I'm sure," Sabina patted Julie's hand. "You and Bonnie have done a wonderful job."

"It's up to Mario and Dave and Mary Jean and, especially Debbie Orloff now. I'm just the producer lady. They're the stars."

And so, with a fanfare and a medley from the orchestra, the curtains opened on the first sold-out USO production of *Anything Goes.*

~~~~~~~~~~~~~~~~

Naturally, the arsonist, who never missed much in the way of local entertainment, was at the show. *It would have been spectacular if I'd been able to burn down the entire Connie Bean Center. But, alas, I just couldn't mange to do it by myself. And listen to that music...heathenish! Singing about birds and bees...The devil's music!* The arsonist fingered the tin badge that was buried in a pocket.

*However, I'll find my next situation and victims soon. And it will be an overwhelming next time! It will diminish my other efforts.* The arsonist was still miffed that the last fire had been extinguished before anyone could die...before it spread to the adjoining buildings. *This one, whatever it may be, will be the fire of all fires!* The arsonist smiled a modest smile and began to hum *Onward, Christian Soldiers*, making sure that no one else in the audience could hear. *This one will go down in history!*

~~~~~~~~~~~~~~~~

Mario didn't forget a syllable. His dancing and his singing brought the entire audience to laughter. Debbie Orloff's renditions of *Anything Goes* and *Blow, Gabriel, Blow* got standing ovations and calls of "Brava! Brava!"

The band was terrific, the dancers sublime, the songs and the music perfect. At the end, when Debbie Orloff had taken her fifth bow, she shushed the crowd and called for Julie and Bonnie to come on stage. "Here are our producers! Let's give them a great big hand!" The audience responded, cheering their hearts out. The evening had been a roaring success.

"And tomorrow, we do it all over again!" Julie faced the crowd, sending a kiss to Pat and Alex. "I can't wait!"

~~~~~~~~~~~~~~~~

There was a lot to do after the show. Cleanup, re-arranging the chairs, making sure that the costumes were hung up to air and get rid of wrinkles, putting the left-over soda pop into the refrigerator, sweeping the floor. Mary Rose and Eunice had stayed on to help..."We'll drive you home," Pat and Julie had assured them. Now, all was finished and the auditorium could rest until tomorrow night when it would blossom forth again.

The last of the clean-up crew went to the door. Mary Rose looked back into the darkened auditorium. "What's the matter?" Eunice asked her as she held back.

"Something...something..." Mary Rose felt a pull in her midsection. A primal tug. "Something." She turned back. "Wait for me. I'll...I just have to check..." and she ran into the bowels of the building.

Alarmed, Julie, Pat and Eunice followed her. "What's wrong?" Pat asked, thinking maybe that Mary Rose had suddenly had a need to use the bathroom.

"Don't know," Eunice pulled him along. "Where the heck did she *go?*"

She turned back to Julie, who was huffing along behind her husband. "She gets these funny thoughts sometimes...." She stopped. "Listen!"

A yell came from behind the stage. "Over here!" Eunice pointed the way. "She's over there!" They ran, not knowing why.

"Hurry! She's just about....!" They stopped short, amazed at the sight before them. Sabina Carter lay on a pile of boat cushions that had been, a half hour before, the boat cushions bolstering the stage-crafted boat in the last act of *Anything Goes.* Kneeling at her feet was Mary Rose. "The baby is coming! It's a boy!" Mary Rose whispered. "There isn't time..." She bent forward. "Eunice, get over here and hold Sabina up! Pat, go away and get some help. Call an ambulance or a doctor!" Pat blinked in astonishment, then, recognizing the voice of authority, ran back to do as bidden.

"Julie, get some newspapers or cloths...anything!" Julie looked around wildly and then stepped out of the long, cotton skirt that she wore. She ripped it from the hem upward.

"Great! Just what we need!" Mary Rose's voice was still in a whisper. "Sabina, honey...hold on. We're gonna get you to the hospital, OK?"

"I don't think..." Sabina began to pant. "It's....I can't..." her voice rose to a shriek. "I'm...it...*Ohhhhh!*"

"Hang onto Eunice. Hang on!" Mary Rose's voice rose slightly, but she was still calm and in control. "I've never quite delivered a baby by myself, but...It's in my blood. It will be fine...well...here we go!"

Sabina grabbed at Eunice's hand and held on hard...and then harder. She panted like an animal and groaned.

"Good girl, Sabina." Eunice didn't have time to pray. "Good girl!"

"Push!" Mary Rose hollered. *"Push!"*

Sabina grunted and moaned. "I'm…I'm pushing! I'm pushing, for goodness' sake!" Her grunt ended in a squeal of effort.

There was a scooping movement and then a frail, thready cry. Mary Rose busied herself as Sabina began to cry. "Is…is the baby….?"

"The baby is fine! He's perfect!" Mary Rose snuffled.

"Is it a boy?" Sabina asked through her sobs.

"If this little knobby thing is what I think it is, yes, it's a boy! I *do* have the power! I *am* a good witch!" Mary Rose whooped, exulting. "How do you feel, Mrs. Carter?"

"I'm just grand, my dear. Exhausted and sticky and crying my head off, but grand." Sabina grasped Mary Rose's hand and held it hard. "Thank you. You saved my baby, I think. How is it that you knew what to do?"

"She's a witch," Eunice crowed, echoing Mary Rose's exultations. "She's got the power!"

"A boy, just like I said." Mary Rose was laughing and crying at the same time. "Eunice, you owe me ten dollars!" She sat back on her heels. "Thank you, God, for helping me! I don't have too much experience in these things, but with Your assistance, we did all right!" Eunice began to cry, too.

The baby, perhaps chilled, or perhaps just joining in, bawled lustily.

Julie, the only one of them who had ever remotely been in this situation before reached out, and holding the remnants of her skirt, dried the baby off and put it in Sabina's arms. The baby immediately stopped crying and nestled against Sabina's chest. Sabina held him tenderly, wrapping him in the folds of her sweater. Julie stepped back carefully. She could barely see, what with her own tears pouring down her face.

"A baby!" Eunice just couldn't get over the miracle. "A baby boy!"

"Is he all there?" Sabina was afraid to unwrap her bundle.

"Well, that one important part is fine. And I think I counted all of his fingers and toes."

The baby, as if in answer, began to cry again, a lusty wail that echoed throughout the entire building. Acting on instinct, Sabina asked Eunice to help her sit up. "I think he wants some nourishment," Eunice suggested.

Sabina's eyes widened. She laughed, nearly hysterical and nodded. "I think I know what you mean." She fumbled with her blouse.

"Did you know? When...?" Mary Rose stood up, knuckling her back. "Ooof, this is tough work!" She grinned and bent to touch the velvet cheek.

Julie leaned over, too. "Sabina?" She just *had* to ask. "Were you expecting this? I had no idea that you were...um, pregnant."

"I thought you were just eating too much," Eunice confessed.

Looking down with a proud and triumphant expression on her face, Sabina again began to cry. "Praise the Lord! I knew. Oh, Lord, I knew! I thought I was just getting fat at first. My clothes were tight and I tried to lose some weight. Lester didn't seem to notice anything amiss. I mean, I'm forty three years old! Much too old for this kind of nonsense!" She bent and kissed the top of the nonsense's head. "I...Then, I began to count and think on it all. I still didn't quite believe it. I tried to ignore what was happening."

"Well, ignore it or not. It happened!" Mary Rose was nearly dancing with glee.

"Looky, looky!" She touched the baby's dark hair. "He's just beautiful!"

The lights in the building suddenly went on. The women blinked in the light, still amazed to find themselves at the back of the theater, huddled around Sabina and her newborn child. There was the pounding of feet and six men, led by Pat Patten, together with a doctor, ran towards them.

'We're here! Where's the lady?"

"Aw, you're just about ten minutes too late," Julie crowed. "We capable ladies coped just fine. It's all taken care of now."

# CHAPTER TWENTY-TWO

**September 5, 1943 – The 503rd Parachute Regiment under General Douglas MacArthur, lands and occupies Nadzab, just east of the port city of Lae in Papua, New Guinea**

**September 6, 1943 – Reggio Calabria hit hard by Allied Forces. 5th Army heads for Salerno.**

The night before the big thank you and farewell party, the girls gathered in the room Mary Rose had made into the dormitory for the four nurses. "We'll do each other's hair, make cute little canapés to eat, do our nails and practice some ravishing make-up, so that the men will be wowed by us tomorrow." Carol trilled, holding aloft a bottle of blonde hair highlight goo that she had purchased at Grannick's Drug Store in Portsmouth. "I plan to blonde myself up. No man will be able to resist me."

"I bought a new shampoo and some sexy perfume. I really need to look va va voom, girls," Eunice cried. "Even though Joe won't be able to actually see me, I want him to remember how good I smelled for the next ten years." She was greeted by hoots of laughter. "And, I want to see if you," she turned to Michelle, "with those magic French fingertips, can fix my hair into a new and glamorous hair-do."

"I will make you *ooh la la!*" Michelle kissed her fingertips and threw her hand into the air. "Even if Joe is blind, he will know...sense through his fingertips...that you are beautiful when I get through with you."

And so, the following night, the girls shampooed their hair with the finest and most expensive shampoos, set their hair on bristling curlers and wound up pin curls, taping them in place. They luxuriated in scented bathwater, painted their toenails lurid red (Michelle and, surprisingly, Eunice) or daisy pink (everyone else), then painted their fingernails to match.

Each girl had chosen her favorite dress to wear, the one that made them feel sexy and feminine.

Andy helped out by bringing Mary Rose's record player and a stack of records up to the dormitory. *"Ohhhh, la la,* Andy!" Michelle purred at him, winding her fingers in his hair. "You are going to be some heartbreaker! Won't you come up tomorrow night and dance with me?"

Andy backed away with horror on his face. "N...no. No thanks. I'd rather be playing baseball!"

"You will change your mind, *mon brave,"* Michelle kissed his cheek, leaving a huge red print of her lips, "And when you grow up, please come and see *Tante* Michelle!"

~~~~~~~~~~~~~~~~

Alex Patten had received his invitation, and, although he had said he'd be there, he was seriously contemplating not attending.

"Why don't you go, honey?" Julie asked with maternal anxiety. "Is it because Dad and I are also invited?" She glanced at his face. "Will we embarrass you if you want to dance with someone and we're watching?"

"No, Mom. Don't be silly. I just...I'm ready to get back on the ship. This has been a very pleasant interlude in this miserable war, but the miserable war is still raging. Look at us! We've just landed in Italy and are about to ramrod the continent of Europe. I've got to get back in the action. There are men and women getting hurt out there. I'm wasting my time here in York Hospital. I'm needed out there...in the operating rooms...out in the middle of the fighting."

"Wasting your time, did you say, my son? Wasting your time helping men like Joe and Jack to walk?" She shook her head. "No, Alex. That's not wasting your time at all."

"Cut out the guilt stuff, Mom. You know what I mean. Jack and Joe and the rest of the wounded men are tops in my book. They're all heroes and I wish them the best in making the rest of their lives better." Alex felt a movement down by his ankles. He stooped and picked up Mystic's suddenly limp body. The cat meowed and patted Alex's cheek with a sheathed paw.

"Even Mystic is champing to get back on the ship, aren't you, Mystic?" The cat promptly wiggled out of his arms and paraded to the front door, tail held high. "See? Mystic is all set to go."

Julie patted her son's back. "I know how you feel, darling. I just wish this damn war would end and that you'll come back home." She smiled, but her eyes were bleak.

"I may not come home after the war is over," Alex muttered. Julie's head whipped around. "I might stay overseas, where they will need doctors more than ever. This is a big world, Mom. I've enjoyed seeing the parts that I have been sent to. Maybe I'll need to see some other places, too."

"Need to?"

"Maybe." She gulped back the retort that was on her lips. Sometimes it was better for mothers to keep their mouths shut. "Well," she said stoutly, "you ought to come to the party anyway. The girls will be very disappointed if you don't drop in."

"I'll most likely be there." He, too, knew that he'd said too much. Sometimes it was better for sons to keep their mouths shut. He hadn't meant to hurt her, but he was a grown man now. It wasn't the same, living at home, as when he was a schoolboy.

~~~~~~~~~~~~~~~

They pushed the beds up against the wall, and the girls brought up cartons from Mario's stock room to put all of their clothing and possessions in. They barricaded the boxes behind a screen. "There!" Mary Rose panted, hot with exertion.

"The room looks great. You'd never know that it slept four women."

Mario agreed. "Four women who never put their stuff away. The dormitory certainly does look different...it looks clean!" Eunice threw a pillow at him.

One by one, their guests trickled in, lured by the promise of a fun time and the poignancy of parting from those who had come to mean a lot. The uncertainties of the war made these eminent separations even more poignant. Who knows what might happen in those far-off places?

At ten o'clock, the party was in full swing, marred only by the fact that Joe, Jack and Doctor Hamilton Zapfester, who was driving them to the party, had not yet arrived. 'Where could they be?" Mary Rose fretted. Eunice, nervous and worried, trotted to the front window every six minutes, looking down the road to be the first to see the headlights of Hamilton's car. She jumped up with delight as a car approached, slowed down, then picked up speed and continued on its way. "Rats. I thought that was them," Eunice gloomed.

She turned away from the window and thus, didn't see the car turn around and slowly return towards the bakery and their dormitory. One of the reasons she might not have seen the car, even if she had been looking, was that the car had shut off its headlights and was driving in the dark. The car passed the bakery, passed the nursery, and pulled far enough into a clump of trees so that its bumper couldn't be seen from the road.

"Get over here and dance with me," Alex grabbed her hand. "I hate it when you pay more attention to Joe than to me!" He whirled her into a jitterbug, laughing at her openmouthed expression.

"If I ever chased after you, Alex," she panted with the exertion of their dancing, "you'd jump over the rail of the ship to get away from me!"

Alex executed a fancy step, then dropped to his knees. "Girls and boys, this woman doesn't adore me!" Everyone clapped and laughed. Alex was well-known as a heart-breaker, but everyone knew, Eunice only had eyes for Joe.

~~~~~~~~~~~~~~~

There was a soft chunk as the arsonist got out of the car, opened the trunk and pulled out a large can of kerosene and a box of rags. Creeping along in the darkness, the arsonist began to splash the perimeter of the bakery with kerosene.

Looking up, the arsonist could see the lights of the dormitory area and watch as the dancers bounced past the windows. Music poured out and the arsonist sang along. *"Braaaa-zil, dad dad dad dad dad dad a daaaa! Braaaa-zil...."* Xavier Cougat's brassy horn blared, covering any noise that was being made.

"Heathens!" The arsonist hissed. "Fornicators. Philistines!" More kerosene was splashed.

The arsonist finished with the bakery area and moved toward the back where the dormitory was built over Mary Rose's bedroom and bathroom. The rest of the kerosene was splashed lavishly here, the arsonist throwing it as high as possible. "The place will go up like a haystack."

~~~~~~~~~~~~~~~

"I'm so sorry. We're going to be late," Hamilton pushed his foot down on the accelerator.

"Don't worry." Joe reached out a hand and found Hamilton's thigh. He patted it. "They're going to be at it all night." He smiled into the darkness. This would be a great chance for him to talk to Eunice. Maybe hold her in his arms to dance, if he didn't fall flat on his face. He'd been practicing, when he thought no one was looking, to do a waltz. *Jitterbugging is out for now*, he laughed at himself. But a waltz, holding on to her, was just possible. And maybe she wouldn't catch on to the fact that he was holding onto her not only because he was afraid of falling, but because he could. He rubbed his chin. It was going to be awful without Eunice around. How was he going to bear it when her ship sailed away?

"They sure have the place lit up!" Hamilton remarked. "Wow! They've probably used every light in the house."

"Wait!" Jack leaned forward tensely. "Those aren't lights!" He gasped. "The damned place is on fire!"

Hamilton screeched to a halt, blowing the horn and crying out. The two men could see the dancers on the second floor dormitory. They could hear the music.

And they could see and hear and feel the fire licking at the entire perimeter of the building. "What's going on?" Joe asked, opening his door and only seeing the black emptiness in front of his eyes. "Where's Eunice?"

"It's a fire, Joe. Stay right where you are! We're going to give the alarm!" Hamilton raced to the doorway, shouldered his way in, leaping over the licking flames. He screamed up the staircase, *"Fire! Fire! Hey, everyone get out! Fire!"* Hollering, he leaped up the stairs, two at a time.

Jack, twisting his body to accommodate his wounded leg, also began to go up the stairs. The two of them heard voices and words of consternation. Then cries and screams. People came to the head of the stairs. ""Come down, quickly. The place is on fire!" Hamilton backed himself flat against the side of the staircase, so that everyone could get down quickly and safely.

As the guests stampeded down, Hamilton called back to Jack, who was also plastered flat against the wall. "I think it's OK. Everyone is coming down. Be careful" The thunder of running feet, all frantic to get down, drowned out the rest of what he was trying to say.

Hamilton backed down, careful not to bump anyone or trip. "I'm gonna put my headlights on." He grabbed Mario. "Call the fire department! Call the cops!" Mario nodded and quickly ran next door to the nursery.

Hamilton slid into the front seat of his car. Joe heard him and, feeling his way, went around the car. "Are they all out? Can you see Eunice?"

"Wait a minute, Joe. I think everyone is out. Let me get the headlights on. Then, we can see."

At the bottom of the staircase, Jack Harrington was worried. "Was Yashiko up there? Did you see her? I didn't see her come down." He grabbed Alex and shook him. "Was anyone left upstairs?"

The headlights pierced the darkness. People grabbed other people. "Come on!" Hamilton yelled. "Let's try to beat out the fire!" He took off his jacket and began to try to extinguish the flames that were now licking up the side of the building. The bakery, they could see, was alight, burning swiftly with the crackly noise that an unstoppable fire makes.

"Eunice?" Joe whimpered. "Eunice?" He could feel the heat and started walking toward it, holding his hands out to protect himself from bumping into anything. "Eunice?" He called again. "Ooof!"

"Joe? It's Michelle. Who are you looking for? I think we are all down."

"Eunice. Where is she? Did you see her?"

"No...no, but she must be down here. Let me look. You stay here and don't move."

*I'm a useless crock,* Joe thought. *Worthless as a man. I can't see! I can't see if Eunice is all right! Where the hell is she?* "Eunice?"

Upstairs, caught by the encroaching flames, Eunice and Yashiko clung to one another. The two of them had left the noise of the party proper for a moment to use the bathroom. When the shouts were heard, Eunice was putting a little more lipstick on and Yashiko had just finished re-braiding her hair. Neither of them heard the warnings. Neither of them knew that all the other guests had fled down the stairs.

They came back into the main room and stopped, astonished that no one was there. It was then that they heard the noise and the shouts, smelled the smoke and realized there was a fire. Horrified, they tried to run, but the staircase was already ablaze. Used to making split-second decisions about life and death, Eunice ran and checked the dormitory's three windows. They were all much too small for a cat to climb through. "What shall we do?" Eunice and Yashiko had been through battles before. They knew enough to keep themselves calm. They'd try to get out. They'd try...

Joe bumped into another person. "Joe? It's Jack. I don't see Eunice or Yashiko down here. I'm going in to get them. You stay here." Jack shook Joe gently, then patted his arm and turned to go into the building. The twisting of his turn re-injured his half-healed leg. He staggered and nearly fell, propped up only by Joe's strong arm.

"Like hell I'm staying here!" Joe hollered. "You guide me and I'll hold you up. Between us, we can get them out."

"Lucky you can't see," Jack hollered back. "There's no way we can get into the building. It's too hot and the flames have gone too far!"

"*Semper fi,* my Marine friend. The flames have gotten too far to get our women out? Never! What are we waiting for?"

"Nothing I can think of!"

With a yell, the two of them blundered into the doorway, "Wait!" Jack halted. "Take off your jacket and put it over your head." Joe swiftly muscled himself out of his jacket. From far off, they could hear the sound of sirens coming closer and closer. "Here comes the fire department," Jack said, "They'll help us."

"They'll be too late! Let's go!" And holding onto one another, unseen by the milling crowd, they started up the stairs.

"Hey!" Alex yelled, catching a glimpse of the men. "What the hell? Hey!" He ran to the doorway, shielded his face against the conflagration, and tried to stop Jack and Joe. "You'll get killed!" He reached for them, but they had, together, somehow eluded his arms and clambered halfway up the staircase.

"Eunice! *Eunice!*" Joe cried.

"*Yashiko!*" Jack screamed. "Can you hear me?"

By holding one another and scrambling like two demented creatures, they reached the top of the staircase. "*Son of a bitch!*" Jack screamed. "There can't be anyone up here alive!"

And then they heard the cries. Nearly mad with fear, Jack dropped Joe's arm. "Stay here! I'll get them out! I promise!" He lurched himself forward through a wall of flames. Alone, feeling the heat and sensing the greedy licks of the fire, Joe was disoriented. Which way should he go? He crouched, touching the red-hot wall and shuffled forward, praying that Plutarch wouldn't let him down. To his left, he heard a crash and a curse. He bent, so as to keep the smoke above him and headed toward the sound. "Jack? *Jack?*"

"Over here, *amigo.* I fell down. Shit! I'm on *fire!'* Jack rolled, trying to get to his feet. As he rolled, he bumped against someone. He grabbed the someone. "Yashiko? *Yashiko?*"

Love is wonderful, isn't it? He recognized her groan. He maneuvered himself around, grabbing her waist, and pulled her and himself backwards until he bumped into Joe's legs. "Joe! Can you pull Yashiko out?"

Yashiko groaned again. Then, "Jack! My darling! Eunice is still there. She was lying next to me. We were trying to crawl out. Find her! Find her!"

Joe pushed himself around them. "I'm gonna find her. Get yourselves over to the stairs and get the hell out of here."

"You can't...you..." Jack shrugged. If a man was really determined to do something, well, he was determined to do it. And Joe was determined to rescue Eunice. "OK, pal." Jack pushed and shoved a few feet more, then located the stair-case. He pushed Yashiko ahead of him and the two of them bumped and rolled down into the freshness of the night air.

"Joe is up there!" Jack babbled to the fireman who ran to him. "He's trying to get Eunice out."

"We'll find him, sir." The fireman ran to his Chief, screamed his report and then began to climb, carefully, back up the stairs into the inferno.

The firemen began to play the big hose on the door and the staircase, cooling them enough, they hoped, to try to rescue the two people still trapped inside.

"Eunice?" Joe roared, swishing his hands high and low. He was lucky, and tripped against her fallen body, banging into her, pinwheeling his arms to keep from toppling over on top of her. "I've got you, honey and I'm never gonna let you go." He pushed and pulled, hoping he could remember where the staircase was. She was limp and heavy and he had great difficulty moving her. He stooped and lifted her, using every muscle he had. Slinging her over his shoulder, his arms extended wide to balance himself, he shuffled towards the sound of the fire hose and the water. He reached the opening and nearly fell down the staircase, sensing the draft of air and stopping himself just in time.

"Hey!" A fireman yelled at him. "We're right here. Let her down and slide her to me."

Joe leaned and slipped Eunice's unresponsive body down. He felt with his foot and ascertained where the top step was, slid her forward and heard the fireman yell, "Got her!"

The noises made him think that they had passed her down, from one man to the next. "Here I come," he hollered to the fireman, guiding himself against the wall. The fireman reached up.

There was a crash as a ceiling beam fell, pinning Joe to the floor. "Mister? Hey, Mister, where are you?" The fireman waved his hand frantically, trying to see through the black and acrid smoke. "Shit!"

He climbed up one more step, his arm shielding his face from the racing flames. *Aha! Got him!* He reached for Joe's arms. He slid Joe's body towards him, knocking the blazing piece of wood off Joe's back. "Hey! Help me get this guy down!"

~~~~~~~~~~~~~~~

They lay in the cool grass. Jack cradled Yashiko in his arms while Alex administered to her wounds. "She's got a fractured leg, I think, lots of superficial burns and maybe a concussion." Alex shook his head. "I can't believe that you got her out alive."

Next to them, lay the unconscious bodies of Eunice and Joe, tended by Hamilton and Alan. "She's got a broken leg, too. Maybe a broken arm, a few ribs cracked and lots of burns. How's he doing?"

"Considering that the guy is blind and has only one leg, *really* well." Hamilton shook his head in disbelief. "How the hell he got up there, found her and got her to the top of the stairs is a miracle. A fucking miracle!"

Joe shuddered and a deep groan burst from his cracked and burned lips. "Eunice?"

"She's right here, Joe." Alan leaned over him. "She's a little beat up, but she's alive and breathing just fine. Stay still and we'll get you all to the hospital. I hear the ambulance wailing now. They'll be here in a second." He patted Joe and got up to direct the ambulance men.

Joe pulled himself to a sitting position. He turned to Eunice and rolled himself over to her, cradling her head in his arms. "Eunice!"

She moved slightly. "Eunice! Wake up!" He gently shook her, unaware that conventional medicine of the time would frown upon shaking a person with a possible concussion.

She opened her mouth, wetting her cracked lips. "Joe?" she croaked. "Joe?"

"Oh, darling!" He crushed her to his chest. "You're alive!"

"I'm...oh, Joe. What happened? I hurt all over!" She raised her hand and touched his cheek. With her heart in her eyes, she stroked his face. "Look at you! You're filthy!" She used her good arm to dust his clothing. She captured his hand and held it to her breast.

Carol ran over to them...and then she stopped.

"Look at *you*," Joe whispered, with jubilation in his voice. He brushed a wisp of hair away from her forehead. "You're beautiful."

"Joe. You don't....you can't..." Eunice raised her eyes to his. She saw his eyes...his poor eyes...and they...they...his eyes were filled with tears that dripped onto her upturned face. Her heart beat like a tom-tom. "Joe?" she said in the most peculiar voice. "Can you...can you *see* me?"

"I can, my darling. I can." He laughed, his voice ringing out in triumph. "Guess the fire knocked my eyes back together." He bent, his lips touching hers with gentle love. "You look just like I thought you would...beautiful. Just beautiful."

Carol took three steps back and then, looking over her shoulder, put out her arm, stopping the ambulance driver from interfering. "Don't go to them for a few moments. Let them have a little bit of time to themselves." She sniffed, wiping back her tears. "Let them have a minute or two together."

~~~~~~~~~~~~~~~~

Grace and Mario invited everyone to their home. "You can't go back into Mary Rose's place. Hell, there *isn't* any Mary Rose's place! Come on, we'll all have something to eat and then, we'll figure out where everyone can bed down."

Before they all could manage to go next door, Andy ran up to his mother and father. "Oh, Mom! I need to tell you..." He gazed at the throng in awe. "Is everyone all right?"

"Andy," Grace chided, "Get back to the house. You're in your pajamas and your feet are bare."

"But, Mom! Oh, Mom!" His young voice cracked with agony. "Oh, Mom! I just called the police!" Andy began to sob.

"The police? Because of the fire? Good boy!" Mario patted him. "No need to cry, son. Everyone is alive, although a few people were injured." He looked over Andy's shoulder at his wife. No need to disturb the boy tonight about the injured.

"No! No!" Andy insisted. Hiccupping his fright, he stuttered out, "I killed him, I think..."

"Killed who?" Grace suddenly started to pay attention. She shook Andy. "What do you mean?"

"I never did what you told me to do about the bushes. The sharp points on the *buddlieas*. I forgot, Mom. I didn't mean to hurt him."

"What are you saying, son?" All of a sudden, everyone was silent, listening to Andy's wail of grief.

"I killed him. The bush poked his eye out and the branch... it stuck in his chest!" Andy's voice rose to a scream. "He's *dead*, Mom. I killed him and he's lying in the bushes!"

"Slow down, Andy. Start from the beginning...Oh, Chief Parks! Thank goodness you're here. Andy, tell the Chief what happened."

Andy saw the bulk of Horace. He shrank back against his mother. His eyes were wide with fright. "I didn't mean to hurt him. I..."

"Slowly, my boy. Slowly. Tell me now, but tell me from the beginning." Horace's steady, measured voice got through Andy's fear.

"I was asleep and I heard the fire engines. I got up to see what was wrong. I saw the fire next door. I could see everyone running out of the building and then the fire engines came. I decided to come over here to see what was going on." He took a deep breath and continued.

"I put the porch lights on. And then I saw the man."

"What man?" Grace interrupted.

"Let him finish, Grace." Horace put out his hand. "Go on, Andy."

"He was hiding, I think. Over there in that clump of bushes. I yelled at him...asked him what he was doing. He jumped up and began to run away. He had some kind of big oil can and it bumped against his legs when he ran. I hollered after him and he ran faster...he ran...he ran right into the *buddlieas.* He tripped, I guess, and fell. I heard him screaming for a minute and then he stopped screaming."

Andy looked down at the ground and toed the grass with his bare feet.

"Go on," Horace encouraged him.

"Well, then I ran over to see what happened to him." The boy looked up at the Police Chief. There was terror in his young eyes. "He...the stick...the pointed stick...it went right though his face...his eye, I think." Andy began to tremble. "And the other one...it stuck in his chest. I know he was dead! There was dark stuff...blood, maybe, or maybe heart and his brains were falling out. I don't know." Andy sniffed and wiped his nose with his pajama sleeve. "I think I killed him..." His voice trailed off.

"Show me, Andy." Horace took his arm. "Show me where he is."

The lights were all on at Mario's...all the lights for the business, the porch and all the lights in their little house. The entire yard was lit, every bush, every flower, every sapling, stood out in bold relief to the blackness of the night.

Andy pointed to a huge clump of *buddleia.* "There. He's there." He leaned back, hard, against his mother's solid body.

She put her arms around him and reassured him. "It will be fine, Andy."

Horace motioned to Andy to stay where he was. Wide-eyed, Andy watched and held hard to his mother's arms. Horace walked to the clump. Indeed, impaled on several sharp, thick and sturdy sticks, like pieces of meat over a barbecue, was a man, face down. Horace bent and listened for a moment.

"Get an ambulance over here right away. He's still alive, but barely." His deputy raced away. "I think we've found our arsonist." Horace pushed his hand in to the *buddleia* clump and showed Mario the empty kerosene can. He backed away, careful to not touch the can at all. "Get my Deputy back here and call the station. Get some fingerprint people here and keep everyone away from this area."

He went back to the clump, bent himself double so that he could see the injured man's face. "Sonofabitch! It's Jimmy Earnest. The man who never could resist a fire. I think we've got our arsonist, the bastard."

He went back to where Mario, Grace and Andy were huddled. "He's alive, son. None of this is your fault at all. As a matter of fact, you may have caught a criminal that we've been after for months. A man who killed a lot of people and set a lot of fires, and most likely, this one, too." He hugged Andy's thin body.

Andy sighed from deep inside his soul. Thank goodness, he wasn't like *La Vedova!*

"Go in the house, my boy and get some slippers on those feet. Let's forget all about this until tomorrow. I'll come by and tell you everything that we find out. I promise. I owe you that much." The Chief patted him on his back.

"Gosh!" Andy's eyes were wide. "Can't I stay and watch, Chief?"

"Sure." Horace had four sons of his own and remembered what it was like to be a kid. "You've earned it. But go and put your slippers on first."

~~~~~~~~~~~~~~~

Mary Rose, Michelle and Carol slept in Andy's bed for the night in borrowed nightdresses. Andy went to sleep, finally, after watching the police remove Jimmy Earnest. "They cut the stick about a foot away from his eye. Then they cut the other stick. Then they turned him over with the sticks still protruding. Yuk!" Andy explained to his mother. "They put him in the ambulance and he was groaning. There was a lot of stuff all over him. Yuk!"

"Go to bed now, Andy." Grace couldn't keep her own eyes open. "We'll talk about all of this in the morning." She brought some sheets down and made up the couch for Andy. She kissed his forehead and went into her own bedroom where Mario was sitting up in bed, just looking at the ceiling.

"What an incredible night! That man with the *buddleia* sticking out of his eye and his chest! I'll never see a *buddleia*

again without thinking of him! Do you think Andy will be able
to sleep? Will he be plagued with nightmares forever?"

Mario sat up and pushed himself out of bed. "Let's check
on him. If he's nervous or afraid, he can come in here and
sleep with me. You can bunk down on the sofa for tonight."
They crept into the living room, expecting to see Andy shivering and frightened. Instead, they saw a boy sound asleep, his
hands tucked under his chin.

Mario took Grace into his arms. "He's quite a boy, our son."

"He is, isn't he? Thank God he ignored what I asked him
to do. Imagine if that man had gotten away."

"Come to bed now, Grace." Mario kissed her, sliding his
palms up and down on the silky material of her nightgown.

"I should be exhausted, but I'm not. Are you sleepy, Mario?"

"Nope." He said, pulling her along with him into their bedroom.

~~~~~~~~~~~~~~~~

In the morning, they all sat on the porch, gazing at the
smoldering heap of ashes that once was The Bread of Angel's
Bakery and Mary Rose's home. "Awful. A complete loss,"
Mary Rose mourned.

"But we're all alive, even that criminal man. Buildings can
be replaced. People can't." Mario brought out coffee for everyone and dispensed it, along with his homily.

"You're right." Mary Rose sipped her coffee and wondered
what was going to happen now. She had plenty of insurance
on her business and home, but how did all of this get settled?

One by one, her employees showed up...Caledonia, Ursula and her husband, Jannus and Agnes Winchell. They stood
in a group, unable to believe their eyes. Mary Rose told them
that she was fully insured. "I even have insurance to pay you
and me our salaries until the business is back up and running.
Clever people, we Sabatinos are. We always buy good insurance."

Another car pulled up. It was Nick, driven by his Texas
buddy, Jessie LaRue. Nick embraced Mary Rose, then stood
silently, surveying the damage.

Shrugging, he spoke with Jessie and then the two sailors,
joined by Jannus, went to inspect the ashes, hoping to find
some remnants of the business or perhaps some of Mary
Rose's personal things that might have been spared.

The group on the porch watched, their eyes riveted in a hypnotic stare as Jannus, with a rake, pulled out a twisted hunk of metal that once was a bread mixer, a burnt lampshade, and, completely untouched by the fire, a brush to clean the toilet.

And yet another car, this one driven by Chief Parks pulled in at the same time a large, flashy new-model Chevrolet made a stop. The Chevrolet was driven by a tall, thin, balding man, the insurance company's representative. "I'm Ed Meyer," the insurance rep introduced himself. "I'm here to investigate just what happened here and see if you have any claim with us."

*He's a snake!* Mary Rose thought. *His eyes are too close together...looks like a weasel. He's going to try to cheat me out of the insurance money! I know men like him!*

"Any claim?" Mario stoutly answered. "Of *course,* she has a claim!"

"We'll see." Ed Myer stuck a toothpick in his mouth and started to inspect the damage. As he turned his back, Grace stuck her fingers in her ears and wiggled them at him. Mary Rose stifled her giggle. It wouldn't be a good idea to make Mr. Meyer angry.

With a roar, yet *another* car drove into the parking lot. This car was a heavily built black sedan, driven by one of the largest men that Mary Rose had ever seen. There were two other men in the sedan, one elderly, thin and scrawny, one young and thick-set. They were all attired in black suits and wore black fedora hats. The young one leaped out of the back seat and ran to open the door of the driver, almost bowing as he did so. The men approached the porch, each doffing their fedora.

"Miss Mary Rose Sabatino?" The heavy set man asked in a soft voice.

"Yes." Mary Rose stood up. "I'm Mary Rose."

"My compliments to you from Don Mantaldo." Heavy set bowed to her. "He sent us up here...these are my associates. Mr. Vincent Lewis," the young man bowed to Mary Rose, "And Mr. Joseph Tripodi." The elderly man also bowed. "I am Charlie LaMonica."

"Don Mantaldo has heard about your misfortune. He is very sad that you have suffered any inconvenience. We are here to assure you that your business and your home will be repaired quickly and at no problem to you. Don Mantaldo has spoken to the insurance company this morning..." He turned to Mr. Meyer, who opened his mouth to protest. "You...please keep silent until I finish speaking to this lady, here."

Mr. Meyer closed his mouth.

"As I said, the matter has been taken care of. Don Mantaldo always takes care of his friends and *paisoni.*" Mary Rose gave a solemn nod.

"Don Mantaldo is a great man," Mario stated.

Charlie LaMonica allowed a smile to crease his face. "Yes. It is a privilege to work for such a man." He stared hard at Ed Meyer, who visibly shriveled before their eyes. "You can get estimates today. I will be by tomorrow morning to talk further with you." He snapped his fingers and young Vincent Lewis ran to the car, returning immediately with a briefcase.

"Here is an advance for you to begin the work." He handed Mary Rose a heavy envelope. "If it isn't enough, I'll bring you more." He bowed to her. "Don Mantaldo swears on the soul of his beloved mother...may she rest in peace...that your business will be up and running within three months from today." He looked at each of them. "Are there any questions?" His eyes stopped for a moment on Mr. Meyer's face. Mr. Meyer blanched as a cramp went though his digestive system.

Nick grinned. His own family knew men like these. They were not to be trifled with, not to be pissed off. "No, Don LaMonica, Sir," he bent his head in respect. "We have no questions at all."

"And who are you?" Charlie LaMonica liked this young man. He knew how to speak properly to authority.

"I'm Nick Cappiello. I'm Mary Rose's fiancée."

"You are a fortunate young man. This is a lovely young girl. Don Mantaldo speaks highly of her." He nodded in approval. "We will be back to speak again tomorrow." Charlie LaMonica made a gesture and the three men got back into their car. With a wave from Vincent Lewis in the back seat, they were off.

"Harrumph." Ed Myer, insurance representative, moved away with a crab-like step. "I'll just check with my office. Um, seems like there will be no problem after all." He jumped in his Chevrolet, gunned the motor and was never seen again.

Jannus, who had been watching the whole performance with goggled eyes, began to laugh. In a moment, *everyone* was laughing. They were all doubled over, holding their sides with tears in their eyes. It was that kind of laughter.

"By da vay, Chief Parks," Jannus, when he got control of himself, "I found somet'ink you might vant to see." He held out a stick. On the end of the stick, dangled a tin badge.

"I didn't touch it." Jannus assured Horace. "Only picked it up vit da stick."

"Thank you, Jannus. Thank you." *If his fingerprints are on it, another nail in Jimmy's coffin.*

~~~~~~~~~~~~~~~

"You're my fiancé?" Mary Rose squeaked to Nick. "What's that all about?"

"Of course, I'm your fiancé." Nick pulled her close. "Nobody else but me is going to marry you, right?" He kissed her while the group on the porch watched with avid interest.

"Right," agreed Mary Rose, breathing hard. "Whatever you say, Nick, dearest."

Nick grinned at his audience, giving them the thumbs up sign. "And I think that we should get married right away, before I ship out and you find some other man to rescue you from a buzzsaw and from a burning building."

"Right," agreed Mary Rose, blushing to the roots of her hair. "Whatever you say, Nick, dearest."

"I'm gonna be here for another two weeks. I'm a good carpenter and builder. By that time, we can have your new bakery started." He kissed her again. "I always hankered to have a rich wife and help her in her bakery right after I knock up a house or two."

"Whatever you want, Nick, dearest." Mary Rose pulled him closer and reached up for another one of those kisses.

~~~~~~~~~~~~~~~

Horace left the group at the scene of the bakery fire and drove himself to York Hospital. There, he spoke with Gideon Balfour, who had been on guard outside Jimmy Earnest's room all night.

"Any change?"

"He's waking up. They gave him a lot of stuff last night. One stick penetrated his left lung and went into his kidney. The other stick pierced his eye and went through part of his brain. They operated in the early morning, but closed him back up again. There wasn't much they could do except stop the bleeding. But the damage has been done. They don't think he's going to make it."

"Has he said anything yet?"

"Nope. Just turned his head away and smiled a nasty smile."

"Let's see if we can get a confession out of him."

They nodded to the nurse, who permitted them into Jimmy's room. "You look pretty bad, Jimmy." Horace greeted him. Jimmy closed his one good eye.

"I spoke with your minister this morning." Jimmy's eye flew open. "He's mighty disappointed in you, Jim. Said some things about God not liking what you've done." Horace shook his head sadly from side to side, tsking his displeasure.

Stung, Jimmy whispered, "But God *told* me that I had to burn!"

"That's not what God told your minister. Listen, even I know the Ten Commandments and 'Thou shalt not kill' is one of the biggies. Why would God tell you to go against his Commandment?"

Jimmy shrugged, wincing with pain. "He told me over and over." Jimmy began to snivel. "I was *supposed* to set the fires!"

"Help me to understand," Horace pulled a chair closer. Behind Jimmy's line of vision, Gideon took out a notepad and a pencil.

"I'm going to die, aren't I?" Jimmy's tears stopped.

"Maybe." Horace looked sad. "If so, you're going to be face to face with God. So let's do the best we can, huh? Tell me how this all started."

"I suppose." Jimmy shifted himself slightly. "I was always a special child, you know. I was always better than the other boys. God told me and my mother and father always told me. They said I was hand-picked...that God had some plan for me. And he did. When I was growing up, I lusted for girls. God told me that I was a bad boy and he punished me."

"How did he punish you?"

"He made me burn myself." Gideon reared back, startled, but made no noise. "He told me to get some matches and burn myself...my hands and my...well, you know, down there." He looked down at himself. Gideon shuddered.

"But I still wanted to touch and play with girls." Jimmy coughed and bloody sputum came from his mouth. Horace reached over and gently wiped the blood away. Jimmy struggled to talk. "I was special, but I was a sinner. My father was fooled by me, but my mother always knew I was bad. Sometimes, she helped God and burned me, too. She would light a match and hold it to my feet until I screamed. Then, if I screamed enough, sometimes she let me go." His voice dropped to a softer whisper. "Sometimes she didn't let me go. She'd make me lie on the bed on my stomach and she'd burn my buttocks."

Gideon couldn't help himself. A small gasp escaped from his lips. Horace glanced over at Gideon and then back to Jimmy, who was trying to sit up. Jimmy's face was grey and ashen. He was going fast, Horace could tell. *And they always want to tell you, at the end, what it was all about,* he mused to himself. *He'll talk until he's finished.*

"I waited until I was older and then God told me to take care of my mother."

"How did you do that?" Horace urged him further.

"I waited until my father was out of the house and hit her over the head." I told her that she shouldn't have burned me. I told her that I was stronger. I told her...And then, I laid her in her bed, face down, and burned *her!* She never woke up, so maybe I hit her too hard. I don't know and I don't care. She never burned me again." He was silent for a moment, thinking back.

"Then...she was a smoker, my mother was. That's why there were always so many matches in the house. I put a cigarette in her hand and lit it...then I put the match on the sheet until the sheet was blazing. Then I went out of the house and went to church to ask God what I should do next. God told me to burn other people." The pencil lay still in Gideon's hand. He shook himself, his face blanched with the horror of Jimmy's story, and began to write again.

"What happened to your mother?" Horace sounded friendly.

"Well, the entire house burned down and she was burned up in it." There was a faint smile on Jimmy's face. "I came back from church and the fire engines were racing to my house. The entire house was in flames. The flames and the fire engines made me happy...excited...better than any girl had ever excited me. The firemen said she had been smoking and must have fallen asleep. They felt bad for me...a child now without a mother. One of them had a little boy and he had bought his son a cap gun and a sheriff's badge. The fireman gave the badge and the cap gun to me as a present. I pinned on the badge and felt very happy."

"And is that why you...?"

"Left the badges at each fire. Yes. It was to remember my mother." He began to cough. "I...don't feel....I don't...." The coughing racked his body, shaking him. Blood dripped from his lips.

"Better get the nurse," Horace leaned forward. Gideon ran out of the room.

"Jimmy? Jimmy?" Horace called to him. "Can you hear me?"

Jimmy stopped coughing. "Yes, mother. I hear you." His voice was high and childlike. "I'll be good from now on. Please...please, don't burn me again...."

The nurse ran in, motioning to them to leave. They got up, but stood in the corner, watching as she tried to give Jimmy a sip of water. He slumped back and the water dribbled down his chin, wetting the sheets.

The nurse stood back, then leaned forward, listening carefully. She put her fingers on Jimmy's neck, pressing to find his pulse. She stood up, shaking her head. "He's gone."

"I wonder how God's going to deal with him?" Horace helped the nurse to cover Jimmy's face.

"He was a real nut-case, wasn't he?"

"Crazy as a mangy dog. Talking with God and all." Horace shook his head.

"The mother was a lulu, huh? Terrible things that some people do to their kids." He made that tsking sound. "The bastard murdered a lot of people, though. Crazy enough and shrewd enough to get away with it for a long, long time."

"But no more," Gideon intoned. "No more."

~~~~~~~~~~~~~~~~

Jimmy's father refused to believe that his son had been an arsonist. "He was always a God-fearing boy. A good boy. We raised him with strictness, just as the Bible told us. He'd never set fire to anyone, and certainly not to his own mother. Why, she loved him! She was strict with him, surely. He needed a strong hand for guidance. He was a good boy. A good boy, I swear to God!"

They found a box filled with tin badges in a battered old toy box shoved against a wall in the attic of the Earnest home. In the box were newspaper clippings of sixteen fires, some that had been declared simply an accident. At the bottom of the toy box, they saw a rusty old cap gun and a roll of rotting caps.

# CHAPTER TWENTY-THREE

**September 10, 1943 – The Italian Fleet surrenders.**
**The Italians brought four battleships, six cruisers and seven destroyers into Malta for the surrender. The Germans, hoping to stop the fleet from surrendering, tried unsuccessfully to bomb the flotilla.**

The police did a thorough search of Tedesco's Restaurant. The neatly wrapped white bundles of meat were sent to the State Police laboratories for further study, and most were found to contain human remains. In a wooden chest, emblazoned with some sort of heraldic engraving, they found the freshly-killed tail of an elderly mule. The tail was wrapped in greaseproof butcher's paper. In addition to the tail, they found several pieces of jewelry, including a gold locket, engraved with the letters 'G-A S-C'. Patricia Fundy identified it as belonging to her sister, Gloria-Ann. Inside the locket was a tiny painted miniature of the face of little Shirley St. Clair."

The chest also contained several bracelets, six rings, none of which were particularly valuable, two brooches, a silver pendant, five handkerchiefs and a red plastic hair slide. The prostitutes thought that one of the bracelets belonged to the girl they knew only as Lena, but they couldn't be sure.

There were three high heeled shoes at the bottom of the chest, all different, and all for a right foot, three silk scarves, and an empty black patent leather handbag.

It was assumed that these were souvenirs that had been removed from the women (and the mule) before their bodies were cut up.

However, the big prize was the radio transmitter and receiver that the men found in the attic of the Tedesco building. As they tried to disassemble the transmitter, it turned itself on and began to chatter.

Horace called Admiral Wither at the Shipyard. "This is beyond me. I think you and some of your code people better get over here and see what we've got."

A group of Military Intelligence officers arrived, all of whom spoke fluent German. Their collective eyes bulged out as they saw the treasure that had been found.

"They listened to the transmitter stuff," Horace told Fanny later that night. "I just stood there like some idiot while they nodded and gesticulated and wrote down things. From what they told me, and they were *very* careful not to tell me much...the radio and the other stuff were transmitting to an enemy station in Nova Scotia. Something about U-boats and a possible invasion of the harbor and even the Shipyard."

"No!" Fanny's hand went to her heart. "He was not only a murderer and a cannibal, but also a *spy?*"

"Sure looks like it." Horace's face was solemn. "They brought a few more men up to the attic. Guys with peculiar equipment and machines. They found some kind of log books and all the messages that Tedesco...I mean...Klemperer had sent and received. They all sat around and planned what to do. I just sat there like a bump on a log, staying quiet." Fanny nodded her approval. "After messing around with the transmitter, they made a few telephone calls." Horace wiped his forehead. "Whew! I think they even talked to President Roosevelt himself!"

Fanny gaped at him.

"And then...you won't believe this, dear...they were going to pretend to be Tedesco himself and send and receive messages. Ha!"

"How clever!"

"Yeah. I think he was a mole planted here by the Germans to spy on the men from the Yard. He'd listen in on the conversations of his customers and then communicate with his countrymen. Who knows what secrets he overheard?"

"So they are going to send fake information to the Germans?"

"Yup. Try and mess them up as best they can. They'll think they're spying on us and won't know that we're spying on *them!*"

"Those butchers and the *wife!* She was the worst. She was evil and they were evil too. Bad men. The worst." Fanny got up to clear the dinner dishes. "I hope at the end of all of this Mister Hitler gets what he deserves."

"He will, darling. He'll get it soon from us and he'll get it when we kill him and he goes to be judged by God. God will fix him."

"We'll fix him first!"

"You bet we will! Now, how about you and me going to get an ice cream cone?"

~~~~~~~~~~~~~~~

The SS *Buchanan* sailed on the morning tide. Left behind, recuperating from the wounds suffered in the fire, were Eunice O'Conner and Yashiko Kobiache. Delighted that the women that they loved and planned to marry were left behind as the ship sailed, Joe Martin and Jack Harrington slapped one another on the back and planned to go out and get royally drunk.

The four of them were on the pier as the *Bucket* sailed away from the Portsmouth Naval Shipyard's dock, the two women in wheelchairs, the two men limping along with the help of canes. But they were all there, together with Mary Rose and Nick, Mario, Grace, Andy and the Pattens.

From the *Bucket's* deck, Alex waved to his friends and his parents. On the dock, Julie and Pat waved back to their son, blowing kisses. Alex bent down, picked up Mystic and waved his paw at the dock. Julie and Pat laughed. Alex, wherever he would go, would be fine…just fine.

Standing along the rail, Alan, Neil and Hamilton waved to the men who lined the dock. Michelle and Carol also waved to the many men, Navy and otherwise, who had enjoyed their company.

The *Old Bucket's* ship's horn tooted its goodbye...the sound getting fainter and fainter. The group on the dock slowly dispersed, more than a few with a backward look as the ship shrank on the horizon.

# CHAPTER TWENTY-FOUR

We shall not flag or fail. We shall go on to the end. We shall fight in France, we shall fight on the seas and oceans, we shall fight with growing confidence and growing strength in the air. We shall defend our island, whatever the cost may be. We shall fight on the beaches, we shall fight on the landing grounds, we shall fight in the fields and in the streets, we shall fight in the hills.... we shall never surrender!

– Sir Winston Churchill

The Town of Kittery erected a marble bench on the dunes of Seapoint Beach overlooking the Atlantic Ocean. The plaque on the bench was inscribed:

To the memory of Eustace Barnes and his faithful mule, Jezebel, who often traveled this way, and who are now traveling elsewhere.
– From the Citizens of Kittery, Maine

~~~~~~~~~~~~~~~

Doctor Alex Patten, together with a platoon of Marines, stormed a prison camp in the Philippine Islands, freeing seven hundred prisoners, many of whom lived because of Dr.

Patten's medical skills. After the war, he published a book featuring the photographs that he had taken during the War. The book garnered a Pulitzer Prize.

~~~~~~~~~~~~~~

Naval Prisoner #27659, Lloyd Williams, under the tutelage of Scott Wanner, was crowned Chess Champion at the New England Chess Competition. Williams and his chess-mate, Nicky Catanzaro, Naval Prisoner #74364, were returned to their units to fight for the Navy. They were both Honorably Discharged in 1946.

~~~~~~~~~~~~~~

Brenda Be moved to New York City where her design consulting business thrives. All of her Beboppers were returned to their Navy units and were released in 1946 and 1947 with Honorable Discharges. Six of them traveled to New York City and found lasting jobs with jazz bands there.

~~~~~~~~~~~~~~

Jack Harrington and Yashiko Kobiache married. Jack's line of Marine Corps inspired leather goods continue to be featured at L.L. Bean, and earned the Harringtons more than a million dollars. Jack was convinced to pursue a political career and was elected Governor of the State of Maine. He is now contemplating a run for President of the United States.

~~~~~~~~~~~~~~

Martin Joseph, recuperated in Kansas, recovered the sight in one eye and incurred the wrath of nearly every nurse and doctor at the Kansas Army and Navy Hospital. Nearly well, he was almost ready to be discharged with a disability. Before the discharge went through, Joseph got into a poker game and was discovered cheating. When called out, he attacked two players and an orderly and was sent to prison. There, his gonorrhea became full-blown and he died in agony.

~~~~~~~~~~~~~~~~

Alan Bowen married his sweetheart, Clair, and is employed with Doctor Jon Eneman at York Hospital. Neil Harmon married *his* sweetheart, Gerry. The two of them operate a schooner in the Maine waters out of Kennebunkport.

~~~~~~~~~~~~~~~~

Nick's former girlfriend really became a notorious "Allotment Annie" and a bigamist. She married six servicemen, three of whom died in battle. The Army's Internal Investigation Unit uncovered her crimes. She was imprisoned for seven years. In addition to her prison time, she also had to reimburse the insurance money and the sum of the monthly allotment checks. The three surviving "husbands," upon hearing of her perfidy, "divorced" her.

~~~~~~~~~~~~~~~~

Doctor Hamilton Zapfester was killed in action while attempting to save the life of a Japanese soldier.

~~~~~~~~~~~~~~~~

Posey McCardle finally returned to her home. She has been visiting her Aunt Dorothy in Fort Kent, Maine.

# AFTERWARDS

October 13, 1943 – The new government of Italy sides with the Allies and declares war on Germany.

November 15, 1943 – German SS leader Heinrich Himmler orders that "gypsies and others be put on the same level as Jews and placed in concentration camps."

December 24, 1943 – US General Dwight D. Eisenhower becomes Supreme Allied Commander in Europe.

September 2, 1945 – World War II ends.

In 1946, the United States declared that meat was no longer rationed.

# RECIPES

## BUTTERLESS BUTTER

1 envelope gelatin
1 tbsp. cold water
3 tbsp. boiling water
1/3 cup evaporated milk

1/3 cup mayonnaise
1/4 tsp. salt
1/2 pound margarine,
  softened

1. Soften gelatin in cold water, add boiling water and stir until dissolved.

2. Stir in milk, then the mayonnaise and salt.

3. Chill until thickened.

4. Beat softened margarine, then gradually beat in mayonnaise mixture.

5. Spoon into a covered container and refrigerate.

# EGGLESS, BUTTERLESS WAR CAKE

1 pound raisins
2 cups packed light
  brown sugar
2 cups water
4 tbsp. lard

2 tsp. salt
2 tsp. ground cinnamon
½ tsp. ground cloves
3 cups unsifted flour
2 tsp. baking soda

1.  Combine raisins, brown sugar, water, lard, cinna-mon and cloves in a 2 quart saucepan. Bring to a boil over medium heat. Cook 5 minutes, stirring occasionally. Cool to room temperature.

2.  Preheat oven to 350°. Grease a 10 inch tube pan. Stir together the baking soda, salt and flour.

3.  Fold dry ingredients into cooled raisin mixture. Spoon into greased pan and bake 45 to 50 minutes or until a toothpick inserted in the center comes out clean.

4.  Cool 5 minutes in pan. Invert onto a wire rack to cool completely.

5.  Might have been iced with confectioners sugar, if you had the ration points back in 1943.

# SCHIACCHATA
## (STUFFED ESCAROLE TORTA)

| Ingredients for Dough | Ingredients for Stuffing |
|---|---|
| 2 2/3 cups flour | 3 pounds fresh escarole |
| freshly ground pepper | 1/3 cup virgin olive oil |
| 1/2 packet active dry | 2 tsp. chopped garlic |
|   yeast, dissolved in | 3 tbsp. capers |
|   1 cup lukewarm | 10 black Greek olives, |
|   water |   pitted and chopped |
| 2 tbsp. lard, softened, or | 3 tbsp. pine nuts |
|   3 tbsp. virgin olive oil | 7 flat anchovy fillets (optional) |

1. Mound the flour on work surface; make a hollow in its peak. Put the salt, black pepper, the dissolved yeast and the softened lard (or olive oil) into the hollow. Pull together and knead for about 10 minutes, keeping the dough soft.
2. Shape the kneaded dough into a ball; put it in a lightly floured bowl and cover bowl with saran wrap. Keep in a warm corner of the kitchen until doubled in bulk.
3. Preheat oven to 350°.
4. Prepare filling. Wash and trim escarole, then chop into 2-inch pieces.
5. Bring 3 quarts of water to a boil, add salt and drop in escarole. Cook until tender (15 minutes), then drain and squeeze to remove as much moisture as possible.
6. Put garlic and olive oil in large sauté pan; turn heat to medium and sauté garlic until pale gold.
7. Add escarole, toss to cover, reduce heat and cook for 10 minutes. Stir in capers and olives. Remove from heat. Add pine nuts and anchovies, if desired. Cool.

8.  Divide dough into 2 **unequal** parts, one about twice the size of the other. Roll the larger piece into a circle large enough to line the bottom and sides of a 10-inch springform pan. To simplify this, you might roll the dough out on a piece of lightly floured waxed paper or parchment paper.
9.  Smear the inside of the springform pan with butter. Transfer the large piece of dough to the pan, center it, covering the bottom, and smooth the edges up the sides.
10. Pour the escarole filling onto the dough in the spring form pan.
11. Roll out the remaining piece of dough into a circle large enough to cover the top of the pan. Lay it over the filling, as if covering a pie. Then, make a tight seal all around.
12. Bake until torta swells slightly and the top becomes golden brown, approximately 45 minutes.
13. As you remove the pan from the oven, unlatch the springform catch and remove the hoop. Allow the torta to settle for a few minutes and then transfer to a serving platter. Can be served either lukewarm or at room temperature.

# TEDESCO'S STEW SURPRISE

Is this a joke in bad taste? No, not really – Tedesco's *did* make a great stew. However, I would be somewhat careful in my choice of meat in this recipe.

¼ cup salad oil
4 pounds beef round or
  stewing beef, cut into
  1-inch pieces
2 tbsp. flour
3 cloves garlic, minced
3 cups good red table
  wine (burgundy is great)
2 cups beef broth
1 stalk celery, cut into
  chunks

3 large carrots, cut into
  chunks
handful of chopped parsley
½ lb. diced salt pork,
  sautéed until crisp
20 small white onions, **or** 2
  medium onions, chopped
20 fresh mushrooms,
  quartered
1 can stewed tomatoes
salt and pepper to taste
bay leaf, if desired

1. Dust meat chunks with flour. If using oven method, preheat oven to 350 degrees.
2. Heat oil in large sauté pan **or** Dutch Oven. When hot, add beef pieces, but do not crowd. Brown pieces on all sides.
3. Stir in garlic, wine and broth. Bring to a boil.
4. Add celery, carrots and parsley. Cover and simmer for 2 hours **or** put covered Dutch Oven into a 350° oven and cook for about 2 hours.
5. Add salt pork, onions, bay leaf, mushrooms and stewed tomatoes. Cook for another 30 minutes.
6. Skim any fat off the top; add salt and pepper to taste.
7. Serve over boiled potatoes tossed with fresh snipped parsley and butter.

# THE KENNEBUNK BANK GIRLS'
## CARROT CAKE
## WITH CREAM CHEESE FROSTING

3 cups sifted flour
1½ tsp. baking soda
1 tsp. cinnamon
½ tsp. salt
1½ cups liquid corn oil
2 cups sugar

2 cups grated carrots
1 8½ oz. can crushed
  pineapple with juice
1½ cups chopped pecans
2 tsp vanilla extract
3 eggs

1. Sift flour, baking soda, cinnamon and salt.
2. Mix oil and sugar.
3. Add half the dry ingredients to the oil mixture.
4. Mix well. Add carrots and pineapple, nuts and vanilla.
5. Add remaining dry ingredients, then add eggs, one at a time, beating well after each addition.
6. Grease and flour a 10-inch tube pan. Pour batter into pan.
7. Bake 1½ hours at 350° or until cake is firm to the touch.
8. When cooked, cool in pan for 10 minutes, then remove and cool thoroughly before frosting.

# CREAM CHEESE
# FROSTING INGREDIENTS

This makes a very thick layer of frosting...delicious!

2 8-oz. packages of cream cheese, at room temperature
1 cup butter (**do not** use margarine!)
2 16-oz. boxes confectioners sugar
2 tsp. vanilla extract
2 cups chopped pecans

1. Mix cream cheese and butter together.
2. Add sugar, vanilla and half of the pecans. If frosting is too stiff to spread, add a few drops of milk.
3. Frost top of cake.
4. Sprinkle remaining pecans on top.

Note: If you only want a meager amount of frosting (though who would?), you can cut this frosting recipe in half – but don't blame me if people complain....

# PUDDLEDOCK BAGELS

1 packet dry yeast
1 2/3 cups water at 110°
3 tbsp. sugar, divided

3 tbsp. barley malt* sugar, divided
4 ½ cups flour, divided
1 tbsp. salt

*Can be purchased nowadays at Whole Foods Markets. In 1943, barley malt sugar would have been purchased at a brewery.

Toppings: poppy seeds, sesame seeds, garlic and/or onion flakes, coarse salt, fennel seeds.

1. In bowl of electric mixer, whisk together the yeast, water and 1 tbsp. of the sugar. Let stand until foamy, perhaps 5 minutes.
2. Attach dough hook. Add sugar, 1 tbsp. malt sugar, 4 cups of the flour and the salt.
3. Knead until soft dough forms, perhaps 1 minute. Dough should be slightly sticky. If needed, add the rest of the flour. Knead dough 5 more minutes.
4. Lightly oil a large bowl. Place dough in bowl and cover tightly with saran wrap. Leave in bowl until doubled in volume.
5. In a large, deep frying pan or stock pot, bring 2 quarts of water to a simmer. Add the 2 remaining tbsp. of malt sugar to the simmering water.
6. Take dough out of bowl and, with a sharp pair of scissors, cut into 8 equal pieces. Roll each piece into a firm ball, then, with your thumb, poke a largish hole into the middle of each piece.

7. Place each bagel on a piece or parchment paper for ten minutes. Bagels will rise slightly and look puffy.
8. Bring the water up to a boil. Preheat oven to 500°.
9. Carefully drop two of the bagels into the boiling water for about 30 seconds, gently flip over and boil an additional 30 seconds.
10. Put the bagels on the parchment paper. While they are still wet, sprinkle toppings on bagel.
11. Repeat with two more bagels, then two more, etc.
12. When all bagels are topped, with care and a spatula, slide them onto a parchment-paper lined baking sheet.
13. Bake 5 minutes, then reduce temperature to 350° and bake for an additional 10 minutes.
14. Flip bagels over and let the bottom of the bagels brown for 5 minutes more.
15. Transfer bagels to a rack to cool.

Breinigsville, PA USA
13 October 2009
225688BV00002B/2/P